"Why is it so important that I rejoin the world?"

Evan demanded. "What's so great about the world, anyway?"

Sarah moved closer to him, and as she did, he stepped back. "It's where the people are, Evan." *It's where I am.* "You can't run away from us forever."

"I could try."

"You could try to change, too."

"Give me one good reason to."

Because I'm attracted to you. Because I want to be a part of your life. Because I want you to be a part of mine.

She wasn't bold enough to say what she was thinking, but there were other ways to make him understand....

Dear Reader,

There's a nip in the air, now that fall is here, so why not curl up with a good book to keep warm? We've got six of them this month, right here in Silhouette Intimate Moments. Take Modean Moon's *From This Day Forward,* for example. This Intimate Moments Extra title is a deeply emotional look at the break-up—and makeup—of a marriage. Your heart will ache along with heroine Ginnie Kendrick's when she thinks she's lost Neil forever, and your heart will soar along with hers, too, when at last she gets him back again.

The rest of the month is terrific, too. Jo Leigh is back with *Everyday Hero.* Who can resist a bad boy like T. J. Russo? Not Kate Dugan, that's for sure! Then there's Linda Randall Wisdom's *No More Mister Nice Guy.* Jed Hawkins is definitely tough, but even a tough guy has a heart—as Shelby Carlisle can testify by the end of this compelling novel. Suzanne Brockmann's TALL, DARK AND DANGEROUS miniseries continues with *Forever Blue,* about Lucy Tait and Blue McCoy, a hero as true blue as his name. Welcome Audra Adams to the line with *Mommy's Hero,* and watch as the world's cutest twin girls win over the recluse next door. Okay, their mom has something to do with his change of heart, too. Finally, greet our newest author, Roberta Tobeck. She's part of our WOMEN TO WATCH new author promotion, and once you've read *Under Cover of the Night,* you'll know why we're so keen on her.

Enjoy—and come back next month for six more top-notch novels of romance the Intimate Moments way.

[signature]

Leslie Wainger,
Senior Editor and Editorial Coordinator

Please address questions and book requests to:
Silhouette Reader Service
U.S.: 3010 Walden Ave., P.O. Box 1325, Buffalo, NY 14269
Canadian: P.O. Box 609, Fort Erie, Ont. L2A 5X3

MOMMY'S HERO

AUDRA ADAMS

Published by Silhouette Books
America's Publisher of Contemporary Romance

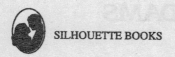

SILHOUETTE BOOKS

ISBN 0-373-07743-2

MOMMY'S HERO

AUDRA ADAMS

loves to dream up her characters' stories while lying on the beach on hot summer days. Luckily, her Jersey shore home offers her the opportunity to indulge in her fantasies.

She believes that falling in love is one of the most memorable experiences in a person's life. Young or old, male or female, we can all relate to those exquisitely warm feelings. She knows that stories of romance enable us to tap into that hidden pleasure and relive it through characters.

An incurable romantic, Audra is in love with love, and hopes to share that optimism with each and every one of her readers.

To my agent, Alice Orr, a classy lady,
a caring friend...this one's for you.

Chapter 1

I'm going to kill Lara . . .

Evan Forester watched the now-empty moving van navigate the ruts in the driveway as it rumbled onto the main road. He swore under his breath as he stared in disbelief at the sight before him. The new tenants had arrived, and to say he was upset would be an understatement.

His dog began to bark and wag his tail. "Calm down, Ralph," he said, running his fingers through the russet hair on the Irish setter's neck.

He slowly made his way to lean against the railing on his back porch. Evan shook his head as he checked out the blue station wagon. It was parked at the other end of the driveway in front of the old house behind his, the only obstruction in his view to the lake.

Why had he let Lara talk him into this? He'd bought the two properties because of the privacy and tranquillity of the setting. He'd built himself a new, modern house on the front lot and had rented the old, smaller, hodgepodge one on the lake.

He'd thought about tearing down the old place when his tenants, the Kellys, passed away this past winter, old Mr. Kelly following his beloved wife of fifty-eight years within months. But his cousin, Lara, the *Realtor,* had convinced him to rent it again.

"It's a great little house. A landmark. There are so few of these old places left in town. Please, Evan, don't destroy it."

Lara had known how to get to him, appealing to his sense of history. No one was certain, but his guess was that the house was at least a hundred years old. He built things for a living, so he knew that as rundown and small as it was, they didn't build houses like that anymore.

Okay, he'd told her, rent it. But to someone older, quiet, a steady person who would preferably go off to work each day. Maybe a pet or two, but no kids. Definitely no kids.

So why was he standing out here on his back porch watching two rambunctious couldn't-be-more-than-five-year-old girls romp around the front yard of the old house?

The same front yard that overlapped *his* backyard.

No, this couldn't be. Lara was pushy and sometimes overstepped her bounds, but she wouldn't directly disobey his order. When he'd signed the lease, she had told him the new tenant was a widow, and he'd thought, great, someone like Mrs. Kelly—homemade chicken soup in the winter and apple pies in the fall.

So there had to be some mistake.

Maybe they were grandchildren of the new tenant, and the kids' parents were helping with the move. That he could handle. Visiting kids were acceptable...if they visited rarely and were kept inside for the most part.

Yep, that had to be it. He was overreacting. As usual. Lara said he guarded his privacy like a miser protected his gold.

These past three years she'd stayed on his case, always coming up with this event or that in an attempt to entice him out of the house. Fourth of July town picnic. Football homecoming. Christmas pageant at the church.

Memorial Day parade through town. It didn't matter the holiday, the only thing that mattered to her was that he attend.

She'd made him her own personal crusade. "Come on, Evan, you have to get out more. You can't expect people to come to you way out here. You have to *mingle*."

But he'd tried mingling many times early on after the accident—he'd tried more than just mingling—and it hadn't worked. It had made him feel like a freak.

No, he liked his privacy. He liked living at the end of a dead-end road in the middle of nowhere. He liked working in his own home, pounding nails, carving wood out in the yard with the sun on his bare back and no one to tell him he couldn't. He liked being alone with no one to bother him, no one to annoy him, no one to look at him. . . .

They could call him a recluse, a hermit, a weirdo. They could call him anything they wanted as long as he didn't have to see them, *mingle* with them. He was content, happy even, and he didn't want to change one thing in his life. Not anymore. The days of feeling sorry for himself were long gone.

Lara knew that better than most. She and her fiancé, Willy, were the only ones left he kept in touch with, and that was more their doing than his. He never visited them, but they always took the time out of their busy lives to check in on him.

Willy had even become a business partner of sorts, arranging new contracts for him, getting his supplies. He'd even recently brokered a deal for Evan with a new custom mail-order house. He liked Willy and was glad he was marrying Lara. Maybe he would teach her something; Willy knew how to keep his opinions to himself.

Yet despite the fact he called Lara a nuisance to her face, he loved her. She, at least, cared.

He watched the children roll around in the grass.

She wouldn't do this to me . . .

Evan pushed himself off the railing and headed back into the house, convinced that when all was said and done, the new tenant would show herself to be exactly what he'd expected—an older, friendly, white-haired woman with a bun in her hair who baked pies and knew the value of minding her own business.

His infusion of confidence was short-lived, however, when his peripheral vision caught sight of the front door swinging open. A woman emerged. A young, fresh-faced woman dressed in a lavender-and-pink flowered sundress that fell to her ankles and clung to her body's curves like an hourglass in motion.

She was smiling as she stepped onto the porch steps, her arms outstretched, her head tilted back as if she were paying homage to the sun. She leaned forward and a riot of more-red-than-auburn curls fell across her face. Then with eyes shut tightly, she wrapped her arms around herself and pirouetted in what could only be called an unrestrained display of pure joy.

Evan's lungs stopped functioning. He felt as if he'd been punched smack in the middle of his solar plexus. He gulped for air, blinking, hoping to dispel the sight. But she was still there. Far enough away that he couldn't make out her features, close enough to know she was heart-stoppingly beautiful. His stomach did a little flip as her hands slid down her sides to rest at her waist. It was an unconscious movement, which made it all the more potent.

Much to his surprise, his body tightened. This couldn't be. Those feelings, those urges, were long gone. By necessity, he'd done away with them systematically and effectively. No one or no thing could make him susceptible to that kind of feeling, that kind of rejection, that kind of hurt, again.

"Alys! Ariel! Dinner..."

She dragged the last word out as she gripped the porch pillar and pivoted down onto the crushed-rock walkway. She didn't walk, she sashayed, completely unaware, he was sure, that her hips thrust forward and swung rhythmically from left to right with each step.

Stopping midway down the walk, she raised a hand over her eyes and scanned the area. He had watched the two little girls disappear into the bushes at the edge of the lawn, but offered no help in her search. Instead, Evan stood stone still, almost willing himself to disappear into the surroundings. He didn't dare move and bring attention to himself. He wished at that moment to be a chameleon, able to change color and blend into the brown stained oak porch that wrapped around the back of his house.

She spotted him, anyway. Tentatively, she raised her hand in a wave of friendship. He knew what he was supposed to do. He was supposed to return the greeting. He was supposed to jump down from his porch and amble on over for a friendly welcome chat. He was supposed to be hospitable. He was supposed to be the friendly landlord, a good neighbor.

Well, he was none of that. He was stunned, and when that wore off he knew he would be angry.

"Come on, boy." He grabbed Ralph by the collar, turned into the house without a word or gesture and slammed the door behind him.

He couldn't believe it.

A woman.

And two kids.

Lara, you're dead ...

Sarah Wyeth's fingers curled into an embarrassed fist. That, she assumed, was the owner and her new neighbor, Evan Forester. He must not have seen her wave. Hesitantly, she continued her search for the girls, then stopped and looked back over at the big, split-level house across the lawn.

He was watching her from inside the house. One thing she had was good eyesight. The hair was going a bit gray here and there, but the eyes were still in excellent shape. She could see his silhouette outlined against the window. Strange. If he'd seen her, why hadn't he acknowledged her greeting? Her mouth puckered with worry.

What had the Realtor told her about him? Oh, yes. He was the town hero. Had saved a whole bunch of people from some sort of catastrophe. A fiery explosion or something. But Sarah had gotten the impression that it had been a while ago.

Lara had spoken about him at length, and Sarah remembered thinking it odd at the time that he owned this old house, yet she hadn't met him. He hadn't shown up at any of the walk-throughs, allowing the Realtor to handle the rental transaction.

She tried to remember something, anything, else about him. He lived alone. Worked at home, crafting custommade furniture. Good with his hands, the Realtor had said. It had been a plus. Twins tended to break things in doubles, and she had no doubt that she'd need his expertise sometime before her rental ran out.

She'd learned how to do a lot of practical things around the house in the past few years. Not that John had been that good with his hands, but they had separated the household chores to "his" and "hers," and John's had always involved the more physical aspects of upkeep. But John was dead, and she was alone, except for the girls, of course, and she had to handle it all now—the "his" and the "hers."

Sometimes that organized, controlled but carefree life she and John had lived as a young, married, city couple seemed as if it had happened to someone else. It was so far removed from her present world, from who she was, from what she was.

She was now, more than anything else, a mother.

All thoughts of her strange neighbor fled as her two ragamuffins reappeared from behind the bushes and frolicked on the lawn. Alys and Ariel played tag, running around each other in circles, giggling as they pitched and pivoted, making themselves dizzy enough to fall down. Their laughter was contagious, and Sarah found herself joining in. She grabbed a handful of her anklelength dress and held it aloft as she plopped herself down on the ground, as well.

But the girls didn't stay near her for long, running off again in opposite directions. Sarah let them go with a wave and a warning, watching as they disappeared around the side of the house. She breathed deeply, savoring the smell of freshly mowed grass as it filled her lungs.

This was something so good for all of them. Giving up the apartment in the city had been a difficult decision. It had been a downstairs walk-in in her parents' house, and a perfect place for newlyweds. But the apartment, which had been small when only she and John had lived in it, was miniscule with two children running around.

But then, they hadn't planned on having children right away. They were going to work, save their money and buy a house of their own in the country. That had been the plan. The plan that died when John suffered his fatal heart attack.

It had happened six years ago, and though her eyes didn't fill with tears any longer, it still stung. He'd collapsed on the street while jogging. That was it. One minute she was waving goodbye as he ran out the door, the next, she was talking to the police about arrangements for the body.

Congenital, the autopsy had said. Had been walking around with the problem all his life. He'd never known what hit him.

Somehow those words were supposed to have consoled her, but all they'd done was make her angry. How could a thirty-year-old healthy man just drop dead? She hadn't been able to understand it then, and for months after refused to accept it. Especially after she'd discovered she was pregnant. It had seemed as if God had taken from her with one hand and given with the other.

Her parents had insisted she stay in that small apartment even after she'd given birth to the girls, and she had found it easier to agree than strike out on her own. It had seemed like her—their—only link to John. For years, she'd allowed her parents, and John's, too, to cluck over her until the concern and attention became so smothering she hadn't been able to go for a walk without calling to tell someone.

It hadn't really dawned on her how bad things were until the girls started nursery school, and she'd discovered that Alys was becoming a bully, and Ariel was so introverted the teachers were thinking about having her tested.

That had shaken Sarah to the core. The girls—she—needed a change. They were starting kindergarten this year, and it seemed a perfect time to make a new start. She wouldn't admit it to anyone, least of all the family, but she was scared to death. She couldn't remember a time when she'd been completely on her own with all of life's responsibilities on her shoulders. She'd gone from her mother and father's house to John, and after he died, it had seemed so easy to let her family and his take care of her. But she had to stand on her own two feet. More than that, she and the children needed a *life*, one separate from John, her family and that which had been.

It was time for her to move on, and though this was by no means a perfect, or even a final, solution, a new teaching job and this house were enough to meet all the criteria she'd set for herself and her girls. For the time being at least. She had a year's contract with the school and a year's lease on the house. After that, she would see.

She'd picked the town of Wayside because it had been the only job offer that met all her needs: a part-time position teaching music for an elementary school that allowed her to work in the same school the girls attended. She'd visited a few times to test the waters and had found she liked the tranquillity of the town and the friendliness of the people.

As she stood and brushed off flecks of grass from her dress, Sarah stole one more glance at the house across the yard. At least she remembered that *most* of the people had been friendly. She made a mental note to ask Lara to fill her in a little more on her landlord.

"Girls! Come on . . . dinnertime."

Alys's little face peeked from around the side of the house. When Sarah waved her forward, she came running up to her with Ariel close behind. "Five more minutes . . ." she pleaded.

Ariel piped in with, "Please . . ."

Sarah looked down at her girls.

"Okay," Sarah said as she brushed Alys's chestnut bangs out of her eyes. "Five more minutes."

They screeched with pleasure as they ran off. She called a word of warning as they ran off in the direction of the lake, even though there was a fence between the house and the dock.

She watched them continue their game for a long moment. They were as alike in appearance as two peas in a pod, but in temperament, no two children could be as different if they had been born to complete strangers. Yet they complemented each other in ways that still amazed her. While Alys was always moving, rushing, running, chattering, Ariel was quiet, contemplative, content to sit in the corner with a picture book or a coloring book and crayons.

They had their own language, exchanging one-word sentences or only a glance before both would bolt a room on a joint quest. Sarah had thought she'd known love before: for her parents, even the short time she'd known John, but nothing in her life could have compared with or prepared her for the feelings she had for these two little girls.

They filled every nook and cranny of her life. To say that they were everything to her would be an understatement.

They were her salvation.

Sarah sighed and turned back to the house. But, she knew, they were no longer enough. They were growing up, and this past year had brought that home to her with crystal clarity. With nursery school three mornings a week, they'd needed her less and less in a physical sense. For the first time in years, she had a degree of freedom, albeit small; yet during those brief respites, she found herself questioning what she would do with the rest of her life, and she knew she had to go back to work.

Sarah swung open the creaking screen door and let herself into the house. She gave the room a quick glance. Her furniture looked strange in this new, more spacious setting. The apartment had been so cramped, particularly after the girls were born, that she'd forgotten how

much she liked the paisley print sofa and love seat she and
John had picked out so long ago. As she passed, her hand
caressed the upright mahogany piano that stood against
the half wall that separated the kitchen from the living
room.

Her love of music was a constant in her life. She'd been
classically trained, but her preference for popular music
always exasperated her teachers. Instead of the concert
stage, she'd opted for the classroom. After the twins were
born, she'd quit, not realizing until recently what a void
that had left in her life until she'd decided to look for
work again.

She circumnavigated the several cardboard boxes containing her books and other personal belongings that lit-
tered the living room. A mess, she told herself. Still, she
loved the room. As soon as she had walked through the
door with the Realtor, she had been hit by its simplistic
beauty. The entire back wall was made of stone, with a
huge hearthlike fireplace built into its center.

Nothing, not even the chaos of moving, could spoil the
image she'd had of sitting down on the rug, cuddling and
reading to her girls by a big fire on a cold night. Warmed
by the thought, but too tired to do anything, she stole a
glance through the door to the kitchen. It was even more
cluttered.

Later, she said to herself. It was June and she had
purposely planned the move to coincide with the end of
nursery school. So she had all summer to set the house to
rights and get her family acclimated to their new life before the new school season began for all three of them.

She climbed the stairs to put fresh linens on the girls'
twin beds. Her goals for today were to feed and bathe the
children and get to bed early. Tomorrow she would make
a game of unpacking, letting the twins help.

Once the rooms were made up, Sarah entered the
bathroom and splashed cold water on her face and hands.
It was a warm day, with the portent of the hot midsum-
mer days that would soon follow. That was fine with her.
She looked forward to swimming in the lake with the
girls, of picnics in the hills beyond, of cookouts in the

backyard—all the things she could never do living in the city.

Her parents would come up during the summer, and John's would visit around the holidays. She would never deny any of them access to the children, but she knew they would try to lure her back. Her parents wanted her to live with them again, and her in-laws had concurred. They had even offered to buy a new, bigger home anywhere she'd choose. But, scared as she was, Sarah longed for her independence. That, as much as moving out of her cramped quarters, was most important.

She had promised them, though, that by the end of this lease, she would make a decision on where she would settle. She shook her head. She didn't want to think about that now. She had plenty of time to make up her mind.

She stared at her reflection, touching the laugh lines around her eyes with the tips of her fingers. She was thirty-four years old and so involved in her children's lives that she had no time or inclination to think of what life had left in store for her.

Who are you, Sarah Wyeth? she asked herself.

She didn't know the answer to that question anymore. Most times she was content to be Ariel and Alys's mother, her life so full there was little time for anything else. But there were those "other" times, as well. The middle-of-the-night times when she ached to be held in a man's arms once again. She missed the touching, the intimacy, the heat of a man's body lying next to hers as dawn crept in with the cool early-morning light. She missed being wanted, desired, but most of all, she missed being needed, not as the children needed her, but as a man needs a woman.

Would there be another love in her life? That would be difficult at best with the twins, yet how that hypothetical man felt about children would play a major part in any decision she'd have to make.

Sarah grinned at her thoughts. Love. Men. That was a joke. This move must be doing something to her sup-

pressed libido, she mused. It was a good thing she was
going back to work in September.

The grandfather clock chimed below, alerting her to
the lateness of the hour. Time enough to wonder about
what was in store for her love life. Right now, it was time
to get the girls inside and put together something resembling a nutritious dinner.

"Mommy! Mommy!"

Sarah ran out of the bathroom at the sound of the girls
rushing into the house and a dog frantically barking
outside. "What is it?" she called out from the top of the
stairs.

"A monster chased us!"

"Yes! A bad monster came after us. He tried to kill
us!"

Sarah rushed down the stairway. "Hold on, both of
you! What are you talking about?"

The twins began to talk and cry at the same time. Sarah
knelt in front of the hysterical girls and cradled one in
each of her arms. Ariel tucked her head into her shoulder and sobbed. Alys started chattering incoherently. As
Sarah soothed her, she turned to Ariel. "Tell Mommy
what happened."

"An ugly monster-man *screamed* at us."

"Where?"

"At that big house over there." Ariel pointed out the
front door.

Sarah's gaze followed her finger. "Mr. Forester? The
man next door?" Both girls nodded. "What did he say
to you?"

"He said, 'Go away, brats, and stay away,'" Alys
shouted theatrically.

"And then he said, 'Don't come near this house
again!'" Ariel added.

"He shouted at you?" Sarah asked.

"Yes," Ariel said.

"Screamed and shouted," Alys added.

"And his big dog almost bit us."

"Yes, the big dog jumped and barked and scratched the door to get at us. He was going to bite us. But we ran fast."

Sarah stood. The girls hugged her legs. She reached down and caressed their heads as her mind began to race and her heart beat double-time with fear and indignation.

Who did this man think he was? She had made an excuse for him, allowing that he hadn't seen her when she waved, but now she wasn't so sure. Perhaps he had indeed seen her and the girls, and had no wish to meet or greet them.

That was fine with her. If he didn't want to be friendly, she could live with it. What she couldn't live with was his frightening her girls. Her "mother bear" instinct kicked in as a surge of protective anger swept over her.

"Wait here," she said to the girls.

"Mommy! Don't go," Alys screamed. "He'll get you!"

"No one's going to get anyone," she said slowly in a reassuring but firm voice. "Now I want both of you to stay in here. I'll be back in a few minutes."

The screen door slammed behind her as she purposely made her way across her backyard property and onto the neighboring lot. She could feel her internal steam building, rising, clogging her ears to all sounds except the ones inside her head. Hands clenched, she took a deep breath and gritted her teeth, preparing herself to confront the girls' "monster."

When she was about twenty feet away from his back porch, the dog started barking again. Sarah looked up, and stopped dead in her tracks.

He was there, hands on his hips, his back resting against the wooden column of the deck. He wasn't looking at her, wasn't watching her approach. Instead, he was turned sideways, staring off into the woods beyond, his masculine form in stark relief against the natural wood background of the house.

The first thing that struck her was what an incredibly beautiful man he was. His chiseled profile and wavy brown hair gave new meaning to the words *tall, dark and handsome*. She had thought he'd be older, gnarled in some way, frightening, even ugly to a little girl's eyes. But no, this man before her was no monster. He was young, vibrant, his long-legged body rippling with vitality and strength, his arms bulging with well-defined muscles peeking through his sleeveless denim vest.

Despite the dog's incessant barking, the sight of him took the wind out of her sails.

Until the sound of her screen door opening and shutting caught her attention.

She turned her head to see her twins holding hands, standing side by side on the porch of her new home, their small shoulders hiccupping in sobbing unison, watching and waiting for her to handle the situation. It galvanized her anew, and she put one foot in front of the other faster still, almost running toward him.

"Who do you think you are?" she asked, and, not waiting for him to answer, continued, "scaring the daylights out of little girls? They weren't bothering anyone—"

"They were on my property."

"So? They have no way of knowing that."

"I don't want them here."

Sarah moved closer to the porch, spinning around to face him, but as she moved, so did he. "They weren't hurting anything, were they?" she asked.

"That's not the point."

"They're children, for heaven's sake. Children run around—"

"Not here. Not on my property."

Sarah leaned forward to get a better look at him. It annoyed her that he wouldn't face her, wouldn't look her in the eye as she spoke to him. "And how do you suppose I keep them off your property? There's no dividing line between our yards."

"That's not my problem. It's yours."

"Not entirely. You're the one who wants to keep them away. It's your property. I suggest you put up another fence. This time on *your* side."

A muscle in his cheek tightened. "I suggest you *move out*. I don't want any children living here."

"How dare you! I just leased this house. From you, I might add. You should have thought of that before you rented it for a year."

"That was a mistake. I didn't know."

"You would have if you had shown up at the Realtor's office. I wasn't keeping my children a secret."

"Lara... the Realtor made the mistake."

"That, Mr. Forester, is not *my* problem. I'm here to stay."

"We'll see about that."

"Yes, we will," she said. "You'll find I don't scare easily." Sarah swung around the banister to face him. He moved away from her again. "Would you please look at me when I'm speaking to you!"

He hesitated a moment, then with slow deliberation he turned to her. Sarah gasped and brought a hand to her chest at the sight of the scarred flesh on the left side of his face. A burn, obviously, from his hairline, past the corner of his left eye down across his cheek to his chin and below, disappearing into the neckline of his vest.

"Happy now?" he asked with a smiling sneer.

Sarah opened her mouth to speak, but nothing came out.

"That's it," he continued, "go ahead. Take a good look. Gawk all you want, I don't care. Just as long as when you're finished, you pack your bags and your kids and get the hell out of here."

Sarah took one step back, then another, slowly retreating to her house. "I... I'm sorry..."

"Save your pity, lady, I don't need it. Just go," he shouted after her as she picked up speed.

The dog began barking again, but his voice reached her nevertheless.

"And till you do, keep those little brats away from me!"

That stopped her cold.

Sarah could feel the blood rush to her head as anger overtook all of the other myriad emotions. She turned slowly. Her eyes met his across the distance. Met, held and challenged as daggers flew through the air. Even the dog stopped barking. With long, purposeful strides, she made her way back to his porch.

This time it was Evan's turn to retreat. He stepped back as she ascended the stairs, reaching behind him for the doorknob.

It didn't deter Sarah one bit. She walked right up to him. Close, so close, he could see the spots of red on her cheeks and the fierce glint in her blue eyes.

Heart pounding, Sarah spoke softly. "I don't care who you are, hero or saint. I don't care what you've done or how you came to be the way you are. I don't even care about your personal problems or what you can or cannot deal with in your life. There are only two things in this world I *do* care about, Mr. Forester, and those are my girls."

"Listen—"

"No, you listen. I have come a very long way to be here. I have a job waiting for me and a lease that is binding for one year. You signed it, and believe me when I tell you that I intend to hold you to it. So, like it or not, we are not packing our bags and going anywhere. You will just have to learn to live with it."

Sarah held his gaze for one long moment, defiantly waiting for him to respond. When he didn't, she nodded imperceptibly, more to herself than to him, turned abruptly and headed down the steps.

"And one other thing—" she looked at him over her shoulder "—don't you ever, *ever,* call my girls 'brats' again."

Chapter 2

Weeks later Sarah stood at her door watching the twins, arms outstretched, literally walk the property line between her front yard and the Forester backyard as if it were a balance beam.

She sighed. She *had* managed to keep the girls away from his property up to now. They had still been leery of him even though Sarah had explained that Mr. Forester was not a monster-man, but only scarred from a terrible accident. She'd told him about his saving people from a fire, embellished a bit about his being a brave hero.

Their natural compassion had made them very sympathetic toward him, and they vowed with "cross-my-heart-Mommy" promises that they would stay away. They'd nodded as she told them he just wanted to be left alone, and for the past weeks, they had complied with her wishes.

Until today.

While Sarah was happy they were no longer frightened, she also should have known that their curiosity was going to overcome any admonishment she'd made *or* oath they'd taken to stay off their landlord's property.

Evan's truck was gone, indicating that, thankfully, he was not at home—for a while, at least. Nevertheless, Sarah called out to the twins, and they immediately ran off in another direction. Away from his house. For now.

Sarah bit her lower lip. Keeping Alys and Ariel away from Evan Forester was going to be a full-time job in itself. But she had no choice. She was committed to staying in Wayside for the next year, and if that meant playing warden to the girls, she would do it.

It was a small price to pay for her independence.

A car horn tooted as it turned into their shared driveway. Sarah pushed the screen door open and stepped out onto the porch, returning the wave. Lara Hanlon, her Realtor, parked her black BMW behind Sarah's station wagon and exited the car.

"Hi, there! Settled in yet?"

"Not exactly," Sarah said, taking Lara's extended hand in greeting. "I still have some boxes to unpack."

"I thought I'd stop by to see if there was anything you needed from me," Lara said.

"Well, actually, there is."

"Shoot."

Sarah's thumb and forefinger formed a mock gun. "Don't tempt me," Sarah said with a purposeful look in the direction of her neighbor's house.

"Uh-oh. I presume you've met Evan."

"Head-on."

Lara had the good grace to look chagrined. "What did he do?"

"He told me to pack my bags, get out and take my 'brats' with me."

"I was afraid of that."

"Lara, *why* didn't you tell me he didn't want to rent to someone with children?"

"Because what he wants is not what he needs."

"Excuse me?"

"I'm sorry, Sarah, to put you in this position, but Evan's my cousin. I've known him all my life. He's really a great guy. He used to love children, love *people*.

Ever since the accident, he's hidden away here like a hermit. He needs to socialize, get a life again.''

"What happened exactly?''

"There was an explosion at a chemical plant in the next town. He was a volunteer fireman at the time, and was one of the first on the scene. He ran into the burning building and pulled out five people. He was going back in when the roof caved in. He was trapped under a burning beam.''

"How awful.''

"Yes. It was terrible. He's had a lot of operations, but finally decided to let it go and live with the scars.'' She hesitated. "Some people . . . didn't understand. So he moved on. That was five years ago.''

"He's been alone out here since then?''

"He built the house about three years ago, and yes, he's been alone. Except for the Kellys, and they were in their seventies.''

"So you moved us in here to rehabilitate him?''

"No, of course not. I thought having a family next door would draw him out of his shell. Especially the girls. They're darling. He'll never be able to resist them.''

"He's resisting them pretty well so far. Scared them half to death.''

"Oh. Yes. His face. I should have told you about that. It's just that I don't even see the scars anymore. No one that matters really does. Only him. He uses the scars to keep people away.'' Lara paused. "Does his face bother you that much?''

"I'd be lying if I said that I wasn't taken aback at first. But once he got me riled, it didn't matter much what he looked like.''

"You told him off?''

"And then some.''

"Oowee! That's great!''

"He didn't think so. And neither did I. I was shaking like a leaf.''

Lara grinned from ear to ear. "But he took it. You're staying.''

Sarah shook her head slowly, but returned the grin. "Yeah. We're staying. Unless he can do something legally to get us out."

"No way. Your lease is signed, sealed and delivered. That's what he gets for going fishing when he should have been in my office signing papers." Lara beamed. "This is just wonderful!"

"We'll see about that."

With that, Lara's attention turned toward the road. "Uh-oh. I'd better be going. That's Evan's truck I hear. He's left a zillion messages on my machine, which I haven't answered." Lara slipped into her car and started the ignition even before she shut the door. "I figure I'll give him another week or so to cool down."

"Coward," Sarah called as the car began backing out toward the road.

"You know it!" Lara answered, with a wave. "I'll call you..."

"What the—"

Evan didn't notice Lara's car until she peeled out of the driveway in front of him. He pulled the wheel sharply to the right to avoid hitting the speeding car before he realized who the driver was. He braked sharply.

"Lara! Lara, you come back here! I have to talk to you," he shouted half hanging out the truck's cab window.

"Not now, Evan," she called. "Too busy." With a wave and a cloud of dust, she was gone.

Evan muttered a string of expletives under his breath as he parked the truck and got out. "Come on, boy," he called.

Ralph jumped out of the cab and bounded past him up onto the porch. Evan took a step to follow him when he caught sight of Sarah at the other end of the driveway.

He stopped. For a long moment, he just stared at her, the distance making it impossible to discern her features, but her defiant stance and hands-on-hips body language told him in no uncertain terms she was once again ready to do battle should he choose to pursue his previous course of action.

But he was in no mood to battle. He'd spent too many restless nights this week, tossing, turning and thinking of ways to get rid of the Widow Wyeth, but not one scenario materialized into any coherent plan.

His mind had chosen instead to picture her as she'd looked the first moment he'd seen her—soft, free and wildly feminine. And then in the darkness of his bedroom, his body had overtaken his mind, and the fantasy of forcing her to move away and leave him alone became as farfetched as the possibility of having a woman such as she lying in bed next to him.

But today she looked different, almost waiflike, not at all like the sensuous woman who'd descended the porch steps. She stared back at him as if she knew this new image she presented would return to haunt him tonight, as well. Yet he couldn't look away.

She was too adorable for her own good. Her body was thin, tall, tight, with just the right amount of curves to make him wonder what lay beneath those baggy denim overalls and white T-shirt. She didn't move, not an inch, but just stood still, allowing his perusal, as if to say, "Go ahead, mister, just try it."

He forced his lips not to twitch into a smile even though he knew she couldn't see him clearly. The tough-girl act was just that as far as he was concerned. With legs too long to be called decent, she looked as if a good, stiff wind could knock her over. Her militant posture would be laughable if she weren't so damned serious.

He was sure she had no idea whatsoever how absolutely desirable she looked. Her mass of curly reddish auburn hair framed her oval face and fell onto her shoulders. Rather than intimidating, the upward tilt of her chin beckoned him to come closer for a better look into those blue, very blue, saucer eyes of hers.

He remembered those eyes from their first encounter, up close and rimmed with fire. Eyes you could stare into forever. Eyes you could drown in...

Ralph licked his hand, the one from which his truck keys dangled. Evan rattled the keys and stuffed them into his pocket. He'd spent enough time on this woman and her children. He had contracts to meet, work to do.

He shook his head. *Don't be even more of a fool than you already are....*

Without a word or a wave, he headed into the house.

What a peculiar man, Sarah thought as she pivoted and started up the porch steps. No greeting, no gesture of any kind, only that same quiet hostility that seemed to emanate from his body toward her.

She should have asked Lara more about him. Not that it would matter much. Her instincts told her that however fun-loving he'd been in his past, this present man was decidedly different—morose, moody.

Sarah stared at the front door for a long moment, then shrugged and returned to the house.

Whatever the case, as long as he left the girls alone, it was none of her concern.

Evan looked up when the dog woofed. "What is it, Ralph?" he asked, moving away from his workbench to the door.

The answer was clear as a serious, little, female, pug-nosed face with a fringe of very straight light brown bangs peered back at him through the screen.

Then she smiled. "Hi. My name's Alys. What's yours?"

Evan scowled and returned to his workbench. He picked up the fine sandpaper and gently rubbed it against the table leg he had been giving the finishing touches to.

His first thought was to chase her, but that hadn't worked the last time. All that had done was bring the mother after him fast and furiously. He didn't need another encounter with the Widow Wyeth. Not if he wanted a good night's sleep tonight.

Maybe if he ignored her, she'd go away.

"Is that dog mean? I don't like mean dogs. A mean one tried to bite me when I was little. Is his name Ralph?

He looks nice. Look, he's smiling at me.'' She waved. ''Hello, Ralph.''

Ralph gave a halfhearted bark at the sound of his name. ''Quiet,'' Evan said to the dog, who, tail wagging, had started to rise, then thought better of it once he saw the look on Evan's face.

''Can he come out to play with me? There's only my sister to play with, and she wants to look at books. I don't want to look at any old books. Mommy wants me to help her put stuff away in the kitchen, but I don't want to. I want to play outside. I can throw sticks and things. Ralph can chase them. Can he?''

''No,'' Evan said finally, hoping that would be the end of it.

''I can play in here with him.'' She reached for the door latch. ''I can pet him and stuff. Is that okay?''

''No.''

Alys's hand dropped to her side. ''Why not?''

''Because I said so.''

''Grandpa says that all the time, but Mommy says that's not an answer.''

''It's the only one I have.''

''What are you doing?'' she asked.

''Working.''

Before he knew what happened, she had let herself in and was standing by his side. ''On what?''

Evan eyed her cautiously. She was a little bit of a thing. Couldn't be more than five, tops. ''A table.''

''Can I touch it?''

''Go ahead.''

She ran her hand over the wood and smiled up at him. ''Nice.''

''Thank you.''

''You're welcome.'' She bent down and began petting the dog. ''Mommy said you weren't a monster-man. You're not, are you?''

Evan felt his lip curl of its own volition. ''No.''

''I knew that. Mommy doesn't tell lies. She said you weren't mean. She said you were sorry you scared me and Ariel. Are you sorry?''

Evan hesitated. "Yes."

"She said you were a hero..."

"And...?"

"And that you were sad. About what happened to your face and all."

Evan stopped sanding. He rested the table leg on his thigh and looked at her. "What else did *Mommy* say?"

"She said it was a *terrible* accident." Alys waved her hands over her head dramatically, then dropped them back to continue petting Ralph. "Was it?"

"Yes."

"Was there a fire?"

"Yes."

"Did you get burned?"

"Yes."

"Did it hurt?"

"Yes."

"Oh, Mommy was right. She said we should be nice to you and not be scared. We should feel sorry for you."

"Well, little girl, you can tell *Mommy* that I don't need—"

"Alys!"

Alys ran to the door and peered out. "Uh-oh, here comes Mommy. I've got to go." She paused and wrinkled her brow. "What's your name? Mommy calls you Mr. Forester, but that's too long."

"Evan."

"See ya, Evan. Bye, Ralph," she said with a quick pat on the dog's head.

The screen door slapped shut behind her as she disappeared with the lightning speed of a guilty child. Evan dropped the table leg onto the workbench and slowly rose. In the distance he could see Alys skipping and animatedly gesturing toward her sister who was waiting on the lawn. Her young, high-pitched voice traveled back to him as she repeated every detail of her conversation with him.

Reluctantly, as if he knew what he would find once he looked down, he moved closer to the screen door. No surprise, Sarah was standing at the foot of the porch steps. His gaze met her contrite one, and he held it for a long moment. She bit her lip, and he followed the movement.

"I'm sorry," she said softly. "I know I promised to keep the girls away, but Alys has a mind of her own."

Evan didn't answer. He didn't know what to say. He'd forgotten how to make small talk with people, especially with women. So instead, he remained silent, safe. The long pause grew awkward. His stomach churned with the turmoil. He watched her as her face turned red.

"I'll talk to her again," Sarah added.

Evan stared at her through the mesh of the screen, but again could not reply if his life depended on it. In some vague, social way, he supposed it did.

"I hope she didn't bother you too much. She's quite a chatterbox."

"Yes," he said, finally forcing out the words, "she is."

His calm reply seemed to ease the tension somewhat. She smiled up at him. It transformed her face, and Evan felt as if an arrow pierced him in the middle of his chest.

She has no idea, he told himself, *no idea at all how she affects you.*

His hand came up to the door latch, and Sarah's body swayed forward. For a moment, she thought he was going to ask her to come inside. She would have refused, of course, but the thought that he might ask her sent a tingling feeling up from the base of her spine to the roots of her hair.

Strangely, she wanted him to, and for the most shallow of reasons. She wanted to get a better look at him. The man she'd confronted weeks ago was a blur except for the scars. The man she viewed this morning from the driveway was too far away, too intimidating with his still-as-a-statue stance.

She wanted to study him, view the real man, the Evan Forester his cousin, Lara, said was buried somewhere inside *this* man who wore his scars like a mask, hiding, pretending to be something and someone he was not.

She didn't know why this sudden impulse was important to her, she just knew it was. If what Lara said was true, he was hurting, and it went beyond the obvious physical hurt he'd endured. She'd always had a soft spot in her heart for those in need, and he seemed like one of the neediest people she'd ever met in her life.

Pity, she supposed, that was what she was feeling. She knew instinctively that he would scorn such a feeling from her, somehow *particularly* from her. He had been handsome before the accident. He had probably also been a bit of a ladies' man. It must have been devastatingly hard for him to become a source of pity.

No, she wouldn't do that to him. She'd respect his wishes, turn around and go back to her house. She'd make a mission out of keeping her children away from him. She'd respect this private world that he'd worked so hard to create. If that's what he wanted, she'd give it to him.

That, and nothing more.

Oddly, the thought of this being all there would ever be between them made her sad. . . .

"I—I'd better be going. The girls . . . I have to go food shopping. Stock up the pantry." She was babbling, she knew, and backed up as the words kept tumbling out of her mouth. "We'll be gone for a while . . ."

"Goodbye," he said.

Sarah nodded. "Yes, goodbye. And again, I apologize." When he didn't answer, she almost tripped over her feet trying to retreat back to her house. The girls were waiting for her on the porch, and she quickly loaded them into the station wagon and strapped them in, all the while feeling the power of his gaze on her back.

Strange, strange man, she thought. Better to do as he wished and stay away. But as she backed the car out of the driveway, she couldn't help but steal a glance at his back screen door to see if he was watching her.

He wasn't.

It didn't happen again for three days. He'd expected it sooner. Even, if he'd admit it to himself, looked forward to it, but no little face showed up at his window. Not until today. And it wasn't one little face, but two.

Alys brought Ariel along to meet the monster-man who really wasn't a monster, after all.

"Hi," Alys said without preamble, "this is my sister, Ariel. She's shy, so she doesn't talk much. But she really wanted to meet Ralph even though Mommy said we weren't ever to come here anymore. But I thought it wasn't fair that I got to meet Ralph and Ariel didn't. Mommy said we should be fair and we should always share. Well, I think sharing Ralph is more important than staying away from your house, don't you?"

Evan didn't answer, but then he didn't have to. Alys opened the screen door and held it for her sister. "Come on, Ariel, it's all right. Isn't it, Evan?"

"Yes, it's all right."

Ariel took two small steps forward and stopped near the threshold. Her eyes were as big as saucers as if she were waiting for him to jump up and bite her.

"I think Ralph's back in the living room," Evan said.

"You wait here," Alys said to Ariel, full of importance. "I'll get him."

Alys brushed past Evan with a smile and headed down the hallway. Ariel hadn't taken her eyes off him since she'd ventured into the house.

Evan cleared his throat. "Would you like to sit down?" he asked, pointing to a bench in the corner of his workroom.

Ariel shook her head.

"Would you like something to drink?"

She shook her head again.

"Are you afraid of me?" he asked.

She shook her head vigorously.

"Here he is," Alys said, leading a willing Ralph by the collar. "See, he's likes me," she added when the dog began to lick her hand.

Ariel stood still, but Evan could read the desire to rush forward and pet the dog as Alys was doing. "Go ahead," he said, "he doesn't bite."

Hesitantly, Ariel moved forward with her hand outstretched. Once she reached Alys and Ralph, she slowly knelt next to her sister and touched the dog's head. She pulled her hand back quickly, but bravely tried again, this time with her full palm against the crown of the Irish setter's head.

Evan watched Ralph move into Ariel's little hand, loving the attention from the two little girls. His tail thumped the floor with pleasure. Ariel looked up at him and smiled.

And with that, he was lost.

She had her mother's mouth. Why hadn't he realized that with Alys? Maybe because Alys never stopped talking long enough to get a good look at her face. But Ariel was different, so much so that she almost *looked* different, which was impossible, of course, as they were identical in every way.

Every way but one. Their souls were different, and it was as evident to Evan as if they'd had different color hair, eyes and skin.

Ariel had a quiet intelligence, and it oozed out of her pores. She could have been a silent-screen actress from days of old. She still hadn't uttered a word, but her facial expressions spoke volumes. He watched as Alys bent her head down to Ralph's ear and talked to him as she enthusiastically scratched his back, while Ariel gently ran her hand across his head in a slow, firm, sure motion that never deviated.

Her eyes would meet Evan's from time to time, as if to reassure herself it was okay to be here doing this thing to his dog. She was cautious, careful and very conservative, unlike Alys who jumped headfirst into things and worried about the consequences later.

It startled him to realize that the girls' personalities were mirror images of his own. Alys, bubbly, vibrant, represented the past him; Ariel, quiet, introverted, represented the present him. He understood both of them, but felt himself more drawn to Ariel's serious eyes.

He knew what it was like to live inside your own head.

He shook his head to clear it, realizing that Alys was asking him a question. "What did you say?"

"Can I have an ice cube?" she asked.

"An ice cube? What for?"

"See—" Alys pointed to Ariel who was yawning. "She's so tired," Alys said to Evan.

"What's that got to do with an ice cube?" he asked.

"We didn't sleep a wink last night. Mommy let us sleep on the porch, but the screen on the window in the middle got ripped. The mosquitoes came in and bit us to pieces. See—" she held out her arms to show off the bite marks "—and they itch a lot. Mommy said don't scratch them. Ariel's not scratching hers, but I can't help it." To prove it, she began scratching the inside of her arms.

"Your mother is right," Evan said. "If you scratch them, they'll only itch worse."

"So can I get an ice cube? Mommy lets us put ice on the bites and it makes them feel better."

"Go ahead," Evan said.

"Come on, Ariel," Alys said and took her sister's hand and led her down the hallway, "the kitchen's this way."

Evan had to smile to himself. The little rascal already knew her way around his house. He looked down at Ralph who looked positively bereft by the cessation of attention. "Go ahead," he said to the dog, who immediately rose and followed the route the girls had taken to the kitchen.

He let out a chuckle at the same moment he heard a light tap on the screen door. Turning, he saw Sarah standing on the other side.

"They're here, aren't they?"

"Yes." He nodded. "They're here."

"May I?" she asked, her hand on the latch.

"Please."

Sarah opened the door and stepped inside. "I'm embarrassed," she began, "and I don't know what to say. You must think I'm a terrible mother, not being able to keep my children under control."

"No," he said softly. "I don't think anyone could keep Alys under control."

Sarah smiled. "No, I suppose you're right, but I apologize, anyway." She looked over his head. "Where are they?"

"Putting ice on their mosquito bites."

"Oh. Yes. They had a pretty bad night." She held out her arms to show her own bite marks. "We all did."

"What the—" A crashing sound sent them both rushing to the kitchen.

Alys was kneeling on the countertop with Ariel standing below. A large ceramic cookie jar was in pieces at her feet. Bits of papers, odd keys and coins were strewn all over the floor.

"Oh, my Lord!" Sarah exclaimed, "what have you done?"

"It wasn't my fault, Mommy. Ariel dropped it."

Sarah eyed Alys impatiently as Ariel whimpered. "And whose idea was it to climb up on the counter?" she asked.

"We wanted a cookie."

"I use it to keep junk in. I'm afraid I don't have cookies," Evan said almost apologetically even though his kitchen looked like a tornado had hit it.

"Of course you don't!" Sarah said. "Why should you?" She took a deep breath. "Get down from there right now, young lady. Back to the house, both of you. I'll deal with you in a minute."

In seconds, the two girls had scrambled out of the kitchen, with a meek Ralph fast on their heels. When Sarah heard the back door slam shut, she turned to Evan. "Do you have a broom and dust pan?"

"There's no need. I'll handle it."

"No, I can't let you do that," Sarah said as she bent and began picking up pieces of the pottery.

"Really, you don't have to do this."

"I feel awful," she said.

"No—"

"I can't believe they did such a thing. They are usually so respectful of other people's belongings. I don't know what got into them—"

"Sarah . . ."

The sound of her name on his lips stopped her cold. She looked up, her hands full of broken pottery. He was kneeling beside her, eye level. His closeness was unnerving. She almost dropped the pieces of pottery, her hands began to shake so.

"Please. Leave this. I'll clean it up later," he said.

"But—"

Evan took hold of her wrist and forced her to drop the broken pieces. "No buts. I'll take care of it."

Sarah looked down at his hand gripping her wrist. The heat of his touch sent waves of warmth up her arm. She lifted her head and, when their eyes met, her stomach blipped like a line on a cardiac screen.

She liked the feel of his fingers around her flesh, firm but gentle. A thought rushed through her head. A man was touching her. The first since John. Why that thought of all possible thoughts should be the one in the forefront of her mind told her more about her mental state than any long, drawn-out self-analysis might later on.

She felt his thumb rub against the soft skin on the inside of her wrist. The pad was rough, callused, wonderfully masculine. Her gaze returned to his hand, and as if he'd just realized what he'd done, Evan pulled away. He rose and walked to the other end of the kitchen.

Sarah felt the loss of energy immediately. "I—I'd better go," she said softly. "The girls . . ."

"Of course."

Sarah pointed to the mess on the floor. "Are you sure—"

"It's all right," Evan said, obviously anxious for her to leave. "No harm done." He tried to smile, but only a half grin creased his face.

Sarah couldn't even manage that. With a weak wave, she was gone, down the hallway, through his workroom and out the back door. As her feet flew across the cool green lawn, only one thought kept repeating itself over and over inside her head . . .

He touched me.

Evan waited a long moment, then returned to his workroom. Looking out the back door he caught a glimpse of Sarah just before she disappeared inside her house.

He moved to open the latch to let Ralph back in when he caught sight of his hand. Fingers splayed, he glanced down at his palm, and only one thought registered in his mind...

He'd touched her.

Chapter 3

The warm afternoon sun filtered in through the open window, casting the living room in a golden glow. Sarah relaxed on the sofa, flipping through a fashion magazine. She was sleepy after a long soak in the tub. Her hair wrapped in a towel, she lounged against the pillows in her pale blue terry-cloth robe.

It was "quiet time," a time she set aside each day to stop and catch her breath. The girls were upstairs either napping or lying side by side talking in whispers as was their habit when their energy level was high and sleep elusive.

Sarah adjusted the volume knob on the one-way portable baby monitor that kept her in touch with the girls' room. Listening intently for a long moment, she heard only the normal, mild static of a silent room. They must have given in to the drowsiness of the day and fallen asleep. Tempted to put aside her magazine and give in to a little nap herself, Sarah tucked her feet underneath her and leaned her head back.

The house was so beautifully still and peaceful, the knock startled her. She looked up from the magazine to peer out the front door. She hadn't heard a car and wondered who it might be. Her mouth fell open at the same moment the magazine slipped from her hands.

Evan.

Sarah rose, but hesitated before walking to the door. She hadn't seen him since the incident in his kitchen even though the girls had gone over to his house again. He hadn't complained, nor had he chased them away. In fact, Alys had told her he'd offered them milk and chocolate-chip cookies, which meant he must have stocked up in anticipation of their next visit.

Such a turnaround in his attitude had surprised Sarah, but the girls had thought that it was perfectly natural. In their short lives, no one had ever really not wanted them around and they couldn't fathom anyone who wouldn't.

In a few weeks' time, the twins had made the area between the two houses their own. It seemed almost useless to forbid them to cross the lawn any longer, especially since the dog had taken to following them, roaming in and out of her house as he pleased, more like their pet than Evan's, as the girls ran around with carefree abandon.

But she was not the twins, and she'd stayed put. She wasn't proud of the reason, either. She was embarrassed at her girlish reaction to his touch. The memory of his hand on her wrist was burned in her brain with such clarity that it frightened her. Unbidden, it would return, and with it, a thrill would creep up her spine, an anticipatory tingle that made her warm and cold at the same time.

Why an insignificant touch would wreak such havoc with her nervous system was a question for which she didn't want to search too deeply for an answer.

But the memory wouldn't go away, nor would the realization that she *liked* the feel of his hand on her. A man's grip, roughened, callused fingers rubbing against the soft inside of her wrist. A man's hand, with all its myriad textures. It had made her heart beat faster, her pulse flutter beneath his fingers.

And all he'd done was touch her. Briefly. Too briefly. So briefly that she hungered for more.

Silly. Foolish. *Desperate*.

The stereotypical love-starved widow who'd been without a man for too long. That's how she felt. Had he guessed? It was all too possible, and that was why she'd hidden away, safely tucked inside her little house, nursing her shame, finding dozens of little tasks to keep her hands busy, to keep her mind from skipping across the lawn and imagining what he was doing, what he was thinking, what, if anything, he was feeling. About her.

The knock came again, and she could no longer ignore it. Slowly, Sarah walked to the door, but didn't open it.

"Hi," he said through the screen.

"Hi . . ." she answered. "Is something wrong?"

"I've come to fix the porch screen," he said, holding up his toolbox with one hand and a mesh replacement with the other. Glancing at the towel on her head, he added, "If it's not convenient—"

"The screen?"

"On the back porch. The mosquitoes? Biting Alys to pieces, remember? She mentioned it again yesterday."

"Oh, yes. The mosquitoes. But you don't have to—"

"Yes, I do." His gaze centered on the V neck of her robe, and Sarah gathered the material together with a fist. "It's in the lease," he added.

"Of course." She pushed at the screen door. "Come in."

Sarah held the door for him, and Evan slid past her. "Please go about your business," he said. "I know the way."

"No, it's no trouble," she said, leading him toward the back porch. "It's 'quiet time.' The girls are napping, and I was just reading a magazine."

He dropped his toolbox in the center of the room and leaned the screen against the wall. "Quiet time?"

Sarah smiled. "Yes. My only demand as a mother. I need an hour or so each afternoon to gather myself together for the next half of the day. It probably sounds strange to you."

"No," he said, "not at all. I understand completely. If I had Alys chattering at me all day, I'd need a rest, too." He paused. "No offense."

Sarah smiled. "None taken." Encouraged that he could joke about her children, Sarah pushed on. "I'm sorry I haven't been able to keep them away from your house. I'll try to do a better job."

His mouth turned down in a frown. "I haven't been doing too well myself. My dog seems to have attached himself to the girls. I hope he hasn't been a nuisance."

"No, not at all. It seems the attraction is mutual." As soon as the words left her mouth, Sarah blushed. She turned her face and tried to change the subject. "Please feel free to chase the girls if they bother you."

"I don't think that will be necessary anymore... Sarah. My cousin tells me I guard my privacy too jealously—"

"No—"

"She's right. Sometimes I overreact."

It was the closest to an apology that she was going to get from him, but the mere fact that he was trying warmed her heart more than she would have imagined. "I think we both may have... Evan," she said softly.

Their gazes locked. She took the opportunity to study him. He stood still in his tight jeans and fitted gray T-shirt, almost defiantly, as if he were gauging her reaction to his face as he granted her permission—or just dared her—to cringe, or pull back, or show some signs of revulsion.

But Sarah felt no such thing. Lara was right. After a while you didn't even notice the scars. From the right, he was a strikingly handsome man, but the marred skin on the left side of his face didn't frighten her in the least, nor did it detract from his masculine beauty. In some ways the imperfection enhanced his looks, providing a stark contrast that made his chiseled features stand out all the more.

He was the first to look away. The test was over, but Sarah wasn't sure if she'd passed or failed.

"Where's the rip?"

It took Sarah a minute to realize he was talking about the screen. "Over here." She pointed to the middle window. "The moving men were a little too aggressive when they delivered the furniture, I'm afraid."

"No problem."

She sat on the edge of the sofa as he turned his back to her and began to pry the torn screen from its molding. The room was hot without even the slightest of breezes coming in through the jalousie windows that faced the lake.

Pulling off the towel from her head, Sarah shook out her damp hair and combed her fingers through it. She knew she should excuse herself and go upstairs to dress, but she didn't want to. It had been such a long time since she'd shared space with a man that she gave in to the impulse to indulge herself and just watch him.

In the still afternoon with the sun beating down on the thin porch roof, she felt more alive than she had in ages. She told herself again that she should leave him alone to work, but the thick air made her limbs too heavy to move. She could almost see the waves of heat in the air. It seeped into her skin with the intensity of a sauna, and she was loath to break the languorous spell.

The muscles in Evan's back rippled as he worked, and his arms glistened with sweat. She leaned forward, and he twisted his head to look at her over his shoulder. He attempted a smile, but it turned out more like a short, almost pained grimace rather than a full-fledged grin.

She was near, perhaps too near, and that might be making him uncomfortable. But Sarah didn't care.

Perspiration dotted his forehead. Sarah fantasized as his gaze met hers. He looked like a rogue from days of old, a pirate, a ravisher. Sarah took a deep breath and her robe gaped open slightly. His jaw tightened, and she watched Evan's eyes move to the swell of her breast, then quickly, almost guiltily, return to the business at hand.

Just my luck, Sarah thought. A modern-day rogue. With a conscience.

She watched him pull out the torn screen from its molding. His fingers fumbled momentarily, and it slipped.

He turned to her in exasperation. "Please don't let me keep you from anything."

"You're not keeping me from anything." She *was* making him nervous. Good.

"You don't have to stay here while I work. I'll be done soon."

"It's all right. I don't mind."

"Oh."

"Unless I'm bothering you. Am I?"

"No. No. Of course not."

"Fine."

"Fine."

Evan wiped his forehead with the back of his hand. Bothering him? That was a laugh. His body was as hot as the blasted sun baking the inside of this room. He didn't dare stand up for fear of embarrassing himself.

What was wrong with this woman? Didn't she realize she was sitting here half-naked with a virtual stranger all alone in the middle of the afternoon in an isolated area where he could do anything he wanted to her and no one within twenty miles would hear?

Sweat began to pour down his back between his shoulder blades. The heat this afternoon was more July than June. He looked out at the inviting water only a few feet away at the end of the dock and wished he could strip down and jump into the still-cool water and shock his body back into submission. But even the thought of taking off his clothes anywhere near Sarah Wyeth made him randy as hell.

Please, he begged, *please leave.*

He glanced at her again and she smiled at him. Why was she watching him? She couldn't possibly think he would take something from the house, could she? No, there had to be another reason she was sitting behind him like an overseer at a work farm.

"Want to help?" he asked, immediately regretting the words as they left his mouth.

"Sure." She jumped up and moved beside him.

Evan made room for her on his right, his good side, a habit he didn't even realize he'd cultivated over the years. She knelt beside him.

"Here," he said, handing her the screwdriver he used to pry off the old screen. He lifted the new screen. "Now hold this with both hands and hang on tight."

Sarah stuffed the screwdriver into the pocket of her robe and grabbed the replacement screen, holding it against the molding as he asked. She was close to him, so close she could see the beads of sweat pool on his forehead. One or two broke free and streamed down his temple onto his cheek.

Her stomach muscles tightened. God help her, she wanted to touch him. She held fast to the screen in an effort to stop her hand from reaching up and wiping away the moisture from his brow. His gaze didn't wander in her direction, and she was sure he had no idea of the turmoil that was going on in her mind.

Looking at this perfect side of his profile, Sarah realized how difficult all this must have been for him. Lara had said he'd had a wonderful personality and had been popular. A handsome, popular man in a small town would have been the center of attention. He must have attracted both the young and old, male and female, with his looks and charm. To lose one by accident and discard the other by choice must have changed his life completely.

He seemed shy, ill at ease, awkward even, yet she knew there was something deep and serious simmering under the surface of that facade. Something so compelling, so utterly male, that it was reawakening feelings in her she'd thought had died with John.

What was it about Evan Forester that intrigued her so? Was it just that he was the first man since John who she actually viewed as a man? Were her man skills so rusty that she needed to practice on someone? Was he the prime candidate only because he lived next door? Was she that hard up? That much in need of sex that she would jump the first masculine form to even remotely attract her?

She didn't like these questions, nor was she one to indulge in self-psychoanalysis, especially where her sexuality was concerned. But she had to admit that sometimes she thought there was something wrong with her.

She hadn't always been a sexual person, but her short marriage to John had changed that. Marital love had been one of the greatest joys in her life. She'd sometimes felt as if she'd been the one to invent it. Their sex life had been active, spontaneous and thoroughly fulfilling. Which was why she missed it so much.

But missing it couldn't totally account for the way she was feeling. In the six years since John's death, she hadn't once experienced this need to touch a man, to want a man to touch her.

Until now.

So...*what* was it about Evan Forester that resurrected these feelings? Perhaps the fact that he was so remote, so unattainable as to be laughable, but therefore... safe.

"Done," he said, sitting back on his haunches to inspect his work.

Sarah didn't move, wanting the proximity to last even though she knew she was being blatantly bold.

Evan turned to her, and their gazes locked. "It's so hot today," she said, her voice as dry as her lips.

His gaze followed the movement of the tip of her tongue as she licked her bottom lip. "It is," he said, wiping at his forehead again with the back of his hand.

Sarah picked up the discarded towel and twisted an end in her hand. "May I?" she asked.

He barely nodded, but it was all the incentive Sarah needed. She slowly daubed his face, first the right side, then his forehead, then hesitantly she moved to pat the side with the scar.

Evan reared back, moving out of her reach. He grabbed her wrist and tugged the towel free from her grasp, finishing the job himself.

"Thanks," he said, and stood.

"You're welcome," Sarah answered.

He held out his hand and Sarah placed her hand in his palm, allowing him to give her a brace up. Standing toe-to-toe, he didn't immediately release her hand.

For a long moment, Evan remained still, watching her, unable to read her mind but just as unable to ignore the burning sensation on his cheek where her touch had been. What was her game? What did she want?

Their eyes met again, and he threw caution to the wind.

"It doesn't bother you." It wasn't a question.

She didn't have to ask what he meant by "it."

"No," she said, "it doesn't."

"Then you're unique."

Sarah shook her head. "No, I don't think so. I think you make more out of it than you should."

He laughed then, a cynical sound that chilled her. "You've been talking to Lara."

"Yes, I have. She told me that you were once very involved in the community, very popular."

He stood and gathered up his tools. "The operative word here is *were.*"

"You need to give people a chance."

"I've taken all the chances I ever intend on taking... or giving," he said.

"But—"

Evan pressed the towel into her hands and swung the toolbox up into his arms. "Thanks for your concern, Sarah, but I like my life just the way it is..."

"And it's really not any of my business?"

His only answer to her remark was a slight tightening of his jaw. She knew she'd gone too far. He turned from her and walked back through the house to the front door. Sarah followed, trying to think up something to say that would make amends, but she never quite caught up with him. She grabbed hold of the swinging screen door as he exited.

"Let me know if anything else needs fixing," he said over his shoulder as he tramped down the steps.

"I will. And...thank you."

Sarah watched him walk across the lawns. Looking down at the bulge in her robe, she realized she still had his screwdriver in her pocket. She swung open the screen door and ran down the steps.

"Wait!" she called.

Evan stopped, turned and waited for her to catch up with him. She came to an abrupt stop in front of him. Out of breath and heart pounding, she knew she looked foolish standing in the middle of the lawn in her bathrobe, which had fallen off one shoulder during her run. She felt awkward, silly even, having given in to an irrational, impulsive need to not let their meeting end.

It couldn't. Not like this.

Before she could open her mouth to speak, a little voice called from the upstairs window.

"Mommy?"

They both turned toward the house.

"The girls are up," he said.

"Yes."

"You'd better go."

"Yes."

But she didn't move. Instead, she stared into his dark, fathomless eyes, wondering what he was thinking, wanting to know so badly that only her staunch pride stopped her from asking him outright.

He reached up and pulled up the lapel of her robe. "Go, Sarah," he said.

It was a simple order that told her more than any answer he might have given to any question she might have asked. It told her that maybe he was not as immune to her as he seemed, that maybe he was feeling something stir within himself, as well, that maybe he—

"Mommy!"

"Coming!"

She held up the screwdriver. "You forgot this."

Evan looked at the tool and grinned. For some reason the grin embarrassed her more than her disheveled appearance. It was as if he knew she'd used any excuse to run after him. Abruptly, Sarah turned and started back to the house, forcing herself not to run.

"Thanks," he called after her.

Pride stiffened her back. She pretended not to hear.

The cool water shocked his naked skin. Evan dived into the shimmering blackness and swam until his lungs were near bursting. He wanted to stay under until all conscious thought was erased from his mind, until he was this close to oblivion, until he didn't—couldn't—think anymore.

It didn't work.

He exploded onto the surface, gasping, drinking in the precious air with huge gulps of breath. All was quiet except for the sounds of his own splashing. He kicked his feet, treading water, going nowhere.

Like my life . . .

The moon was full, and it cast a long pale gold shadow that drew a straight line from it directly to him. He could feel the waves he had created lapping against him, licking every pore on his skin.

He raised his arms and dived under again, swimming faster, farther out toward the raft near the center of the lake. He pulled himself out of the water and laid down flat against the floating island. Water streamed off his body in rivulets, and he wiped his face with his hands.

Naked and alone, he stared at the black sky. A plethora of stars engulfed him. He studied them for a long, long time as he would a painting in a prestigious museum, looking for the hidden meaning, trying to figure out how he fit into all of this.

This soul-searching was not new. He'd engaged in this very exercise on many, many occasions since he'd moved out here by the lake. Sometimes he spoke out loud to the sky, the stars, the universe. God. Sometimes he felt solace, sometimes he found a reason. Sometimes he didn't. Tonight was one of those nights.

Tonight, there was no answer.

His wet body became chilled against the night air. He didn't care, accepting the gooseflesh as a small price to pay for this complete privacy. He rolled over onto his belly, the cool wooden surface of the raft chafing his skin as it rocked gently back and forth.

It was the dead of night. The old house in the background was as still, dark and silent as the night itself. The twins were asleep, and so, too, was their mother.

Sarah...

A light breeze came down from the north side of the lake. It caressed his face, breathing her name in his ear as it threaded through and ruffled his hair.

Sarah... Sarah... Sarah...

He shut his eyes against the sound in his head that was weaving its way in and around him, making his body ache with a want and a need he'd suppressed for so long, he'd thought it gone. But it wasn't gone, only sleeping, seemingly awaiting the one person who would reignite that flame of desire in him.

Sarah...

He didn't need it, didn't want it. There was no room for that kind of desire in his life anymore. He had order if not passion. He had his work, which gave him satisfaction and validation. It had taken a long time, but he'd managed to convince himself that was enough.

He'd had to. The women in town were not exactly beating a path to his door. After Maureen... no, don't think of that time, that horrible, humiliating time. That was over, forgiven if not forgotten. And, he had to admit, there was no comparison between the two, between the Maureen who was and the Sarah who is.

Sarah...

She was too beautiful, too sweet and, for all her years as wife and mother, too innocent, as well. The way she'd let him in the house today dressed in that blue robe— fresh faced, wide-eyed and so damned tempting his mouth had watered.

He'd wanted to kiss her. He'd wanted to take her into his arms and taste her on his lips, on his tongue. He'd wanted to bury his face in the curve of her neck and feel the softness he knew would be waiting there for him.

Evan took a deep breath to dispel the image. It was a mistake. He could almost smell her damp woman's scent in the air around him. His body grew hard. He squeezed his eyes shut and audibly groaned in frustration as he tried to clear the memory.

Impossible . . .

He rolled off the raft, falling silently into the black water, almost willing it to take him away somewhere where it didn't matter what he looked like, but only who he was.

But that place was not here, not Wayside, not anywhere on earth that he knew of. He was what he was and he looked as he looked, and never the twain shall meet. For all her sweetness and compassion and words of advice, Sarah Wyeth was no different from other women.

It was easy to talk the talk . . . just ask Maureen.

He swam to shore with long, slow freestyle strokes that stretched his muscles and relaxed him at the same time. Pulling himself onto the dock, Evan slipped into his worn cutoffs, sat back and brushed the wet hair from his face. His fingers came in contact with the rough skin of his scar. His hand stilled and he checked the palm, as if by some miracle the scar had rubbed off onto it.

Laughing out loud at his fanciful thought, he stood and ambled down the path along the lake, passing close by but not too close to the old house on his way back home.

He tried not to look up at her window and he almost made it, but at the last moment he stopped, unable to deny himself. Scanning the second floor, he found the master bedroom, window open, white lace curtain billowing in the breeze.

And then he saw a figure. Sarah. Only a shadow against the curtain at first, but he was sure it was her. He pivoted, and moved closer.

She was watching him.

In the dark, he knew, she couldn't see details. He would look whole to her in the dark. Unblemished. His body was in good shape—hard and tight from running, working out and just plain swinging the hammer.

He tried to imagine what he looked like from her perspective. Shiny wet in the dark, his skin slick, gleaming in the moonlight with the wetness from the lake.

She stepped forward into the moonlight. Though he couldn't make out her features, he knew by her posture that her gaze was centered on him. The white of her nightgown gleamed like neon, her outline pristine and stark against the night.

He wanted to say something, but couldn't speak. She was too beautiful, too *perfect,* too out of his reach in more ways than this distance between them. Yet he longed for her. Ached for her. Wanted her in a way he couldn't remember ever wanting a woman. Not even Maureen.

No comparison. He was older now, wiser, and he knew himself better.

That breeze again. *Sarah . . . Sarah . . . Sarah.*

Don't do this to me, woman, he begged mentally. Don't tease me with the impossible, entice me only to remind me later on that I can't have you or anyone like you.

She had looked at him today without the reserve he usually saw in a woman's eyes. But that meant nothing other than that she was compassionate, kind, perhaps even a little farsighted.

He smiled to himself. Yes, that was it. Had to be. Sarah Wyeth was blind as a bat. She must be to stand there this long staring at *him.*

But what if she wasn't?

He felt a chill run down his spine. The breeze was picking up. A cloud obscured the moon. Suddenly, all was black around him, and he could no longer be sure she was standing at the window. He turned and started back toward his house, quickly, without a backward glance.

Fantasy, he told himself, some damn moonlight fantasy. *Go home, and go to sleep.* Tomorrow the sun will be out, and the real you will be visible once again.

Scars and all.

Chapter 4

Sarah loaded the girls into the car for her first real trip to town. She had many things to do today, all of which demanded her undivided attention.

So she was more than annoyed with herself for the side glance she gave over to Evan's house, hoping for a glimpse of him, a wave maybe or, *miracle of miracles,* a word of hello. But even though his truck was parked in its usual spot, he was nowhere in sight.

So much for fantasies.

Grow up.

Evan had seen her last night, she was sure of it. He'd stopped directly below her window on his way back from the lake. At first, she'd thought something had distracted him, but then he'd looked up. At her. It had almost been as if he'd sensed her presence.

He couldn't have known that she'd seen him arrive at the dock for his middle-of-the night swim. She'd been too keyed to sleep, and the ribbon of moonlight across the lake had lured her to the window. Her first inclination had been to look away when he dropped his cutoffs and plunged into the black waters, but something had compelled her to stay.

He'd seemed possessed, swimming hard as if in an Olympic race, and she'd wondered what demons he was banishing with such exertion. By the time he'd reached the raft, he'd been only a dim figure in the distance, but she'd continued to watch as he'd stretched out and paid homage to the twinkling ebony sky.

When the silence of the night had once again prevailed and his prone figure became too difficult to discern, she had chided herself for her juvenile behavior. He'd remained on the raft for a long time, long enough for her to abandon her attempt at voyeurism and climb back into bed.

She'd dozed, until one of those illusive, indecipherable, exaggerated night sounds had roused her once again. Like a thief in the night, she had scurried back to her place at the window. Drawn to see what it could be.

Drawn to him.

And there he was right below her window. At first, she'd inched back behind the curtains, embarrassed at being caught, but when he took a stand and stared up at her, she'd moved forward into view. She'd wanted him to see her, wanted him to acknowledge her and, in some very basic way, just . . . wanted him.

To do what, she wasn't exactly sure.

Not then, not now.

Sarah drove the car out onto the main road and turned toward town. The girls were chattering in the back seat, but her mind was still on last night and what might have been. Like…what if she had called his name? Would he have answered? Would he have invited her to come down and join him? What would have happened if he had?

That was the real question, the one she was afraid to answer. She wasn't impulsive by nature, but last night she had felt impulsive, daring, and had to grip the windowsill to stop from calling out to him. There had been electricity in the air, a static that pricked her senses long after he'd disappeared back into his house, long after she'd slipped back into her bed. Her body had been charged with it, tingled with it, and still today, there remained a dangerous residue.

She wanted to see him, knowing that it would do her little good once she did. No matter what his eyes said to the contrary, Evan Forester was made of stone.

Her mind was in overdrive, and she wished she knew more about him. Lara had called her several times since she'd moved in, and she hoped that they were becoming friends of sorts. But while she certainly was a good source of information about Evan, all her answers were guarded, as if she'd been charged with protecting that privacy he held so dear. Perhaps today, in town, she would be able to find out a bit more.

Suddenly, finding out what made Evan Forester tick became an important mission if only in her own mind.

Her first stop was the rectory. She'd wanted to enroll the girls in Sunday school, but also inquire about the organist position that was available. Lara had mentioned it to her during one of their early interviews, and the idea had stuck. Working at the church would be a great opportunity for them to become involved in the community quickly, and Sarah was anxious to introduce herself and show her interest.

Edith Winthrop was the pastor's wife, and she greeted Sarah and the girls at the rectory door. "Come in, come in. It's so nice to meet you," she said after Sarah introduced herself and the girls.

"I hope we're not intruding," Sarah began. "Lara Hanlon told me about the opening for church organist, and I was wondering if the position had been filled."

"No, not yet," Edith said. "Mrs. Mallory hasn't retired yet, though her age is showing, poor dear. She's determined to stay until summer's end, and then the reverend will have to make a decision as to who will replace her."

"So I'm not too late."

"Heavens, no. I'm sure my husband will be conducting tryouts soon. Why not leave your name and number so that he can call you?"

"That would be wonderful," Sarah said as she scribbled her name and telephone number on the pad Mrs. Winthrop provided. "I look forward to hearing from you."

Mrs. Winthrop looked down at the paper Sarah handed her. "I see you're living out next to Evan Forester."

"Yes, I'm renting the old Kelly place."

"I'm surprised he rented again. That young man seems determined to be alone."

Sarah looked Mrs. Winthrop in the eye. "That's something we're working on."

"You and the girls?" When Sarah nodded, she continued, "Well, Mrs. Wyeth, if you can get Evan Forester to accompany you to church one Sunday, you'll have my husband's undying gratitude. He's been after him for years!"

Sarah laughed. "That, I'm afraid, would take a miracle, Mrs. Winthrop."

"Well, this is the right place for them! You never know."

"That's true," Sarah agreed, thinking about how much Evan had changed already in his attitude toward the girls.

Lost in thought, Sarah didn't realize she was still standing in the doorway.

"Can I offer you and the girls some refreshments? Lemonade?" Mrs. Winthrop asked.

The girls' eyes lit up, but Sarah had too many errands still to run to take a break quite yet. "No, thank you, Mrs. Winthrop, I'm on my way over to the school."

"Registering the girls?"

"Yes, for kindergarten, and myself, as well. I'll be teaching music this year to the elementary-school children."

"Yes, I heard about that. Well, good luck to you, Mrs. Wyeth—" she extended her hand to Sarah "—and I look forward to seeing you in church on Sundays."

"We'll be there."

Sarah said her goodbyes, promising the girls ice cream as they walked over to the school where she made quick work of registering the girls for kindergarten and introducing herself to the staff. The principal, Sam Johnson, was very cordial and friendly, and after her tour of the school, they sat in his office for an informal chat while the girls charmed his secretary.

"We're all looking forward to the new term," he said. "This is the first time our district has had funding for the arts at the elementary-school level. We hope you're as excited as we are, Mrs. Wyeth."

"I certainly am, and please call me Sarah," she offered.

"And I'm Sam," he said with a friendly smile, which Sarah returned. "Well, September will be here before we know it. I'll send you a letter outlining your specific duties, days, times, that sort of thing, and if you have any questions, we can straighten it all out before school starts." He paused as he checked her file. "You're living out in the Kellys' old rental by the lake, aren't you?"

"Yes, next door to Evan Forester."

"Oh, yes. Evan."

"Do you know him?" she asked.

"Evan and I went to school together. Played ball together. We go back a long way."

"Then, you're friends?"

Sam chuckled. "No, I wouldn't exactly say that. *Friends* is a heavy word where Evan is concerned. He's been a bit on the ornery side since the accident."

"I hear from his cousin that he was quite a hero."

"My, yes. The man's a near legend around these parts. Evan risked his life and saved a lot of people. Paid dearly for it, too."

"You mean the scars."

"Yes, it's terrible, isn't it?"

"Oh, I don't find them all that bad," she said with a smile.

"Of course not," Sam said with a half grin. "We must consider all he went through."

Sarah's smile faded a bit. "Yes, we must."

She said her goodbyes, took the girls by the hand and made her way out of the school, a vague feeling of discontent lingering after her conversation with the principal.

Is this what Evan put up with each time he came to town, this patronizing courtesy? No wonder his trips were few and far between.

Her thoughts on Evan, she distractedly took hold of the girls' hands to cross the street and came up short as the oncoming car stopped for her. She recognized Lara and smiled.

Lara rolled down her window as she passed. "Sarah! Wait up for me."

Sarah nodded her agreement as she trotted the two girls across the intersection to the other side of the street and into the ice-cream parlor. She'd promised the girls cones, and made the purchase as she waited for Lara to park.

"How are you?" Lara asked when she caught up with them.

Sarah wrapped the bottom of each cone in a napkin and handed them to the girls as they sat on the bench outside the storefront.

"Great! And you?" she asked, perusing the younger woman's hassled look. "A bit frazzled?"

"Don't you know it!" Lara said, running a hand across her brow. "I've been running all day. This wedding is going to be the death of me."

"Wedding?"

"Didn't I mention I'm getting married Labor Day weekend?"

Sarah shut her eyes and nodded. "Yes, of course you did. Don't mind me. Wally, isn't it?"

"Willy," Lara corrected, "and he's part of the problem. We started out with this real small affair, and now we have over a hundred people. I swear, he keeps inviting everyone in town he bumps into. We'll never fit all these people into the house we've bought, and it's too late to arrange for a hall."

"What are you going to do?" Sarah asked.

Lara made a face. "I was thinking of asking Evan if I could use his house. He's got plenty of room and the yard's twice as big if you count his back and your front."

Sarah's eyes widened. "Do you think he'd agree to it? I mean, knowing how he is about his privacy and all?"

"Not in a million years. Evan would rather spontaneously combust than have to deal with a house full of people."

"So what are you going to do?"

"Ask him, anyway. I don't really have a choice." Lara hesitated, shifting her weight from one side to the other. "I was hoping you'd help."

"Me? What could I possibly do?"

"Oh, I don't know. But he might respond better to you. He did adjust very well to the girls."

"Well, you were right about that. They're great friends now."

Lara eyed Sarah speculatively. "You know, this would be just the thing to solve both our problems. Evan's and mine, I mean."

"What thing?"

"Evan keeps teasing me about trying to arrange an 'event' to bring him back out into society. Like a debutante's coming-out party. He always laughs at me when I come up with something, telling me, 'No, that's not it,' but this might just be . . . *it*. What do you think?"

"You *are* his cousin, Lara. And you're in a jam. How could he refuse you?" Sarah asked, warming to her idea of having the wedding take place next door to her.

"Oh, I'm sure he'll think of a way. He's not too big on weddings. Marriage in general, for that matter. Told me that if I had to do it, I should just elope. But I'm willing to give it a try." Lara pursed her lips. "Will you help?"

Sarah wanted to ask what Evan had against marriage, but held her tongue. "If I can," she offered instead.

Lara bit her lip. "This won't be easy. We'll have to brainstorm."

"Come on over later in the week. We'll come up with something."

"Then attack," Lara said with a mischievous grin and her hands formed into claws.

The thought of attacking Evan—but not quite in that way—skittered through Sarah's mind, but she let it go. "We'll get the girls to help."

"We can make them flower girls!"

"Oh, Lara, you don't have to do that!" Sarah asked.

"Why not? It would be great fun. It won't be expensive. The wedding's going to be informal. They can wear dresses they already have."

"If you're sure..." Sarah said.

"Look, we have enough people in this wedding party to start a parade already, two more won't matter one way or the other! That is, if it's all right with you."

Sarah looked over at her twins. They sat side by side on the bench, swinging their legs through the air with alternating rhythm. Their faces and hands were sticky with vanilla ice cream and sprinkles. She dipped into her bag for wet-wipes and tried to imagine them in pink organdy dresses. "I'll talk to them tonight, but I'm sure they'd be thrilled."

Lara extended her hand. "Deal, then?"

"Deal," Sarah said. A shimmer of excitement ran through Sarah as they shook hands and sealed their bargain.

But what would Evan think? Was she poking her nose where it was none of her business? Would he think she was trying to worm her way into his life via his cousin?

And... would he be right?

The phone was ringing as she unlocked the front door. Sarah ran inside, dropped her bag on the sofa and raced to catch the call before the machine kicked in.

"Hello!"

"Are you all right?" It was her mother.

"Hi, Mom. I'm fine."

"You're out of breath."

"Just got in. I registered the girls for kindergarten this morning."

"Oh."

Hearing her mother's peevish tone, Sarah rolled her eyes. "What is it, Mom?"

"I guess that means you've decided to stay."

"We've been through this before. I signed a lease for a year."

"I know," her mother said with a sigh, "it's just that your father and I miss you all so much. We're used to seeing you and the girls every day. It's been very hard."

"We miss you, too, but you'll be visiting soon."

"Yes, well, that's why I called. Dad and I wanted to move up the date and come the first of July instead of the fifteenth. Then we can stay for a whole month. How does that sound?"

A whole month? "Let me check the calendar," Sarah said as she swiveled, wrapping the cord halfway around her waist.

She bit her lip. There was no calendar to check. She needed time to think. July first was a week away. Sarah felt as if she'd just arrived in Wayside and already her parents were about to descend on her.

And take over.

She loved them dearly; together with her in-laws, they had been her lifeline after John's death. But in these few weeks away from them, she'd gotten a taste of freedom, and she found that she more than liked it, she thrived on it.

"I don't know, Mom. That first week of July is kind of busy. The holiday weekend and all."

"We won't be in the way. We can help you."

They would help, she knew that. She also knew that they would smother her. Her summer had been planned in her mind, and having to face them sooner did not sit well with her. But how did she tell her mother without hurting her feelings?

"Let me check again," she said, stalling.

As her mind raced, she caught sight of the twins in the yard with Evan. He was getting ready to cut the grass on the rider mower, and the girls were vying for his attention. He'd begun to make a habit of letting them ride with him on his lap, one at a time, and the girls had come to look forward to his weekly lawn maintenance.

She looked at their smiling faces. They were in the process of forming a new life, distinctly different from the one they had in the city. They were happy, healthy and . . .

Suddenly, Sarah knew what she had to do. Hurt or not, she had to tell her mother no. She needed this extra small bit of time alone with the girls, and, if she was perfectly honest, with herself . . . not to mention her growing interest in Evan.

She wanted to get to know him better, and her parents, particularly her mother, would be a definite deterrent to that. Instinctively, she knew that her mother would not approve of any kind of relationship with him, or anyone else for that matter. She was overprotective, and it had taken every morsel of strength Sarah had to break away from her and come this far.

Sarah steeled herself. It hurt her to hurt them, but in this case, she knew she must. "I'm sorry, Mom, but it's just not going to work out. Let's keep the date to the fifteenth as planned, okay?" Silence. "Mom? Is that all right?"

"If it's too much trouble for you, of course it's all right. We wouldn't want to put you out."

Sarah held her tongue. "Great. I'll call you next week and we'll firm up the plans."

"Your father will be so disappointed," her mother added.

Sarah ignored the barb. "I'll call you."

She cradled the phone, and shut her eyes. Her heart was pounding as it always did when she forced herself to do something that was difficult for her to do. Yet each time she made the effort, she felt stronger, more confident and ready to take on the next challenge. She was moving in the right direction with her life, she felt it in her bones.

Turning back to the window, she noticed that Alys's turn was over, and she was hopping off the rider mower. Evan motioned her back to the porch as he lifted Ariel onto his lap to take her place. As the mower lurched forward, Sarah could hear Ariel's screech as she held on to Evan's arms for dear life.

Sarah came out onto the porch and put her arm around Alys, who was sitting patiently, waiting as Ariel took her turn. That in itself was a miracle. Ariel giggled with delight each time Evan swerved into a turn, and Sarah couldn't help but smile, too. Her shy little girl was blossoming with the extra attention.

This is right, she said to herself. This is the way her girls should be, not spoiled and withdrawn, but happy and sharing. She felt a small pang of regret at hurting her mother's feelings, but she was convinced it had to be done. She needed this time, for the girls, for herself . . . and for Evan.

He slowed the mower down to a crawl and maneuvered it closer to the porch. Slipping the gear into neutral, the engine idled as Ariel slipped off his lap. Once she was safely on the ground, Evan looked up. His eyes met Sarah's, and his gaze caressed her face. She felt herself grow warm with its intensity, and wondered if he was thinking about last night at the lake.

"Mommy's turn!" Alys shouted gleefully.

It took Sarah a minute to understand what her daughter was suggesting. "Oh, no, you silly thing," she said with a laugh. "I'm too big!"

"No, you're not! Is she, Evan?" Alys continued, warming to the idea of her mother going for a ride on the mower. "You can fit next to him. See?" She pointed to the small space at the edge of the mower's bench seat.

It was true, there was room—barely.

"Can she, Evan? Can she?"

Evan looked at the expectant faces of Alys, then Ariel, and finally Sarah. "I don't know if that's such a good—"

"Oh, please, Evan," Ariel asked, her eyes as big as saucers.

Two identical little faces stared up at him. "Uh, sure. If she wants . . ."

Alys grabbed hold of Sarah's right hand and Ariel took her left. Together they pulled her down the steps right up to Evan and the mower. "Go on, Mommy. You'll see. It's so much fun!"

Sarah shook her head. "I don't think—"

Evan held out his hand.

Not having a clue as to what was going through his mind, Sarah hesitantly placed her hand in his palm and accepted the invitation. As he helped her on board, she told herself she was doing this just to please the girls, but that wasn't entirely true.

She was doing this because she wanted an excuse to touch him.

"You don't have to do this," she said as she attempted to squeeze into the small space next to him.

"Oh, no?" he asked, motioning to the twins who were jumping up and down with joy and giggling their heads off in anticipation of their mother's ride around the lawn.

"Okay," she said with a grin, "once around."

"Show time," he said and put the rider in gear. "Hold on."

Evan increased the throttle, and they took off at top speed.

The girls squealed their delight as Sarah lurched forward, gripping the edge of the seat.

"Faster," Alys screamed, "faster!"

Evan gave her a sideways grin that said "get ready," and as they rounded into a turn, he downshifted. Determined to survive this ride, she hung on tightly.

"You okay?" he asked, and all she could do was clench her teeth and nod.

He directed the rider down the width of the yard and made another, wider turn, and this time she was not okay. She lost her balance. As she felt herself flying sideways through the air, an arm wrapped around her waist and pulled her to safety.

Onto his lap.

Evan wasn't sure which one of them was more surprised by his instinctive action. She was lying full across him, her legs hanging straight out over the side, her head tucked in the curve of his neck, her body flush against his. She locked her hands behind his neck for balance. He held her firmly around the waist, and with his free hand he managed to downshift to a mere crawl.

He had her. *They were safe.*

And then their eyes met.

Or were they?

Everything hit him at once. The low growl of the motor, the smell of the freshly cut grass, her long auburn curls spread across his shoulder. Evan took a deep breath to clear his head, but her natural woman's scent filled his nostrils, obliterating everything in his consciousness but her.

Her softness was nestled in his lap as if he had personally directed her to the one spot on his body that corresponded perfectly with the one spot on her body where they were destined to come together.

He felt it all, each sensation separate and potent: her hands on his neck, her arms resting on his shoulders, her eyes, big, blue pools of wonder wide enough to drown in. Desire shot through him, burning him with a heat as searing as the fiery beam that had scarred him for life.

He was gone, lost, trapped in a space, time, place somewhere between heaven and hell....

Sarah was shaking. Well, she'd wanted to touch him, and she'd gotten her wish.

Be careful what you ask for...

Sarah's fingers curled into the longer hair at his nape, and as if they had a will of their own, her fingers began to thread themselves through it. Inching closer still, she pressed herself into him, savoring the feel of her breasts against his muscled chest. Her heart skipped a beat when his hand dropped from her waist to her derriere. He lifted her more snugly onto his lap. Eyes never leaving his, she wiggled to settle in to the new position.

He slanted his head. She lifted her chin. Their faces were so close, his vision blurred and only the soft creaminess of her skin registered in his mind. And her lips. Full, ripe, parted, waiting. He opened his mouth, ready to take what was so temptingly offered...

Somewhere in the background, he heard a noise, a shout, a warning, a bark— "Evan! Watch out!" And then a scream, "Mommy!"

He looked up.

Too late.

They crashed into the fence.

Evan released the throttle and the engine stopped dead just as the green cyclone mesh completely encompassed the lawn mower. Evan and Sarah held on to each other and, as if in slow motion, watched in horrid fascination as the rider tipped onto its side, taking them, locked in each other's arms, with it.

He landed half on, half off Sarah. His left thigh was securely wedged in between hers. Her arms were still around his neck, holding on even more tightly than before, and her breasts were pressed up against his chest so snugly he could feel her heart beating in tandem against his. One of his hands rested at her waist, the other cradled her leg behind her knee.

She wiggled against him and even that minute friction set his blood to pounding. He lifted himself onto an elbow and looked down at her. "Don't move," he breathed into her hair, making it sound like a command that had something to do with life and death, rather than a plea not to rub her soft, deliciously female body up against his again.

Their position was so intimate that if they were in a bed instead of in the grass with a section of fence over them, it would seem that they were assuming the position for making love.

His body tightened as his head spun with the image.

It took a split second for it all to register to Sarah. With the girls screeching and the dog barking in the background, she abruptly separated herself from Evan and immediately sat up. Her face was flushed, her hair as wild and unruly as her skipping pulse.

"I'm okay," Sarah called breathlessly to reassure the girls.

But was she okay? She wasn't sure. What had started out as something light and playful had suddenly turned into something else. Pretending to smooth down her dress, she slowly raised her eyes to meet his, and he returned the gaze with an intensity that took her breath away.

Nothing happened, she told herself. And, of course, nothing did. But they'd touched more than mere hands this time. She'd felt his body against hers...and she'd felt him become aroused.

Evan knew he should say something, but for the life of him could not think of one appropriate thing. The girls saved him by attempting to pull the fence off the tipped mower and forcing him into action.

"Stay put," he said to them as he pushed the fence back so that it was no longer encasing them. "Give us a minute and we'll be right out. Quiet, Ralph," he ordered the dog.

The barking stopped, but the chattering didn't. "Can you see Mommy?" Alys asked, trying to peer over the tipped mower.

"I can't see Mommy," Ariel answered, squatting to get a look through the wheels.

"Can you see Evan?" Alys asked.

"No, I can't see Evan, either," Ariel answered.

Their little voices served as background noise as Evan turned to Sarah. Her hair was in complete disarray. He reached for her, gently combing back stray strands from her face with his fingers before cupping her head in his hands. Holding her still, he looked into her eyes.

"Are you all right?" he asked.

"Y-yes . . . yes . . ."

Evan leaned into her, and she placed her hands on his wrist. She lifted her lips to him. They were close, so close their breaths mingled. He didn't know what he was doing, or why. To say he was out of control was an understatement. Lost in this hot little cocoon of intimacy, he struggled to keep his mind on the problem at hand—one mower, a section of fence, two worried little girls and one hell of a beautiful woman so close to him his body was throbbing with such a ferocity he wasn't sure whether it was desire or injury.

He studied her face for a long moment and wondered if she recognized what was in his eyes . . .

Hunger . . .

It was blatant and so *there*, Sarah's heart pounded with its force. That this man could want her was scary, heady and so exciting she could hardly hold his gaze. She began to tremble. From the fall or the man—at this point she didn't know or care—the effect was the same.

She wanted him to kiss her.

She shut her eyes and breathed him in, and as she did, a dizziness washed over her. She felt him lean closer to her . . .

"Mommy?" It was Alys. "Aren't you coming out?"

Evan reared back, releasing the last bit of fence that trapped them in the process. The girls dropped to their hands and knees and peered inside. Ralph stuck his nose in between.

"There you are!" Ariel exclaimed.

"Here." Evan held out his hand. "Let me help you."

Sarah accepted the help and crawled out of the mangled mess of machine and fence. Evan was close behind. They stood side by side and assessed the damage.

"It was my fault," he said. "I wasn't watching where I was going."

"No, mine. I distracted you."

Evan let that slide. "Yeah, well, whatever." He ran a hand through his hair. "I'll have to order a new section of fence. It'll take a while before I can fix it."

"I'll keep the girls away."

Evan moved over to the mower and right-sided it.

"Do you need some help?" Sarah asked.

He turned to her as he lifted one end of the mower. The girls were standing on either side of her like bookends, hands gripping her dress in little fists as they watched him work.

"No, you all go on inside. I can handle this."

"Okay, if you're sure."

"I'm sure."

The three turned in unison with his traitorous dog trailing behind. He watched a second longer than he should have and, because of that, couldn't help but notice the slight sway of Sarah's hips as she made her way back to the house. The very same hips that had been snuggled against him.

"Oh, yeah, man," he muttered to himself as he resumed working, "you can handle this. But can you handle *that?*"

Chapter 5

Evan was up at first light. He'd become a creature of habit since he'd moved out here, and though Sarah Wyeth and her twins were greatly disrupting his life, he knew the wisdom in coping with such distraction and intrusion would be to find safety in his old routine.

So he was going fishing. It was Friday, and Friday was fishing day.

A beautiful morning, the dew was damp on the grass and the sun was just beginning to peek over the horizon. A mist hung over the lake, promising another scorcher. Fishing pole in one hand, bait bucket in the other, he and Ralph left the house.

With only a cursory glance toward the broken section of fence, they wound down the hidden dirt path off the side of his house that led to an inlet only he knew about.

He kept a rowboat there, pulled way up behind a makeshift dock he'd improvised with odd pieces of wood left over from various jobs. It was a hodgepodge place, but the natural clearing provided a peaceful sanctuary away from it all.

He liked that, liked knowing it was there for him if he needed it.

Not that many people had ventured back to his dead-end street over the years, but there had always been the chance someone would make a wrong turn, get lost and arrive on his doorstep on one of those days when he didn't want to be disturbed. Of course, that was before the Wyeth females had descended upon him, wreaking havoc with his solitude, and his peace of mind—or more exactly, his mind in general, which he wasn't at all sure he wasn't losing.

Especially after yesterday afternoon. He'd known temptation before in his life—he'd even given in to it a time or two—but nothing could have prepared him for the effect Sarah had on his senses as she'd sat in his lap, lain in his arms, not to mention those precious moments when her body had felt so right beneath his.

Maybe it was because it had been such a long time since he'd been with a woman. Maureen's departure had devastated him enough to swear off them for good. He didn't want one in his life, and had managed to convince himself that, in this day and age, celibacy wasn't such a bad idea, after all.

Lara had set up some so-called "dates" for him way back when all that hero stuff was still going on around town, making him desirable for his celebrity status if not for himself. He'd obliged her. He'd gone out to dinner. He'd shown up with a date at a party or two. He'd *mingled* his ass off, but the effect was always the same.

They wanted him to talk about *it*. "How does it feel, Evan?" *How the hell do you think it feels?* he'd wanted to answer, but never did. They'd wanted to get inside his head, and at that point in time, it wasn't a place even *he* wanted to be. Besides, it was no one's business, and the more they'd asked, the more reserved he'd become. So he began to say no to one setup after another, until Lara— and everyone else in town—began getting the hint.

Like the Great Garbo of old, Evan Forester wanted to be alone.

Not that Lara ever really gave up, as evidenced by her small sin of omission in mentioning the age of the Widow Wyeth, but she'd learned, at least, not to talk home, hearth and marriage to him anymore. He'd even managed to convince her that being alone wasn't as bad as she made it out to be.

Alone was good; alone was safe; alone didn't have to answer any questions.

Which made this little alcove, this secret place, all the more special. As many Friday mornings as possible in spring, summer, fall and even winter, he'd watch the sun rise and push out in his boat for some early-morning fishing.

The first time he'd seen the place, it had brought back a memory of Friday mornings at dawn with his grandfather, and he'd been hooked. Old Grandpa Forester had been a mixture of sturdy English and Scottish stock. When Evan was not much older than the twins were now, the old man would take him along on his dawn fishing expeditions, teaching him how to bait a hook, catch a fish, clean it and bring it home to Grandma to marinate in a lemon, butter and pepper concoction that had been handed down the generations.

Those fishing trips always took place early Friday so that the fish would be sufficiently flavorful for that evening's dinner. Grandma had called her husband of fifty-odd years a "papist," but she had never failed to cook up however many perch, bass or shiners he'd catch.

So as Evan prepared to push off in his rowboat, thoughts of family were strong in his mind. His grandparents were gone now, his parents moved away. He loved Lara, but she and Willy would be married soon, and have their own lives to live and family to raise.

Those long-ago dreams of children of his own were shattered with the accident—or more correctly, with Maureen's defection. No more little Foresters in Wayside; the name would die with him. That was okay. It had taken a while after the accident to come to terms with all the effects, but he now knew and accepted the value of his own self-worth, and that was more than enough to keep him going. He seldom thought about it anymore, yet at moments like this the fact became crystal clear that for all intents and purposes, he was alone.

Not quite.

The hairs on the back of his neck rose, and his senses told him someone was watching. Stepping out of the rowboat, he perused the line of trees that circled the alcove. A double take later, he saw her.

The littlest face, the biggest eyes. Ariel. He knew it was her immediately. From day one, Evan hadn't had any problems telling the twins apart.

"Come on out," he said in a gentle but stern voice.

Meekly, Ariel stepped from behind a bush, barefoot and clad only in a long-sleeved white cotton nightgown that stopped short of her ankles.

"What in the world are you doing here this time of morning?" he asked.

"I saw you and Ralph," she answered, as if that said it all.

"Does your mother know you're here?"

Ariel shook her head.

"Then, come along. I'll have to take you back." Evan walked toward her and held out his hand for her to take on the trip back through the woods.

Hands behind her back, Ariel remained firmly planted. "They're still sleeping."

"If your mother wakes up before you get back, she'll be worried."

Ariel shook her head again. "She won't wake up."

Evan glanced at his watch. It was barely 6:00 a.m. and there was more than a good chance Ariel was right. He looked at the child, then at the rowboat. "Want to come with me?" he asked.

A broad smile broke out on her face, and she nodded enthusiastically.

"Okay," he said, "but only for a little while, then you have to go back home."

"Okay."

He helped her in the boat as Ralph jumped around wagging his tail on the dock. "Stay," he ordered as they pushed off.

Ariel waved, and the dog circled with a final yelp and whimper before sitting down, his tail thumping against the slotted wood as the rowboat drifted out into the deeper part of the lake.

Evan watched Ariel study him as he rowed the boat to a spot where he'd been lucky before. "Now pay attention," he said to her, and Ariel leaned forward on the seat, knees locked together, elbows resting firmly on them with her face in her hands as she studied his baiting technique.

He held up a wiggling worm on the hook and she recoiled a bit, but not totally. "Icky, isn't it?" he asked, and she gave a forceful nod as agreement. "Want to throw it into the water?"

Her eyes lit up. "Oh, yes."

Evan leaned forward and took her hand, demonstrating the proper way of throwing the line into the water. Then he let her do it herself. Very carefully, she followed his instructions. When the hook and the bait disappeared into the green water, she looked up at him and smiled, pink spots of pride on her round cheeks.

His heart swelled. There were probably brighter, funnier, more adorable or entertaining children in the world, he was sure, but this little one had captured a heart he didn't think he had anymore.

Most Fridays he caught something, but there was always that odd day that he did not. For this reason, he wanted today to be a particularly fruitful one. He wanted to see the expression in those big blue eyes when she pulled a fish out of the water.

Within minutes, the line began tugging away. "Okay," Evan warned, "this is it." He lifted the pole and held it with her as together they reeled in their first catch of the day.

Evan offered a small prayer of thanks to the heavens as a medium-size perch wiggled ferociously on the hook.

He was rewarded with a little-girl shriek and the biggest, baby-toothed smile he'd ever seen.

After repeating the process several times in the next half hour, Evan rowed them back to the shore. They'd thrown back the small ones, but managed to catch two good-size perch, which he promised to cook up with his grandfather's famous marinade and let her taste.

Ariel was silent on the walk back, but Evan could tell by the skip in her step and the intensity with which she held his hand that her excitement was close to the surface.

The sun was well up as she slipped her hand from his, hugged Ralph and ran up the front porch of the quiet old house. "Is this a secret?" she whispered over her shoulder.

"If you want it to be," Evan answered.

"I do," Ariel said. She smiled once again before silently slipping behind the screen door.

"I do, too," he said out loud, to no one but himself as Ariel disappeared.

Or so he thought.

"You do what?"

Evan spun around. Sarah stood behind him, her unruly, auburn hair bunched in a makeshift ponytail on top of her head, more down than up. She wore old cutoffs, a faded, blue T-shirt and, from what he could tell, little else. Remembering the feel of her through that light cotton sundress yesterday made him come to the conclusion that the woman had a distracting habit of underdressing.

He diverted his attention back to her face. "Where were you?" he asked.

"Around the side of the house. I woke up early and got this bug to start a garden." She held up the hoe. "I've been digging."

"I can see that."

"And you've been . . . ?"

"Fishing." He held up the bucket for her inspection. As Sarah peered inside, he added, "With Ariel."

She looked up quickly. "What did you say?"

"I said, I had company. Ariel followed me, and I took her out in the rowboat for a little while."

"She snuck out of the house?"

"Yes. Don't be angry with her."

Sarah shook her head. "I'm not. At least, I don't think I am. Yet. But I'll have to talk to her about leaving the house and going off on her own."

"She didn't go off on her own. She saw me leave my place with Ralph and followed. No harm done."

"Not this time."

"This isn't the city, Sarah," he said with a half grin. "And I don't think you have to worry about this becoming a habit with her. Ariel isn't particularly adventurous."

"No, I suppose not, but—"

"No buts. Please don't say anything to her. I promised I'd keep it our secret."

Sarah opened her mouth to continue this conversation, to let him know that as a mother she had responsibilities to her children that he did not. But the look on his face reflected a peace she hadn't seen before, and if she knew her daughter, Ariel was probably floating on air from the experience, as well.

Thinking better of it, she smiled and nodded. "Thank you."

"I would have let you know about it."

"I'm not thanking you for telling me, I'm thanking you for taking her with you."

Evan smiled. "It was my pleasure." There, he did it, he thought. He'd been downright neighborly. This wasn't as hard as he'd thought. Neighborly, he could do.

"Truly?"

"Truly." ·

"Sounds like you had fun."

"We did. You should try it."

"Is that an invitation?" Sarah asked.

Evan was taken aback. He'd meant she should try it with the girls, not *him*. "Sure," he said politely.

"Maybe I'll join you sometime. When do you go?"

He hesitated. "Most Fridays at dawn if at all possible," he said. "Just follow the path and you'll find me."

"I may do that."

He nodded.

She nodded.

Searching for something else to say, Evan pointed over to the spot where they crashed yesterday. "I've ordered the section of fence," he said.

The reminder of yesterday's escapade made her face turn pink. "Oh. Yes. Good." Sarah grinned—like an idiot she thought, unable to say anything intelligent about the incident.

Evan retreated a few steps backward. "Well, I'd better get to cleaning these," he said, indicating the bucket.

"Are you going to cook them up?" she asked.

"Yes. I promised Ariel a taste."

"Want me to do it? Cook them, I mean?"

Evan stopped. This was going a little too fast for him. It was one thing to take the child out in the rowboat, another to get conned into issuing an invitation to Sarah to come alone someday, but having her cook up the catch . . . well, that was a bit too cozy in his mind, and he wasn't ready to take this new socializing bit quite that far. Neighborly was one thing, cooking him dinner was something else.

"I'm sorry. I didn't mean to be so pushy," Sarah added after noting the look of abject panic on his face.

"No," Evan said hastily, "you're not." *It's me, not you,* he wanted to say, but didn't. But how could he explain that yesterday on his lap and today in his house was more than he could handle? "It's just this family recipe of mine . . ."

"Another secret?" she asked with a smile, trying to lighten his mood.

"Sort of." He paused, feeling foolish as he thought of a way out. "Maybe the girls can come over and I'll show them how to do it."

The girls, he'd said, not her. "Sure," Sarah said with false enthusiasm. "They'd love it."

"Great," Evan said with an almost audible sigh of relief. "I'll let them know when I'm ready to cook them up."

They exchanged waves, and Evan trotted back to the house. He placed the bucket on his workbench and ran a hand through his hair. He was perspiring, though the morning air had yet to reach a temperature to justify it.

That was close, but he was proud of the way he'd handled it. He'd call the girls over later on and they could help him prepare the dinner. It would be a treat for Ariel, knowing she'd had a hand in catching the fish, and Alys would be happy just to boss him around his own kitchen.

He looked out the window to the spot where Sarah had been standing. A small wave of guilt assailed him as he recalled the look on her face when he all but disinvited her to dinner. He'd make it up to her. He'd send some over for her to taste. That would be just the right thing to do, he told himself.

Neighborly.

"Did you really like the fish, Mommy?"

Sarah helped Ariel from the bath and wrapped the towel around her. "Yes, it was very tasty," she said as she squelched a smile.

This was at least the tenth time Ariel had asked the question since she'd run over to Sarah late this afternoon with a paper plate containing a morsel of Evan's famous dish.

"I helped dip it in the flour," she added.

"And you did a wonderful job," Sarah said.

She knew Ariel was warring with herself as she attempted to keep her morning jaunt with Evan to herself. Her daughter wanted more than anything to bask in the glory of her achievement and shout from the rooftops that *she* had caught that fish, but once announced, her secret would be no more, and she would, no doubt, have to share her next fishing expedition with Alys.

Obviously, she wasn't quite ready to do that.

Sarah bit her tongue in sympathy. Quite a dilemma for a five-year-old, and though she wanted to help her out, she also had to respect her daughter's wish to keep this special event all to herself. Ariel would tell when she was ready.

Alys padded barefoot into the hallway in her pink pajamas. "Are you done yet?" she called to her sister.

"Almost," Ariel answered as she buttoned up the top of her matching purple set. Once dressed, she ran to catch up.

"Let's play a game," Alys said.

Ariel yawned. "What game?"

"Candyland."

"No. I'm too tired. I want to go to sleep."

"Play one game," Alys urged.

"No. I got up early this morning."

"I got up earlier than you," Alys answered.

Ariel's eyes widened. "You did not! I got up earlier than everybody!"

"Not Mommy."

"Mommy, too."

"No, you didn't."

"Yes, I did!"

Sarah shook her head as their banter faded into their room. Poor Ariel. She was finding out that keeping secrets was hard work. Picking up the dirty clothes and damp towels, she made her way downstairs. She'd give them some time, then it would be lights out. Sarah had a feeling, that at least for one of her darlings, hitting the pillow would be no chore tonight.

By the time she returned to their room a half hour later, both were fast asleep. Sarah leaned over to kiss each of them on the forehead. She extracted a metal toy car from Alys's hand and covered Ariel with a light blanket before turning off the light and tiptoeing out of the room and back downstairs.

She poured a glass of iced tea from the pitcher in the refrigerator, squeezed in a wedge of lemon and set it on the kitchen table. She adjusted the knob on the baby monitor and set it next to the tea. Sitting down, she picked up a magazine and laid it out in front of her. She didn't look at it.

Sarah was restless. The girls were in for the night, and she was at loose ends. Having risen early, she should be tired, but she wasn't. Summer reruns on television didn't entice her, and she was too keyed up to read.

These were the times she dreaded. Those in-between times in her life when there was nothing that had to be done, no one that needed her and no hope of concentrating enough on busywork to help her unwind.

These were the times when she thought about herself, her life and where she was going. It was on a night such as this that she had made the decision to leave the city and move away to be on her own.

These were the times when her impulsiveness kicked in, when her mind went off on tangents and created all sorts of scenarios that she knew could never be.

They'd been coming more and more often in the past year. This vague feeling of discontent troubled her because she truly felt her life was on the right track. She was a happy, fulfilled mother, and soon would be working again. There was only one part of her that seemed neglected, and up until now, she hadn't even realized that it might be the source of her occasional anxiety.

Who are you?

Sarah, the woman.

What do you want?

Evan, the man.

She picked up her iced tea and headed toward the front door. His truck was parked in its usual spot, but only a dim light shone from the other side of Evan's house. She wondered what he was doing. Was he thinking about her the way she was thinking about him? Did what happened on the mower affect him at all? She was still suffering from the aftershocks of being held in his arms.

It had felt good. No, wonderful. Heady, sexy stuff had been filling her head all day. Unsolicited, uninvited, it would creep into her mind, making her flush with a warmth that had nothing to do with the heat and humidity of the day.

"Admit it," she said out loud to herself, "you want to have sex with Evan Forester."

She laughed at her own bold words. She wondered what he would do if she marched over to his house right now, knocked on the back door and announced, "Evan, how about it? Want to make love with me?"

He'd die. Absolutely, positively pass straight away. Why, he couldn't even bring himself to invite her to dinner. She could just imagine his reaction if she came on to him.

Not that he wasn't interested. She wasn't so brain-dead that she didn't know when a man was turned on. And Evan had been thoroughly and completely aroused. She'd felt it, and her insides had twisted with empathy for his need. For hers was as great, if not greater.

It was pretty apparent what kind of life he lived. In the short time she'd been here, there had been no female visitors and, except for his cousin, no visitors at all. He may not be a total recluse, but he was borderline.

So maybe it was just a case of two people who had been without too long. Maybe that's why they'd reacted so strongly to each other's touch. Maybe that's why her head was still swimming with thoughts too risqué to even verbalize to herself. She could understand all of that, and if it were true, okay, she could handle it. Fantasizing was as good for the soul as it was for the body. It was also a healthier life-style in this day of AIDS.

She could go on waving at him, occasionally touching his hand, his arm, his . . . whatever. She could even pretend that he was just about to kiss her yesterday when the girls interrupted. That was okay, too. As long as she kept her thoughts to herself. As long as she played her little game without him knowing about it.

As long as *he* played, too.

"Stop it," she told herself as she turned away from the door. "Go do something useful." She put down her glass on the end table and glanced at the piano. "Like work."

Rummaging through the bench seat in front of the piano, she found her sheet music. She told herself she should be practicing some of the more difficult, serious pieces, especially now with the church organist position a possibility. But as she sorted through the papers, she

came across a stack of show tunes she had collected before her move here. As usual, all thoughts of ''serious''
practicing fled her mind.

She lifted the stack onto her lap and rummaged
through it, rationalizing that playing music that you loved
didn't mean you weren't practicing. Besides, one of her
plans this coming school year was to introduce the children to both classic and new Broadway shows in addi-
tion to the more traditional children's and holiday songs
she'd be expected to teach during the year, so in a way,
this *was* work.

Leafing through the stack of sheet music, she came
upon one of her favorites, *The Music of the Night* from
Phantom of the Opera. She sat, lifted the cover and ran
her fingers lovingly across the keys....

Evan checked his watch. Ten p.m. He yawned, shut the
book he'd been reading and snapped off the living room
lamp. It had been a busy day today, and an early one to
boot. He stretched as he stood, listening to the steady
drone of the air conditioner, and suddenly he needed
some fresh air.

Opening the back door, he stepped out onto the porch.
The moon was rising, obscured by a few drifting clouds.
He walked back and forth a few times to work the kinks
out of his legs, then settled in the bentwood rocker he'd
made for himself and listened to the sounds of the crickets chirp.

He tried not to look across the yards, but of course, he
knew he would. The upstairs lights were off. The girls
were probably down for the count. On the first level a
soft light filtered through the curtains of the living room,
but no movement was discernible.

He wondered what she was doing. Not that it was any
of his business. Not that he even cared. He chided himself as his lip curled with self-contempt. Who are you
kidding, Evan, old boy? You can't get the woman out of
your mind.

She'd invaded his turf, his space, his sanctuary. He'd
come here to get away from people. Lara said to hide

from them, but that wasn't exactly so. He'd gone to town when there was cause. He wasn't a hermit, no matter what everyone said. He just liked his solitude, liked to get away from all the hustle and bustle of the life he'd left behind. The life that hadn't worked.

But there was no getting away from the ever-present Sarah Wyeth. He'd thought his biggest problem would be the twins running around his yard, disrupting his work. But the girls had turned out to be a joy, and he found that he looked forward to seeing what they were up to each day.

Sarah was something else. Whenever he looked at her he wanted her, it was as simple as that. And she was everywhere he looked. All the time. Even when she was in the house, like now, she was there, with him, beckoning him with her very presence to come closer.

So? What was he to do? This was home; he'd made it so, and he was comfortable here. He wasn't going anywhere—there was nowhere to go. He'd have to live with it. Live with her.

He'd just have to find a way to do that.

The music came out of nowhere. Drawn by the sound, Evan rose from the rocker and allowed the clear, pure notes to drift over him. The melody was familiar, a sad, haunting lament that grabbed hold of him and wouldn't let go.

The moonlight peeked from between two pearly gray clouds and he took a step down, moved by the purity, intensity, of the sound, and awed by its source.

Sarah was playing the piano.

Evan leaned against the railing. Alone and far from the probing eyes of the world he so wanted to avoid, Evan allowed himself the luxury of absorbing the music. He breathed in the sound, letting it travel through him, invade his system and take over.

It was strangely seductive, this private concert she didn't realize she was giving. Evan liked to think that she played for him and him alone. His body reacted to the idea, and he felt himself stir. Another fantasy to add to his library of Sarah dreams, he mused. He shut his eyes for just a moment, fighting the restlessness that tended to plague him each and every night he picked one of those dreams off his mental shelf and took it to bed with him.

He rested his head against the wooden column of the deck and stared up at the stars. They seemed to form scales, rolling through the heavens like a ribbon of musical notes in time and rhythm to the song being played. The longer he stared, the clearer the image became, until he was filled with a feeling of both peace and liberation as the final notes faded into the darkness.

Afterward, the silence was ear-shattering. He had to reattune himself to the normal night sounds, as once again the crickets and other insects performed in their own symphony of nature. Evan returned to the rocker, and just as his bottom hit the chair, Sarah's front door swung open and she emerged. She took a deep breath and let the spring-driven screen door swing shut behind her.

Surveying the yards, she didn't spot him. Evan willed himself not to move an inch, to blend into the scenery of the night. He wasn't sure why, but he didn't want her to see him. Not tonight. Not after his reaction to her music. It was a dangerous time for him; much better if she turned around and went back inside. Out of sight, if not out of mind.

As if she heard his wish, Sarah reopened the door and went back into the house. He exhaled a breath of relief he hadn't realized he'd been holding. Better call it a night yourself, he told himself, and pulled himself out of the chair once again.

As he did, Sarah's door opened once again. Without any preliminaries of any sort, she bounced down the porch steps, carrying something with an antenna in her hand. She waved as he stood to his full height, and reluctantly he returned the greeting. A half minute more and he would have been in the house, but now it was too late.

Sarah was coming to him.

Chapter 6

"Hi."

"Hello."

"Warm night."

"Yes, it is."

"Mind some company?"

"Uh, no," he said, "come on up."

As she climbed the steps onto Evan's back deck, Sarah smiled shyly. But Evan didn't smile back. Suddenly, her idea to join him seemed reckless. She'd seen him when she'd stepped outside for a breath of fresh air, and the urge to join him for some adult conversation must have replaced whatever common sense she usually had. Come to think of it, he hadn't acknowledged her presence. That alone should have warned her that he wasn't in the mood for small talk.

But playing the piano hadn't sapped enough energy to cure her restlessness, and she truthfully hadn't given a thought to his reaction to a surprise visit. She should, of course, have known better. Especially where Evan was concerned. Their little "accident" with the lawn mower seemed to accentuate the awkwardness between them rather than relieve it. The fact that he hadn't included her in his little fish dinner exercise with the girls was proof enough of that.

She glanced up at him as she passed him on the deck. He was wearing his standard jeans and T-shirt, his hands half in, half out of his front pockets. He followed her progress with his eyes, his look pensive, and she wondered if he was only being polite with his invitation to join him.

She could never read his moods from his facial expressions; he held himself too rigid for that. She hesitated and thought about making an excuse and leaving. But while she didn't want to be a pest, the thought of returning to her quiet house was less appealing than making a fool of herself, if indeed that was what she was doing.

This is where you want to be, Sarah. So stay.

Resting the children's monitor on the railing near to where he stood, Sarah turned to him.

"What's that?" he asked.

"It's a baby monitor. An intercom, really. It connects me to the girls' room. I can hear them if they call, but they can't hear me. Probably a little overprotective at their age—" she shrugged "—but I can't help it. Mind if I sit?"

"No," he said, offering the rocker, "try it out."

Sarah ran a hand over the arm of the fruitwood-stained bentwood rocker before sitting down. "This is beautiful. Did you make it?"

"Yes."

Evan held the rocker as she sat. The smell of lavender drifted up to him as she shimmied in the seat and made herself comfortable. It took him off guard, and he quickly stepped back to the railing. It didn't help. By now, her scent permeated the very air around him.

Sarah glanced up at Evan and smiled again. This time he returned it, halfway at least, which somewhat relieved her feeling of awkwardness. She curled her fingers around the curved wooden armrests and sank back into the cushion as she rocked back and forth a few times.

Sighing, she rested her head on the high back of the chair and shut her eyes. "Mmm. I could get used to this. What a great chair." She opened her eyes and met his gaze. "You're very talented."

"Thanks."

"How'd you get started with this work?" she asked.

"I worked in construction years ago. This seemed like a natural offshoot. I wanted to be on my own, and I liked to work with my hands."

Sarah's gaze fell to his hands, which gripped the railing, before returning to his face. "And you're successful at it."

Evan shrugged. "It pays the rent."

Sarah waited for him to continue, perhaps to go on a bit about how he crafted the furniture, but he didn't. After a few moments she cleared her throat. "I made fried chicken for the Fourth of July picnic tomorrow in town. Would you like to join us?"

"No, thank you. I don't go to the town picnic."

"Oh," she said, "well, I can leave you some if you'd like."

"You don't have to bother."

"It's no bother," she said.

"Then . . . sure. Thanks."

"You're welcome."

Sarah smiled. Evan did, too. Again, that feeling of awkwardness overcame her. "I wasn't interrupting anything, was I?" she asked.

"No, I was just enjoying the music."

"I hope it didn't disturb you. I forget how sounds travel at night."

"No, it was beautiful."

You're beautiful, he wanted to add, but, of course, did not. But she was, beautiful that is. Her hair was as wild as ever, and her floral print dress as oversized as most of her clothing, but nevertheless, she was the most beautiful, perfect specimen of woman he had ever laid eyes on. Maybe too perfect. A bittersweet ache wrenched his insides. At least for him.

Sarah smiled. "I've made it my summer project to practice myself back into musical shape. I have to be ready for September."

"September?"

"When school starts. I'm going to teach music at the elementary school."

Evan looked surprised. "I didn't know."

"I thought Lara might have mentioned it to you."

Evan made a face. "Lara never mentioned very much to me about you except that you were a widow."

"So I wasn't what you expected?"

"A little old lady with white hair who baked? No."

Sarah chuckled. "Is that really what you thought?"

He nodded. "Lara conveniently left out a lot."

"Including the girls," Sarah said with a knowing grin. "I know. I could have strangled her, too. She put me in a very awkward position with you."

"You handled it," he said, "and then some."

"If you're looking for an apology for my actions that first day, you're not going to get it."

Evan laughed. "If anyone should apologize, it should be me."

"Yes, it should." Sarah waited for a long moment. "Well?"

"Well, what?"

"Aren't you going to apologize?"

"I thought I just did."

"That wasn't an apology, Evan. That was...nothing."

"Okay, how's this?"

Without thinking, Evan moved over her and placed a hand on each side of the armrest, effectively trapping her as he stopped the rocking chair in mid-stride. He was about to jokingly tell her how infinitely sorry he was for calling her two angels brats, when all of a sudden he realized what he'd done, how close he was to her, and how much he wanted not to apologize but to pull her out of this chair and carry her into the house and make slow love to her.

What the hell was he doing? he asked himself as he looked down into her surprised face. Her beautiful, surprised face. Her beautiful, surprised face that was lifted up to him with parted lips offering an unconscious invitation for him to kiss her. His heart thumped in his chest.

Now who's surprised...

He fought the urges that were bombarding him fast and furiously—to close the distance between them, to plunge his fingers into that glorious auburn hair, to rub his mouth against those pouting lips, to taste her on his tongue. It took all the control he had to remain still. But then, control was something he'd spent a long time perfecting.

Evan pushed off the chair, and it started rocking again. "I'm sorry, Sarah," he said softly and turned his back to her as he returned to lean against the deck railing.

For what? she wanted to ask, no longer quite sure what they had been talking about or what he'd apologized for—his rudeness that first day, or what that sexy, heavy-lidded gaze had just done to her insides. Her heart was skipping wildly. Did he have any idea the effect he had on her?

"Apology accepted," she answered in a voice not quite her own.

Clouds hid the moon, and it was very dark except for the dim lights shining out from both houses. The stillness of the night hung between them as Sarah continued to rock on the chair. The silence became thicker, but still, Evan didn't turn around. She tried to think of something to say, but was at a loss for words. She didn't know what had happened, what, if anything, she had done, but she gave up the pretense of companionable silence and rose from the chair.

Evan turned to her. "What's wrong?"

"I think I'd better go."

"Why?"

"You seem to want to be alone. I don't want to bother you."

"You aren't." How to tell her. Inside the house or out, she bothered him. Her very existence *bothered* him. "Stay."

"Evan—"

He took a step to the left and blocked the stairs. "Please." For a long moment, they stared at each other. Evan was the first to look away, somewhere over Sarah's shoulder into the night. He ran a hand through his hair. "You'll have to excuse me, Sarah. I'm not very good at this small talk thing. But I'm trying." He moved around her and held out the chair again. "Please."

Sarah hesitated, then sat. "Okay. But just for a while longer."

"So tell me," Evan began in an attempt to start anew, "about this teaching job."

Sarah eyed him suspiciously. "Do you really want to know?"

"Yes," he said emphatically, "I really want to know."

"Well, it's teaching music to kindergarten through fifth grade," she said. "It's one of the reasons I chose Wayside to live. It was the only job offer that let me work and have the same hours as the girls. They'll be starting kindergarten in the same school."

"So you're all set?"

"Not quite. I need to get specifics on the curricula. That's where I went today. To the elementary school." When he didn't comment, she added, "I met the principal. Sam Johnson. He says he knows you?"

"Hmm."

"He says you went to school together."

"Yup."

"He says you were friends."

"That would be pushing it."

Sarah leaned forward. "You don't like him?"

"I didn't say that. It was a long time ago. I don't really know him anymore."

"If you liked him in school, you'd like him now, wouldn't you? People don't change."

"Yes, they do."

"No, they don't."

"Trust me. They do."

Sarah met his gaze. "Oh, you mean because of the accident. I think I understand. He was a bit patronizing when I mentioned you. It kind of ticked me off."

Evan's face creased into a half smile. "Did it really?"

"Yes, it did. He made it sound like you were strange or something."

"I am strange."

Sarah bit her lip, then shook her head slowly. "No, that's not true. Oh, I thought so when I first met you, but not anymore. In some ways, you're the most *un*-strange person I've ever met."

"Then you've led a very sheltered life."

Sarah nodded at that. "Yes, I think I have. There's always been someone to watch over me. It sounds wonderful, but sometimes I think it's part of my problem."

"I can't see you as having any problems at all."

"Oh, you think my life's so great?"

Evan shrugged. "On the average? Yeah. Pretty damn great."

"You think so?" She seemed genuinely surprised by his statement. "My husband died never even seeing his daughters. I'm alone and raising two girls on my own. You think that's great?"

"So what's your point?" He asked. "Your husband didn't leave you on purpose. He had no choice. He died. But at least you have the girls. My wife just left me." He made a dismissing motion with his hand. "Up and gone." He shrugged. "That's life."

"You were *married?*"

"Don't look so surprised. I didn't always look like this."

"I didn't mean that! I meant . . . it's just . . . well, Lara said—"

Evan pushed himself off the railing. "Lara said what?"

Sarah noted the defensive stance, but didn't back down. It was a good time to find out what she wanted to know. Like it or not, Evan Forester was going to talk about himself. "That you weren't a big fan of marriage. We were talking about her wedding, and she said you told her that if she had to go through with it at all, she and Willy should just elope."

He nodded. "And I stand by that statement."

"But that's not possible! She has all the plans made
already. And all those people Willy's invited. She's desperate."

"To get married?"

"No, silly. To find a place to have the wedding."

"I thought they were having it at that new house they
bought?"

"Too small. They need a bigger yard." Sarah tilted her
head and surveyed the huge piece of property between
their two houses.

Evan followed her line of vision, then his eyes returned to hers. Sarah lifted her eyebrows. It took him a
moment to realize where this conversation was leading.

"Oh, no. No way. Absolutely, positively not. Forget
it."

"Evan, why?" she pleaded, jumping from the rocker
to confront him. "She's your cousin."

He nodded. "That's why. She should know better."

Sarah shook her head, dismissing his answer. "She
needs you. When you needed her she was there for you,
wasn't she?"

"Yes, but that has nothing to do with this."

"It has everything to do with this!"

"Sarah—"

She held up her hand. "I know, it's none of my business. And you're right. It isn't. I'm overstepping my
bounds. I know how you feel about your privacy. I know
that better than most. But this once, won't you bend just
a little?"

"One hundred people in my yard isn't bending, Sarah,
it's suicidal."

"You won't have to do a thing."

"Do I have to be here?" he asked.

That shut her up. She hadn't thought of that. A wedding at his house without him. "Where would you go?"

"Away."

"But where?"

"Does it matter?"

It does to me. And she realized in that instant that it
did indeed matter to her. She wanted him at the wed-

ding. There would be nothing to look forward to if he wasn't going to attend. It was an event she wanted to share. With him. Eat with him, drink with him, maybe even dance with him. The idea of his arms around her sent a shiver down her spine. Yes, it mattered to her. Very much.

"Yes," she said, "it does."

Evan looked into her eyes and saw that she was serious. He saw something else, too, a question, a desire to take this neighborly business a step further. He felt his throat close as his pulse picked up speed. He turned away and leaned his head back against the deck column. "It shouldn't."

"But it does. It matters, Evan." She walked over to him and forced him to look at her. "It's time."

"Time?"

"For your coming-out party."

He laughed, a mocking sound that had no joy in it. "You've *really* been talking to Lara."

"Yes. And she's right. Even the pastor's wife, Mrs. Winthrop, mentioned you today."

"And what did she say?"

"She charged me with bringing you to Sunday services." Evan made a face at the suggestion. "You can't go on living this way, you know."

"Why not? Did it ever occur to any of you ladies that I might actually *like* living this way?" He pushed off the column and began pacing in front of her. "And what the hell is *wrong* with the way I live? I'm not bothering anyone, am I?"

"No..."

"Then what is it? Why is it so important that I rejoin the world? What's so great about the world, anyway?"

Sarah moved closer to him, and as she did he stepped back. "It's where the people are, Evan." *It's where I am.* "You can't run away from us forever."

"I could try."

"You could try to change, too."

"Give me one good reason to."

*Because I'm attracted to you. Because I want to be a
part of your life. Because I want you to be a part of mine.
And I'm part of that world.*

She wasn't bold enough to say what she was thinking,
but there were other ways to make him understand. There
had to be.

Sarah took another step toward him, and this time he
ran out of room as his back hit the outside wall of the
house. "Because Lara's asked the girls to be flower girls.
They'd be terribly disappointed if you weren't there."

"That's blackmail."

"Yes, but it's true."

"Sarah, I'm sorry the girls will be unhappy, but it's not
enough."

"Then, do it—" she wanted to say "for me," but
thought better of it "—because it's the right thing to do.
Because I'm asking."

Evan strained to maintain the small distance between
their bodies. "Don't ask."

She reached up and touched his chest with the palm of
her hand. His skin was warm through the thin cotton of
his T-shirt. She splayed her fingers and gently massaged
the spot over his heart. His body was hard and well-
toned, but she could feel his muscles contract beneath her
hand. "I am asking," she said softly.

He placed his hand on top of hers to stop her, but his
fingers wouldn't obey. Instead, they curled around hers
and held her to him, halting the circular motion that was
driving him crazy. But he didn't pull her hand away.
"Sarah... don't do this."

"Don't do what? Ask?" She lifted her other hand to
join the first. "Or touch you?" Her heart was pounding
with excitement, and a little bit of fear. She looked into
his dark eyes and saw her own raw need reflecting back
at her. Throwing caution to the wind, she swallowed past
the lump in her throat. "I've wanted to, you know. From
the first time I saw you. Right here, in fact, on this deck.
Do you remember?"

"Yes... I remember."

She lifted her face to him, and because he couldn't help himself, he rubbed the back of his knuckles against the smooth, silky skin of her cheek. He looked down at her. Her face was flushed, and her blue eyes sparkled with life. God, how he wanted to kiss her, to slant his mouth across hers and taste what was so willingly being offered to him. To fulfill a fantasy, to create a dream. It would be heaven, he knew, while it lasted. It would be hell later when it was over and done. It would return to haunt him.

Don't start something that can never be finished, he warned himself. But she was too close and he was too needy to listen to his rational side intellectualize all the reasons why this was so wrong when, God help it, it felt so very right.

His hands moved to her waist, and he pulled her to him. His insides twisted with desire long denied as her body came up against his. At the feel of her taut nipples grazing his chest, Evan pulled her tighter still, fitting himself into the cradle of her hips.

She let him.

Okay, Sarah, if this is what you want, you've got it.

Maybe it was all for the best. He was sure the minute he kissed her, the minute she saw how hungry he was for her, she'd run for the hills. Better to do it now and get it over with. Better to scare the holy hell out of her, so that she'd leave him alone, to himself, just like he'd been before she came crashing into his life.

He reached up with both hands and threaded his fingers through her hair. Holding her head in place, he bent his head to her. She parted her lips and their breaths mingled. "Sarah . . ." he whispered.

Kiss her. Do it. Go ahead. She'll run back to her house never to darken your door again. You'll be safe again. Go ahead. Kiss her. Go on and kiss her and watch what happens . . .

Impatiently, Sarah pushed herself up onto her toes to close the small distance between them. She brushed her lips against his in the most blatant invitation she had ever, ever given a man.

What was happening to her? Where did this desire come from? She didn't know; she didn't care. She wanted this right now, and was only coming to realize how powerful this kind of need could be. So powerful it was taking over, taking control, making her ache to touch him, feel him, taste him. All of him. His body touching her body in all the places that hadn't been touched in such a long time.

Kiss me...

She got her wish. Evan captured her mouth in a man-woman kiss that snapped her head back and took her breath away. His tongue swept inside and slowly, thoroughly roamed, explored and stroked everything she had to offer. Sarah's eyes fluttered shut as a dizziness washed over her. Her fingers curled into fists, scrunching the material of his T-shirt as she held on for support, and more.

She opened her mouth wider for him and held nothing back. She pressed herself into him, trapping him between her body and the house. Her thin cotton dress offered no protection from the hardness of his body. She rubbed herself against him like a cat, winding her leg in between and around his, loving the strength of him, the feel of him, the masculine smell of him.

Tears formed behind her eyelids. She hadn't thought she would ever feel this way again with any man. She wanted to tell him somehow, show him how much this kiss—this reawakening—meant to her...to know she was still alive... still a woman.

Lifting her hand from his chest, Sarah tried to caress his face. But before she could touch him, Evan's hand shot out and grabbed her wrist, stopping her cold before she could make contact with his scar. At first she didn't realize what had happened, but as they broke apart, her eyes met his, and she saw the fear. She shook her head, mouthing a silent "no" to him even as he held her hand firmly away from his face.

Evan watched her confusion, shared it. Even in the throes of desire, he couldn't let it go, couldn't forget about the scars. They were there, always, reminding him that at any given moment she would see them, *really* see them, and run from him. It was irrational, he knew, but he couldn't help it. The fear was so deeply embedded in his psyche, it was part of him. In his mind, the fact was irrefutable: if she touched the scars, she'd leave.

But then, wasn't that what he wanted? For her to go?

Yes... and no.

He brought her hand to his lips, kissed the palm, then rested it back onto the spot on his chest where it had been before. He released her, giving her every opportunity to step away from him, to end this craziness, to go home. But she didn't move, just continued to stare up at him like a little lost soul who'd been abandoned.

But it was Evan who was lost. Taking her by the waist, he spun her around so that now her back was up against the wall of the house. He watched her eyes as his hands traveled up her sides to gently cup her breasts. Sarah sighed as his thumbs made small circles around her nipples. They hardened at his touch. She shut her eyes and gave herself up to the sensations his fingers aroused.

It was all too much for Evan. His mouth devoured hers, and she responded by boldly touching her tongue to his. Want, need and desire snaked through him with lightning force. He felt as if he were one raw mass of senses out of control. Her lips were so soft, her mouth so warm and welcoming. His skin burned where their bodies met. He could hear every sound of the night reverberate in his ears, amplified by the blood pounding through his veins. The smell of night air filled with the scent of woman swirled in, out and through him.

But it was her taste that was taking him to a place he hadn't known existed, a place where beauty and light lived, where passion ruled, where hope prevailed. A place he had never been before and couldn't imagine ever wanting to leave.

Sarah felt his growl of approval vibrate against her as he slanted his head to get better access. She whimpered into his mouth, and he rewarded her ardor by deepening the kiss even more, a feat she hadn't thought possible. Until now.

This wasn't just a kiss. He was making love to her with his mouth, his tongue, just as truly as if their bodies were joined together. And her body responded to each thrust of his tongue as a slow, hot, melting sensation gripped her insides.

His hands caressed her back, then drifted lower to her hips, and down still lower to cup her bottom and virtually lift her off the deck as he fit himself in between her legs. He was so hot, so hard, so aroused, Sarah's head spun with the intimate feel of him rubbing himself against the one spot where she wanted so badly to be touched by him.

The intrusive sound of the static didn't hit her at first. She thought it was some annoying insect that was hovering around the two of them, but then she heard a distant, fretful "Mommy . . ." and realize immediately that it was the monitor.

They broke apart. Breathing labored, Sarah pointed to the little box on the railing. "The girls . . ."

Evan stepped out of her way. "I know . . ."

"I've got to—"

"Go. Please."

Sarah grabbed the monitor and took off across the yards. Evan turned his back to her, rolling his forehead against the frame of the door as if he were in pain. He heard her screen door slap shut and shut his eyes, trying for the life of him to remember how all this had started. Something about Lara, the wedding, his coming-out party, her wanting him to be there . . .

Yeah, that's right. He was going to show her. It was supposed to work like this: He'd kiss her; she'd run like hell.

Evan exhaled a breath he felt as if he'd been holding for a lifetime. Without a backward glance, he strode into his house, shut the door securely behind him and turned the bolt.

That's it. Run like hell.

Who, man? You or Sarah?

Chapter 7

*O*ne step at a time.

That's what Sarah told herself as she dressed for the town's Fourth of July picnic. She should be mortified about her behavior with Evan last night, but she wasn't. Instead, she felt wonderfully alive and gloriously happy that he wanted her.

And Evan *had* wanted her. She grinned as she checked herself in the mirror. There were some things a man couldn't fake, and for all his quiet reserve, Evan Forester *had* been very turned on.

By her.

For the first time in a very long time, Sarah felt the power of her femininity. It probably didn't mean much to anyone except herself, but the fact that she could feel anything remotely resembling passion was a major accomplishment. She had buried those feelings with John. No man—until this man—had sparked the least bit of interest in her. Why that should be, she didn't know. All she knew was that she liked it.

But she had a feeling that Evan wasn't going to be as pleased with what had happened as she was. He would avoid her, no doubt about that, just as he did after the lawn mower incident. It seemed that for every one step forward, there had to be two steps backward.

Not that she exactly knew what she wanted from him in the first place. Last night as she lay in bed waiting for sleep to take her, she'd questioned herself. This move to the country was supposed to be a test, an opportunity to see if she could live and function with the girls without the help and support of her family.

So far, so good, she told herself as she made her way to the kitchen, but what else did this little experiment entail? It was certainly nice that her sexuality was being reawakened with her attraction to Evan, but just how far was she willing to go?

All the way...?

She didn't know about that. What was worse, she was more than fairly certain that Evan wouldn't be interested in more than a brief, uncomplicated fling, preferably all sex and little or no emotional commitment. Was she ready for that? A little country affair with one of the locals, as her mother might say?

She wasn't sure she could handle a short-term affair, but her life was too unsettled to think beyond that. Besides, she seriously doubted that Evan would just roll over and let her have her way with him. This privacy thing with him was a major obstacle in any and all decisions about a future relationship.

Sarah shook her head as she packed the picnic lunch she'd prepared the night before. She'd have to give a lot more thought to this attraction before letting it go any further...before letting it get out of control. After all, she wasn't a girl anymore, she was a mother, not to mention the new elementary-school music teacher and a prospective church organist. Decent, mature women didn't make hasty decisions where men were concerned, and attraction or not, she couldn't afford to let Evan Forester or any man distract her from her main goal of total independence.

Pleased with her new sensibility, Sarah lifted the basket, grabbed her pocketbook and headed for the door before remembering the separate serving of chicken she'd left in the refrigerator that she'd promised to Evan. Wishing for an extra hand, she ran to get it, juggling all the items as she attempted to open the front door.

She was running late, as usual, and knew that they wouldn't get a good spot on the park's grounds if she dawdled much longer. And she was determined to go to this picnic in town. Evan might not need people in his life, but she certainly did. Being brought up in a city had conditioned her to the hustle, bustle and congestion of crowds, and while she would have enjoyed spending the day with Evan and the girls, she felt it was more important to follow through on her original plan.

She liked people. And she was going to prove it. To herself as well as to him.

Sarah glanced over her shoulder as she locked the door behind her. The girls were playing with Ralph as they waited for her by the car. To her surprise, so was Evan. So much for his avoiding her. Suddenly, it was she who felt like digging a hole and crawling into it.

Their eyes met. His expression was tight, his jaw clenched. He looked as if he hadn't slept very well. She knew why. The image of him tossing, turning and *wanting* her flashed before her eyes. For all her bravado, Sarah felt her face turn red and her stomach clench. God help her, but she wanted him. She wanted to touch him, to kiss him again, to share this beautiful blue-sky day with him. Alone.

So much for maturity, distractions and her innate love of crowds.

"Good morning," she said as cheerfully as possible.

"Morning," he answered. "Here, let me give you a hand with that."

"Thanks," she said as she handed him the heavy picnic basket. She strapped the girls into their seats in the back of the car as Evan set the basket down on the front seat.

"This okay?" he asked.

"That's fine."

"Anything else I can do for you?"

Don't ask. "Just the cooler up on the porch."

Evan nodded. "Pop the back, and I'll get it."

Sarah shut and locked the rear doors and did as she was told. Evan lifted the cooler off the porch and carried it to the car. "There," he said as he placed it in the back of the station wagon. "You're all set."

"Thank you."

"No problem."

Evan walked her over to the driver's side. He held the door open for her with one hand and Ralph's collar with the other.

"Did you change your mind and decide to join us?" Sarah asked hopefully as she climbed into the driver's seat.

"No." Evan shut the car door as he shooed the dog away.

"Then you'd better take this."

Evan took the paper bag from her. "What is it?"

"The fried chicken I promised."

He held up the bag and took a sniff. Ralph jumped up, and he laughed as he held it out of reach from the barking dog. "Smells great. Thanks. I'll...I should say *we'll* enjoy it." He backed away from the car to allow her to pull out.

"What will you do all day?" she asked, wondering why she was prolonging this when she was already late.

"Don't worry about me," he said.

She wasn't worried about him, she was worried about herself. And why the prospect of spending the day without him was so distressing. She turned the ignition key. "Well, okay, then. Goodbye."

"Bye." He waved into the back seat at the girls. "Have a good time."

The girls returned the wave and began chattering about what they would be doing all day. Sarah backed out of the driveway, watching Evan as she did. He gave her a final wave with the hand holding the bag of chicken, which she returned before turning the wheel to bring the car onto the road.

All during the ride to town, her stomach rumbled with a mixture of fear, excitement and indecision. She'd wanted to go to the picnic in town, wanted a day out with the girls where they could mingle and perhaps meet some new friends their own age.

But she wanted to be with Evan, too.

When she pulled into the municipal parking lot and found it near full, her mind began to rationalize. It was so late. She wouldn't get a good spot. She couldn't park this far away, carry the basket and the cooler and watch out for the girls all at the same time.

"It's really crowded, Mommy," Alys said, vocalizing Sarah's concerns.

"Yes, it is, honey," Sarah said. "I don't know where we can park the car."

"Too bad Evan couldn't come with us," Ariel said. "He could've helped carry stuff."

"Yes," Sarah answered distractedly as she drove the car up one row and down the next searching for a space closer to the park grounds, "too bad."

"I'll help you, Mommy," Alys said.

"Thank you, sweetheart, but first we have to park the car."

"Do they have a lake here, too?" Ariel asked.

"Yes, it's the same lake, just the other end. But I'm afraid we won't get a spot near the lake anymore."

"Can we still go swimming?" Alys asked. "I want to go swimming."

"We'll try," Sarah said, finally finding a parking spot toward the back of the lot.

Pulling into the space, Sarah stepped out of the car. Waves of heat rose from the asphalt. It was hotter here in town than it had been out by the house. She ran the back of her hand across her brow and perused the distance she would have to trek with the girls to get to the park's entrance. Opening the rear door, she let the girls out.

"Where's the lake?" Alys asked.

Sarah pointed to the trees that represented the beginning of the park. "Over there." The three of them scanned the sea of cars in the municipal lot.

"That's real far," Alys said.

"Yes, it is."

"Mommy?"

"Mmm?"

"I want Evan at our picnic, don't you?" Ariel asked.

Her patience wearing thin, more with herself than with the children, Sarah took a deep breath. "Yes, Ariel, I do, but I asked him, and he said no."

"But—"

"No buts," Sarah interrupted stubbornly. "Evan didn't want to come here to the picnic." *And we're going to have a good time on our own. With people.*

"But," Ariel began again, "can't we give him the picnic there?"

Sarah looked down at her daughter. "Do you mean, bring the picnic to him?" Ariel nodded. "By our lake?" Ariel nodded again.

"Then we can go swimming!" Alys said.

"Yes," Sarah said, attempting to resist the warm feeling the thought evoked, "then we can all go swimming."

"And we can sit on a blanket right by the water," Alys said, "all for us."

"And it won't be crowded," Ariel added.

"No—" Sarah glanced at the jammed parking lot and the crowds of people milling around "—it won't be crowded at all."

"Can we go back, Mommy?"

"Can we?"

Sarah looked down at the two anxious faces and wondered why she was fighting this battle that no one—herself included—seemed prepared to wage. She brushed their bangs out of their eyes one at a time. "Is that what you both really want to do?"

The girls nodded in unison.

"Okay," she said, "why not?"

Within minutes, they were on their way back home. Sarah unpacked the car while the girls went running to Evan's to call him to join in the "new" picnic. They checked inside, out and around the house, but Evan was nowhere to be found.

Sarah fought a sinking feeling in her stomach as she looked over at his truck parked in its usual place. "Where could he have gone?" she asked out loud.

"I don't know," Alys said with a big sigh.

"I do."

Sarah and Alys turned to Ariel. "You do?" Sarah asked. "Where?"

Ariel smiled. "Fishing."

Evan stood in the rowboat and cast out the line. The day was hot and humid, probably too hot and humid to be fishing. But for some reason, he didn't want to work today, nor spend the day inside the air-conditioned house. It was the Fourth of July, a holiday he used to enjoy very much as a kid. A fleeting picture of Sarah and the girls at the festivities in town caused a thin wave of nostalgia to wash over him, but too meager to make him wish he'd gone along.

No, you could still see the fireworks from this side of the lake, and he had no doubt that later on he'd mosey on down to the dock to watch his fill and satisfy those old memories.

It was satisfaction of a very different kind that was on his mind right now. What had happened with Sarah last night had just about blown him out of the water. He hadn't even entered his bedroom, knowing it would be a total waste of time trying to sleep. Instead, he'd poured himself a brandy or two—maybe three, he didn't remember—hoping to sufficiently numb himself into not thinking, not feeling, not needing, not wanting.

It hadn't helped a bit.

God, Sarah, what have I let you do to me?

And he didn't kid himself; he had allowed it. He had let her in, the first person since the accident with whom he felt at ease; the first woman since Maureen that he actually felt he might be able to trust. This, he knew, was a recipe for disaster. People were not always what they seemed, and each and every one of them had a hidden agenda.

Though he'd tried not to become cynical, life had shown this to be true, and once that inalienable fact had sunk into his dense brain, he'd taken himself off to this remote little area of the lake and hidden away. He had become self-protective to a fault, he knew, but then it had seemed the only viable way for him to continue living his life. And nothing, not even the unexpected arrival of Sarah and the girls, had given him any reason to think anything had changed.

But he couldn't deny that being with Sarah gave him a sense of peace he had forgotten existed. Even with Maureen it hadn't been this comfortable. Not from the first. They had known each other, it seemed, forever, and had married young. But that marriage soon metamorphosed into an extension of their teenage years together. There had been no growth, and as it had turned out, no depth.

Maureen had always been the quiet one. She had called him "Mr. Personality" and had deferred all the arrangements for their social activities to him. He'd readily taken on the role. He loved being "out there," loved being the center of attention, loved the idea of people crossing over the main street just to say hello to him.

All that had changed with the accident. While Maureen had been suitably nurturing during his recovery, a new personality emerged once his story of heroism had hit the media. The reporters came out of the woodwork. They started camping outside the house for the hourly, then daily, updates on his condition. The shy, quiet Maureen learned to shine and, more importantly, learned to like the attention. Especially from one seemingly earnest and very persistent reporter.

At first he'd tried to discourage the hype, but Maureen would have none of it. A day didn't go by when she wasn't quoted in a newspaper. Her serious, sometimes teary face had showed up on the local news more often than not when he'd turned on the television in the hospital room.

Once he'd become conscious of what had been happening, it had more than annoyed him. Soon he forbade her to give any more interviews. But by then it had been too late. She was enjoying the notoriety too much, and his reluctance to provide the fodder for her next scheduled appearance soon turned her secretive.

But it was hard to control someone who didn't want to be controlled, especially from a hospital bed. The more he reprimanded her, the more defiant she'd become. She would make things up that Evan had supposedly said. She'd even gone so far as to take a snapshot of him while he was sleeping so that her reporter friend could have an exclusive photo to go with his copy.

A fish tugged his line. No, Evan told himself, don't dig up old Ansell Walcott. He shook his head. He didn't like thinking about that sleazy tabloid monger who popped in and out of his life like a yearly recurring rash, and had no intention of resurrecting those feelings from days gone by. Though the man had out-and-out used Maureen, she had been a more-than-willing participant. He hadn't discovered how willing until months later when he'd left the hospital to find the man all but ensconced in his home. And in his bed.

Evan waited for the pang that usually twisted his insides whenever he thought of that time in his life. Only it didn't come. He felt nothing.

And he knew why.

Sarah had taken over.

Sarah had swept over him like a tidal wave, washing out the old furies and replacing them with a warm hope that scared the holy hell out of him because he knew in his heart that it was one-sided, that it could never really be. Hope was such a dangerous thing.

She was too perfect, too beautiful, too full of life and love and joy to want to spend any part of her life with a shell of a man like him. She needed more, *deserved* more, and though she may enjoy the feel of his arms, the taste of his kisses, he knew that sex would only fulfill a need in her that had been denied since the death of her husband. In time she would realize that there was just not enough in him to satisfy her long-term needs.

And she would be right.

The fact was he couldn't love anymore. He could want, he could feel, and Lord knew he could desire, but he no longer had the capacity to give himself fully. One of those therapists early on after the accident had told him that he had to learn to love himself again. Maybe that was the problem. He'd loved the before-Evan; he was content with the after-Evan.

But it didn't stop him from dreaming about her. It didn't stop the scenarios from forming in his mind night after night, day after day like some misty scene from a bad fifties B-movie melodrama.

She'd appear before him, all soft and silky in a sexy, transparent gown, looking like an angel, her body ripe with want, desire written in her eyes. She'd hold out her arms to him; she'd call his name . . .

"Evan . . . Evan . . ."

Like a mirage, he saw her standing by the edge of the water. Blinking quickly, the scene faded from an erotic invitation into a woman in jean shorts with two little girls standing on the shore waving their arms in the air to get his attention. His dog, who he'd left lounging on the dock, rounded out the group.

Eyes never leaving the scene, Evan pulled his line out of the water and began to row toward shore, not even realizing a fish was attached to the hook until it started flapping at his feet. As he reached the dock, he unhooked the catch and threw it back into the water. The grateful little shiner swiftly swam away.

"What happened?" he asked as he jumped from the boat onto the makeshift wooden dock.

Sarah stepped back to make room for him. "We decided to have our picnic back here instead." She pointed to the red Radio Flyer wagon loaded with both the picnic basket and cooler he'd helped her with earlier.

"Too crowded, right?" he asked with an I-told-you-so grin.

"I like crowds," she answered with a lift of her chin.

"Couldn't get a spot, could you?"

"I didn't try. The girls wanted to come back." *Sure, blame the twins.*

"Uh-huh."

"What's that supposed to mean?" Sarah asked, hand on hip.

"Nothing." Evan turned from her and hunkered down in front of the girls. "What do you say?" he asked Ariel and Alys. "Want to go for a ride in the boat?"

"Wow! Could we?" Alys asked, examining the rowboat as if it were the *Queen Mary.*

Evan nodded. "Yup, I know a special clearing just out over that way that's perfect for picnicking. There's even a tire swing." He looked over his shoulder at Sarah. "If your mom says it's okay."

"Can we, Mommy?" Ariel asked.

Sarah eyed the rowboat. "Can we all fit in that thing?"

Evan stood to his full height. "Sure, with a little maneuvering, it'll be fine."

With a second look at what she considered a rickety, less-than-water-worthy vehicle, she acquiesced. "Well, okay, if you think—"

Evan clapped his hands together. "Great," he said. "Alys, you and Ariel bring me that basket of food and I'll get the cooler. Ralph? Here, boy."

Before she knew it, the food was packed, the girls in place at the narrow end of the boat with the dog sitting at their feet and Evan was helping her into the opposite end. Facing him. She tried not to watch the play of muscles in his arms as he rowed them out first into the middle of the lake, and then off to the side into a copse of trees that nestled a small clearing framed by a jutting section of rock that extended into the water.

It was beautiful. To Sarah's mind, a more perfect place didn't exist on earth. Dappled sunlight filtered through the huge oaks, maples and pines that were set back just enough to offer shade without blocking the sunlight on the lake.

"Oh, Evan," she said as she turned to him.

His eyes were on hers in an instant. "Better than the park in town?"

"Yes." She nodded at his teasing eyes. "It's perfect."

The excited girls began to jump up and down on their seat, causing the boat to rock precariously as they floated toward the shore. In no time at all, they'd unpacked the boat, fed the dog and laid out the blankets with food and drinks.

Evan played ball with the girls and had them running back and forth vying for the chance to be the one to catch each throw. They lunched on cold chicken legs and potato salad, the girls too excited to eat much, and Sarah feeling the same, but for different reasons. After lunch, Evan and the twins climbed trees and Sarah pushed them on an old rubber tire swing that hung by a rope from a low, sturdy maple tree branch.

After a respectable waiting period, Sarah allowed the girls to swim in the lake. She lounged on the blanket and watched Evan take turns tossing the girls into the water. Ralph barked every time they flew through the air, but though they screeched like banshees, the twins didn't seem to mind being thrown around one bit.

They hadn't previously had a man in their life young enough or vigorous enough to offer them this type of rough play. Her father had tried, as had John's, but they hadn't had the stamina to provide the interplay necessary to keep up with two young girls.

She knew then with a certainty that she'd made the right choice in moving away. The twins needed this. Her eyes slid over Evan's trim form. And so did she.

"Sarah, come on in," Evan shouted, breaking her reverie.

Jumping up from the blanket, Sarah stepped out of her jeans and pulled off her shirt to reveal a black-and-purple bathing suit underneath. Without a second's hesitation, she dived into the cool lake water to join in the fun.

It was a forever day, one that seemed to move in gloriously sweet slow motion. Sarah didn't realize it was coming to a close until the sun disappeared from the lake and a cool shade covered their space on the blanket. She lifted an exhausted Ariel into her arms and rocked her as she leaned back against the base of a huge oak tree. Ralph, always loyal, followed close behind and found a spot at her feet.

Somewhere beyond her range of vision, she heard Alys giggling as Evan pushed the seemingly tireless child on the swing again. Sarah felt Ariel's body sink into hers. She shut her eyes and began to relax when she felt Alys's little hand on her forehead.

"Where's Evan?" Sarah asked.

Alys pointed toward the water. "Swimming."

Sarah made room on the blanket. "Here—" she pointed Alys to a spot on her lap "—lie down and rest for a little while."

Alys did as she was told, and Sarah began to stroke her hair. Within minutes she could tell that Alys had joined her sister in slumberland. She tried to shift her weight to get a glimpse of Evan swimming, but the girls and the dog had her wedged against the tree. Giving in, she shut her eyes again, letting the late-afternoon heat lull her, as well.

She was just dozing when she felt drops of water on her legs. Her eyes opened to Evan lifting a towel off the edge of the blanket.

He was dripping wet, but his T-shirt was back on. The only time he took it off was when he was swimming, making sure to put it back on as soon as he emerged from the water. She knew he was overly conscious of the scars on his chest, and while they didn't bother her in the least, she respected his feelings and looked away.

"Sorry," he whispered as he dried off.

"It's okay," she whispered back. "Since I couldn't get free, I decided to join them in a nap."

"Do you want to sleep?" he asked.

"Not necessarily."

Evan slowly extricated Ariel from her arms as she slipped Alys off her lap. He extended his hand to Sarah and pulled her off the blanket. She leaned over and rearranged the girls next to each other on the blanket.

"They're out like lights," Evan said. Ralph lifted his head unenthusiastically at the sound of his master's voice.

"They should be. You gave them a heck of a work-out. I haven't ever seen them have so much fun."

"It was for me, too," he said, and their eyes met. He held out his hand again, and she took it. This time he threaded his fingers through hers. "Let's sit over by the rocks," he said, and Sarah nodded. "Stay," he said to the dog who was only too happy to oblige.

Without letting go of her hand, Evan led her to the rock formation that jutted out into the water. It was close enough to see the girls, but far enough away to afford them some privacy. Evan chose a flattened overhanging stone to sit. He patted the spot next to him and Sarah sat. She stretched and rubbed the back of her neck.

"Mmm. Heaven," she said as she dangled her feet in the water.

"Neck hurt?"

"Just a little kink. Ariel had me cornered." Sarah rolled her head from side to side and grinned. "She's not as light as she looks anymore."

"Come here," he said and twisted his body to make room for her between his legs.

"What for?"

Evan held up his hands and wiggled his fingers in the air. "Massage. I'm great with my hands."

Sarah didn't doubt that for a moment. She smiled at his comment and scooted over to him. He splayed his hands across her shoulders, but didn't move for a long moment. "Well?" she asked, turning her head to look at him.

"Just testing."

"Testing what."

"The fit."

"The fit?"

"Yeah, you know, how much area I can cover with my hands. You've got to have the right fit."

"And is it?"

He dug his thumbs into the base of her neck and began a deep massage. "You tell me." Sarah groaned out loud. Evan laughed. "I guess that means it's okay."

"Oh, yes. Don't stop."

She leaned into him as he continued to manipulate her sore muscles. "You're too tense."

"Mmm . . . am I?"

"Yes, try to relax."

"I'm trying."

"Try harder."

Sarah slumped back against him. "That enough?"

Her hair hit him in the face and he reached up and pulled the band holding her ponytail. Curls cascaded over him. "Yeah. Perfect."

Sarah turned and grinned at him over her shoulder.

"Stay still," he said, "or this won't work."

"Yes, sir." Returning to her original position, she settled into the space between his legs more firmly.

He worked in silence, loving the soft feel of her beneath his callused fingers. Her skin was lightly tanned and as soft as satin. Evan breathed in the fresh shampoo scent of her hair, and had to stop himself from leaning forward and planting kisses across her nape.

"Oh," she sighed, her head tilted to give him better access. "This is too fabulous."

"What did I tell you?"

For the longest time, he worked in silence, giving her a deep massage until her muscles loosened to the point where she fell back against his chest. His touch gentled as his hands worked their way back up to her shoulders. It was evident that the massage was over, yet she didn't move away. Hesitating for a brief moment, he gripped her shoulders and gave her a chance to do so. When she didn't, his fingers moved down to caress her collarbone where they lingered before slowly descending to graze her full cleavage.

Still, she didn't move.

Toying with the straps that held her bathing suit in place, Evan slipped his fingertips under them and gently stroked the sensitive skin they covered. Sarah opened her eyes, aware that the tone of the massage had changed. Her body on red alert, she felt each movement of his hand as if he were leaving a scorching trail in his path.

She could stop him right now. All she had to do was say something, or move away, but she did neither. Instead, she held her breath and silently willed him to go beyond, willed him to touch her as intimately as he dared.

She arched her body, and the top of her suit gaped, giving an unrestricted view of all she had to offer. Evan's hands stilled, and she knew without looking at him that his eyes were riveted on the sight below. Her nipples tightened in response, and she could feel as well as hear his intake of breath.

She shifted again, and this time, the straps of her bathing suit fell from her shoulders, trapping her arms at her sides. She gripped the muscles of his thighs with her hands. There could be little doubt about what was being offered, and Evan wasted no time in accepting the gift.

He dipped his hand into the front of her suit, tenderly cupping one breast. Sarah shut her eyes and lifted herself into him. With slow deliberation, he massaged her, flicking the pad of his thumb against her nipple as he paid homage to her body.

He peeled down the top of her suit, and his other hand joined in the love play. Two sets of eyes stared down in fascination as if they were detached, observing but not participating in this sensual game. But the feel of him was all too real, and the melting sensation inside Sarah was all too powerful to deny.

She squirmed against him, thrilling to the heat and hardness of his arousal against her buttocks. Her suit slipped lower with her action, exposing even more of her to his gaze. She didn't care. She wanted all he was willing to give. More.

One hand crept down, and he rubbed his palm against her belly. Sarah's breathing became more labored, and her heart picked up speed in anticipation.

"Sarah . . . oh, Sarah, you feel—" his raspy voice hesitated "— like heaven."

His breath was hot on her neck and in her hair. It sent shivers down her spine. Sarah turned her face to him, and without a moment's hesitation, he captured her lips in a soul-searing kiss.

There was no rhyme or reason to what he was feeling, no thought or hesitation, none of the fear or trepidation. There was only Sarah, open, willing, waiting for him, the sweetest-tasting woman there ever was, too soft to be real, too perfect to be his.

But right now, this one perfect moment, she was.

His.

Evan drank her in, probing her mouth with his tongue as he wished to with his body, letting his imagination go wild as she eagerly met him more than halfway. His hand drifted lower to her nest of curls. She opened herself to him, and he brushed the tips of his fingers across the tiny bud that seemed to be waiting for his touch. She whimpered into his mouth, and that was all the encouragement he needed. He began to stroke her, dip into her, then stroke her again. She was so ready for him, he could feel her body pulsing beneath his touch. Her hips began to undulate with the rhythm of his hand . . . and then he felt the spasm overtake her.

She broke the kiss and gulped for air. He turned her body around to face his. Chest-to-chest, her breasts exposed, her lips swollen and wet from his kisses, Sarah sat before him for the longest moment, allowing his inspection. He ran his hands up her arms, then grazed her taut nipples with the backs of his knuckles. Her eyes fluttered shut as he felt her tremble from his touch. It made him feel powerful, almighty. It made him feel like a man.

Again.

He wrapped his arms around her, and she reached up to link her hands behind his neck. Slowly, she pulled his head down toward hers. Her chest heaving, Sarah opened her eyes and stared into the depths of his dark brown fathomless gaze. Tilting her head, she nibbled at his lips, until obediently he opened his mouth for her. And then, she touched her tongue to his.

With a groan that seemed as if it came up from his toes, Evan kissed her back, slanting his mouth and devouring hers as he maneuvered them to lay upon the flat rock. He tried to hold himself away from her, resting his weight on one elbow as he deepened the kiss, but Sarah would have none of it. She wanted more, to give more, to get more. Wrapping her arms around his torso, she nudged him on top of her, loving the feel of him as she rubbed her aching breasts against his chest, all the time wishing he'd kept the T-shirt off so that she could feel his skin against her.

Nestled in the cradle of her legs, Evan was going crazy. Hands in fists, he fought the urge to strip off their suits and bury himself inside her the way he'd dreamed so many nights in the dark shadows of his room, the way his body was demanding right now, right this moment, he take her, use her, if only to put himself out of this seemingly eternal misery. He looked into her big blue eyes glazed with desire but innocent still, and he knew she was willing. More than willing; she was issuing an invitation.

And that alone was enough to stop him from going that one step too far. Too far to turn back, too far to stop.

And if he didn't stop... then what?

Sarah had no idea the battle being waged in Evan's mind. Somewhere deep in the recesses of her own, Sarah knew she was probably going to regret her wantonness, yet she was unable to stop herself from rejoicing in the reawakening of her body. She had been so ripe for this, so ready, she couldn't deny herself the pleasure he offered, no matter what her rational mind told her.

When Evan broke the kiss and lifted himself from her, she was bewildered. When he replaced the straps of her bathing suit into their proper place, she was embarrassed. But as she attempted to cross her arms protectively across her chest, he pulled her hands away.

"No..." he said softly as he sat up and drew her to him, holding her tightly against his chest. For a long moment he buried his face in her neck and tried to regain control over his wildly aroused body.

Slowly, gently, Evan extricated himself from the embrace. He had to move away. He was wound as tight as a coil about to spring, and he knew he had to break contact or he would fulfill his every desire and make love to her here on the rocks by the lake with the girls sleeping . . .

The girls.

He rose to his knees. His head spun around as he checked them with a backward glance. They were still asleep with Ralph at their feet. He exhaled and ran a hand through his hair.

Sarah sat forward. Still slightly dazed, she turned to Evan. His eyes were ringed with black and filled with a desire so blatant her heart skipped a beat. He returned her gaze for the longest moment, but when she opened her mouth to say something, he pushed back from her and stood.

Resting her weight on her arm, Sarah looked up at him. His body was tight, well-muscled and strained. The bulge in his bathing suit gave testament to how strained. She wanted so much to touch him, to press her palm against him, but of course, she could not, would not. Instead, she looked up at him, following his line of vision to the picnic blanket.

The dose of reality was like a splash of cold water in her face. Sarah turned and glanced over at the tree. The girls were side by side, asleep. That he should have to be the one to remind her of her children's presence shook her to the core. Sarah felt the rush of blood return to her face as she heard a splash. She turned and watched Evan swim away with long, sure strokes, most likely to insure he would get away from her as quickly as possible.

Sarah stood on wobbly legs and readjusted her bathing suit. Physically sated, but emotionally empty, she made her way back to the blanket. It was getting dark. Without hesitation, she woke the girls and began packing up. Once they were through, she called to Evan, and without a word or a look, he loaded the boat.

The ride back to the fishing dock was silent except for the burst of fireworks that were visible from across the lake. Evan attempted to rouse the girls, but they were still half-asleep, and their interest was minimal at best. But Sarah was thankful for the diversion. She sat fascinated, staring at each and every burst of fireworks, too mortified to look at Evan or even say a word.

They loaded the empty basket, cooler and sleepy girls into the wagon and headed down the path to the houses, a very subdued Ralph tagging along. It was pitch dark as they came into the side yard. Sarah noticed the lights on upstairs in her house. A quick look at the festivities below told her even more. Her heart sunk at the very familiar but not particularly welcome sight.

Sparklers were stuck in the soil at the base of the porch, spraying colored bits of light all around. Sarah took a deep breath to steady herself and regain control as the girls opened their eyes to the commotion.

"Grandma!"

"Grandpa!"

With a renewed burst of energy, the twins jumped from the wagon and ran into the waiting arms at the foot of the steps.

"Who the . . . ?" Evan asked as he stopped short.

Sarah turned to him. "My parents."

They exchanged a look, his perplexed, hers resigned. She walked away from him, leaving him with a tired dog, a loaded wagon and an uneasy feeling that things were about to drastically change.

Chapter 8

Sarah stepped into her mother's outstretched arms.

"Surprised?" she asked.

"A little."

Her mother held her at arm's length. "It was your father's idea," she said in her who-cares-if-everyone-hears whisper-voice. "He missed the children so much there was no living with him! So this morning I just said, 'Enough, let's pack up and start our visit early.'"

Sarah glanced at her father, who met her eyes, then diverted his attention back to the twins. She knew that despite their phone conversation, it was her mother's idea to push up their arrival date and not his.

From time immemorial, it had been this way. Lenore Hudson used Ted as her excuse to do whatever she deemed necessary, and he allowed it.

"Mom, Dad," Sarah said, "I'd like you to meet Evan Forester, our neighbor. Evan, my parents, Lenore and Ted Hudson."

"How do you do?" Evan said, extending his hand to Ted, who readily accepted the gesture. Lenore, on the other hand was not as forthcoming. She smiled primly, but stood her ground and nodded her greeting.

A long awkward moment followed, and Evan saw by the look on Sarah's face that this was not something she'd expected to deal with tonight, and since she hadn't mentioned any forthcoming visit, probably not anytime soon for that matter. The best course of action as far as he was concerned was to leave.

So he did. After a quick head rub for each of the girls, he made his excuses, whistled for his dog and headed back to his house. He was halfway across the lawn when Sarah called out to him. He stopped and waited for her.

"Did I forget something?" he asked when she caught up with him.

"No," she said a little breathless, "I did. I forgot to thank you for today."

"I'm the one who should be thanking you," he said with a half grin. "You gave up the great American picnic."

Sarah gave him a playful punch in the arm. He grabbed hold of her wrist. Their eyes met, and the smiles faded from their faces. "I had a wonderful time," she said. "I just wanted you to know."

Evan swallowed. He knew he should say something like, "I did, too," but for the life of him, he couldn't get the words past the lump in his throat. He was going to dream about this moment tonight, and in that dream he would say something clever, something so deeply moving and terribly romantic she would swoon at his feet, but for now he could only nod his head.

"I have to go," she said.

Evan released her wrist. "I know."

"Good night," she said over her shoulder as she began to walk away.

"Good night," he called after her.

He stood in the middle of the lawn, watching her retreat. He was just about to turn when he caught the eye of Sarah's mother. Lenore Hudson's face was stone cold, her eyes slitted as if he were a strange, threatening, new organism she were examining under a microscope. And she didn't like what she saw.

He returned the look a little defiantly, which was a decidedly wrong approach if he was of a mind to win her over, but he couldn't help himself. He knew what she was saying with those assessing eyes: "Don't get any ideas, mister. You're not good enough for my daughter." And while part of him heartily agreed with her, he had enough sense of self-worth and pride left to bristle at the sentiment.

He knew well-meaning, righteous people like Mrs. Hudson. He'd met hundreds of them while the "hero-worship" thing was still going on. They had fawned all over him while he had been healing, had praised his selflessness and expressed their undying gratitude as they stood by his side to have their picture taken with him. Then, once the bandages were off and all the hoopla had died down, they could barely manage a nod in his direction.

Suddenly, he understood Sarah's need to take her children and run off on her own, her need to assert herself, her need for independence.

He turned on the judgmental, probing eyes without another backward glance, but with a new understanding of what it must be like to be Sarah Wyeth caught in that loving cocoon of parental concern.

For her part, Sarah had no idea what had passed between her mother and Evan. She was too riled right now to even care. As she escorted her family into the house, it became apparent that her parents had been here for quite some time. They'd arrived early afternoon and had already settled in. Sending them a duplicate key seemed to be a most grievous error in judgment. Her mother announced that she had taken it upon herself to unpack and take over Sarah's master bedroom, relegating Sarah to the third and smallest bedroom in the house.

Lenore had also rearranged the couch and love seat so that they faced each other instead of the fireplace because "it looks more cozy this way." And she had managed to cook a hot meat-loaf dinner, which required using the oven. Unfortunately, the house now felt like a sauna.

Sarah fixed a smile on her face that was as phony as a three-dollar bill, but worked well enough to fool her parents. She loved them dearly and deep down was glad to see them, but she wished her mother had not surprised her with this unexpected visit. Her stake on independence was still too fragile, and their hold on her still too strong. She wasn't ready quite yet to face what she knew would sooner or later have to be done.

For she and her mother were on a collision course. That had become apparent from the day Sarah had announced she was moving away. Her mother had fought a long, hard battle to keep her nearby, but she had lost. And Lenore Hudson did not take loss well. Outwardly resigned to the move, inwardly she had continued to undermine everything Sarah was doing.

While Sarah saw it for what it was—her mother's intense love for her and the girls—it still rankled her that at thirty-four years of age, she, for all intents and purposes, had yet to cut the umbilical cord.

After bathing Alys and Ariel and putting them to bed, Sarah descended the stairs to find her mother sitting alone in the kitchen, two mugs of hot tea steaming on the table in front of her.

"Dad's gone to bed. He was just exhausted from the drive today. Do you know how far this godforsaken place is from the city?"

Not far enough obviously.

Sarah dismissed the unkind thought from her mind. "I know, Mom, it is far."

"You look exhausted yourself. Drink your tea."

"It's too hot for tea, Mom."

"Oh? Well, then, let's ice it." She jumped up and poured the tea into tall plastic cups and added ice cubes. Then she placed one of the cups in front of Sarah. "There you go. Iced tea. Fresh brewed and just the way you like it. I'll send Dad into town tomorrow for some fresh mint. But this should do for now. Go ahead, take a sip." Sarah took a sip to please her. "How is it?"

"Good, Mom. Very good."

"There," she said as she sat again across from Sarah. "I'll bet you haven't made any fresh-brewed iced tea for yourself, now have you?"

"As a matter of fact, I have."

"Really? I am surprised. You were never much of a cook, dear. Why, that was one of my biggest worries about you moving away. I wondered how you and those poor children would fare with your limited menu."

"We're doing just fine. Truly."

Her mother folded her hands in front of her. "Well, that's fine . . . just fine . . ."

"And . . ."

"No and."

"Nothing to add?"

"Well . . . perhaps . . . something."

"Like?"

Lenore sat forward. "I must admit I was a bit shocked to see you and the girls with that man tonight."

"Evan's become a good friend to the girls."

"Only the girls?"

Sarah met her mother's eyes. "No, to me, too."

"I see."

"Do you, Mother?"

"Yes, I think so. You found a friend, and from that defiant look on your face that I know so well, Sarah Wyeth, I'd say you're telling me to mind my own business."

Sarah shut her eyes and shook her head. "That's not it at all. Evan's . . . he's . . ."

"What?"

"Good for us."

"But his . . ."

"What?"

"Face."

"Mom—"

"My God, Sarah, don't tell me you can ignore the scar?"

Sarah shrugged. "No, like you, I was taken by surprise at first—" her face creased with a slow smile that
she hid behind the cup "—but he kinda grows on you."

"What happened to him?"

Sarah's eyes lit up. "He's a hero."

"Hero?"

"Yes, he saved people from a fiery explosion and was
hurt himself in the process. There was quite a big to-do
about it up in this area a few years ago. Perhaps you read
about it. You're usually up on those things."

"Hmm...I seem to remember something...what? Five
years ago or so? The papers had a picture of a man all
bandaged . . . CNN did a special or something."

"Yes, I'm sure that was it. From what I hear, Evan was
dogged for a long time afterward. It changed his life
completely."

"Well, I'm sure that it was all very noble of him, but I
still don't think he's appropriate company for the girls."

Sarah's back straightened. "Why not?"

"Because...well, he must frighten them. They'll have
nightmares—"

Sarah stood and poured the remaining iced tea down
the drain. "Don't be ridiculous. Evan is the best thing
that's ever happened to the girls. You should have seen
him today, tossing them in the air in the lake. They were
having the greatest time." She turned to look her mother
in the eye. "They need a man in their lives, Mom."

"They have your father. And John's."

"A young man. A man who can do things with them.
A role model."

"You don't mean to tell me that you expect this...this
hero-person to fill that gap?"

Sarah folded her arms. "His name is Evan, and I expect nothing. I've just arrived here, and I'm starting to
make a life. As my neighbor, Evan is part of that."

"And that's all?" Her mother's eyes studied her.

Sarah lifted the tap. She washed out the plastic cup,
wiped her hands and turned back to her mother. "That's
all." *For now.*

"I thought you might be a little tired of this experiment by now."

Sarah laughed. "Not in the least."

"I just thought—"

"Mom, we've been through this a hundred, no, a thousand times. Why can't you accept that I need to do this?"

"Because it's wrong for you to be this far away from your family. John's parents—"

"John's parents are at least trying to be supportive. So is Daddy. The only one who is having a problem with this is you."

Her mother opened her mouth, then shut it. Sarah hadn't meant to be so direct, but her parents' surprise arrival tonight of all nights was more disruptive than her mother could ever know. Sarah didn't know what she'd planned for later this evening once the children were asleep, she only knew that she had planned on seeing Evan again, perhaps out on the back porch later tonight. And after what happened this afternoon, well, she was more than disappointed that she would have to postpone whatever might have happened between them later on.

Postpone it indefinitely.

Sarah turned the conversation to family gossip, and soon both women called it a night. Sarah stood at the window in the little room upstairs. Like the girls' room, it faced the front of the house. She sat for a long time in the dark, staring across the lawns at Evan's. No lights were visible from here, and for the first time, she wondered where his bedroom was located in his house. She'd been on the first level, but at that, had only seen his workroom, hallway and kitchen. She had no idea what the rest of the house looked like.

So she used her imagination. Shutting her eyes, she pictured him lying in his bed, white sheets gleaming in the moonlight. Would he be naked? Sure, why not? It was her dream, she could make him anything she wanted. His hands would be crossed behind his head and he'd be staring at the ceiling thinking of her... thinking of today...thinking about the way she responded to him when he touched her.

I'm great with my hands...

That, Mr. Forester, was an understatement. Sarah buried her face in her hands. She couldn't believe she'd behaved so brazenly, with her children no more than fifty feet away no less. Was she that sex-starved? Is that what he thought? Was he only being kind, fulfilling a need he felt she had?

She opened her eyes and resumed her fantasy. No, in her fantasy, he wanted her as much as she needed him. He was a willing participant. More. He was all over her, commanding, demanding, taking her to places she'd never been before. They would be alone, blissfully secluded from the eyes of the world, and this time he wouldn't stop.

This time, they would make love.

Sarah rose and moved to the single bed. She lay on top of the light blanket, crossed her arms under her head and stared at the ceiling in much the same way she'd imagined Evan doing. She was tired and needed to sleep. Her mother was an early riser and she had no doubt the house would be jumping in the morning.

Her eyelids fluttered shut, and she turned her head in the direction of Evan's as if that small gesture would bring her closer to him. Was he thinking of her or was she fooling herself? The answer lay somewhere out there in the darkness, somewhere in the space between her dream and his.

All she could hope was that someday the two would meet in reality.

"Breakfast!"

Sarah opened one eye at the sound of her mother's voice. By the time she had the energy to open the other, she heard the pitter-patter of the girls descending the stairway in a mad dash to the kitchen to have some of her mother's—what was it today? She sniffed the air—pancakes and those skinny melt-in-your-mouth sausages.

Three weeks had passed since her parents' arrival, and a new routine of sorts had arisen from the loose structure in which Sarah had lived before. Her mother, bless her, had all but taken over the kitchen. This was one thing that Sarah didn't mind in the least. Lenore was right about her not being the best of cooks, and the kitchen was her least favorite room in the house, so she was just as happy staying out of her mother's way. It was amazing how quickly she'd fallen back into her old habits.

That wasn't the only change that had taken place. Her conversations with Evan had become almost nonexistent. He waved to her from his porch; she waved from hers. Twice they'd met in the middle of the lawn, but hadn't gotten past the small talk before her mother and father, or the girls, had interrupted.

With every day that passed, she felt more deprived, as if her body was undergoing withdrawal, lacking some essential vitamin and slowly deteriorating. It was murder to see him and not be able to touch him...or have him touch her. She felt as if she had run a very long distance and had a great thirst, but when she arrived at the water supply, there was an electrical fence around it and she couldn't get to it. Evan was the water and her parents were the fence, and if something didn't happen soon, she would surely shrivel up and die right in front of all of them.

She was sure, of course, that Evan had no idea what she was going through. He must be happy, she thought, not to have to deal with her anymore. He certainly wasn't knocking her door down to see her. Sometimes he didn't appear all day long, and at those times, she didn't know which was worse—seeing him from afar or not seeing him at all.

The weather had cooled down at bit and the humidity eased. They were full into the thick of summer, and though she felt as if she were walking a tightrope between what she wanted and what she could realistically have, the bright, sunny days did make her feel energized. It was as if all her senses were on alert and waiting, for what she didn't know.

Sarah ambled downstairs just as everyone was finishing breakfast. She poured a cup of coffee and watched as the girls pulled their grandfather out the front door to show him something or other. She smiled at their antics and, at that moment, felt a warm rush of love for her parents. Evan or no, in some ways it was good to have them with her. Her emotions were on an up-down roller coaster that she didn't seem able to control. So she decided not to fight it.

She walked over to her mother and gave her a hug. "It's good to have you here, Mom."

Lenore smiled. "I'm glad to be of help—"

"What in the world—?"

A loud clanging sound interrupted them. Both women ran to the front door to see what the commotion was all about. Sarah spotted her father, the girls, Evan and another man by his truck. He'd dropped the gate and was in the process of unloading as she opened the screen door and stepped onto the porch, her mother close behind.

Evan stopped when he saw her. "The fence is here," he called out to her. "Willy's going to help. Say hi to Sarah, Willy," he added, and Lara's fiancé waved his hello.

Sarah returned the greeting and called the girls away. "Alys... Ariel, back here, girls, while the men are working."

"What's he doing?" her mother asked as the twins made their way back to the porch.

"A section of fence broke, and he's fixing it."

"Will you look at your father? I swear that man never thinks about that back of his." She waved her arm in his direction. "Ted? What do you think you're doing?"

"I'm giving the guys a hand with the fence," he called back to her.

"Your back—"

"Back's fine."

"Stubborn old coot," she said out loud enough for him to hear. Still it didn't stop him from helping the two men unload the section of fence. Lenore shook her head. "He's going to kill himself—"

"Mommy broke the fence," Alys offered as a way of joining the conversation.

"What did you say, dear?" Lenore asked, looking down at her granddaughter.

"Alys...that's not true," Sarah warned.

"What's not true?" Lenore asked, thoroughly confused.

"That Mommy broke the fence," Ariel added. "Mommy *and* Evan broke the fence," she said in defense of her mother.

Lenore turned to Sarah, who offered a small smile and a shake of her head. "It was nothing, really."

"Nothing? The entire section is gone. What were you doing to cause that?"

"It was Mommy's turn on the lawn mower. We had our turn, then she had one—" Ariel began to giggle "—but she almost fell and Evan had to grab her."

"Yes." Alys began giggling, too. "Mommy went flying in the air—" she demonstrated with outstretched arms, "—and Evan had to catch her, but the mower went wiggle-waggle and crashed into the fence."

Lenore smiled benevolently at her grandchildren. "And that was it?"

"No," Ariel said seriously, "they fell."

"On top of each other. But nobody got hurt, right, Mommy?" Alys added.

"Right, nobody got hurt," Sarah confirmed, turning her attention to the work being done across the yard.

Her mother stepped up behind her. "Riding on the mower?"

"The girls wanted to see me do it. It was a silly game that got out of hand."

"How out of hand?"

"What do you mean, Mother?"

"Just exactly what is going on between you and this man?"

"Nothing is going on. And his name is Evan."

"Nothing?"

Sarah looked her in the eye and did something she never thought she'd do. She lied outright to her mother. "Nothing."

Lenore smiled her approval as Sarah knew she would. As she turned her attention back to the work being done, she noticed her father, Evan, and Willy laughing. At least one of her parents didn't find him unappealing or a threat.

"Look at your father. I swear he's going to be bent over like a pretzel by the end of the day," she said. "Ted? Ted? Do you hear me? That's enough now, come back up here."

Sarah watched as her father held the section of fence for Evan, his back to her in defiance. She grinned. She'd always thought that she'd taken after her mother, but now she wasn't so sure. She was suddenly seeing her father's quiet acceptance of Lenore in a new light. He didn't argue with her or ever cause a ruckus of any kind. What he did was more subtle, and in some ways, much more effective.

He ignored her and did whatever he wanted to do.

That works for me, she thought as she wrapped a supportive arm around her mother's waist.

The three men were still laughing as Ted escorted Evan and Willy into the kitchen a few hours later. They walked right past her and her mother as Ted offered them each a cold beer.

Sarah could see by the look on her mother's face that her father would pay for this insubordination one way or another, but for now Ted was having his own way, knowing his wife would rather die than air their dirty laundry in front of strangers.

And Sarah had no doubt which one was more the stranger as far as Lenore was concerned.

"Would you like some lunch?" Lenore asked sweetly of the men.

"How about it, Evan, Will? Lenore makes a healthy turkey sandwich."

"Uh, sure. If it's not too much trouble," Willy answered.

Evan's reply was limited to a speculative eye on Lenore's pasted-on smile.

"No trouble at all. You three wash up and I'll get started. Sarah? Would you set the table?"

Sarah pushed herself off the counter. "Sure thing."

In no time, Lenore had the table laden with sandwiches, salads and pickles. She directed the men where to sit, and after arranging the twins on stools at the kitchen counter, Sarah joined them.

"How are the wedding plans coming, Willy?" Sarah asked as she took a bite out of her sandwich.

"Uh, pretty well," he said with a side glance to Evan.

"It's okay, Willy," Evan said. "Sarah has already asked me."

"Asked you what?" Lenore joined in.

"My cousin Lara and Willy are getting married in September. They've asked to use my house for the wedding." Evan looked straight at Sarah's mother. She didn't avert her eyes. She was getting better.

"What a lovely idea," Lenore said.

"I haven't said yes," Evan added.

"Why ever not?" Lenore asked.

"Evan doesn't like people," Sarah said.

Evan didn't answer her barb, but gave her a dirty look. She smiled and took a sip of her freshly brewed, minty, iced tea. No one seemed to know what to say after that, so the subject was dropped. Willy looked relieved. Sarah wouldn't be surprised if Lara had sent him out here to help with the fence as a way to further her case along. Labor Day was just around the corner, and judging by the sound of Lara's voice the last time they spoke, she was sure the invitations were sitting ready to be mailed.

Her mind wandering on about the fate of Lara's wedding prospects, Sarah almost missed Willy's comment about a furniture show he'd attended the week before and about Evan going away somewhere.

"Evan's going where?" she interrupted.

"Supply outlet," Willy answered. "Evan always goes away this time of year." He glanced at Evan and grinned. "He hates when the papers dredge up all that anniversary stuff."

"Anniversary of what?" she asked.

"Nothing," Evan said. "I'm just going out of town for a while. I need supplies for the new designs Willy picked up for me."

"How long will you be gone?" she asked, feeling all eyes on her, but not being able to stop herself from asking. She knew that with conditions the way they were, it would be impossible to have a conversation alone with him. Audience or not, this would have to do.

"A week . . . maybe two . . . I'm not really sure," Evan said, eyeing Sarah as he spoke. She looked distressed and he wondered why. She might be afraid to be alone out here with just the girls, but with her parents here, that wouldn't be the case. "I was going to ask you to look after Ralph for me." When she stared blankly at him, he became concerned. "Is something wrong, Sarah?"

"No. Of course not," Sarah answered, sitting back in her chair and faking a smile. "The girls will be thrilled to have Ralph around full-time."

Evan watched her closely. The look in her eyes belied the smile on her face. What could be her problem? As far as he could figure, if she wasn't going to be alone, there was really no other reason for her to be upset about his leaving.

Unless . . . she were going to miss him.

The idea sent a jolt through his system.

Their gazes locked, and what he saw there squeezed his heart as if in a vise. No, it couldn't be that, he told himself. There was something else going on in her mind, and he was misreading it. His heartbeat eased. Yes, that was it. He was seeing something that really wasn't there. And why should that surprise him? He didn't even know how to act around women anymore, let alone read their minds. He smiled at Sarah in hopes of easing whatever tension she was feeling.

"When are you leaving?" she asked.

"After I drop Willy off this afternoon. I wanted to get the fence finished before I left."

"And you're all done." It was a statement, not a question.

"Yeah." He patted Willy and Ted on their backs. "I had a lot of help."

"Well, have a good trip," she added with feigned enthusiasm. "Just let Ralph loose when you leave, and I'll call him in later."

"Thanks. I'll leave a bag of his food on the porch."

Sarah smiled. He smiled back. Ted passed the potato salad and everyone began talking about something else. Sarah wasn't paying attention. She pushed her dish away and patted her lips with the paper napkin. Lunch was over. For her, at least.

She'd just lost her appetite.

After coffee, Lenore and the twins cleaned up as Ted and Sarah escorted Evan and Willy to the door. She waved her goodbyes to the two men from behind the screen door, but didn't move away even after they disappeared into Evan's house.

Her father's arm crept around her shoulder, and she looked up at him and smiled. "Thanks for helping with the fence, Dad, but I'm afraid Mom's on the warpath about it."

"I can handle your mother. It's you I'm worried about," he said.

"Me?"

"Yes, you. I heard how that fence got broken."

"Oh. It was just a silly game that got out of control."

"That's all? Just a game?"

"Yes, of course. Why do you ask?"

He reached up and ran a finger in the small space between her eyebrows. "Because of what's going on right here. Every time something was bothering you when you were little, you would crinkle your face. Just like it is now."

"What could be bothering me?" she asked with a dismissive shrug.

Just then, Evan's back door opened and the two men emerged. They were talking as they walked to Evan's truck, but Sarah couldn't hear about what. She watched Evan throw a suitcase into the back. He gave Ralph a farewell pat, and shooed him away from the truck as he swung open the driver's door. Just as he was about to step into the cab, he turned and looked at Sarah's house over his shoulder. Their eyes met across the distance. He hesitated for a moment, then, lifting a hand, he waved. She waved back.

As the truck pulled out of the driveway, she couldn't suppress the sigh that escaped her lips.

"He'll be back soon," he father said softly.

Sarah read the understanding look on his face. "Oh, Dad, am I that transparent?"

"You are to me," he said and hugged her to him. She turned to him and hugged him back. They looked at each other and smiled. "Just one thing," he added.

"What's that?" Sarah asked.

"Don't tell your mother."

Chapter 9

The only other time in her life Sarah could recall watching the calendar this intently had been when she was counting the days to her seventeenth birthday in anticipation of getting her driver's license. This was worse.

It had been a little over a week since Evan had left for his business trip. It was already the beginning of August, and her parents showed no signs of leaving. She and her mother were getting along well enough, and the kids were having a summertime ball with the small inflatable kiddie pool her father had set up for them at the side of the house.

Everything was fine. Everyone was happy. Except her.

She waved to the twins as they splashed each other—and Ralph—unmercifully. "Careful," she called with a smile.

Sarah sighed out loud, folding one leg under her as she sat on the lawn chair in her bathing suit and cutoffs watching the girls frolic. The latest, bestselling paperback novel was sitting at her feet untouched. She couldn't summon up enough energy or concentration to read.

The setting was new but the problem was an old one.
It had been so easy to fall back into the old routine with
her parents, of allowing them to take care, protect, nur-
ture and oversee every aspect of her life with the girls.
Her greatest fear of moving away from them had been
that she wouldn't be able to cope with everything involved in raising the twins without the help she'd come to
know and depend on.

Yet she had been coping. No, better than coping. She'd
been thoroughly enjoying herself. Granted, a lot of time
hadn't passed since her move, but the fact was that she
had been doing very well on her own. And she liked it.
She liked the autonomy of coming and going as she
pleased, cooking or not cooking, making her own
schedule for herself and the girls, not fitting into someone else's.

And she liked the privacy. That, if she were honest with
herself, was at the crux of her discontent. She liked having the early mornings to herself before the girls awoke,
and most of all, she liked the freedom of the night after
they'd gone to sleep. No one parent or the other to call
her to watch a television show she had no interest in, or
to play a game of cards to pass the time, or to indulge in
mundane conversation of the events of the day.

Those things had been fine before, but no more. She
wanted the quiet of the evening back, wanted her new
habit of roaming outside onto the porch to think, to view
the stars, the moon, and... to be with Evan.

Admit it, that's your real problem.

She missed him. Simple, silly Sarah. She'd known the
reserved, reclusive Evan Forester little more than a month
and yet he'd become an important, even vital, part of her
life. A day, an hour, a minute didn't go by when a
thought or image of him didn't skip through her mind.

This wasn't the way it was supposed to be. *She* was the
one intruding on his life, not the other way around. But
somewhere between scaring the twins half to death and
proving how truly great he was with those talented hands
of his, she had begun to feel things for him she hadn't
thought possible to feel for another man ever again.

Since he'd been gone, she'd awakened each day with a hollow ache inside, and by the time the morning fuzzies cleared from her head, she'd realize the reason for it: she wouldn't see Evan today.

Each time she fed or petted Ralph, she felt a seamless connection to him. Long after her parents and her girls were asleep at night, she'd sneak down to the porch. The dog would always follow her, and as she sat alone in the darkness, she'd find herself talking to Ralph about Evan, asking and answering inane questions about how he might be doing and when he would be back, reassuring the Irish setter that they all missed him, too. Once the one-sided conversations were over, she'd feel as foolish as she was sure she looked for talking to a dog.

But now that more than a week had passed, the ache was changing, replaced by a tingling feeling of anticipation. Soon, very soon, he would be home, she could feel it. When she'd awakened today, the sky looked a little brighter, the air a little clearer, and her heart beat a little faster as morning blended into afternoon.

How should she react when she saw him? A kiss? No, not if her mother was watching. A hug, maybe. Yes, that would do, a friendly offered handshake followed by a short, quick, welcome-home embrace. She'd bring Ralph out to him, and they'd talk about his trip. Maybe later on in the evening, he'd come out on his porch, and then she could nonchalantly cross the lawns and climb his deck steps and they could—

"Penny for your thoughts."

Sarah looked up. "Hi, Dad."

"Want me to take over here?" he asked.

"No, I'm okay. Where's Mom?"

"She's lying down upstairs. Got a bit of a headache. Why don't you go ahead and take a break, too. I'll watch the girls."

"In a little while, maybe," she said as she patted the seat of the lawn chair that was set up next to her.

Her father sat. "Saw the pickup pull into the driveway a while ago." He turned to Sarah who became instantly alert. "Looks like Evan's back."

Sarah's heart began to pound. "Really?" she said with as much disinterest as she could manage. "I wonder how his trip was?"

"Why not go on over and ask him."

She shook her head. "No, he's probably busy or he would have come over to get his dog."

Ted watched the sopping wet Irish setter jump in and out of the blue plastic pool with the shrieking girls. "Ralph doesn't look like he's in any hurry to go home. Why don't you let Evan know where he is?"

Sarah turned to her father. "Dad, if I didn't know better, I'd think you were giving me permission to go after Evan."

"I just want you to do what you want to do."

"And that is?" she asked with a grin.

"Go after Evan."

They both laughed out loud. "You are too much," Sarah said as she leaned over to kiss her father's cheek. "But thanks."

She rose and began walking painfully slowly toward the front of the house, feeling her father's eyes on her back, counting each step that she took. But as she rounded the corner, her impatience got the best of her and she picked up speed, her demure walk breaking into an all-out run.

And she smacked flat into Evan coming around from the other side.

"Whoa!" He grabbed her by her upper arms to stop the collision.

"Oh!" She held onto his forearms for balance.

And then they stopped moving long enough to look at each other.

If eyes could only speak...

Sarah gazed into the deep, dark pools of his and wondered what was going on in his mind. Had he thought of her at all this week? Had he wondered how she was doing, what she was doing, if she were thinking of him? Did he know how much she'd missed him, could he see it in her eyes? She was sure he could plainly read the gamut of emotions his arrival evoked.

Her gaze drifted down to his chest. He was wearing a white dress shirt, sleeves rolled up, with two buttons opened at the collar exposing just enough of his tanned chest to make her want to run her finger down the slit. Her hand curled into a fist. *God help me, I want him.* She looked up at him again and felt herself blush with the direction her thoughts were taking.

He saw the twin spots of red on her cheeks, and Evan reluctantly loosened his grip. His hands slid down her arms. As he did, the fingers of her right hand hooked his left and held. He didn't pull away.

"Welcome back," she said softly. *I missed you.*

"Thanks." *I missed you, too.*

His eyes drank their fill of her. He hadn't thought it possible to feel physical pain from missing someone, but that's how he'd spent his time away. An ache had begun somewhere in the vicinity of his solar plexus the minute he'd pulled out of the driveway last week, and since then it had blossomed into a full-grown pain that seemed to have taken root.

She was here now, facing him, touching him, and he took a deep breath, willing the pain to subside, but it did not. Instead, it became sharper, more urgent, as if it were being chased by the fear that she now would leave him the way he'd left her. Stupid, irrational, he knew, but still he couldn't let her go.

Not that Sarah was pulling away from him. In fact, she seemed to be leaning into him. God, he wanted to kiss her. He wanted to forget where he was and who might come upon them and take her in his arms, kiss her, cup her luscious bottom in his hands and lift her into him...

"How was your trip?" she asked. *I want to touch you.*

"Productive. I was able to pick up most of the supplies I need," he answered, surprised at the neutral, calm sound of his own voice. *Let me hold you, feel you. Let me...*

He smiled to hide his thoughts, and she smiled back. It didn't work. The fantasy had intensified since he'd been away. All he could think of was what it would feel like to have her soft body beneath his, to run his fingers

over her silky skin, to press his lips in the little nook behind her earlobe, to feel her open up to him, to bury
himself inside her.

The thought itself was enough to make him hard, and
he thought about it all the time. All through the business
trip, he'd felt like an automaton, controlled by these
erotic thoughts and images, moving by rote in a perpet-
ual state of sexual readiness.

It had to end; he had to end it. Somehow or other he
had to get control of himself . . . or let himself go completely. Living like this in the middle, on the fence between feigned disinterest and total arousal, was driving
him stark raving mad.

What would she do if he asked? What would she do if
he *didn't* ask, just acted? But he couldn't do that. She
had to come to him. He didn't have the luxury of calling
the shots. He couldn't exactly pound on her door in the
middle of the night and invite himself in. That first move,
if there was to be one, was up to her.

"You look tired," she said.

"A little stressed out, I guess," he answered with a
short laugh that didn't quite make it.

Lord, what was he going to do? He was wound as tight
as a coil and ready to pop at any given moment. He
needed time with her, and space. Privacy. He almost
laughed out loud to himself. Here he was living in the
most private, protected area around and he couldn't find
the space to be alone with the woman he . . . wanted.

"Evan! Look, Alys, Evan's back," Ariel called to her
sister as she ran around the side of the house.

As if on cue, Ralph bounded up the walkway, passed
the oncoming girls and, without breaking stride, jumped
up onto Evan with such force he almost knocked both
him and Sarah over. Sarah took an initial step back in
self-defense, then tried to control the dog by grabbing his
collar.

It was too late. Evan's white shirt and dress pants were
immediately dotted with muddy paw prints and bits of
wet grass. The twins were close behind and not to be
outdone. Each girl took hold of one of Evan's legs and

jumped up and down with the excitement of his arrival, completely wetting his trousers on both sides.

"Good Lord!" Sarah exclaimed, trying to shoo the dog and the girls away from Evan.

"It's okay," he shouted over the noise.

"But your clothes—"

"Doesn't matter—"

"Come see our new pool," Alys said as she tugged Evan toward the side of the house.

"Yes, come see," Ariel added. "Ralph's been swimming with us."

"I can see that," Evan said as he attempted to extricate himself from the dog's enthusiastic greeting and the girls' persistent tugging. "Okay, okay, I'm coming."

He raised his chin to Sarah to catch her eye. "I'll see you later?" he asked.

"Tonight?" she asked.

He nodded. Her eyes told him, "Later." His said, "Soon."

"What was that commotion all about?"

Sarah turned to her mother's voice. "Evan's back."

"Oh." Lenore rubbed the bridge of her nose. "I should have known."

Sarah chose to ignore her mother's caustic remark. She was too full of joy to let Lenore ruin what was in her heart right now. He was back, and she would see him tonight. Maybe, if she were lucky, they'd even have some time completely alone. The idea made her stomach clench with anticipation.

"How's your headache, Mom?" Sarah asked.

"It was just going away when all that noise started."

Sarah smiled to herself as she put her arm around her mother's shoulders and led her to the house. "Come on, I'll get you some iced tea."

"Is there any mint left?" Lenore asked as she allowed her daughter to guide her back to the house.

"I think so."

"I hope there is. I can't drink that tea without mint. It's too acidy for my stomach. The mint seems to soothe..."

Sarah's mind wandered as her mother went on and on about her digestive problems. It didn't matter. Nothing mattered right now except the fact that she would see him tonight. What she would do, she wasn't yet sure, but something was about to happen. She felt it in her bones.

She held the screen door for her mother and entered the house with a stupid grin on her face.

He's back.

Frustration gnawed at Evan like a cancer. He paced back and forth in his workroom and stared through the windows at the sky. A storm was brewing. The wind was picking up and distant sounds of thunder boomed from the other side of the lake, moving slowly but surely in their direction.

He'd spent the better part of the evening watching the storm's progress as he sat on his back porch, rocking and waiting for Sarah to appear. She hadn't, and around eleven he'd gone back inside, tired of fighting off the mosquitoes that hovered around the yellow insect light over his doorway.

But he hadn't given up. He'd checked several times out back, pretending to watch the approaching storm, hoping beyond hope that Sarah would come to him. But now it was late, and as time passed, it became more and more apparent he wouldn't see her.

He wondered what had kept her indoors tonight of all nights, this night of his return, the night he had dreamed of since he'd left. Perhaps she was fearful of storms and was hiding away. But even with the little he knew of her, that was hard to believe. Maybe one of the girls was sick. That would be a logical explanation, but unless it was something serious, he knew she would at least let him know she couldn't make it.

Up until a few moments ago, the lights on the first floor had been shining through the windows. Now the house was dark; it was apparent everyone had gone to bed.

He felt his stomach sink.

He'd been so sure she'd come. He'd seen the welcome in her eyes, and had even convinced himself that she had missed him a little. Nothing like the way he'd yearned for her, of course, but a small amount at least—she *had* been happy to see him.

The thought crossed his mind to just walk across the lawn and knock at her door, wake her up if necessary, and ask what had happened. At least then maybe he'd be able to sleep. As things stood now, it would be another of those endless nights where his overactive mind would keep his overcharged body from finding even the smallest amount of peace.

Another hour passed, and the storm was full upon them. Thunder and lightning raged as ferociously outside as desire, want and need warred within Evan. There was no use waiting any longer. Sarah was gone for the night, and his plans to hold her, touch her, kiss her—and more—were shot to hell.

He stripped out of his clothes and donned his reliable old cutoffs before heading out the door. It was insane to go swimming on a night like this, but he didn't give a damn about personal safety. He felt crazy and so full of excess energy that if he didn't do something physical soon, he'd explode.

He steeled himself not to look up at her room as he jogged passed her house, keeping his eyes straight ahead, fixed on the lake. When he reached the dock, he stepped out of his cutoffs and dived naked and visibly aroused into the black churning waters.

Lightning flashed, thunder boomed, but he didn't care. That raw energy inside him seemed to feed off the electricity in the air. His body was tight, hard, and so in need of release he just might have to give in and take matters into his own hands . . . so to speak.

Go ahead, make jokes, he told himself as he swam hard and fast in the direction of the raft. Pulling himself upon the hard wood surface, he lay back flat, knees bent, arms outstretched, and paid homage to the powers of nature raging above him. The shafts of lightning were coming closer now, almost overhead. He watched the flash, then shut his eyes and counted slowly to four as he waited for the thunder to follow. Even knowing it was coming, his body still jerked at the deep, rumbling sound.

The lightning struck out again, closer still. "Go ahead, hit me," he dared the elements, then shut his eyes to wait for the inevitable.

Sarah couldn't believe she was doing this. It was one thing to sneak out of your house in the middle of the night when you were a teenager, quite another to do it when you were closing in on thirty-five. But sneaking she was. Gripping the collar of her blue terry robe in one hand, she tiptoed past her parents' room on her way down the stairs, thanking every myriad and sundry deity ever worshipped since time began that the thunder was muffling the sounds of each creaking step she took.

She carefully closed the screen door behind her so that the spring wouldn't snap shut. Once she was outside, she exhaled the breath she'd been holding and breathed a sigh of relief. Which was short-lived. The streak of lightning that flashed across the sky almost scared her half to death. She stepped down from the porch and crept around the side of the house, glancing at the route she'd seen Evan take just moments ago as she'd watched from her bedroom window. She'd tried to get his attention, but the thunder had drowned out her whispered plea and her vigorous arm waving went unseen.

Standing midway down the path to the lake, she scanned the area. He was nowhere to be found, which meant only one thing. The man had to be a maniac. To choose to go for a swim in the middle of a storm was absolute lunacy. What would prompt him to do such a thing? He had to be crazed.

And so was she.

She made her way down to the dock and stared out into the black, churning waters. It was too dark to see anything clearly, but she had no doubt that the speck of light she saw on the raft was Evan.

Sarah bit her lip. She'd wanted more than anything to see him tonight, but for some reason her mother had been in a demanding and talkative mood. The nap that afternoon had refreshed her enough that she had no desire to go to bed, even after her father had hinted several times that she should join him.

It made Sarah think that Lenore was reading her mind, that her mother knew exactly where she would go and what she would do once everyone was asleep. A hundred times during the endless evening, Sarah had started to say something about going outside for a breath of fresh air. She'd even gotten as far as the door once, when her mother had announced she would join her. Quickly, Sarah had changed her mind, citing the coming storm as a reason to stay inside.

She dropped her terry robe. Okay, she said to herself, clothing or no clothing? Evan's cutoffs were at her feet, which meant that he was naked. Her throat closed and her pulse raced. She was only wearing her thin cotton nightgown and panties, having thought she might catch him down here at the dock, but such was not the case.

Decision time, Sarah. If she swam out to him completely and utterly naked, her message would be loud and clear. She knew very well what would happen.

Was she ready to go that far?

She'd given this a lot of thought, consciously or unconsciously, since the birth of the twins. Though she'd had no plans to jump in the sack with the first man who came along, she also hoped that someday she would meet someone who would make her *want* again. She had even prepared for that day, agreeing when her doctor had recommended a new contraceptive. But one year seemed to glide effortlessly into the next and sex had become nothing more than a cherished memory that had faded with time. Now she was faced with the reality of a situation that had only seemed a distant possibility.

Evan was out there, on the raft.

And all she had to do was join him.

Her heart began to pound so loudly in her chest it drowned out the thunder in her ears. Her hands began to tremble as she untied the string at the neck of her nightgown. Even if she chose to dive into the water like this, it would offer little to no protection, and besides, it might hamper her, drag her down, slow her up as she swam to the raft.

That's it, Sarah, indulge in a little healthy rationalization.

Her whole body was trembling now. She wasn't even sure she could make the swim in the condition she was in without some help. A light bulb went off in her head, and she ran over to the kiddie pool to grab one of the small plastic tubes her father had bought for the girls.

As she returned to the dock, tube in hand, she shrieked out loud as another streak of lightning, another clap of roaring thunder sounded overhead.

Sarah Wyeth, you are (a) nuts, (b) stupid, (c) sick, (d) love-starved or (e) all of the above.

"I pick (e)."

She shut her eyes and jumped into the black waters.

Evan heard nothing but the sound of black churning waters slapping against the raft interspersed with claps of thunder. The storm was right overhead now, frightening in its power and glorious in its fury. He lost himself in it, letting the hot, wet wind take his frustrations, fears and disappointments and blow them away into the night.

"Help..."

He opened his eyes, thinking he'd heard something, then shut them again. Another streak of lightning flash, another clap of thunder. The air was wetter now. Rain was imminent.

"Help..."

There it was again, a plaintive sound, a cry. He pushed himself up onto his elbows and looked around. Must be a bird lost in the storm, entangled, maybe, in something...

"Evan...please..."

He leaned over the edge of the raft and saw her. "Holy—" He reached down and pulled her out of the water and onto the raft. Dripping wet, they faced each other on their knees. "What the hell are you...?"

And then he realized that she, too, was naked.

Lightning flashed in the sky above, illuminating her face, her lashes wet and spiked, her blue eyes bright and stark against the paleness of her skin. And then the thunder clapped around them, ferocious in its intensity, loud enough to drown out his thoughts let alone any words he might want to utter.

But there were no words to say; none were needed. Like a gift from heaven, Evan didn't question it. He dipped his head and took her mouth in a searing kiss. Sarah's head snapped back initially with the strength of it, but then she responded measure for measure, giving him back everything he offered her, and more.

She caressed his back, his waist, around to his chest, then lower. Her fingers were wet and cool from her swim; his skin was on fire. Slowly, her hand continued its caress, and then she touched him intimately. He was hard, smooth, wet, and so hot her hand trembled.

Evan shut his eyes and wrapped his arms around her. Their bodies touched. Wet and slick, they slid against each other as they came together. Her body cooled his heated skin. Her pebble-hard nipples grazed the hard flesh of his chest. He couldn't move, couldn't think, only feel. For the longest time he held her, letting his beating heart tell her more than his inadequate vocabulary ever could. And then, when he didn't think he could stand it anymore, he pulled her down onto the raft.

Rain began to fall—huge, splattering drops that were erratic at first before taking form into tingling, prickling shards of water that pelted them in sheets from all directions. He lifted himself over her to protect her. She responded by spreading her legs to accommodate him, offering herself on this floating altar of love as she had never been offered before.

For a long moment he stared into her eyes, then reached up to smooth the wet, clinging, curly strands of auburn hair back from her forehead.

Evan's eyes asked questions. "Do you want this? Are you sure?" Sarah could only nod firmly in response.

Evan lowered himself onto her, nestled himself in the cradle of her hips. Without warning, he drove into her in one smooth, singular motion. Her eyes widened as he filled and stretched her; his shut with delight at the warmth and tightness that welcomed him.

Evan fleetingly thought he should have waited. There should be some preliminaries, some seduction, some foreplay. He was sure there was some kind of unwritten women's law about that. But as he pulled out almost to the tip before joining them back together, he noted that Sarah lips were parted with pleasure, her eyes were a fire blue, dilated and did not seem the least bit concerned that he had missed a step or two.

He moved again with a full thrust that caused their bodies to jointly shift toward the edge of the raft. He kissed her, his tongue invading her mouth in tandem with the thrusts of his body as they shimmied across the raft.

It was then he realized there was no need for foreplay. Not this time. Their entire relationship since day one had been foreplay of the most erotic kind. And as she arched her back to accept him again and again, Evan lost his train of thought and gave himself over to feeling.

If there had been another time in his life when he had felt this way, he couldn't remember it. If there had been another setting so perfect, another night so dangerously charged, another woman as soft, sweet, hot, wet, ready and yielding, the memory had somehow gotten lost in the sensual haze that now controlled his body, his brain.

But the answer was that there had never been a time like this, a night like this . . . a woman like this.

Sarah couldn't get enough of him. She brought her knees up and wrapped her legs around his back, but still she wanted more. She ran her fingers, her hands, all over him, from the top of his head to the tops of his thighs, as far as her reach would allow, and still it was not enough. Finally, she pushed at him, pulled at him, until he got the message that she wanted to be on top. He wrapped his arms around her and rolled them over.

Like a cat, she stretched her arms over her head as she straddled him. He was exactly where she wanted him to be: open and available and deep inside her. She thrust her hips forward, and he groaned.

The rain had lightened in its intensity, but was still coming down hard enough to drench them. She slid her wet hands across his chest. He grabbed her wrist when she encountered the scar, but she would have none of it. She was in control tonight. She was his master. She pushed his hand away, giving herself free reign to do as she pleased.

And then she dipped lower, finding her way to where their bodies were joined together. His fingers joined hers, burrowing his way into her nest of curls, finding that one spot on her body that was swollen and needy and ached with want for him.

He touched her, feather light, but enough for her to cry out. As he rubbed his thumb against her, she began to rock back and forth to the rhythm he set. Her hands on his shoulders, she lifted herself up and down against him. She felt it coming, tensed with anticipation, but still it surprised her with its intensity. The brightness of the lightning was nothing compared to the all-out blindness of her climax.

She rode him hard, hearing his plea to stop, to let him pull out, to go more slowly, to make it last, but she didn't heed it. She didn't want to leave him, not now, not when she was so perfectly fulfilled, so absolutely satisfied. She wanted to share this feeling with him.

Evan gave up the fight. His head spun as his body stiffened, then exploded into hers.

She lay down over him for a long time afterward, intertwining her legs with his, running her hands through his hair, and he caressed her back, her thighs, her buttocks.

The rain had lightened and was now only a light drizzle. Without moving, Evan whispered in her ear, "The storm's over."

Sarah pushed herself up onto her elbows and looked down into his dark, penetrating eyes. She shook her head and brushed her lips against his. "No, I don't think so. Not quite yet."

Chapter 10

The morning after...

Evan ran a hand over his face. Though he hadn't had a drop to drink, he felt as if he had a hangover. It wasn't his head that hurt so much as everything else.

A sex hangover... Was there such a thing?

He hadn't remembered making love as being so strenuous an activity, but he'd awakened with some very interesting aches in some very unusual places. He was definitely out of shape—celibacy, it seemed, had its drawbacks—though he was sure he could attribute a few of those straining muscles to that warp-speed swim he'd made in the middle of a storm.

Lying in bed he stared at the sunlight filtering through the vertical blinds and knew it was nearly noon. But he was in no hurry to rise. What he was, was satiated. Like a fat pasha stretched out and naked on his throne of sheets and pillows, Evan was replete and so damned relaxed he felt more like a bowl of jelly than a man.

But last night, he'd felt all man. And Sarah had been all woman. More woman than he'd ever hoped to have in his life. He shut his eyes to conjure up the image of her lying beneath him on the rocking raft. He saw it all, as clearly now as it had been last night: her parted lips, her rain-soaked hair, the lightning reflected in her eyes. His stomach twisted with the flash of her face, chin slightly uplifted, registering her pleasure as he'd entered her.

A shiver ran through him and his body tightened. Hell, it had been like a scene from some erotic video on MTV. His face split into a wide, self-satisfied grin. And he was *the star*. He glanced down at the tented sheet. So much for celibacy. It seemed that when he got back in the game, he dived right in . . .

He jumped when the phone rang, the sound reverberating through his entire being. Gingerly, he lifted the receiver without otherwise moving an inch. "Hello?"

"Evan, old boy! How are you?"

Evan winced, shut his eyes and shook his head. He'd expected this. Lara had let him know the cretin was in town asking his yearly questions, but he didn't think the man would have the gall to dig up his unlisted number and call him directly.

He should have known better. Ansell Walcott had no class, no decency, no conscience, having proven that years ago when he'd taken advantage of his distraught, attention-craving young wife. To think he had changed one iota in the ensuing time would make Evan as naive now as Maureen had been then.

"What do you want, Walcott?"

"Just checking in. Saying hello, that sort of thing. Thought you might like to talk," the silky, phony, British accent sounded crystal clear through the usually staticky portable phone Evan kept beside his bed.

"I have nothing to say to you."

Ansell laughed. "Not to me, crazy man. To the *people*. They want to know how their hero is faring. They're dying to find out what happened to you since the explosion."

"I doubt that."

"That's your problem, Forester, you've no sense of what the masses find interesting. But then, you don't have to. That's my job. Just let me come on out and we'll

chat a bit about life, liberty and the pursuit of custom-
furniture making.''

"Not interested."

"You're missing a great opportunity. Think of the
publicity! Think of all the new customers clamoring for
one of your rustic coffee tables or country rocking
chairs."

"I'm doing fine without it."

"Still hibernating, aren't you? Can't understand it for
the life of me. If I had your face and your story, I'd make
a million. Why the talk shows alone—"

"I'm hanging up."

"No, please, not yet. Evan, come on, for old times'
sake. Invite me out there so I can take a look-see at your
little haven for myself. Maybe then I'll understand what
the attraction is all about."

"Save yourself the time. Go back to the city, Ansell.
There's nothing for you here."

"You really mean that? You won't talk to me? I
thought this year—"

"Not this year. Not any year. Stop wasting your time."

"Well, it is my time, Evan, though, isn't it?"

"Walcott—"

"Maureen says hello," Ansell said softly.

Evan laughed out loud. Though Maureen had left
Ansell after the first few months, he had kept up the
pretense that they'd kept in touch. He had used it before, and once or twice, at the beginning, it had actually
worked well enough to rile Evan to anger. But now—especially after last night—he felt nothing but pathetic humor. "Give it up, Ansell, *old boy*."

Ansell feigned a loud sigh. "Oh, well, you can't blame
me for trying." He paused. "Are you absolutely sure,
Evan? A short, sweet piece, a few snapshots, would make
a great human interest—"

"Forget it."

Evan hung up without waiting for the reply. He knew
that no matter what he did or said, there still would be
some sort of story published about him, but as had happened in the past, Ansell Walcott would have to make a

lot of it up as he went along, interviewing townspeople and shopkeepers and such to get enough fact to mix with his fiction.

He pulled the plug on the phone, knowing all too well that this would be the first of many calls Ansell would make before actually giving up.

Evan forced his legs over the side of the bed and ran his hands through his hair. It was his own fault for being here. He usually made it a point to be away the two or so weeks before the anniversary of the accident to avoid being hounded by photographers and reporters, but in the past two years, the number of interested media people had dwindled to a trickle, and most were gracious enough to take his no for an answer. Ansell, of course, being the exception to the rule.

But he hadn't stayed away very long this time, pushing himself to do twice the work in half the time, so that he could rush back home. To Sarah.

Each hour, each day, she haunted him. He'd missed everything about her—her scent, the sound of her voice, the look on her face when he'd touched her for the first time.

He'd missed all those other things, too, things he'd thought would annoy the hell out of him, but had instead become as important to him as the air he breathed. Those inane, simple things, like the clap of her back screen door slapping shut, alerting him to the fact that she'd come out onto the porch. He even missed the girls intruding on his work, poking their little noses into whatever he was trying to do.

He'd missed every small nuance, every tiny word, gesture, glance. They had become necessary to him, and anniversary or not, he'd had to get back to his life here as soon as possible.

Perhaps what Lara had claimed all along was true. He'd always known his need for privacy was a form of self-preservation; he'd never argued that. But he had thought everyone overreacted to him, exaggerating his wanting to live alone out here by interpreting it as a withdrawal from society in general.

He'd never thought of himself as a hermit.

But maybe that was true. Maybe he had kept himself out of the mainstream of life. Maybe he was hiding. Maybe they were right, after all. Because suddenly, with Sarah and the girls, his life had taken a new course. It had become . . . unpredictable. At any given moment in time, someone could interrupt him, distract him, reach out to him . . . touch him.

He'd thought that kind of living-on-pins existence would have driven him crazy, and maybe it did, just a little. But along with the craziness came a new meaning. His blood was pumping faster these days and the wall around his heart was cracking. Feelings he didn't think he'd ever had before were seeping into spaces he hadn't known were there, finding their way inside . . . changing him. Not again, as he had been before the accident, but in a different, deeper way.

And now, after last night, it would be much worse. Because something else had happened other than the fact that he'd had sex for the first time in more years than he'd like to admit. He had stopped thinking long enough to feel again. He had let himself go completely, renewed himself, healed himself, in her, through her and with her.

Perhaps it had something to do with the uncontrollable elements—the lightning, the thunder, coupled with the incredible way she'd come to him and offered herself—but making love with Sarah had almost been a religious experience for him.

He was still dazed. Sarah represented to him all that was sweetness and light, while he'd only thought of himself in terms of night when it was too dark to see clearly, when he could pretend he was as he used to be.

But she knew him, the day-him as well as the night-him, and she still wanted him, accepted him . . . and proved it last night when she followed him to the lake and gave herself to him.

He thought he'd imagined the invitation he'd seen in her eyes on those nights on the porch, when he kissed her, or when she touched his hand and wouldn't let go. She'd seemed ready, willing even, to accept him as a lover. But never did he think it would actually happen. Never did he think it was more than testing herself, her feminine power, her sexuality.

To him, it was impossible because it made no sense.

Because unlike him, Sarah had choices. She could have any man she'd choose. And as much as he enjoyed the pleasures of last night, he was still confused about that.

Why him?

The best answer he had was that he was here, now, and based on his past celibacy, he was safe. That would be an issue with Sarah, as well it should be. But somehow being the ''safe'' choice to reinitiate herself into the world of loving didn't exactly sit well with him. His passion for her was too great for that, his wants too raw, his desires too broad.

But he'd take whatever she was offering, and enjoy it as long as it lasted. He knew this was not a forever thing. Once she saw, really understood, the extent of his needs, the depth of his hunger, she'd run so fast and so far he'd never see her again. Besides, the more involved she became in the community, the less she'd need him. She'd meet other men. Men who would fit in, men who would offer her things that were no longer available for him to offer.

She'd *date*.

The thought caused his insides to twist in pain. Don't think about that....

He took a deep breath and headed for the shower. Last night had been fantastic, but the rest was up to her. She'd made the decision to take him as a lover, but she still had to decide if this was to continue, because he sure as hell was in no condition to do it. His desire was too strong to be rational, and he'd be willing to take anything and everything she offered.

Here I am, Sarah. Come and get me ... He turned the spigot to cold and let the water hit his face.

Anytime. Anywhere. Anyhow.

Sarah sneezed as she sat across the kitchen table from her mother.

"Bless you," her mother said. "You aren't getting one of those awful summer colds, are you?"

"No, Mom." She sneezed again. She gave her mother a sheepish grin. "At least I don't think so."

"Well, that storm last night certainly cooled things off. The temperature must be twenty degrees lower today. I hope you didn't catch a chill."

She'd caught a lot more than a chill. After she and Evan had swum back from the raft, a cool breeze had replaced the warm, wet winds of the storm. She'd shivered with cold as they'd said a long, lingering good-night that almost turned into another bout of lovemaking against the side of the house. She hadn't wanted to leave him, but it was too cold to stand outdoors soaking wet. He'd asked her to return to his house with him to warm up, but as curious as she was to see what his bedroom looked like, she held on to her senses long enough to know she'd better wake up in her own bed.

So they'd parted.

It had taken a long time for her to fall asleep. Too many questions kept popping into her head, questions with no simple answers. Like, why did she do it? Why did she follow him? Why did she bare herself to him with such blatant invitation it would have taken a eunuch to refuse the offer?

She had been crazed last night, no doubt about that. She had been upset by being thwarted by her mother and not seeing him, propelled by missing the heck out of him while he'd been gone.

She fidgeted in her seat as much from her thoughts as from discomfort, then smiled at her mother who was looking at her peculiarly.

"Are you all right?" Lenore asked. "You look rather peaked."

"I didn't sleep well last night," Sarah admitted. She wouldn't mention the large wooden splinter she had embedded in her backside. Somehow she didn't think Lenore would take well to how it got there.

"You can take a nap when we get back later this afternoon."

"Get back?"

Lenore tsked. "From the church. I swear, Sarah, your memory is getting worse than mine."

Sarah put her head in her hands. "Oh, the audition! I forgot." Folding her arms onto the tabletop, her head collapsed onto them. She shut her eyes, trying to block out all thoughts and sound. Particularly her mother's instructions.

It didn't work.

"Yes, and you should look presentable. Why don't you wear your blue dress? The one with the buttons? It's summery, but proper enough to meet the reverend." When she didn't budge, Lenore added, "It's after twelve, Sarah. You'd better get moving . . ."

Her mother continued talking, but Sarah tuned her out. She wanted to daydream some more, but life was intruding. The Reverend Mr. Winthrop had called the other day to introduce himself and advise that he was conducting auditions for the new church organist. Sarah had promised to stop by this afternoon to show him what she could do, and she had to get herself ready as quickly as possible.

Reluctantly, she lifted her head and nodded at something her mother was saying. It must have been the right response, because she nodded in return. Sarah rose and walked out of the room. She had to put her thoughts in order, and get back into the teacher-mommy-prim-and-proper-matron mode. It certainly wouldn't do strutting into church thinking of Evan and what happened last night!

She amazed herself at how quickly she showered and dressed. She attempted to extricate the splinter, but while she could see it in the mirror, attempting to maneuver a tweezer to handle the delicate operation was an exercise in futility. She would have to live with the discomfort until she found someone to help her get it out.

That, of course, was going to be the real problem.

She couldn't very well ask her mother without an explanation. "Oh, yes, Mom, you know that wooden raft out in the middle of the lake? Well, I got the splinter

while making love with Evan on it during the storm last
night. Could you get it out for me? It's really uncomfortable.''

Definitely not an option.

Her father, God love him, would die of embarrass-
ment if she so much as said the word *derriere* out loud to
him let alone actually pulled down her panties and
showed it to him. And the girls were too little to be of any
help.

That left Evan. A slow smile creased her face as she
loaded everyone into the car for their trip to town. His
reaction might be the most interesting of all. That is, if
she had the nerve to ask him.

As she passed his house on the way to town, she
glanced over and noticed that, though the truck was in its
usual spot, the back door to his workshop was locked
shut. There was something to be said for his protective
life-style. At least when he wanted to withdraw from the
world, there was no audience waiting in the wings.

Her mother kept the girls busy while she auditioned.
She played the most popular and well-known hymns first.
Reverend Winthrop was gracious and very polite, but
noncommittal, advising Sarah that he had other appli-
cants to audition before he would make a final decision.
She'd left with a quick nod to an unsmiling Mrs. Mallory, the retiring organist who had sat in and directed
which pieces Sarah should play. It seemed the older
woman was going to have a lot to say as far as her replacement was concerned.

Sarah breathed a sigh of relief when it was over and she
was back out in the sunlight. Her mother had gotten the
girls ice cream while they waited. Of course, they were a
sticky mess by the time Sarah met them.

"I'll be right back," Lenore said to Sarah. "I just want
to run across to the greengrocer's and get some more
fresh mint."

Sarah rolled her eyes. Her mother and that mint were
going to drive her crazy before this visit was over. As she
waited for Lenore to return, she hunched down to wipe
the girls' faces with a tissue.

"Excuse me."

Sarah looked over her shoulder at a pair of knobby knees. Slowly, she looked up to find they were attached to a man dressed in short blue shorts, a madras-print sport shirt and a backward baseball cap.

"Yes?" she asked, rising from her squatting position.

"Are you Sarah Wyeth?"

"Yes, I am. Who—?"

"Ansell Walcott, at your service." He flashed a press pass too quickly for Sarah to examine. "Do you mind if Joseph here takes your picture? How about one of the girls, as well?"

The man called Joseph began clicking away. Sarah stood with her mouth open. Ariel hid behind her leg, but Alys preened with her hand on her hip, a broad, baby-toothed smile across her face as if she were posing for the cover of *Vogue*.

"Wait one minute." Sarah held up her hand in front of the camera lens. "What is this all about?"

"I'm Ansell Walcott."

"Am I supposed to know who you are?"

"Most people do."

"Except me."

"How presumptuous of me, then. I'm a free-lance reporter for a variety of media, Mrs. Wyeth, and every year I return to Wayside on the anniversary of the horrible accident that took so many lives to update our readers on the life of the town hero, my great friend, Evan Forest—"

"You're a friend of Evan's?"

"Oh, heavens, yes. We've known each other for—" he paused and tapped his index finger to his bottom lip "—let me see...oh, it must be years and years. He's never mentioned me?" Sarah shook her head. He looked hurt. "I can't understand why. Evan and I have shared so much—"

"I've only just moved here, Mr...."

"Walcott."

"Mr. Walcott. I'm sure Evan would have mentioned you sooner or later."

"Of course he would . . . and will, I'm sure. Now. Can we get on with this interview?"

"Interview?"

"Why, yes, every year I do a human interest story on Evan. I'd like to interview you as his new neighbor. Get your perspective on how he's faring, that sort of thing."

"I don't know . . ."

"Don't know what?"

Sarah turned to her mother. "Oh, Mom, there you are. This is Ansell Walcott—"

"The reporter?" Lenore asked.

"How do you do?" Ansell held out his hand palm up. Lenore placed her hand in his and he kissed her knuckles. She giggled.

"Yes, you know him?" Sarah asked in disbelief at her usually sensible mother's girlish behavior.

"Of course. Everyone knows Ansell Walcott. He writes for that paper I buy in the supermarket every week. And he's on that TV events show I watch every night."

"That sleazy—!"

"Now, now, Mrs. Wyeth, let's not be judgmental. Many fine people find my work to be very informative as well as entertaining." He smiled at Lenore. "Your mother, for one."

"Yes, well. I don't think I should be granting any interviews about Evan."

"He wants to know about Evan?" Lenore asked.

"Yes, Mother," Sarah said, giving her mother the very same stern-eye look of which she was usually the recipient. "But you know how Evan feels about his privacy. I don't think—"

"Nonsense. Evan should be proud of what he's done."

"He doesn't want to talk about it."

"Well, if he doesn't, then someone should. Perhaps we can help you, Mr. Walcott?" Lenore asked.

"I was hoping you'd offer," he said with a smile. "Why don't we go and sit by the park bench over there so Joseph can snap a few shots."

"Of all of us?" Lenore asked, her hand to her chest.

"Of course," Ansell answered. "You know Evan, too, don't you?" He ushered Lenore toward the bench as he spoke.

"Well, just slightly. Although I did make lunch for him one day, didn't I, Sarah?"

"*Mother...*"

"Oh, Sarah, come along. I don't think Evan will mind a few pictures. After all, you are his neighbor." Lenore turned to Ansell. "Will our pictures be in the newspaper?"

"That will depend on the article. If I have enough information to write about, then we'll need a lot of pictures to go along with it. Let's sit and chat awhile, shall we?"

Lenore sat on the bench with one of the girls on each side. "Sarah?" Ansell motioned her to stand behind her mother. "How about over here. A nice family shot."

"No, go ahead, take the girls and my mother."

"Sarah, come here right now," her mother said, "and don't waste the man's time." Sarah blew out a breath and obeyed. "Sometimes she's so obstinate," Lenore added as an aside to Ansell.

"Ready," Joseph said, then snapped a few in a row.

"Now then," Ansell began, "tell me about Evan. How did you meet?"

"Sarah moved next door to him," Lenore said, "and they hit if off right away."

"Is that true, Sarah?" Ansell asked.

Sarah grinned. "Not exactly."

"He scared us," Alys piped in.

"But not for long," Ariel added defensively. "And we love Ralph."

"Ralph?"

"His dog," Sarah advised, wondering if he knew Evan that well why he didn't know about Ralph.

"Oh." Ansell jotted that down, then looked up again. "So after he scared you, then what?"

"Then we all became friends," Alys said.

"Yes, he lets us watch him work," Ariel said.

"And we ride on the lawn mower with him every week—" Alys giggled "—even Mommy."

Ansell's eyebrows rose. "Mommy?" He turned to Sarah who was blushing. "Tell me about that, Sarah."

Sarah waved her hand dismissively. "Oh, it was nothing. We had a little accident—"

"A little accident!" Lenore exclaimed. "Why they knocked an entire section of fence down! My husband, Ted—that's Ted Hudson—he had to help—"

"How did that happen?" he asked.

Alys waved her hands in the air. "They were looking at each other and not where they were going. And they crashed."

"Crashed?"

"Yep. Right into the fence. Me and Ariel helped them get out."

"And Ralph, too," Ariel said.

"Interesting," Ansell said, staring at Sarah, whose blush deepened.

"Not really," she said. "It was a silly game. For the girls. That's all."

"Hmm," Ansell said with a grin, then he turned back to the girls. "Tell me more."

Alys shifted in her seat. "He plays with us in the lake, and he climbs trees with us—"

"And takes me fishing!" Ariel added.

"Fishing? Really. Sounds like fun."

"It is. He has a special fishing spot. And I know where it is," she said.

"Where is it?"

"Off the path on the side of Evan's house," Alys said importantly.

"You shouldn't tell," Ariel said. "Now it won't be special anymore."

"I won't tell a soul," Ansell promised, making a cross against his heart with his index finger. "I promise."

Ansell sat back. "Well, I must admit I'm a little surprised. Evan has been somewhat of a recluse these past few years. I can hardly believe all this . . . friendliness."

"Well, he must be changing," Lenore said. "Yes, that must be true. Why just the other day at that luncheon I gave? He mentioned having his cousin's wedding at his house. A hundred people, for goodness' sake. Now does that sound like a recluse?"

"Mom, Evan hasn't agreed to that."

"But he will, you'll see."

"Would that be his cousin, Lara Hanlon?" Ansell asked as he scribbled more notes.

Lenore nodded. "Yes, I think that's her name. Sarah, isn't that his cousin's—?"

Sarah had had enough. "I think we'd better be going," she said, holding out her hands for the girls to take. They jumped down from the bench and obeyed.

"But I haven't finished telling Ansell about the luncheon we had," Lenore said.

"I think Mr. Walcott has enough," she said with a tight smile.

Ansell stood and faced Sarah. "Yes, thank you. I wonder, though, if I may have your telephone number. Just in case I need to verify some facts?"

"I don't think so—"

"Here," Lenore said. Taking a slip of paper out of her purse she scribbled Sarah's number down. "Don't hesitate to call if you need anything else. I'll be here for a few more weeks."

Sarah's mouth gaped at her mother's words, but Lenore ignored her. It was already August. To date, her parents' visit had gone way beyond the original plan. While she hadn't pushed them for a departure date, she was sure it would be soon. Like this weekend.

Ansell scribbled a note on the scrap of paper Lenore had handed him, then looked up at her. "Why thank you . . . Mrs . . . ?"

"Hudson. Lenore Hudson. That's H-U-D-S—"

Sarah pulled her mother's arm. "Mom. Let's go."

"Oh, well, thank you again, Ansell." Lenore shook his hand. "And I look forward to seeing the article in the papers."

"I'll send you a copy," he said.

"Oh, really. Why, how nice of you!"

"Mother! We're leaving."

"Well, goodbye," Lenore said with a wave.

"Goodbye." Ansell waved back.

Lenore caught up with Sarah. "Won't Evan be thrilled when he hears about the article?"

Thrilled wasn't exactly the word Sarah would have chosen to describe Evan's reaction to this whole thing, but you never knew. "I hope so."

Ansell Walcott stood watching the retreating women cross the street to the municipal parking lot. He nodded, lost in thought for a moment before turning to Joseph. "Makes you wonder what's really going on out there in the woods, heh, Joey? What say we wait a day or two, then take a peek?"

"Sure, boss."

Ansell grinned broadly, thoroughly pleased with himself and his new train of thought. "Oh, and don't forget to take along your zoom lenses."

Chapter 11

Sarah stepped out onto the porch and let the screen door snap shut behind her. It was "quiet time." The girls were upstairs, her father was reading the paper and her mother was watching the soaps.

She, on the other hand, was simmering with anger—at Ansell Walcott for being so pushy, at her mother for once again ignoring her and taking charge, but most of all, at herself for being such a pushover.

Again.

She'd thought she was getting better. She'd thought that she had learned something. She'd even been feeling a little bit smug at the way she'd been able to still do her own thing despite her parents never-ending visit. But it was plain to see that old habits died hard. And now she'd have to pay the price for being a doormat.

She'd have to tell Evan what happened.

Sarah sat on the steps, not quite ready to face him. She knew he wouldn't be happy about her talking to a reporter. It was clear now what Willy meant at lunch about Evan always going away on business around the "anniversary" time. The anniversary of the accident, of course. He neither needed nor wanted any reminders of that time in his life.

After her run-in with Ansell Walcott, she could see why Evan planned things that way. She could see a lot of things now that she hadn't a clue about when she'd first laid eyes on him. He pretended to live this almost boringly normal, isolated life, yet no matter how hard he tried, he couldn't put that one day, that one act of heroism, behind him.

It was clear to her that he hid behind his scars in more ways than the obvious. He was protecting himself, to be sure, but beneath that mask was a man with deep feelings. Whether he knew it or not, last night on that drenched piece of wood in the middle of the lake, he had bared parts of himself that she wasn't sure *he* even knew existed.

No words had passed between them, but his body had spoken to her most eloquently. She still was feeling the aftereffects of the way he touched her. The possessive, sure stroking of his hands on her wet flesh had given her more insight into him than an hour's worth of conversation.

And she loved the power of the message so much she wanted to hear more . . . so much more. She wasn't quite sure if he was even capable of sharing more than his body with her, yet she could see now that if the possibility did exist, it would be left to her to make it happen. She was sure that, to Evan, having sex and sharing a life were two distinctly different and unrelated things. While he might want the former, she had a feeling he would fight her tooth and nail on the latter.

He had established his life-style. She was the interloper. If she wanted more from him, she would have to coax it out of him slowly. But after last night, it didn't seem as hopeless as she'd first thought. He had been an incredible lover, generous and demanding at the same time. It had seemed as if something inside him had been freed, let loose, and like the storm, he needed to conquer all around him.

Conquer her. And he had. She'd never been made love to with such urgency, such passion, such pure masculine animal magnetism.

Perhaps it had been the storm and the accompanying overwhelming darkness that had brought it out in him. He liked the dark, she knew that. He was much more at ease with her in the evening on his porch than he ever was in the light of day. He'd created this world, an almost negative image of the real one, so that in his own mind he could travel freely. But for all his pretense, he couldn't run away from who he was. Each day he saw its results in the mirror, and whether he wanted to or not, each year people forced him to relive it.

And she had now contributed to that by talking to a reporter about him. She stood and smoothed her sundress with her hands as she made her way across the lawns. What could she say to him to let him know that none of this mattered to her? That what he looked like was inconsequential?

Beauty's only skin deep . . .

It sounded so trite, but it was so true. He was beautiful to her, but only with time would she be able to prove that to him. For now, she had to deal with the matter at hand—Ansell Walcott and the article he was sure to write about Evan.

She took a step up onto his deck. His door was opened wide and she could see him through the screen, his back to her as he sat on his workbench bent over a piece of wood. As she climbed the steps, he heard her approach and spun around.

"May I come in?" she asked, her hand on the latch.

"Sure."

She slipped inside and stopped near the door. He stood as she entered, the furniture leg he had been working on in one hand, his carving tool dangling from the other. It was their first meeting since kissing him good-night—or more accurately, good-morning. With her mind on last night and what she had to tell him about the reporter, she hadn't given a thought to how she'd react or how bittersweet the ache inside would feel once she came face-to-face with him again.

His gaze skimmed over her, and Sarah felt herself blush from the inside out. "Hi," she said softly, feeling her toes curl inside her espadrilles at the sight of his hard body in cutoffs and a tight T-shirt.

"Hi," he answered, his eyes stopping here and there, refreshing an already unforgettable memory.

Their eyes met and all thoughts of Ansell Walcott fled Sarah's mind as a haze seemed to settle over the room, obscuring everything except Evan. Her lips parted, and he dropped the tool and piece of wood he'd been carving onto the bench.

He took a step forward. So did Sarah. Into his arms.

Evan didn't think, didn't need to. He wrapped his arms around her and pulled her tightly against him. She molded herself to him, fitting every curve to every angle so perfectly he felt as if he'd just been reconnected with the other half to his whole.

He hadn't thought she'd come to him. Not so soon, anyway. He thought she'd need to hide away for a while and think about what she'd—they'd—done last night. He was sure she'd be having second thoughts about now, embarrassed at best, remorseful at worst, but whatever, she would avoid him until enough time had passed to put her one crazy impulsive act into its proper perspective.

But no, she was here now, and though he would try not to read too much into it, he also wasn't about to pass up the chance to hold her again, kiss her, feel her body on his. She buried her face in the crook of his neck. He shut his eyes, felt her breath on him and wanted to devour her whole. "Sarah..."

"Tell me it was wonderful," she said, her whisper muffled against his body.

He lifted her chin to look at him. Her eyes were crystal blue and moist with emotion. "You have to know... Sarah, it was... so... it was... the best..."

He wanted to say so much more, but the words were lodged in his throat, stuck in bumper-to-bumper traffic, stumbling over one another, unable to get free.

So he kissed her instead, letting his lips, his mouth, his tongue, tell her what he wanted her to know about how she made him feel about being a man to her woman, about how much he wanted her now, especially now, after last night, after having had her, tasted her . . . been inside her.

He groaned into her mouth, overcome with lust for her and some-unnamed-thing else that he couldn't even dare entertain at this point in his life. She touched her tongue to his, wrapped her arms around him and dug her nails into the muscles of his back, holding on to him so tightly he didn't know where his body began and hers ended.

This was worse, far worse than before. He knew it would be, but he hadn't known how intense the need would now become, how powerfully hard his body would respond to seeing her, touching her.

He had made a decision to wait for her to make the first move, to decide if what they shared last night was a mistake that would never happen again or was only a prelude to something better, deeper, stronger. Had convinced himself that was the only way.

But there *had* to be more. And if she would let him, he would take all she was willing to give—anytime, any day, anywhere . . .

Evan lifted her off the floor away from the door and carried her, feet dangling uselessly as a puppet in her master's hands, to lean her against the far wall of the workroom. He set her down, trapping her between the wall and his body, and cupped her face in his hands.

And then he just looked at her. Her hair was its usual, glorious mess around her face; her cheeks were pink and her eyes were wide, luminous and welcoming. He had to touch her. Like a blind man, his hands felt their way down her neck, just grazing her chest, her breasts, on their way to her waist where they held her still and steady as he nestled her against him, serving no purpose except to drive himself crazy.

He undid the front buttons of her sundress, one at a time, fumbling on the third one when he realized she was braless, until her hands joined his, aiding him in his plight. He pushed aside the material of the dress, exposing her breasts. He watched her nipples harden as his hands cupped each one gently. And then he bent his head down to kiss their plump roundness before opening his mouth and suckling one pink and pouting nipple.

Sarah arched her back and gasped as each tug of his mouth caused a corresponding contraction in her womb. She felt herself melt inside as she surrendered to the pleasure he offered. He moved to the other side, and she ran her fingers encouragingly through his hair, unable to stifle the whimpering sounds coming from her throat.

Evan was wild for her. He dropped to his knees, unbuttoning the remainder of her sundress on his way down. With an upward glance, his eyes asked permission even as his fingers insinuated their way into the waistband of her panties. With no objections on her part, he skimmed them down slightly. His hands splayed across her thighs, softly massaging the soft flesh until his thumbs met in the center.

As he kissed her nest of curls, her woman's scent catapulted him into a sensual world beyond his wildest imagination. He crossed over from the here and now into a place where only the two of them existed, where she belonged only to him and he only to her. Only Sarah. Only Evan. And in this special place all their own, he wanted more than anything to please her as she had never been pleased before.

Sarah gasped his name when he touched her intimately, groaned when she felt his breath moistening her and cried out when his tongue found that one tiny spot on her body that craved all the attention he could give. He held her by the hips as she gripped his shoulders for support. His mouth worked its magic on her, and Sarah opened herself to him. She shut her eyes, willing the rest of the world to fade as she felt herself burn from the inside out, as hot and as fearsome as any real fire could be.

Her climax was shattering. She accepted it, let herself feel it, thrilled to it, gloried in it, and finally was left shaken and unable to stand.

As Evan rose, he kissed her belly, her breasts, her chest, her neck, on the way up to her lips. When he kissed her, she tasted herself on his lips and felt tears form in her eyes. At that moment she knew that what she was feeling for Evan Forester was deeper and stronger than anything that had come before.

Even John.

A shiver ran through her. Fear, sudden and urgent, washed over her, and she reached for him for support.

Evan wrapped his arms around her and cradled her head against his chest. He whispered into her hair, "Sarah, sweetheart, I need you..."

He was as hard and aroused as a man could get, and the woman in her wanted to give him everything he had given her. More. She rubbed herself against him, urging him on, inflaming him.

Evan needed no encouragement. He cupped her bottom in his hands and lifted her onto him as he kissed her again.

But then he squeezed.

"Ouch!" Sarah exclaimed, passion flying out the window on the heels of pain.

"Ouch?"

"Yes, ouch."

A dazed, mortally aroused Evan blinked twice and navigated a space between them. "What'd I do?"

"It's not you. It's me," she said. As she yanked up her panties with one hand and buttoned up her dress with the other, she twisted her body around to look at her sore backside. "Know anything about splinters?"

Evan felt as if someone just threw a bucket of cold water on him. He took a step away from her and ran a hand through his hair. "Splinters?" he asked in disbelief.

"Yes, splinters. Have you ever had a bad one?"

"I'm a carpenter, remember? I've had my share. What's the problem?"

"I have one."

"A splinter? Where?"

"Here." She pointed to the spot on her right buttock.

He grinned. "You're kidding."

"I wish I was."

"How in the world did you...?" Sarah raised her eyebrows and jerked her head in the direction of the lake. Evan's eyes lit up with understanding, and he nodded slowly. "Oh, yeah. The raft. Sorry."

"It's not your fault," she said.

"But I should have known. That wood's rotting and...hell, I just wasn't thinking much last night."

"Neither was I."

Their eyes met and that dreamy haze started filling the room again.

Evan cleared his throat. "Can I...I mean, is there anything I can do?"

"You can get it out."

"You mean...?"

Sarah nodded. "I have no one else to ask."

"Your mother?"

"And explain how it got there? No thanks."

"I see what you mean."

Sarah toyed with the hem of her sundress, lifting it slightly. "So...would you?"

Evan swallowed. "Sure," he said, not sure he could touch her right now without throwing her down on the workroom floor and burying himself inside of her. *Count to ten,* he told himself through gritted teeth, and proceeded to do so as he straddled the workbench before sitting and beckoning her over to him. "Let's take a look."

Sarah lifted her dress and peeled her panties down halfway on one side. Evan was quiet for a long moment as he examined the splinter. As she felt his thumb rub over the sore spot, she peered at him over her shoulder. "How does it look?"

"Probably like it feels."

"That bad, huh?"

"Yep."

"Can you get it out?"

"I think so. Come on over to the table, and I'll get the tweezers and some alcohol." Sarah did as he asked as he disappeared into the adjacent bathroom. When he returned, he stepped behind her. "Bend over."

Sarah eyed the large tweezers skeptically. "I don't like the looks of those."

"If you don't get it out, it might get infected. Then what will you do?"

The thought of going to a doctor in town and having to explain how she'd come to have an infection from a splinter in her backside was enough to make her obey. "Okay," she said, turning away from him. She leaned over, shut her eyes and gripped the sides of the table. "But be gentle."

He was. Very gentle. So gentle she hardly felt a thing except a tiny pinch and then the coolness of the alcohol-drenched cotton swab. And then his hands as he caressed the curve of her hip before pulling her panties back up. She straightened, coming right up against his front with her back.

"Sarah," he whispered in her ear as she leaned against him, "I want you so much . . ."

"Oh, Evan . . ."

They never heard the footsteps on the porch, never knew someone was standing at the door until a discreet cough sounded behind them.

"Dad!" Like two guilty children, they jumped apart.

"Excuse me," Ted said through the screen door, "but your mother sent me over to get you. I'll tell her you're busy."

"No! I mean, it's okay. I'll be right there."

"Take your time," Ted said, quickly descending the steps.

Evan blew out a breath he hadn't known he'd been holding. "I don't know who was more embarrassed, him or us."

Sarah shook her head. "My mother will definitely get this out of him."

"You're a big girl, Sarah. You shouldn't have to answer to your mother anymore."

"Yeah, I know." Sarah sighed, her gaze drifting out the door toward her house. "I'm still working on that."

He pulled her into his arms. "And here I was ready to give you the grand tour."

"Of the house?"

"Among other things."

A small smile creased her lips. "Upstairs and all?"

"Upstairs and all."

She met Evan's eyes, and he saw how troubled she was. "Some other time, then," he said, deflated in more ways than one. He released her and took a self-protective step back.

"But I never told you why I came over in the first place!"

"There was another reason?" he asked with a half grin.

Sarah blushed. "Yes, there was."

"What was that?"

Sarah bit her lip. "I ran into someone today who said he knows you. But he didn't know about Ralph, so now I'm not so sure."

"Who?"

"He said his name was Ansell something-or-other. A reporter. Pretty well-known, I guess, because my mother seemed to know who he was. Do you?"

Evan smirked. "I know him."

Sarah smiled, a bit relieved that maybe this wouldn't be so bad, after all. "He said you and he went back a long way. Shared a lot of things."

"My wife for one."

"Your wife?"

Evan walked over to the workbench and sat. He picked up the table leg he had previously discarded and smoothed his hand over the partial carving. He spoke without looking at her. "I found him living in my house when I was released from the hospital. Seems Maureen got a bit lonely, and he was only too happy to keep her company, so to speak."

"How awful! You must really hate him." Sarah kept to herself her thoughts on her opinion of his ex-wife.

Evan shrugged. "It was a long time ago. I don't hate or love him. I just wish he would leave me alone." He looked up at her. "So did you talk to him?"

She bit her lip. "Yes. My mother, too. I'm afraid she told him you were having Lara and Willy's wedding here. It'll probably be in the article."

"At least that won't be a lie."

"You decided to say yes?" she asked excitedly.

"Yes, I decided to say yes. But I won't be here."

"Oh, Evan."

"Don't 'oh, Evan' me, Sarah. I told you how I feel about that. Be satisfied that I said okay to the wedding."

Sarah frowned. "Well, I suppose that's something."

"Trust me, it's a lot."

"That's not all," Sarah added. "He had a photographer with him. He took some shots of me and my mother. The girls, too."

"At least you'll get your pictures in the papers."

"Then you're not angry with me?"

"Why should I be? If not you, he'd find someone else. It happens every year. You'll have to deal with it more than I will."

"What do you mean?"

Evan stood. He carefully laid the table leg on the bench, and, hands on hips, he turned to her. "Have you ever had a write-up in the newspaper?"

"Once. After John died. A local newspaper did a story on him."

"And?"

"And he did a very nice piece."

"And every word was true? You were pleased?"

"Yes, I was. It was very complimentary."

"Then I hope you're as happy with what Ansell writes."

"You say that as if I won't be."

Evan shook his head. "I have no way of knowing what he'll say. I never do."

"But you don't trust him."

Evan laughed. "Ansell Walcott?" He shook his head. "No, I don't trust him at all. He's a little weasel, and what he can't force you to say, he'll make up."

"What could he possibly say about *us?*"

Evan turned from her. "We'll see, then, won't we?"

He picked up his carving knife and began working on the table leg again, all thoughts of passion whisked away by the mention of Ansell's name.

Sarah felt herself bristle at his know-it-all attitude. She was convinced that he was overreacting about Ansell. Walcott's viciousness. After all, he was prejudiced after what happened with his wife and all. But that was years ago. The man seemed perfectly harmless to her. And to her mother, too, for that matter, and no one put anything past Lenore Hudson.

Which reminded her about having to face her parents right now. She knew her father must have told her mother by now about catching Sarah in Evan's arms. Not that her father would have wanted to tell, but her mother had a way of wheedling these kinds of things out of people, and she knew poor Ted would be hard-pressed to keep this to himself. Thank goodness he hadn't come minutes earlier. She didn't want to think of what she would have done if her father had seen Evan on his knees and...well, it was too dreadful to even imagine!

Like it or not, she had to go back to the house and face the music. She felt like a teenager sneaking home after curfew, and was annoyed with herself for feeling so.

The sound of the girls' voices reached her, and she looked out the door. Evan heard them, too. "The girls are up. I'd better be going."

Evan stood and grabbed her hand as she went to leave. "Will I see you later?"

"I don't know. I'll try."

"Try hard."

Sarah looked into his eyes and saw a raw need. She knew she was the cause of that, a direct result of it, in fact, and she wished she could stay right now and satisfy him in ways she had only fantasized about. "I'm sorry about before."

"Before?"

"Being interrupted. I wanted to...I mean, what you did for me, but I didn't..." She threw up her hands. "Oh, you know what I mean!"

Evan chuckled at her discomfort. "Yeah, I do." He ran a finger down the side of her face. "You owe me one."

The look in his eyes made her swallow, hard. "I do?"

"Yes, ma'am. And I mean to collect."

To her surprise, her father had not told her mother a thing. Lenore was waiting on the porch as she returned from Evan's. Sarah braced herself for a barrage of questions and accusations, but none came. Instead, Lenore was sullen.

"Mom? What's wrong?"

"Your father, that's what's wrong. I think he's going through his second childhood."

"What happened?"

"He wants to take the girls to that new amusement park that opened up last year."

"So? What's wrong with that?"

"He wants to go on rides, for heaven's sake. The man's sixty years old, and he's thinking about roller coasters. Don't you think that's odd?"

Sarah suppressed a smile. "When does he want to do this?"

"Tomorrow! Do you believe it? He wants us to pack up and drive to this ridiculous place and spend the day eating hot dogs and standing in line. And then he wants to *stay overnight*."

Sarah's mind began to race. "Sounds like fun to me."

"Then you go with him! I think he's lost his mind!"

Sarah bit her lip. She didn't know what her father was up to, but this sudden urge to go to an amusement park with the girls—and stay overnight—meant only one thing as far as Sarah was concerned. Her father was giving his tacit approval to whatever was going on between Evan and her. So much so that he was willing to give her a free night to pursue it.

Her heart skipped a beat. A free night. My Lord, what would she do with it?

Silly question.

"Well, never mind that for now. So tell me? What did Evan say about the reporter?" Lenore asked.

"He's not bothered."

"I told you so."

"Yes, Mom, you were right," she said because she knew her mother wanted to hear it. "Where are the girls, by the way?"

"Out back with your father. He's decided to barbecue tonight." Lenore audibly exhaled. "Well, I'd better go and pack a bag. He's probably already told the girls we're taking them. I don't know why we all don't go. Wouldn't it be better, Sarah, if you came along, too?"

"I don't think so, Mom. I have a lot of things to do. Getting ready for school and all. I'd really appreciate a day to myself." Endless possibilities swirled through her mind and her stomach twisted with excitement and anticipation.

"Well, if you need me to stay, your father can take the girls by himself. You might need my help."

I don't think so.

Everyone went to bed early that night, Sarah included, and even though her mind was racing with what tomorrow would bring, she fell asleep quickly. The next day she rose early and saw everyone off, waving goodbye from the porch as her parents' car pulled out of the driveway. Her father caught her eye, and she mouthed the words *thank you* for him to see. He smiled and nodded, and she wondered if he truly knew what she had planned to do with her day of freedom.

She stood for a long while after the car pulled away, almost afraid to get started until she was absolutely, positively sure that they would stay gone. She glanced toward Evan's house. His truck was missing, which was just as well. She needed several hours at least to get herself ready.

Ralph sat at her feet, and she scratched his head absentmindedly as she charted her next course of action.

"Come on, boy," she said as she ambled up the steps and opened the front door. "Let's have breakfast together and talk."

It had been years since she'd had this much time for herself, and Sarah took full advantage of it. After breakfast, she made fast work of straightening up the house before diving into a warm bubble bath where she soaked for almost an hour. Throwing on her terry robe, she peered out the front bedroom window to see if Evan was back.

"Not home," she said to herself, then shrugged. She had a long way to go before she was ready to present herself to him, and she began preparing herself for a deep-cleansing facial, followed by a manicure and a pedicure.

Checking the driveway again, she was dismayed to see that Evan still had not returned from wherever he had gone. Determined not to let it get to her, she rummaged through every drawer she had in search of her special cache of sexy underwear. Holding up a matching set of shimmering satin turquoise bra and panties, she tried them on and modeled for herself in front of the mirror.

"Not bad," she said aloud as she vamped, turning this way and that to get a better view. Giggling, she pointed to her image and warned, "Watch out, Evan!"

It took an hour to get her hair and makeup done to her liking, and almost as long to pick out what she wanted to wear, finally deciding on a sleeveless pale yellow silk wraparound dress that she kept around for special occasions and had originally planned to wear to Lara's wedding.

Somehow, today was more special.

By noon, Sarah was ready. She was bathed, polished and dressed as alluringly as she was ever going to get. But Evan was still not back.

So where was he?

Sarah frowned. All dressed up and nowhere to go, she thought as she sat in the living room leafing through a magazine, trying to pretend it didn't matter that he wasn't available. After all, she rationalized, he had no way of knowing she had a free day.

Free day that was already almost half-over. As one hour became two, her ebullient mood turned sour. Wouldn't it be ironic if it turned out her mother was having a better time at the amusement park than she was here?

The sound of the truck door slamming alerted her. She jumped up to peer out the window and saw Evan climbing his back steps with his arms full of grocery bags. He struggled with the door, then disappeared inside.

She bit her lip and wrung her hands a time or two. Should she go right over or should she give him some time to get settled?

No, a little voice said, *time's a'wasting, girl. Go for it.*

She forced herself to put one foot in front of the other slowly so as not to ruin her beige high-heel sandals, but after taking a few steps, she decided she didn't need shoes. She kicked them off, then threw them back onto her front porch. Barefoot was better. When she climbed his deck steps, she looked in through the screen door. Evan was nowhere in sight.

"Hello?" she called.

His head peeked around the hall wall. "Hey! Sarah, come on in. I'm in the kitchen."

She let herself in and followed the hallway down to the kitchen. Evan was engrossed in stocking his cabinets and barely glanced at her over his shoulder as he continued to empty bags.

"How you doing?" he asked conversationally.

"Fine. My parents took the kids to the amusement park today."

"Sounds like fun."

"Yes, I'm sure they're having a ball. They left early this morning."

"What have you been doing?" he asked as he opened the refrigerator door.

"Oh, getting ready."

"For?"

"The grand tour."

"The what . . . ?" He glanced her way.

She stood leaning against the doorjamb, one hip thrust out provocatively, her arms hanging at her sides, her head tilted, resting back against the woodwork.

"I was hoping the offer was still open. You know, for the grand tour of your house?" She paused and licked her lips. "Is it?"

Evan swallowed audibly. "Sure. Anytime. When would you like to do it?"

"How about now?"

Chapter 12

Evan blinked, then *really* looked at her. "Now," he said with a nod. It wasn't a question.

"Yes."

Their eyes met. Like a toy puppy in the back of a car window, he continued to nod with slow exaggeration. He slipped the milk he'd been holding onto the upper shelf of the refrigerator and shut the door. He turned around to face her, leaning against the kitchen counter as he did.

She had to know what she was asking. They'd joked about it only yesterday, and he knew *she* knew what he'd meant by "the grand tour."

Upstairs.

His bedroom.

His bed.

He looked at her again. She stared back without blinking.

She had to know.

His mind began to race. She *did* look seductive. He would never have used that word to describe Sarah Wyeth, but standing there, barefoot in that soft yellow dress, her come-hither look was as tempting as any pouting centerfold's might be.

Was this an act? Was she trying to test him? Turn him on? She had to know, too, that it would take little to nothing to arouse him to that state, especially now, after having missed her last night, after having tossed and turned, praying for dawn to break so that he could justify getting up, making coffee, mulling around the house, finding some alternate outlet for his excess energy that really only wanted to lose itself in one very specific place.

Ah, Sarah... you've got to know ...

So was she here now to make up for standing him up last night, causing his sleeplessness, winding him so tight he was ready to spin out of control, or... what?

Okay. Let's see.

He took a step closer, then another. He glanced down. Her hands were trembling ever so slightly. A slow smile spread across his face. So much for the woman-of-the-world stance.

He kept moving slowly toward her. "Are you sure you're ready for this?"

"Yes. I'm sure. Unless you... can't."

Evan stopped only inches away, so close he could feel the heat of her body, far enough so as not to even slightly come into contact with her. He said softly, "I can if you can."

She licked her lips. He watched her throat move as she swallowed. "Yes, I want to... see the house."

"Then..." He extended his arm to lead the way.

Sarah slipped past him, hoping he couldn't hear the pounding of her heart. She walked slightly ahead of him, more than aware of the feel of his palm against her back as he ushered her down the two steps that led into the dining room.

Furnished with a bleached-oak dining room set made up of a breakfront, a rectangular table and six chairs, the room wasn't large, but was open and airy. It was also so spotless that Sarah was sure he'd never once used the room to either eat in or entertain.

The next room over was similarly formal. Two steps up
from the dining room, the living room faced the rear of
the house. Sarah roamed the room, touching the backs of
the furniture as she moved through the shafts of light.
Again, windows abounded, and the pale green walls were
a calming contrast to the masculine, taupe leather couch,
love seat and chair.

"You haven't said a word," Evan said as he led her up
a short flight of stairs to the next level. "What do you
think?"

"Lovely," she said.

"But...?"

She looked up at him. "But lonely, I think. These
rooms don't get used much, do they?"

"They don't get used at all."

She wanted to ask why, but she supposed she knew.
Evan liked it that way. He liked his privacy, liked living
alone, liked his isolation. The real question to Sarah was
why he'd built such a big house to begin with if he never
had any intentions of filling it with people. As beautiful
as it was, it seemed too impersonal.

But then, the next step up set her opinions upside
down. The recreation room was large, friendly and well-
lived-in. One side housed a huge stereo system, while the
entire wall on the other side boasted a large-screen TV
with all the trimmings—expanded speakers, video games,
VCR, satellite hookup—and more. An alcove in the corner was stocked with an array of books behind a lounge
chair, lamp and table that made up a small reading area.

Sarah turned to him with a big smile on her face. "This
is a fabulous room. The girls would love this."

"They've already seen it. They play Sega all the time.
Getting very good at it, too. They almost beat me the
other day."

"You mean my girls have had the grand tour and not
me?"

"No, your girls have seen the house. You, on the other
hand, will get *le grand tour*." He turned her toward him.
"And then some..."

Sarah leaned into him, and he brushed his lips against hers. "Unless later on we're interrupted by the pitter-patter of little feet. And I don't mean Ralph."

"Don't worry about the girls."

"Your parents?" Evan asked.

"Uh-uh. Them, too."

"What time today will they be back?"

"They won't."

"Won't what?" he asked.

"Be back today."

"They're gone all day?"

"Yes. And all night. Back tomorrow. Not too early, either. Stopping for breakfast and all that."

"All night?" He sounded like a parrot, but the implications were too great not to be absolutely sure he was hearing her correctly.

"All night."

He whistled; she giggled. He pulled her more tightly to him and ran his hands up and down her back. She wrapped her arms around him and did the same. Then she grabbed his buttocks, one in each hand and squeezed.

He jumped. "Sarah Wyeth, what would your mother say?"

"I don't want to *think* about my mother. Or the girls. Or anything. Except this."

"And 'this' is . . . ?"

She kissed him, quick and hard. "*This* is this."

She tried to step back, but he stopped her. "You can do better than that," he said, and slanting his head, he took her mouth in a deep tongue-kiss that made her head spin with its all-consuming intensity.

"Better?" she asked when he broke away.

"Definitely. And there's more where that came from."

"More," she pleaded, leaning into him with her eyes closed.

He held her back. "Later. You haven't finished the tour."

She opened her eyes. "Where does it all end?"

"Where do you think?"

"Your bedroom?"

"My bed."

"Oh."

"Yeah. Unless you don't want it."

"Oh, I want it."

He chuckled. "How much?"

She rubbed her palm across his knuckles. "As much as you have to give."

He took hold of one of her hands and placed it on his arousal. Her eyes widened. "That enough?" he asked.

Boldly, Sarah cupped him, then traced the length of him with her fingers. It was his eyes that widened this time. "It'll do," she said with a sly smile.

Evan slapped her hand as he removed it from his pants. He held on to it in self-defense. "You're dangerous when you have no kids to keep you in line."

"And no mother and father."

"*And* no mother and father. I wonder if Lenore and Ted know about—"

"The tour, what happened to the tour?"

Evan grabbed her hand. "Third floor, coming up."

This was all strange to him. It had been a long time since he'd exchanged any sexual banter with a woman. But he couldn't wipe the stupid grin off his face, nor could he admit that he was having a good time. Fun. *Good Lord, Evan, when was the last time you had fun with a woman?* He couldn't remember and didn't want to try. There was no one like Sarah, no one to compare her to, no one in his life past, present or, he was sure, future who could hold a candle to the way she made him feel.

Normal.

He spun her around as they reached the top step. "Shut your eyes," he asked, and she did so. Then he manipulated her so that she was standing at the threshold of his room. "Okay. Open."

Her initial gaze swept the entire space. The room faced the front of the house. And each side of the house, as well. It was huge, literally half of the top floor. A side glance told her that the bathroom took up the other half.

She caught Evan's eye. He was waiting for her to say something, so she did. "Big."

"Yes, come on in and look around."

She did. Stepping over the threshold, she spun around. Curtainless windows abounded, completely engulfing the room with light that poured in from all directions. And while the view of the woods was magnificent from this level, there was only one thing more impressive than that.

His bed.

It was a perfect square. A perfect, *large* square, to be exact. King-size, maybe bigger, she couldn't tell. Four-postered, it dominated the huge room, sitting in the center all by itself as if everything else should dutifully revolve around it. The bed itself as well as the posts were hand carved, made entirely of redwood, connecting like a cube below and above, a canopy frame minus the fabric, both decorative and Spartan at the same time.

"So what do you think?" he asked, obviously about the bed since it was virtually the only piece of furniture in the room.

"It's very unusual."

"I'll take that as a compliment."

"You made this, didn't you?"

"Yes."

"Why so big?"

To contain my fantasies. He thought it, but didn't say it. "I . . . like big," he said with a self-deprecating smile.

"That wasn't what you were going to say."

"How do you know that?"

"Because I can tell. By the look on your face. What is it?"

"Do you really want to know?"

"Yes," she answered with a nod, "I really do."

Evan hesitated. "It provides the space I need for my . . . thoughts."

"What kind of thoughts?" she urged.

Okay, he thought, *here goes.* "Fantasies."

Sarah nodded slowly. "I have them, too."

"Do you." Not a question.

"Yes."

"Is that why you're here, Sarah?" he asked softly. "To act them out?"

It took her a long moment to answer, but then her eyes met his. "Yes."

"What do you want from me, then? Tell me."

Sarah's head fell back, and she gazed at the ceiling. "I don't know what to say."

"It's up to you, Sarah."

"All up to me?" she asked.

"Yes, ma'am. It has to be. You call the shots."

She looked at him again. "Anything I want?"

He hesitated for a short moment, but there was really no other answer. "Yes."

It was the middle of the afternoon, and in Sarah's sexual scenario, it had been evening, with candles lit and the moonlight pouring through the windows. This bright, cheerful daylight seemed decidedly unsexy as far as Sarah was concerned. Still, she only had this one day and night, and she didn't want to waste a minute of it. So daylight or no, she would go ahead with her plan. This was, after all, what she had come for.

She'd never felt this daring in her life. She wanted to experience as much as possible. *So many things, so little time*. She had a feeling of desperation, as if this might be the one and only time in her life when she would have access to him like this, when she would have his full attention and vice versa with no chance of interruption.

There was part of her that was still so unsure of herself.

"Sit," she ordered, and with a raised eyebrow Evan obeyed, sitting on the edge of the bed as she paced slowly like a lioness back in forth in front of him, deciding what her next move should be.

She glanced at him. His arms were folded in front of his chest. He was waiting for her to make the next move. She bit her lip. There was so much she wanted to do for him, she didn't know where to start. She'd taken so much time to prepare herself for this, there was part of her that just plain wanted to show off, to say, hey, look at me . . .

She stopped. That was exactly what she wanted to do. Show off. A little at a time. A private showing. What would he say if she told him?

No, don't tell him. Just do it.

Turning to him, she positioned herself so that she gave him a full frontal view for the show. "May I?" she asked as she toyed with the knot at the side of her silk dress.

Evan's stomach tightened. He hadn't thought he could get more aroused than he already was. He was wrong. He uncrossed his arms and gripped the edge of the bed. "Please," he urged softly.

She slipped one side, then the other, through the loop of the knot. The dress fell open, partially revealing her turquoise bra. With a graceful twist of her body, she reached inside to undo the hidden button at the waist of the dress. Shrugging it off one shoulder, then the other, she shut her eyes as she got ready to shed the confines of the dress. Then she did, letting it fall off her body and onto the floor into a shimmering lemon puddle at her feet.

Standing before him in her satiny undergarments, Sarah opened her eyes to look at Evan. His face was serious, his jaw tight, his eyes dark, penetrating. She bit her lip. "Okay so far?"

He cleared his throat. "Fine."

She pivoted slowly, one foot in front of the other as she spun around, showing him her back. Watching him over her shoulder, she slipped first one, then the other bra strap down from her shoulder with a wink and an exaggerated shimmy. Evan laughed at her shenanigans. She did, too.

Then she undid the front clasp and the bra fell to the floor.

He stopped laughing. Sarah shut her eyes again and said a quick silent pray that she wasn't making a complete and utter fool out of herself. Then she opened her eyes, put on a big smile, spun around with arms extended and exclaimed, "Ta-daa!"

Evan was in shock. Where did this woman come from? In what closet had the shy, reserved Sarah Wyeth kept this wild woman hidden? And then the shock wore off as quickly as it had come, and he looked at her. She was glorious, beyond beautiful, her heavy, full, pouting breasts creamy white with the largest, pinkest nipples he had ever seen or imagined on a woman.

He'd seen her before, of course, at night in the storm, in his workroom, but this was different. Now, with the bright summer sun filtering through the windows, she was magnificent, and he was on fire, as hot, as randy, as insane with desire as he had never even imagined possible.

He stood and started toward her.

Sarah held up her hand. "No, not yet. I'm not finished."

"Then finish," he said, in no mood to wait a minute longer to bury himself inside her.

"You're no fun," she said.

"This isn't fun anymore," he answered.

"It's not?"

"No, come here."

"Not yet."

"Sarah—"

"One more to go," she said, toying with the elastic band of her bikini panties while her heart was beating triple time at the wild look in his eye. She remembered thinking him a pirate the first time he'd come to her house to fix the screen. Then he had been cool and controlled. Not so now. She had never been ravished before, but she had a distinct feeling she was about to the learn the true meaning of the word.

"Do it," he ordered.

"Sit down first."

Evan ran a hand through his hair, but he obeyed. Sitting barely on the edge of the bed, he motioned for her to get on with it.

Sarah smiled as seductively as she could manage with her heart in her throat. Never in her life had she been this sexually excited. She hooked her two thumbs into the waistband of the panties and pulled them down. The wetness she encountered as they skimmed past her thighs only heightened her aroused state.

She stepped out of them when they reached her ankles. Bending over at the waist, she picked them up and threw them to Evan. He caught them in one hand. "Nice catch," she said in a hoarse voice that barely sounded like her own.

"Thanks," he answered. Eyes never leaving hers, he brought them to his face, burying his mouth and nose in the silky fabric.

Sarah's insides melted down to a creamy hot liquid. She swallowed, excitement and desire making her unsteady and dizzy. She swayed toward him.

"Come here," he ordered, and like the robot that she was, she obeyed, moving slowly but surely to stand between his legs.

Evan dropped the panties onto the floor and brought his hands up to her waist to hold her in place, insuring in his mind, at least, that she wouldn't run away now that she had driven him to the brink of a sexual abyss so deep, so dark, he wasn't sure what was on the other side.

He reached up with one hand, encircling her neck ever so gently with his splayed palm, then running his hand, thumb up, down the middle of her body, in between her breasts to her belly button and beyond, not stopping when he reached her auburn curls.

When his thumb teased her, Sarah's head lolled forward, and if not for the grip of his thighs, she would have fallen on top of him.

"You are so perfect," he whispered as his fingers probed and pleased her.

"Evan . . ."

"Tell me." He stroked her deeply, intimately.

"I want . . ."

"Keep talking." He felt her contract beneath his fingers. "Don't stop . . ."

"No . . . don't stop . . ."

"I won't."

He didn't. He stayed with her, his fingers never leaving her, never lessening their pace, even when she leaned

into him, even when she offered herself to him. Even
then, he didn't stop. He wanted to please her. When she
called out his name over and over again in a litany of
delight, he knew he had.

She leaned her body over his. "Oh, Evan...I want..."

He buried his face between the pillows of her breasts.
A faint sheen of perspiration greeted him and he breathed
in her scent. "What do you want, sweetheart, tell me."

"You. I want you so much. I want to touch you all
over." She reached down his back and pulled at his
T-shirt, lifting it high as she tried to pull it off.

"No," he said, dropping his hands from her body.

Bereft of his touch, Sarah pulled back. "Why?"

Evan stood and set her back from him. He walked
away, putting distance between them. "Sarah, don't. You
know why."

"You can't mean the scars." When he didn't answer,
she met his gaze square on. "Are you telling me you
won't let me touch you because of your scars? That's
absurd, Evan. I've seen them."

He turned his back to her. "It was dark then."

"So? And now it's light." She went to him, forcing him
to turn and look at her. "Evan Forester, don't you dare
shut me out like this."

He stood silently in front of her, head bent, obviously
aroused, and as dejected as any man she had ever seen.

"Look at me," she ordered, and slowly, reluctantly, he
lifted his head. "Do these turn you off?" she asked running her fingertips across the faint stretch marks that
crisscrossed her belly.

"Of course not."

"Do they make you think less of me?"

"Sarah..."

"It's the same for me, Evan. Your scars or mine, they
don't change who we are." She took his palm and rested
it against her stretch marks. "Let me touch you. Like
this. Please, let me..."

He didn't move when she reached up and under his
shirt. She felt him shudder as she ran her fingers over the
thicker skin of his scars. She urged the shirt higher, and

finally he helped her pull it over his head. He watched her when she threw it into the corner of the room, and shut his eyes as she splayed her hands on his chest, slowly, surely, touching her way across his body, until she reached the scar, then slowly, gently, tracing every inch of its diagonal route down his body where it disappeared into his waistband.

"How much farther does it go?"

"Not much."

Her hands reached in to unbutton his jeans. "May I?"

"Go ahead."

She held his gaze as she undid the button, took hold of the zipper tab between her thumb and index finger and slowly pulled it down. He didn't move an inch, holding her gaze, almost willing her not to continue. But she was committed to end this taboo right here and now. She looked down. He was right. The scar ended almost abruptly right below the waistband.

As if reading her mind, he said, "I had on a big old western belt buckle that day. It saved more than I like to think about."

Sarah's eyes moved up to his as she reached inside his jeans and caressed the width and length of his heavy arousal. "Mmm, remind me to bronze that buckle."

He chuckled, but as her ministration grew more heated, he warned, "Sarah..."

"Mmm?"

"You'd better stop now."

She smiled up at him. "Or what?"

"Or I'm going to throw you down on that bed and make mad passionate love to you."

"Uh-uh."

He shook his head in disbelief. "You don't believe me?"

"It's not that. You promised. This is my fantasy, not yours."

"When do I get my turn?" he asked.

"Not quite yet," she said, then took him by the hands and led him back over to the bed. This time she sat down on the edge, positioning him in front of her. She tugged at his jeans, pulling them down to his thighs, taking his short boxers along, exposing him to her gaze as well as her busy hands. She licked her lips as she looked up at him. "But soon."

Then she took him into her mouth.

He gasped at the shock of the wet heat. Reaching up, he grabbed on to the top beam of the bed frame for support. His back arched, his body, of its own volition, undulated along with her as she pleasured him in a way he hadn't dared dream about.

He bent his head down toward her and begged, "Sarah...please...you have to stop...now..."

She raised her head, and as their eyes met, her tongue poked out of her mouth to lick the tip of him. A shudder ran through his body, and then, for Evan, there was no more thought at all. He let go of the beam, kicked off his remaining clothes, and levered himself over her, pushing her down onto the mattress as he effectually trapped her in between the pillars of his arms.

"My turn," he said, and there was no argument.

Sarah spread her legs, raised her hips and accepted him into her body. Together they watched the erotic show as he slowly, by degrees, joined himself to her. Reeling with the feeling of perfect fullness, she shut her eyes and lifted her face to him. He kissed her, and she opened her mouth for him, accepting his mimicking tongue as it thrust into her mouth as surely and thoroughly as his body possessed hers.

There was no day, no night, no sunlight, no darkness, no bedroom, no bed. Nothing. She felt as if they were no longer in the real world, but in another dimension, one ruled by the senses where only feeling mattered. There was no right, no wrong, no should or shouldn't, only the perfection of the moment.

And it was perfect. Sarah opened her eyes to meet his. They were black with passion and so alive they made her already trembling heart beat faster. Those eyes were talking to her, saying things she knew she would never hear from his lips, things he couldn't—wouldn't—say to her even if he could find the right words. His eyes were eloquent, though, as they watched her watch him, as his body pounded into hers, releasing its force, its power, its need, its very soul.

She felt him stiffen above her, felt herself melting with the pressure. "Evan!" His name tumbled from her as her body joined his in one perfect climax that took not only her breath away, but the last of her reservations, as well.

Sarah shut her eyes tightly as he rested his weight upon her. She let the tears seep through her eyelids. There was no more doubts of what this was all about. She was more in love than she had ever been in her life.

Scary.

Evan lifted himself from her. "Are you all right."

She smiled. "Yes. Are you?" She ran a hand across the scar on his face. He let her.

"How can you ask that?"

"I want to hear it."

"Women," he said with a smile. "They always need the words."

"Such imperfect creatures we are," she said.

"Not you. You're perfect." He kissed her forehead, her nose, each eye, then brushed his lips across hers.

"I'm starved."

"For me or food?"

"Food."

He rolled over onto his side, taking her with him. "Fickle girl."

"Let's go to town for dinner. Lara said that new steak house that opened up is fabulous." She didn't think twice about suggesting it. He'd let her touch him, let her run her hands over his scars. It had been a big breakthrough. She felt sure of it. Things were going to change. Hope sparked in her heart. They could have a life together.

"Uh-uh. No town. If you want steaks, I'll barbecue. I've got some in the freezer."

"What's the matter? Too tired?" she teased.

"Mellow," he said softly, and pulled her to him, brushing his mouth against hers. "Besides, I want you all to myself tonight."

She couldn't resist that offer. "Okay," she said as she sat up. "What can I do?"

"Do?"

"Yeah, you know, to help make dinner."

"You can watch. I'll serve you tonight." He rose and slipped into his jeans, but didn't zip them.

"This'll be a treat."

Evan extended his hand and pulled her up. "On one condition."

Sarah walked over to her pile of clothing. "And that is?"

"You don't get dressed."

She raised her eyebrows. "You want me to stay like this?"

"Just like that."

"Mmm, you do dinner, and I suppose I get to be dessert."

Evan grinned and pulled her along out of the room. "Now you got it."

They never quite got to barbecue those steaks, managing instead to satisfy themselves in other ways. Ravenous, they made do with cheese and crackers after midnight, after a long, leisurely, naked swim in the lake. Exhausted, they returned to the bedroom where sleep became even more elusive. It seemed he couldn't keep his hands from her, nor hers from him. They made love again. And again.

Evan awoke first the next morning. He opened his eyes, then shut them to be sure it hadn't been a dream. No, Sarah was still there lying next to him, her head cushioned on his pillow, her hand under her cheek, her lush, creamy, soft body half-covered by his sheet. A leg hung out of the covering to rest across his thigh.

He didn't want to wake her but couldn't resist touching her, so he ran a finger gently down her cheek. She opened her eyes and looked at him for a long moment before a slow smile spread across her face.

"Good morning," she whispered as if there were a roomful of people and she wanted only him to hear her greeting.

"Hi," he answered, still amazed that this woman had chosen him. That she was really waking up in his bed as he'd fantasized so many times. "Sleep well?"

"Uh-uh. Something kept poking at me all night."

"What could that be?"

"Oh, I don't know," she said, reaching under the sheets to find him already half-aroused, "maybe...this?"

"Maybe."

He leaned over and kissed her. She kissed him back. It was about to start all over again, when Sarah started to giggle. "Are you ever going to feed me?" she asked.

"You mean I haven't fed you yet?"

She shook her head. "No, and I have to tell you, I get mean when I'm hungry."

"I'm scared."

"You should be." Sarah rose onto an elbow. "I know. Let's get dressed and go into town. The diner has a great breakfast special. My parents and I took the kids—"

"No. No town. I'll make something."

Sarah sat up. "What do you mean 'no town'? You said that last night. Is that like 'no town' *today* or 'no town' *ever*?"

"Sarah, you know how I feel. I don't do the town. Not socially."

"Yes, but that was before..."

"Before?"

"This."

"Why should *this* change anything?" he asked.

"Because it does."

"Not to me."

"Evan...this is ridiculous. Do you mean to tell me that you never intend to go to town with me, to go to a restaurant with me, a movie—?"

"I don't go to town, Sarah. You know that. Nothing that's happened changes that."

Sarah looked at him for a long moment. Then she made a sound that was supposed to be a laugh, but didn't quite make it. She didn't know why she even attempted to laugh, she just did. It seemed better than crying.

"You call this 'nothing'?"

Evan got out of bed. He walked over to where his jeans were lying on the floor and picked them up. "I'm just saying that making love with you doesn't have anything to do with my going or not going to town, that's all."

"I think it does. I think it has everything to do with it. I think you should question why you need to hide away out here even when you have no reason to."

He laughed a mirthless laugh. "My reasons are my own. You've been talking to Lara too much." He slipped into his jeans, but didn't zip them. "Is that what this is all about? Some conspiracy you and Lara concocted to get me to go to town?"

Sarah sat up, pulling the sheet over her breasts. "What are you saying? That I made love with you to get you to go to town? That I *planned* . . . this?"

He swooped down and picked up her silk dress and held it out to her. "You came here yesterday dressed to kill," he said. "What am I supposed to think?"

Sarah swallowed hard, trying to get past the lump in her throat. "You're crazy," she said and scrambled out of bed.

"Sarah . . ."

It took a while for her to find her underwear, but when she did, she slipped into her panties so hastily they were on inside out. Her hands were shaking too much to do more, so she carried her bra. She walked over to him and grabbed her dress out of his hand as she made her way toward the door. Evan, jeans gaping, attempted to stop her, but she managed to outmaneuver him.

"Sarah, don't leave like this."

She didn't answer him. What a fool! How could she believe that he would change for her? That he would abandon his reclusive behavior all because she'd chosen to sleep with him? Just like that? Overnight? But in her mind, she had thought so. She had thought they were embarking on a relationship, and part of that relationship would be people, socializing . . . living.

This was not living. She wanted to be part of the world, and she wanted her children to be, too. If Evan wanted to hide away, that was fine. For him. But not for her. And, obviously, not for them.

Forget it, there was no *them*.

She stood by the threshold and turned to him. "I'm going home. I don't know what to say. Thank you for the sex, maybe? I'm sorry. I'm not really up on 'morning after' etiquette. You'll have to forgive me."

"Sarah, come back here."

She shook her head and was surprised to find her cheeks were wet. She was crying. How ridiculous. "No, I'm going home. I have things to do before the girls come back." She turned toward the door.

"We need to talk," he said. "You need to understand."

She spun around. "How about going to the diner for a cup of coffee? It's a great place to *talk*."

"What is it with you and this diner? Why can't we talk here?"

"Because you can't talk *there*. I can talk both places. And that's the problem. I want a life outside of these two houses, Evan. These two yards."

"Then have it."

Their eyes met and held. Sarah felt her stomach drop as if she were riding on a runaway elevator. Minutes ago she had awakened elated, so joyous of the night they'd spent together she couldn't put her feelings into words. And now she felt as if she'd been smashed in the face with a sledgehammer.

"Goodbye, Evan."

"Sarah . . . please don't go like this."

She heard the regret in his voice. Heard it, but didn't stop for it. Instead, she flew down each flight of steps, breaking into a run as she hit the hallway to the workroom and the back door. She barely touched the deck steps as she ran, clutching her clothing to her bare breasts, across the lawns. The tears ran down her face, and her sobs blotted out every sound around her.

She didn't hear the clicks, they were too far away, nor did she see the two men hiding, not too well, in the bushes by the side of the property line. All she heard was her heart breaking as she slammed her front door behind her.

"Get that?" Ansell asked from behind a particularly thorny bush.

Joseph nodded, stood and capped his camera lens. "Yup."

Chapter 13

The phone was ringing as Sarah entered the house. She couldn't answer because she was sobbing too hard, so she let the machine pick it up. Instead, she headed for the stairs and ran into the bathroom. She dropped her clothing on the floor in front of her, the once beautiful yellow silk dress hopelessly wrinkled, indicative, she thought, of her once beautiful fantasy.

She leaned against the door and allowed the tears to flow unabated. Between gulps of air, she heard a noise. Catching her breath, she opened the bathroom door a crack to listen. Someone was knocking—no, pounding—at the front door.

"Sarah!"

Evan.

"Go away!" she screamed at the top of her lungs.

There was a split second of silence, then she heard the front door open and footsteps enter the house, stopping at the foot of the staircase.

"Sarah? Where are you?"

"Leave me alone!"

"I'm coming up."

Sarah shut the bathroom door and turned the lock as she listened to him take the steps two at a time. She couldn't face him now. She needed time to think before she saw him again. It was imperative that he go away and leave her alone.

For a long moment, there was no sound, and she thought maybe he'd turned to leave. She placed her ear against the door and knew instantly that was not the case. She could feel his presence on the other side, almost hear his labored breathing.

"Sarah?"

His voice was soft and loving. She shut her eyes against the feeling it evoked. "Go away."

"I need to talk to you."

"You have nothing to say that I want to hear."

"I didn't mean what I said. Not the way it sounded."

"Yes, you did."

The doorknob rattled with his frustration. "Sarah, damn it, open the door. I can't talk to you like this."

"Then don't. Just leave."

"You're being unreasonable."

"Manipulative conspirators usually are."

"I said I didn't mean—"

"Don't say that. You meant every word of it. Now go away and leave me alone!"

She could feel the anger emanating from him even through the thick wood of the bathroom door. She didn't care. She was angry, too, and hurt...very, very hurt. Here she had offered him all she had, her heart on her sleeve...her body, and he'd thrown it back at her like yesterday's leftovers.

"This isn't over," he said with quiet determination.

But Sarah didn't answer. Instead, she picked up her wrinkled dress and neatly folded it. Her heart sank as she heard his retreating footsteps.

Well, what did she want him to do? Stand outside her bathroom all day until she came out, then convince her in no uncertain terms that he was wrong and she was right, to say he loved her with all his heart, the way she loved him?

Yes, that's what she wanted.

The snap of the screen door shutting alerted her to the fact that he was gone. Tentatively, she cracked the bathroom door and looked out. No one was there. She tiptoed to the girls' room and peeked out the window just in time to see the clouds of dust kicked up as his pickup truck took off down the main road.

He was gone. That was what she wanted, wasn't it? Then why was she crying fresh tears? Like a robot, she moved out of the girls' room into her own. Lifting her terry robe off the hook on the back of her closet door, she shrugged into it and went downstairs to the kitchen.

As she put on a pot of coffee, she noticed the answering machine light blinking and remembered the ringing phone. She pressed the button and listened.

"Sarah?" The disembodied voice said, "It's Sam Johnson. It's, uh, just a few weeks till school starts and all, and, uh, I was wondering if we could meet and go over your assignments. You know, as we discussed? But, well, I thought maybe you'd like to have dinner next Saturday night? There's this new steak house in town that's supposed to be good. So, uh, if you can make it, let me know."

Sarah's mouth dropped open. Sam Johnson was asking her for a date! She listened as he left his number and when he'd be available for her to call back. By the time the beep sounded, she was completely dry-eyed.

Before she had time to think of all the ramifications of Sam's invitation, the machine regurgitated another message. Reverend Winthrop's voice came through, awkwardly declaring that she'd been picked as the new church organist.

Wiping the tears from her face, Sarah took both calls as signs from heaven. She had to get a grip on herself. She took a deep breath, squared her shoulders and looked at herself in the little fake mirror the girls kept in the kitchen to play makeup.

Okay, Sarah, you made a number-one fool out of yourself. It's not the first and probably won't be the last time in your life you do it. Evan is great, the sex is fabulous, but that's not enough. What you want is a life. With him and the girls. So face it. It isn't going to happen that way.

She turned away from the mirror. She should have seen it from the first. Did she really think that just because she was attracted to him—okay, *more* than just attracted—she could change him? That a little talk and a little sex could undo in a few short weeks what had taken him five years to build? That she was going to be his great savior, luring him out of this hideaway and back into the real world? She shook her head. How could she be so naive?

People *don't* change. She'd said that to Evan on the porch one night, and he had argued with her. But it was true, especially where he was concerned because it seemed that nothing—not even the love she wanted to give him—could make him change his mind about reentering the world.

But that was his problem, not hers. Lord knew, she had enough of her own. She'd moved out here to prove a point to herself and everyone else. When had she begun to be sidetracked by that? From the first day she laid eyes on Evan Forester, that's when.

It had to stop. She had to stop it. She had to get back on course. As much as she wanted him—and even now, she ached for him—she owed it to her children to regain her focus, regain control. For with or without him, *she* had to move on, and this interaction with the townspeople at church would be a step in doing so.

By the time she showered and dressed, she was feeling decidedly better. She'd even managed to convince herself that last night was just a much-needed sexual release and nothing more. She was human; she was allowed a mistake or two. And she could also forgive herself. Whatever it was she was feeling for Evan was not enough to build a life on. For that, it had to be returned in full measure. And obviously it was not.

If Evan Forester wanted to live his life like a hermit, so be it. If he wanted to use his scars as an excuse to retreat from society, that was his business, but it wasn't for her. She'd moved here to be part of the world, not secluded or protected from it. If she'd wanted that, she could have stayed in the city with her parents and let them move her into that cocoon of a bigger house they always kept dangling in front of her nose.

No, she wanted more than that, the whole shebang, as her father would say. All the things she felt she had been robbed of with John's death. This was her second chance, and she was going to do it right.

Sarah raided the refrigerator. She wasn't kidding when she'd said she was starved, and cooked herself a big breakfast of eggs and French toast. Satiated, she sat over her second cup of coffee and ruminated for a long time in the overly quiet kitchen.

She decided the best course of action was to stay away from him. From the first she'd had an attraction to him, and she knew the more she saw of him, the harder it would be to keep to her convictions.

She wished she could do the same with Alys and Ariel, but she knew it was too late for that. They had developed a relationship with him, and for better of worse, she was going to have to live with that.

But that was all she had to do. She didn't have to talk to him, sit on the porch with him at night, swim in the lake with him, and she certainly didn't have to make love with him.

She ignored the ache in her heart. *It's over. He's not for you.*

The beeping horn broke her out of her reverie. The girls were home. She jumped up and ran to the front door. So were her parents. She laughed out loud with delight at having them home, and waved as they exited the car. Her father was grinning from ear to ear. Her mother, on the other hand, was as sourpussed as she'd ever seen her.

After hugging and kissing the girls and hearing a jumble of tales of their adventures at the amusement park, Sarah put an arm around her mother. "Mom? What's wrong?"

"Wrong? Nothing's wrong! Your father is a maniac, that's all. Traipsing me all around that park as if I were sixteen. My back aches and my feet hurt."

Sarah led her into the kitchen. "Here, Mom, sit down and relax. I'll get you a glass of iced tea."

Lenore sat, but didn't let it deter her from her litany of complaints. "And I didn't sleep a wink in that lumpy motel bed all night..."

Sarah pretended to listen as she poured the tea from the pitcher into a tumbler. She was just about to shut the refrigerator door when she remembered the infamous mint.

It was then it came to her. As she broke off a sprig and added it to the drink, she knew the time had come to make her stand. Her mother was tired and vulnerable, and while a dim, niggling voice in her subconscious told her she was taking unfair advantage of the situation, Sarah wasn't about to look a gift horse in the mouth.

Today seemed to be the day to assert herself.

Braced with her new resolve, Sarah placed the glass onto the table. She sat down in the chair opposite her mother. "Mom," she said, looking her in the eye, "I think it's time you went home."

Lenore looked startled. She shook her head. "Sarah, I wasn't complaining about being here. That park—"

"I know, Mom. This has nothing to do with the trip to the amusement park. It has to do with me. You and Dad have been here over a month. School's going to start soon, and I need to get my life in order. I can't do that with you here."

"But I thought your father and I were helping you...with the house, the girls..."

"You are! But, don't you see? That's part of the problem. I need to do this on my own. That was the main reason I moved away from the city in the first place."

"But—"

"Mom, listen to me. Please. *Listen* to what I'm saying." She reached across the table and squeezed her mother's hand. "I want to have my own life, separate from you and Dad. I love you both, but I have to move on. And so do you."

"I don't know what to say. If you want us to leave, then, of course, we'll leave."

The hurt, huffy voice was back. Sarah looked away for a moment trying to find the right words, if there were any as far as her mother was concerned.

"Do you remember when John died?" Sarah asked.

"Of course. It was a horrible, horrible time in all our lives. How could I forget? You were devastated."

Sarah nodded. "That's right. I was a basket case. And I needed you and John's parents to coddle me. I can never thank you all enough for being there for me at that time." She shut her eyes tightly for a second, then looked at her mother again. "But I've gotten beyond that, Mom. John's dead, and I'm alive. The kind of life I have with the girls now is so far removed from the one I had before. I'm a different person, and I need you to respect that."

"I respect you, Sarah. Haven't I told you time and again how very proud of you I am? You've come so far..."

"Yes, but I'm capable of more. And I need the space to grow."

Lenore opened her mouth to say something more, then shut it. She stared back at Sarah for a long time, then pulled her into a hug. "I think you may be right," she said softly.

They stayed that way for a long time, until Sarah's father entered the kitchen carrying a suitcase. "Where do you want me to put this, Lenore?" he asked.

"Back in the car," she said.

He grinned. "Are we going home?"

"If you're up to the ride back."

"I'm up to it."

Sarah watched her parents smile at each other. She knew now that her father had maneuvered this little trip with the girls for more than one reason. He not only wanted to give her some much-needed time alone, he also wanted to drive home the point that it was time for them to leave, to get back to their own home, their own lives.

As her father set the suitcase down on the floor, Lenore walked over and wrapped her arms around his waist. "Let's go home, Ted," she said, resting her head on his chest.

Unbidden tears filled Sarah's eyes at the sight of her parents, still so much in love and so much a part of each other after all these years of marriage. This was what she wanted. A relationship that had staying power, a relationship where things were shared, where one partner knew the other so well they could work around their shortcomings, compromise and meet on some common ground.

Her parents stayed for lunch, then took their leave. It was particularly poignant for Sarah this time, much more than when she left them in the city. For this leaving was the more decisive one. When she'd moved up here, it was an experiment, one even she was not sure would work. But now she knew this was where she wanted to be. She wasn't afraid anymore; she'd proven she could handle the girls and a house on her own. This time, she knew she wasn't coming back.

And so did they.

"We'll see you for Thanksgiving?" her mother asked as she slipped into the passenger seat.

"Yes, John's parents are coming up, as well. We'll have a real family holiday," Sarah said.

She kissed her father goodbye. "Thanks, Dad," she whispered in his ear.

"Take care of yourself," he answered, his eyes roaming toward Evan's house as he spoke. "I don't want to worry about my little girl."

Sarah followed his line of vision. Evan was back. He was standing on the porch. She squared her jaw. "There's nothing to worry about. Nothing."

Ted ran a finger over her furrowed brow. "Your face is telling me otherwise."

Sarah graced him with a sad smile. "I'm fine, Dad, really. There can never be anything between Evan and me."

"Don't be too hasty. We men don't always have it together as well as you women do. We need a little extra time sometimes."

Shaking her head, Sarah said, "I don't know, Dad. There are some things that even time can't change."

"What are you two talking about?" Lenore asked from inside the car.

"Just saying our goodbyes, dear," Ted answered. He squeezed Sarah's hand as he got into the car.

Sarah had a lump in her throat as she and the girls waved. As they pulled out of the driveway and passed Evan's, the car stopped and Evan stepped down from the porch to say his goodbyes, as well.

Once the car disappeared, Evan turned to look at her. Sarah felt the tears, which had been so close to the surface, threaten to overflow. She wouldn't give him that satisfaction.

It was then she made the decision to call Sam Johnson back and accept his invitation.

"Let's go inside," she said to the twins. Turning, she entered the house, slamming the door behind her.

Evan paced, back and forth, back and forth, stopping now and then to look out his door to see if Sarah might make the first move. Her parents had gone, and there was no reason for her not to just come on over to talk things over with him.

But as the days passed, she didn't appear. And deep down, he knew, she wasn't going to.

For the first time in a very long time, Evan didn't know what to do. From the moment she'd entered his life, Sarah had been turning it upside down. She made him think about himself as he hadn't thought about himself since before the accident. He hadn't realized how comfortable it had become being thought of as a freak until she forced him to start thinking about himself as a man again.

She *wanted* things from him. He'd become too used to no one wanting anything from him, no one expecting anything from him. She pushed; she prodded; she forced him to think about the future, a time he never dwelt on for fear of falling into despair. But despair was better than this, for what she was offering was hope, and hope scared the hell out of him.

He didn't want to hope for things, he didn't want to plan for the future. He hadn't done that sort of thing since before the accident. He lived his life from day to day, much as he had when he was a teenager and life seemed a huge, open, endless void somewhere way ahead of him.

This insistence that he get back into things—into life—
was more than a pain in the ass, it was threatening everything he had painstakingly built over the past five
years.

He didn't *want* to go to town, it was as plain and simple as that. To him, it represented everything he'd had
and lost. He'd finished with that, with the pity-glances
from those who had known him all his life, with the
gawking from those who had not. He'd told himself time
and time again that all he wanted was to be left alone to
do his work and enjoy the things he liked to do.

By himself.

But there was no more "by himself." Now, there were
the twins . . . and there was Sarah. He had thought he
could live out this year of her lease without getting too
involved with her, without her weaving herself into even
the perimeter of his life. But somehow when he wasn't
paying attention, she had taken over a place inside of him
he hadn't known existed—his soul perhaps, he didn't
know. All he knew was that he wanted her as much as he
wanted his privacy.

But Sarah wanted the town, the people, the socializing, the life he'd left behind. The thought made him ill.
It was a dilemma he never dreamed he'd have to face no
matter how many times Lara had lectured him. He'd
made his decision, and he'd been happy with it.

He wasn't happy anymore. He'd watched Sarah turn
her back on him and slam the door behind her on the day
her parents had left. Now she was alone with the girls, but
she wasn't changing her mind. She wasn't about to give
in on this one, he could feel it in his bones. And he had
to ask himself some very important questions: Was his
privacy more important to him than Sarah? Was it worth
losing her for? Would it satisfy him as much as the mere
presence of her by his side did? Was he willing to give her
up for it?

The answer was no, he was not. Okay, so he'd have to
go to town with her, maybe the girls, too, to ease the
burden. He'd have to make an effort, go to dinner, or go
to that stupid diner she seemed so hung up on. Do whatever it took to get her back.

How was the question. He couldn't very well walk over there and say, "Okay, let's go to town." He knew what she'd say to that. Something like, "Don't do me any favors." Especially after what he'd said to her. He hadn't meant it the way it sounded, but maybe she was right, maybe he did feel that she was manipulating him with sex to get him to do what she wanted him to do.

There were worse ways to be manipulated, he told himself with a wry smile, but that wasn't the point. He'd become annoyed with her insistence that they go out. What was wrong with being here? As long as he was with Sarah, he was happy, it didn't matter where.

Then go to town with her, stupid, and end this nonsense once and for all.

He knew his inner voice was giving good advice, but again, he wasn't quite sure how to approach her with his new-found affection for the town. She wouldn't believe him, not for a minute, if he just said he'd changed his mind. She'd think there was an ulterior motive. And, of course, there was. He wanted that look back in her eye, the one she'd had when she'd sashayed into his kitchen and asked for the grand tour.

So there had to be a better, more delicate way to introduce the suggestion, to let her know he was serious and not just making the offer to get her back into his bed.

He shook his head. He wasn't quite so sure that wasn't the only reason he was willing to make this great sacrifice. Because no doubt about it, he wanted her back in his bed. There had never been anyone who made him feel the way she made him feel, and there was no way on earth he could imagine giving that up, especially with the torture that seeing her every day would bring.

He needed time to think.

He walked over to the shed and rolled out the rider mower. As soon as he finished with the lawn, he'd march on over there and find a way to tell her. He had to form what he would say and how he was going to say it. It had to be just right, something told him, for her to agree to come back to him.

And she had to come back to him. The ache in his chest wouldn't subside no matter what he did. It had only been a matter of days since she'd stormed out of his house early that morning, but it seemed as if months had passed. The night they'd spent together was surreal, a fantasy come true. His bed was no longer just his bed. He'd never be able to sleep in it again without thinking about her and what they shared. She was more than he could have ever imagined, and his stomach twisted into knots at the thought that he would never have her look at him that way again, touch him, take him with her to a place only she knew how to get to.

He turned the ignition key. As the engine roared, the twins appeared out of nowhere, their hearing uncanny when it was something they wanted to do.

"Can I go with you?" Ariel asked.

"I want to ride first. You went first last time," Alys said.

"No arguing," Evan said. "You can both ride. Come on, climb up one at a time."

He sat one girl on each knee. As they started moving, both girls put their arms around his neck, nearly choking him, but they couldn't hear him complain over their own incessant chatter. He managed to maneuver the mower and loosen their hold while listening to them tell him every single detail of their trip to the amusement park. He nodded a lot, his mind more on their mother than on their tale.

"Grandma said she was going to take us to see a movie, but now she's gone home, so we can't go," Alys said.

"Uh-huh," Evan replied as he rounded a curve halfway through the lawn.

"Mommy will take us," Ariel said.

"But she can't go on Saturday," Alys argued.

"That's right, she's going out Saturday," Ariel agreed.

"*If* she gets us a baby-sitter," Alys reminded her.

"Maybe Evan would watch us," Ariel suggested.

"Would you, Evan?" Alys asked. "Evan?" She tapped him on the shoulder.

"Huh?"

"Would you?"

"Would I what?" he asked.

"Watch us."

"Sure. When?"

"Saturday."

"What's happening Saturday?" He spun the mower around for the last turn.

"Mommy's going out."

"Where's she going?" Evan asked.

"On a date."

He pulled to a dead stop. "She's *what?*"

Ariel and Alys dropped their arms from around his neck. "Going on a date," they said in unison.

"With Mr. Johnson," Alys added.

Ariel made a face. "And if you don't watch us, we'll have to stay home with a *baby-sitter*."

"But she doesn't have one," Alys said, "so would you?"

"Please?" Ariel added.

He looked from one twin to the other, his head spinning with what they were telling him. Sarah. On a date. His worst nightmare come true. And with Sam Johnson, no less, the biggest bore this side of . . . town.

Well, she wanted to go out on the town, and she certainly didn't waste any time making arrangements, did she? In his bed one morning, out with Sam Johnson the next Saturday night. He felt his blood come to an incoherent, jealous boil.

Okay, fine. She wanted to date, let her date. Let her see what was out there, *in town*.

He gritted his teeth. "Sure," he said.

"Yea!"

The girls jumped off his lap and ran to their house. His back to the door, he heard rather than saw it slam shut. With a patience he didn't really have, he sat, glaring at the woods beyond, tapping his fingers on the steering wheel and waiting for what he was sure would be the inevitable response to the girls' announcement.

He wasn't disappointed. Within seconds, the door swung open again and Sarah flew out. He turned, and she stopped in mid-step. Their eyes met. Slowly, she stepped down from the porch and walked toward him.

"Is it true? Have you told the girls you would baby-sit them on Saturday night?"

"It's true. I wouldn't want you to miss your *date*. Not wasting any time, are you?"

Sarah lifted her chin. "I don't have the faintest idea what you mean by that."

"I mean that my bed isn't even cold yet, and you're making plans with another man."

"I could slap you for that."

"Go ahead, but it won't change anything."

"I'm going out to dinner with my new employer. A friendly dinner to discuss my assignments." Evan made a derisive sound. "It's true," she added, "not that it's any of your business, anyway."

Evan felt his stomach twist with anger and frustration. "You're right. It's not my business. In fact, I want you to go. See what the old town has to offer on a Saturday night. And Sam's just the man to show it to you."

"What's that supposed to mean?" she asked.

She looked the way he felt, as if she were about to implode. "Just what it sounds like. He was a bore in high school, and he's a bore now."

"But people change, you told me so yourself. Maybe Sam is very exciting now. Maybe he's a regular *ball of fire*."

"Don't count on it."

"I'm not counting on anything. What I am doing is going out. To a restaurant. In town. Something that doesn't appear to bother Sam at all. So what is it, Evan? Will you watch the girls, or should I start looking for a baby-sitter?"

"I said I would."

"Fine. My house, seven o'clock, Saturday night?"

"I'll be there."

Evan watched her walk back into the house. He opened his mouth to call her back, to say something, anything, that would alter what had already been decided, but she moved too fast, and he was at a loss for the words that he really wanted to say.

Like, *call the jerk and cancel. I'll take you to dinner in the damn town if that's where you feel you have to go.*

But the door slammed shut, and he didn't say a word. Instead, he boiled in a stew of his own making.

Chapter 14

"Then, *after* college, I taught junior high. But you know how kids that age put you through a wringer ... so I applied for the first administrative position that opened up—" he lifted his coffee cup in a self-toast "—and here I am."

"Here you are," Sarah said. Her pasted-on smile seemed appropriate but was becoming increasingly difficult to manage.

Evan was right. Sam Johnson was a bore. A nice man, but very, very boring. All he talked about was himself, the school and his life as it related to the school. As he began telling her about his first year as principal of the elementary school, her eyes wandered as well as her mind.

The Early American decor of the restaurant was cozy and the homey atmosphere conducive to conversation. She knew she was being picky, but she'd been unimpressed with the service and the dinner was mildly adequate, not fabulous as Lara had claimed.

About the only good thing the evening had offered was the opportunity to meet a lot of townspeople Sam knew who'd stopped by the table to meet the new music teacher. A mere mention of the fact that she was also the new church organist seemed to instantly put her in the good graces of the general population of Wayside.

Sam couldn't have been prouder to be with her, and he made no secret of the fact that he wanted a repeat of this night again soon. She kept telling herself how good she should feel about that, but all she really felt was empty. Her heart wasn't in this date, if that's what it could be called. Her heart was miles away on a dimly lit back porch out at the edge of town in the hands of a man who didn't want any part of it.

Sam droned on, and her vision clouded over as Evan's face flashed before her mind's eye.

Oh, Evan, it should be you here with me. We should be sitting in this candlelit room, holding hands, gazing into each other's eyes, making promises that can only be fulfilled later on when we are alone.

She knew why she was being so critical, of Sam, of the dinner. She had a hunger of a different kind tonight, and no meal or restaurant was ever going to be enough to satisfy her. There was only one thing she wanted and only one person who could give it to her, but the way she'd left him at the door didn't bode well for her hopes becoming reality anytime soon.

Evan had been angling for a fight the minute he walked in the door to mind the girls, and she had responded in kind. She had no reason to believe that his mood had improved over the three hours she'd been gone. The fact was, he was probably worse by now.

"Sarah?"

"Umm . . ."

"I asked if you'd like an after-dinner cordial," Sam said.

Sarah looked up. Then blinked. It was Sam, not Evan. "Oh, no, no thank you, Sam." She checked her watch. "You know, I hadn't realized how late it was getting to be. I think we'd better be going. Evan's watching the girls, and—"

"Evan again."

"Excuse me?"

"He's all you've talked about all night. Did you know that?"

"I don't think—"

He held up his hand to halt her denial. "It's okay, don't be embarrassed. It's only natural that you're curious about him, living so close and all."

"I hadn't realized ... Evan's become ... a friend, and I suppose, other than Lara, I haven't made many friends since I arrived."

"Perfectly normal while you were settling in. But now that the school year is starting, you'll be in town every day, and you'll see how quickly you get involved in the community."

"I hope so."

"You will, you'll see. And all for the better. It's so isolated out on that side of the lake. You'll get lonely after a time, especially when winter sets in. Besides, having only Evan for company is not saying much. He *can* be difficult at times."

Even though she was the last person not to agree with him, Sarah felt her back go up. "I don't know what you mean."

Sam waved his hand dismissively. "All that reclusiveness, not talking to anyone unless he has to. People think he's a little crazy. He's gone from town hero to town bogeyman. Mothers use him to keep their kids in line. I'm surprised the girls aren't frightened of the way he looks."

Sarah was slowly seething. She clenched her teeth and said, "The girls love him. He's been wonderful with them, patient, caring..." Unable to hide her disgust, Sarah stood and tossed her linen napkin on the table. "And I have no idea where you get the notion that he's reclusive. Why, just the other day we were having a conversation about coming to town to the diner for breakfast."

Sam stood, too. "I-I'm sorry, Sarah. I didn't mean to upset you. It's just that Evan is—"

"One of the kindest, most generous, best people I've ever met in my entire life. And I resent you calling him a bogeyman just because he's scarred." She picked up her purse and headed out of the restaurant.

"Sarah, wait! I haven't paid the check—"

Her hands were shaking by the time she reached Sam's car. She was sorry she hadn't driven herself and met him at the restaurant. He had asked to pick her up and, at the time, she'd wanted to rub Evan's nose in it a little, so she'd agreed. But now he had to drive her home when all she wanted to do was be alone to think.

About why she felt compelled to defend Evan to Sam.

It was insane really. One minute she resented him, the next she was standing on a soapbox, defending him. Her mind was in turmoil. She'd kept going back and forth all week about keeping this date with Sam. One day she wanted to go, the next she dreaded the idea. Right up until the last moment, she had been flip-flopping so that she was late getting ready.

But then Evan had arrived. Fresh from the shower, he looked so devastatingly masculine, her mouth had actually watered. At that moment when his eyes met hers and her stomach dropped to her feet, she would have done anything he'd asked of her, including calling Sam with some lame excuse to cancel the date.

Instead, he had an attitude. He came early, ostensibly to help her with the twins, but all he really wanted to do was harass her. Her fantasy crushed, she'd let her temper get the better of her, and instead of dressing in the casual gray pants suit she'd planned to wear, she slipped into a mandarin-collared Oriental-style emerald green jacquard silk dress that buttoned all the way down the front, making sure to leave the last four buttons undone to show just the right amount of leg.

He'd taken one look at her descending the stairs, and his usually opaque black eyes had gleamed like onyx tiger's eyes in the night. He'd paced back and forth in the living room as she'd readied herself. He'd been ornery and difficult, glaring at her as she put on her makeup in the hall mirror. His belligerent attitude had cemented her resolve not only to go out with Sam, but to have a good time, as well.

Even if she hated every minute of it.

She knew he was jealous, and she supposed that if the tables had been turned and he'd been taking someone else

out, she would have felt the same. No, she wasn't a red-
head for nothing, *she* would have gone *ballistic*.

As she'd waited for Sam to arrive, self-doubt had her
questioning the wisdom of accepting this date to begin
with, but it was too late. She was committed, and when
she saw Sam's car pull into the driveway, she'd flown out
of the house to meet him before he could exit and come
to the door. The last thing she'd needed was a confron-
tation between the two men, especially with the mood
Evan was in. She hadn't given a backward look to Evan,
who had been standing behind the screen door watching
her. She'd felt those eyes on her back as if they were
searing laser beams.

Sarah took a deep breath. And now the night was a
disaster. She'd made it so with her constant chattering
about Evan and her juvenile defense of him. She was
feeling too much, and to add to the confusion, she didn't
have the foggiest idea what to do about it . . . him—Evan
Forester, as flawed a hero as they come.

But she couldn't deny what she was feeling for him. If
this was love, it was a new and different strain of which
she had no familiarity. She and John had always been in
sync, always of the same mind. She had no experience
with someone who was stubborn as well as diametrically
opposed to her way of thinking.

Yet she knew that it was because he was such a challenge that she'd found him so interesting in the first place.
It was true that, like everyone else, the scars had initially
intrigued her. But then the man himself took over and the
scars seemed to melt away. As Lara had rightly stated,
only he saw them, not her, not the girls. And that was the
key to her problem. Making what was invisible to her invisible to him, as well.

Could she do it? She didn't know, but she was beginning to think that if she didn't try, she'd never know if she
were throwing away the chance to have something very
special and precious in her life.

"I'm sorry, Sarah," Sam said as he caught up with her.

Sarah looked up and shook her head. "No, *I'm* sorry.
I got carried away. I'm sorry I ruined your evening."

"You didn't. I had a wonderful time. I hope we can do it again some time."

Sarah smiled a weak smile, but couldn't bring herself to agree. She had other things on her mind that were more pressing. She pulled open the passenger side car door. "Please take me home, Sam."

Evan tried not to keep looking out the window, but by the time ten o'clock rolled around, he was borderline psychotic. Dinner did not take this long and, unless they went somewhere afterward, she should be back by now. Here, in the house, with him and the girls where she belonged. Not out gallivanting with the boring but persistent Sam Johnson.

He racked his brain trying to recall if there was any place in town where they might have gone afterward. Dancing? The thought of Sarah in Sam's arms was enough to make him want to jump in the pickup and drive up and down the streets of Wayside looking for her.

He had no memory of ever agonizing over anyone or anything in his life the way he agonized over Sarah and this date. He couldn't believe the way he was reacting to her being out with another man. He felt frustrated, more so than when he'd been lying on his back in the hospital for months on end. Not even Maureen's defection with Ansell had left him this drained, this anxious, this . . . crazed.

He knew why, though he hadn't yet admitted it to himself, hadn't yet said the words even in his mind. It didn't matter, they were there, lurking in the shadows of his heart, and he knew he was lost. He wanted her home so he could show her if not tell her. She belonged to him, with him. His. Period. And he'd never been the sharing type. So no more dating, no more other men, no more nights away from him. Whatever it took to keep her, he was ready to do.

It was amazing how this stupid little date with Sam Johnson put everything in perspective with crystal clarity. His resistance to going to town, the aversion to people gawking at him, all seemed so trivial right now, a stupid reason for them to argue. If that's all it took to keep her with him, he'd do it. Hell, he'd undress in Martin's Department Store window on Main Street if that made her happy. It didn't seem to matter anymore. Nothing did. Except Sarah.

Had she planned it that way? He doubted it. Sarah was guileless; she acted on instinct, impulse. She wasn't calculated enough to concoct this night just to show him what was really going on between them.

And *love* was what was going on. True love. Real love. There, he'd said the word, even if it was only to himself. He uttered it inside his head, his brain, and once done, a warmth seeped into every nook and cranny of his body.

"I love you, Sarah." He said it out loud, testing the words on his tongue, liking the way they sounded, not rusty like some pimple-faced teenager, but like a man who knew his own heart and mind.

"Come home, and I'll say it again. In bed. Inside you." He shut his eyes at the thought, feeling himself swell in his jeans.

Where the hell was she?

He thought of calling Lara for information about the nightlife in and around town, but then he'd be giving himself away, and he wasn't yet quite prepared to play the blatant jealous fool he knew he was.

I'll give her till eleven.

He went upstairs to check the girls. They were fast asleep, having run him ragged for the first two hours, demanding everything from playing hide-and-seek outside at dusk, to piggyback rides, to reading the same storybooks over and over again before they would lay their heads down on the pillows. He tucked the light covers around each girl and headed back downstairs to the living room.

And the incessant ticktocking of the grandfather clock.

What was she doing this long? That she might be having a rousing good time made him sick to his stomach. The thought that anything more than that was going on blew his mind.

Suddenly, he wished he'd kept up with the local gossip around town, wished he'd listened to Lara's constant updates instead of tuning her out. Did Sam have his own apartment? House? Was Sarah there with him now, sipping a brandy, laughing, joking...*kissing?* Unthinkable! He strode to the door for the umpteenth time, but this time he was rewarded. Car lights glared from the road beyond.

He opened the screen door and stepped out onto the porch, moving down to the opposite end from the driveway to sit and wait on the lounge chair Sarah used for sunning herself. It was set back far enough and low enough so that they couldn't see him.

The car pulled all the way up in front of the house. There was silence. For a minute, two, then three. He was losing that loving feeling—fast. He wanted to jump up and go over there and ask them what they were doing, but he knew Sarah would have a fit and a half if he did, and besides, he didn't want to confront Sam tonight. He just might punch him in the nose.

So he waited.

Sarah turned to Sam. "Don't get out. You don't have to see me to the door."

"I want to."

"It's not necessary."

Sam remained quiet for a long moment. "Does this mean you won't see me again, Sarah?"

"I don't think it would be wise for us to date, Sam, with us working together and all."

Sam nodded. "But that's not the real reason, is it?"

"I don't—"

"It's Evan, isn't it?"

Sarah turned and looked him in the eye. "I honestly don't know," she said softly. "I wish I did." She got out of the car. "Good night, Sam."

As she headed for the walkway, she didn't turn to wave when she heard Sam back out. She hoped he wasn't too upset. It was better this way; there was really no future there. She hoped, too, that this wasn't going to affect her teaching position at the school. Sam didn't seem like the vindictive type, but one never knew.

With an audible sigh at the absolute mess she seemed to be making of things lately, she grabbed hold of the railing and pulled herself up the porch steps, trying to mentally ready herself to confront Evan again.

"Did you have a nice time?"

Sarah almost jumped out of her skin. Searching, she found the source of the sarcastic voice at the edge of her porch, sitting low on the lounge chair. A hand to her chest, she took a deep breath to steady her raging heartbeat. "Yes, I had a very nice time."

"Must have been some night. It's almost eleven."

"I wasn't aware I had a curfew. Are the girls all right?"

"The girls are fine. What were you doing all this time?"

"Talking. Not that it's any of your business."

"Just talking?"

Sarah shook her head incredulously. "Why don't you tell me what you *think* we were doing?"

Evan lifted himself off the lounge chair and walked over to her. A slim shaft of light from the living room window poured out onto the porch. His hair was tousled, his face was drawn, and though it wasn't bright enough to make out his features, from her vantage point he looked like a man possessed.

"I'd prefer you tell me," he said.

"I don't have to answer to you."

"Ah, then something did happen. What was it, Sarah? Did old Sam take you back to his place for a little after-dinner tête-à-tête?"

"You're crazy," she said as she tried to walk around him to the front door.

He grabbed hold of her arm to stop her. "Tell me."

"There's nothing to tell. We went to dinner at the new restaurant. We talked about work. That's all."

"Did he try to kiss you?"

"What is this, twenty questions?" she asked. Slipping her arm from his grasp, she opened the door and entered the house.

Evan followed. "Answer me. Did you kiss him?"

She dropped her purse on the chair. The house was dimly lit, with only the small lamp on the end table illuminating the room. She still couldn't see his face clearly. She'd missed him tonight, not realizing how much until this very moment, and wanted to move closer to him. But she didn't dare. To hide her cowardice, she put her hand on her hip and stood her ground. "Now which is it? Did *he* try to kiss me, or did *I* kiss him?"

"Either."

"You're being ridiculous."

"That's no answer."

Sarah straightened the cushions on the couch and fixed a stack of magazines on the coffee table.

"Sarah . . ."

She looked at him over her shoulder. "What was the question again?"

"I asked if the two of you kissed."

She laughed out loud. "Oh, yes, we just kissed and kissed. Tongue in the mouth, the whole nine yards. I can't even remember how many kisses. Hundreds."

"That's not funny, Sarah."

Her eyebrows arched. "If you don't believe me, then why did you ask?"

"You couldn't have been eating dinner for three hours."

"It was a long dinner." She wasn't about to add, a long, *boring* dinner; he didn't deserve the satisfaction. "I have nothing more to say about it. I'm going up to check the girls." She did just that, turning her back to him, though her heart was beating triple-time as she climbed the stairs to their room.

The girls were fast asleep, but Sarah took an inordinately long time checking on them. She felt like trapped prey, with the predator somewhere nearby, waiting for her to show herself. She wasn't frightened; she was excited, for she knew what would happen if he caught her.

As she descended the stairway, she saw him standing in front of the screen door, arms folded across his chest, looking out into the night. The perfect, chiseled features of the right side of his face were bathed in moonlight. He seemed so forlorn, lonely even, and her heart split in two at the sight. Who was she kidding? She was in love with this man. Irrevocably and forever, no matter what the future held, no matter what she had to do or sacrifice to keep him in her life.

A calmness settled over her as she walked up behind him. With slow deliberation, she wrapped her arms around his middle, resting her head in the curve between his shoulder blades. He didn't move at first, then his big hands reached up and completely covered hers.

"Thank you for watching the girls tonight," she said softly as he ran a callused thumb against her knuckles.

Evan looked at her over his shoulder. "Never again," he said.

Sarah shook her head. "No, never again."

"And I don't mean watching the girls. No more dates. Not with Sam. Not with anyone."

"Except you."

"Except me."

He turned around, and she slid into his arms. He held her close to him for a very long time. She shut her eyes as she rested her head against his chest. "I love you, Evan."

He pulled back and looked down at her. "Sarah..."

The amazement in his voice was not lost on her. She put her fingers to his lips. "Please don't say anything. Not right now. I needed to tell you. Tonight while I was sitting in the restaurant I realized that I only want to be with you. It doesn't matter where—here, in town, on the moon for all I care. And I knew at that moment that I loved you. I guess I've been falling for a long time, probably since the first day we met, but now I know for sure. And I wanted you to know, too."

Evan felt his throat tighten with emotion. There were no words in him to describe the unparalleled joy her declaration brought to him. He felt as if his own personal genie had slipped out of its bottle and granted him his heart's desire. It wasn't something he'd expected to hear, not from any woman in what was left of this lifetime, but especially not from Sarah. She was too perfect to love someone like him. Desire him, yes, he could understand the hungers that drove the body, but love...that was something distinctly different, sacred even, and he'd given up on the possibility of it ever entering his life.

He'd told himself that was okay; he accepted his fate. But hearing the words made him realize how much he'd been kidding himself all these years, how deep his feelings truly ran, how desperately important it was that she mean it.

He wanted to say something in return, but if he blurted out he loved her, too, it would sound shallow, as if he felt compelled to say it because she did. He didn't want her to misunderstand, so he said nothing, hoping there would be a time when the words would flow so naturally from his lips she would not doubt them in any way.

Instead, he kissed her, his tongue sweeping into her mouth and taking total possession of her. She touched her tongue to his, and he went wild. She tasted like Sarah, an indescribable warm whiskey woman-taste that smoothed out all those jagged edges in his soul. When he slanted his head and deepened the kiss, her tiny responsive whimper sent a bittersweet arrow of yearning to the core of what made him man. He swelled against her, feeling himself grow harder with each caress of her tongue.

He reached between them and unbuttoned the top button of her dress, then the next, the third, the fourth...

Evan broke the kiss and looked down at his progress. "How many damned buttons does this dress have, anyway?" he asked impatiently.

Sarah giggled, unaware that her eyes glowed with the joy of being here with him like this. "I don't know." Her hands joined his. "Why don't we count? I'll start at the bottom, you—"

Evan pulled her back into his arms and buried his face in her neck. "I want you," he whispered. "I know we can't, but—"

Sarah extricated herself from his embrace. She extended her hand in invitation.

"What—?" he asked as he took hold of her hand.

"Upstairs. My bedroom. My bed."

"But the girls..."

"Are sleeping. But we'll have to be quiet."

Evan grinned mischievously. "You can always tape my mouth."

Sarah leaned over and brushed her lips against his, the tip of her tongue enticing his lower lip as she withdrew. "Maybe later..."

He followed her upstairs, cringing with each creaking step on the way to her bedroom. They both checked the girls as they passed their room, and were delighted to hear simultaneous minisnores coming from the beds. Smiling at each other, they tiptoed out of the room, shutting the door behind them.

Sarah switched on the child monitor next to her bed, then turned to Evan. He was standing in the doorway, waiting for her to make the next move.

"You're slacking off, Mr. Forester. There must be a dozen or more buttons you missed."

Evan walked over to her and immediately went to work, popping each successive button with an Olympic-type speed. Sarah teased him with her hands, running them down his sides, around to his abdomen, which contracted from her touch. With the tip of her index finger, she outlined his arousal through the material of his jeans, making him groan out loud.

"Shh," she warned with a taunting smile. "Or I will have to tape your mouth."

"Not yet," he said as the last button was released.

He pulled her to him and kissed her with a passion that took her breath away. Without any effort on her part at all, the dress slid off her body, followed in rapid sequence by her bra and panties.

And then he began to *really* kiss her. First her mouth, then her cheeks, her neck, the warm hollow behind her ear. Then all over. His mouth was hot and wet, and he used his tongue to guide his progress, dipping in the valley between her breasts before turning his attention to her sensitive, pouting nipples. First one side, then the other. He suckled her, deeply, so deeply that her womb contracted with the pleasure of each tug of his mouth.

Sarah's legs gave way, and she lost her balance. Evan grabbed her by the waist and guided her safely down onto the bed, landing on his knees before her open, waiting, wanting body.

He ran his hands, palms spread, down from her waist past her navel, around the source of her desire to the soft, smooth skin of her inner thighs. Her legs spread of their own volition, and she shivered as he touched her inti-

mately with his thumb. Gratified at the warm wetness he
encountered, Evan bent his head and kissed the slight
roundness of her belly. "You are so beautiful . . . so absolutely perfect. Oh, Sarah . . ."

And then his lips and tongue replaced his thumb. She
writhed beneath him as he feasted on her, holding her
hips still with his hands as his mouth worked its magic.

Sarah was wild, ignoring her own edict to be quiet, she
begged him to stop, not to stop, to end this mad pleasure
that bordered on pain . . . to never end it.

Her climax was powerful, seeming to rise from her toes
to overtake her in a shattering, blinding burst of light.
She shut her eyes tightly and bit her lip to stop from crying out, grabbing handfuls of the comforter as she pulled
herself back to reality.

When she looked up again, Evan was leaning over her,
one arm on each side of her head, grinning from ear to
ear. "Pleased with yourself?" she whispered.

"Yup."

"Don't look so smug."

"Why not?"

She pushed him back and sat up halfway. "Because
now it's your turn."

Reaching down, she unzipped his jeans and dipped her
hand inside the opening to caress him. He was hard,
smooth, hot to the touch, and she felt herself melt into a
pool of want and need. Suddenly, touching him was not
enough, and she pulled and pushed at his jeans in an effort to get them out of her way.

"Let me," he said, rising to a standing position. He
disrobed so quickly the night air barely had time to chill
her skin before his body was back on top of her.

Sarah lifted her knees, hugging the edge of the bed with
her heels, and he nestled himself between her legs. With
deliberate slowness, he rubbed himself against her, back
and forth, until her body blossomed, so willing and
wanting she thought she would die if he didn't fill her.

"Easy," he whispered, easing himself into her, so
teasingly slowly that she lifted her hips high off the bed
to meet him more than halfway.

And then he was there, buried deep inside her, throbbing, unmoving and so potently male that her heart leapt with anticipation of how she knew he would make her feel.

Evan reached up and entwined her fingers through his. He lifted her arms high over her head and at the same moment pulled out almost all the way, then, his eyes never leaving hers, he thrust back into her. One, twice, again, so many times that her legs began to tremble so she had to wrap them around his thighs.

Sarah arched her back to accept him, her eyes fluttering closed with the sensation of fullness each thrust carried. He leaned over and kissed her, a kiss so blatantly sexual she knew that he was close, very close, to his own release.

"Oh, yes, Evan," she urged, using her mouth, her lips, her tongue, her words, to make it as good for him as he'd done for her. "Now, oh, please, now...now..."

She felt him pulse within her, then lost sight of all around her as her body responded to his release with one of her own.

Evan let go of her arms and rested his weight on top of her. She welcomed him, wrapped her arms around his back, running her fingertips up and down his lightly perspired skin. She loved the feel of him, the combined smell of him, the night, their lovemaking, all like sweet perfume to her overwhelmed senses.

"I love you," she whispered again, and felt his lips curl into a smile at her breast. When he said nothing, she tugged at his hair playfully. "Now would be a good time to say it," she added.

"Say what?" he asked without lifting his head.

"To say you love me, too."

"Why?"

"Why what?"

"Why is now a good time?"

"Because...it just is. It's the perfect time."

"I don't agree," he said, pushing up on his elbows. "I think if I said it now you wouldn't know if I really meant it or if I were just saying it because we've made love."

"No, I wouldn't. I'd believe you."

He grinned and kissed the tip of her nose. "No, you wouldn't." He pulled at the comforter and rearranged them side by side under the cover.

"Yes, I would."

"Trust me on this. When I say it, you'll understand what I mean." He opened his arms to her, but she didn't come into them.

"In all my thirty-four years, I've never heard—"

Evan sat up. "You're thirty-four?"

"Yeah, why?"

"I didn't know you were that old."

"What do you mean old? How old are you?"

"Thirty in October."

"Thirty? You're only thirty? Why didn't you tell me?"

He shrugged. "I didn't think it mattered. Does it?"

Sarah looked at him. "No, I suppose not. It's just that . . ."

"What?"

"I feel like an old lady now."

He reached under the cover and found the one place he was looking for and gently stroked the tiny, still tingling bud. "You sure as hell don't feel like an old lady."

Sarah slapped his hand, but when he removed it she felt bereft. "Don't stop," she said, and returned his hand to where it had been.

Evan bent over her and brushed his lips against hers as his fingers continued their sensual assault. "Don't sound like an old lady, either."

Then he kissed her, and all thought, as well as conversation, was forgotten in the pleasures of this very special night.

Chapter 15

*C*hurch bells were ringing...

Sarah was dressed in an ankle-length, cream-colored dress. She was smiling as she floated toward him in slow motion, flowers braided through her rusty curls, one hand clutching a bouquet with streaming ribbons, the other raised high over her head in a wave. He reached out for her, and the bells kept ringing...

Evan opened one eye and squinted at the digital clock on the nightstand by the bed. It was barely 8:00 a.m. It took him several seconds to focus on the sound and to react to it. It was the doorbell, not the church bell, that was ringing repeatedly.

It had been a beautiful dream, and he was loath to let it go, but whoever was on the other side of the door was not fooling around. He swung himself out of bed and grabbed his jeans, slipping into them as he hopped from one foot to the other down the flights of stairs to his front door.

"It's about time," Lara said, pushing past him into the kitchen.

"What the—"

"You need to look at this," she said.

Evan turned around slowly. "Do you know what time it is?"

"Yes, it's already eight o'clock. I tried to get you all last night, but no one answered the phone. If you'd only break down and get an answering machine, maybe I wouldn't have to traipse out here every time there's an emergency."

Evan ran a hand through his hair in exasperation. "What's the emergency this time? The caterers cancel? Rain in the forecast? Or did Willy get cold feet?"

"This isn't funny, Evan."

Evan looked at his cousin. Her face was dead serious and very concerned. "Did someone die?"

"No, worse. Ansell Walcott called me. About this." She held up a manila envelope.

Evan didn't take the envelope. Instead, he ambled over to the kitchen counter and set to scooping coffee into the machine filter. "I have no interest in anything that man has to say, you know that."

She nudged his arm with the envelope. "I think you'll change your mind once you see these."

Evan filled the container with water and set it in place in the machine. Turning to her, he reluctantly accepted the envelope. "What is it?"

"See for yourself."

He flipped open the catch and pulled out the eight-by-ten color photos. Of Sarah. Naked. Well, almost naked. And running away from his house, wild red curls flying in the wind. Four shots, far enough to be questionable, near enough to be damning.

He blew out an exasperated breath.

He knew when they'd been taken. The morning of their argument about going to town when she'd run out of the house. The bastard must have been waiting in the bushes. He wondered how many times that had been the case in the past few weeks, and felt his skin crawl at the thought that he and Sarah had been watched all this time.

"How did you get these?" he asked.

"Ansell called me yesterday afternoon. Said he had a deal to talk to you about. He knew you wouldn't give him a chance to speak, so he contacted me as an intermediary. I told him to get lost at first, just as you would, but he sounded too smug for me to dismiss him completely. So I went to meet him.''

''And what does he want?''

''He wants an interview with you, exclusive, one-on-one, photos of you, the house, the whole works, and if you don't agree, he'll print these...with a story of his own making.''

''I see.''

''Do you? Evan, this could ruin Sarah, you've got to know that. She's not only a teacher at the elementary school, she also is going to be organist at the church. Do you really think Reverend Winthrop will find it in his heart to overlook something like this?''

He shook his head slowly. ''No.'' He slipped the photos back into the envelope.

''The pictures are obviously fakes, but however he staged it, they're damning enough to cause a ruckus and a half. Wayside may have cable TV, but it's still a small town at heart.''

''I know that.''

''Then what are you going to do?''

Evan stared at his cousin for a long moment. ''I don't know.''

He walked over to the door and jammed his hands into the front pockets of his jeans. So this was it. His moment of truth, maybe even the most defining moment of his life. A wry grin creased his face. There should be some fanfare, he thought, a clashing of cymbals or a trumpet blaring to herald the occasion. But no, only this deafening quiet and peaceful view of the sun-kissed woods dappling light into his kitchen.

He felt Lara's presence behind him, sensed the force of her will waiting patiently for him to say something that would make it all right, make it all go away. But he wasn't prepared for this and he needed time to think. In all the years with all the talks he and Lara had had about his reentering society, he hadn't realistically entertained the idea that he'd have to face this kind of decision.

He'd held life at bay for so long by the sheer isolation of his existence. That one act of heroism which had thrust him into the spotlight, had been just that—an act. He hadn't given a second's thought to rushing into that burning building. But he had *chosen* to withdraw, to slink away into this hideaway, untouched by people, protected, he thought, from the pain of life.

But Sarah had changed all that. She and her children had forced him back into a world he'd never thought to inhabit again. And now she was forcing him to do something else. She was forcing him to face his demons head-on.

He should be feeling fear, apprehension, frustration, disgust at the idea of having photographs of his scarred face splashed across the front page of who knew what number of media outlets, of having to deal with Ansell Walcott on his terms again. But as he stopped to gauge his feelings, none of those were present. Only a pure unmitigated sense of . . . relief.

It's over. No more running, no more hiding. Face your devil, and he will go away. . . .

"Evan—"

"Hi, you two!"

Evan and Lara turned to see Sarah standing in the doorway with a plate of steaming pancakes in her hand. She stopped dead at the look on their faces. "I-I hope you don't mind. The back door was open, and I made these for the girls, and thought . . ."

"Sarah, come on in," Evan said.

"Hi, honey, how're you doing?" Lara asked.

"Good." She looked over at Evan and their eyes met and held. *Real good.* Turning to Lara, she said, "And are you all set with the wedding plans? Only a week to go!"

"Yes, we've really got everything under control." Lara smiled stiffly.

Lara turned to the kitchen counter and took a coffee mug out of one of the cabinets. Pouring a cup, she handed it to Evan. As he accepted it, they exchanged a glance that said "tell her now."

"Great," Sarah said. "I can't wait, and the girls are jumping out of their skin with excitement! While you're here, maybe you can come over and let the girls model the dresses for you. I know you've seen them, but we made some alterations. We've added a little pink ruffle on the bottom.''

"They sound wonderful. Sure, I'll stop in.''

An awkward silence followed, and Sarah set the plate down on the kitchen table. She could feel something palpable going on in the room, and for some strange reason it made her uncomfortable. Her mood had been so good when she'd walked in, part anticipation at seeing Evan again—even though he'd left her bed little more than two hours ago—and part nervousness. She had declared herself last night with her body as well as her words, and he had been fairy-tale wonderful. But sometimes in the light of day things changed.

She wondered if that was the case here. Perhaps he had called Lara to come over to talk about this terrible mistake he'd made. A fear washed over her, and she felt herself go cold. She faked a smile. "Well, you two look like you're in the middle of something important, so why don't I just leave this plate and see you later.'' She looked over at Evan, finding it hard to believe this stone-faced man was the same one who'd been so loving just hours ago. "Don't let them get cold.'' She turned to go, but before she could reach the door, Evan stopped her.

"Sarah...I think you'd better sit down,'' he said as he held out a kitchen chair for her.

She hesitated, then took the proffered seat. Evan moved away from her, leaning his back against the kitchen counter. Sarah glanced from Lara to Evan and back. "What is it? Is something wrong?'' she asked.

"Yes,'' Lara added. She took the envelope out of Evan's hand and held it out to Sarah. "A little present from Ansell Walcott. You'd better look at these.''

Sarah pulled the photos from the envelope. Her eyes widened for a nanosecond, but then she studied them, one at a time, slowly and carefully.

Lara put a hand on her shoulder and set a steaming hot cup of coffee on the table in front of her. "He probably superimposed your head on someone else's body,'' she said with unchecked anger. "I don't know how he managed it, but the setting is real enough to fool anyone.

Phony or not, if he prints them, you're going to have a problem."

"They're not phony," Sarah said softly.

Evan pushed off the counter. "Sarah, you don't have to—"

"What do you mean they're not phony?" Lara asked with a chuckle. "You mean to tell me you've been running naked between Evan's and..." Lara's words trailed off as she looked first at Sarah, then at Evan. "My Lord, you mean the two of you are lovers?" she asked incredulously.

Sarah's eyes met Evan's. "It's all right." Then she turned to Lara. "Yes, we are."

Lara whistled, then broke into a huge grin. She punched her cousin on the upper arm. "And you didn't tell me, you rat? I can't believe it! How wonderful! How perfect! Well, I certainly didn't plan on this happening. But I can't say I'm sorry."

"Neither am I," Sarah added. "But I'm not so sure Evan is feeling the same way right now."

Lara turned to her cousin and repeated her earlier question, "So... what are you going to do?"

Evan's gaze moved from Sarah to Lara, then back again. The look on Sarah's face melted his heart. She was worried about him, not herself, he could see it in her eyes. And he knew then, there really was no choice. Not for him. He was in love with her. She was a part of him, body and soul. And she needed help. He'd run into a burning building for strangers, surely for the woman he loved he could expose himself, if need be, to one knobby-kneed reporter.

"Give him what he wants," Evan said matter-of-factly.

"What does he want?" Sarah asked.

"An exclusive interview with Evan, photos of him and the house, the whole bit."

"And if Evan says no?"

"He publishes the photos of you running from the house. He also has some shots of the girls and your mother, too. He said he'll do a whole profile on Evan's little paradise."

Evan's face was stone cold. "Give me his number," he said to Lara.

"It's on the envelope, but he won't be available until next week. He's going out of town on a story. He said he'd give you a few days to think it over," Lara said.

"But that's when the wedding is," Sarah said, and her face turned pale at the thought. "Lord, does he plan to run the story then?"

Lara shrugged. "I don't know what he's planning."

"That's the problem with Ansell," Evan said. "You never do."

Evan walked over to Sarah and lifted the envelope out of her hand. She held on tightly as he tried to tug it free. "No. You don't have to do this," she said softly.

He pulled it from her. "Yes, I do."

She took hold of his hand. "But this is your worst nightmare come true," she said. "And I brought this on myself. You warned me, but I didn't believe you. I won't let you subject yourself to this."

"You're not letting me, I'm choosing to do it."

"Oh, Evan, why—"

"Because I love you."

She'd meant to say, "Why did this have to happen now?" but was glad he cut her off. He hadn't said it last night after she had declared herself, nor after they'd joked about it, and though she knew it in her heart, the words, said so easily by him now, meant so much more. He'd been right, she believed him more thoroughly than she ever would have if he'd said them in the heat of passion last night.

With a small, sad smile, she stood and wrapped her arms around his neck. "Oh, Evan, I love you, too. So much."

They stared at each other for a long moment. Lara cleared her throat. "How about I leave you two alone for a while? I'll go over to your place, Sarah. The girls can model their dresses for me." When Sarah didn't answer, she added in a mocking voice, "'Okay, sure, no problem. See you later, Lara.'"

Neither heard her leave; neither cared. When Evan kissed her, Sarah opened her mouth for him. The way she knew he liked. The way that turned him on. Her, too. It was a sweet, poignant kiss of promise laced with some regret that it had to be this kind of situation that precipitated it.

Sarah pulled back. "I want to handle this myself, Evan. I have to."

"I don't understand why, Sarah. This is happening to you because of me. He and I have a long history. I know how to deal with someone like him."

"Then it's time I learned, too." He looked away from her, exasperated at her insistence to handle this on her own. She took his chin in her hand and forced his eyes to meet hers. "Don't you see? All my life someone has been taking care of me, *protecting* me. The whole idea of moving away from my parents was to set myself free, but with that came responsibility to handle my own problems." She nodded slowly at Evan. "*This* . . . is *my* problem."

"No, sweetheart, that's where you're wrong. What affects you affects me. It's *our* problem."

"Okay, I'll accept that. Then we should solve it together."

"Sarah . . ."

"No, don't 'Sarah' me. I know what I'm doing. I can deal with Ansell Walcott. I'm not afraid of him, or of those—" she pointed to the envelope on the table "—photographs. I can handle him."

"Nobody's saying you can't. All I'm saying is that I know this guy. I know what makes him tick. For some strange reason, ever since the accident and what happened between him and Maureen, he's made keeping tabs on my life his own personal crusade. I used to think it had something to do with her, something she may have said about me, but as the years have gone by I've come to realize that what happened here not only changed my life, it changed his, too."

"What do you mean?"

Evan waved a dismissive hand. "Ansell was an aggressive free-lancer with a lot of promise when he happened to be in the right place at the right time. He was here when the plant exploded, and he became a local celebrity because of the extensive coverage. It was his finest hour—nothing's been as good for him since. He'd thought he'd be going on to the big time, when in reality, he ended up doing sleazy tabloid pieces. It's all been downhill since then. In some sad way, I understand him better than he knows.''

"So you think he comes back here every year to recapture some of his past glory with a story about you?"

"Something like that."

"Then why bring me into this?" she asked.

"He probably sensed something when he interviewed you in town. Believe it or not, he started out as a legitimate reporter, and he has the instincts. He's just warped himself over the years by dealing with the sensational. So that's how his mind works now." He kissed her on the tip of her nose. "And sleaze sells, sweet."

Sarah wrapped her arms around his neck and leaned into him. "So how are we going to handle him?"

Evan placed his hands at her waist and pushed her back. "*We* are not going to handle anything. I'll take care of Ansell."

"Evan Forester, haven't you heard a word I said?"

"Every single syllable. Problem is you haven't been listening to *me*." He paused, and their eyes met. "You don't have to be supermom and superwoman all rolled into one, not for me. I know you want to assert your independence, and I respect that. But part of loving is trusting." He held up his hand to silence her. "Sweetheart, this is as new for me as it is for you. From time to time, there'll be things you'll need to let someone else take care of for you. This is one of those times, Sarah. You've got to trust me on this."

She knew what he was trying to say. Independence was fine, but common sense should rule. Having him handle Ansell didn't diminish her in any way because she was part of him, and they were in this together. She touched her lips to him, feeling stronger already knowing that there was someone like him standing by her side.

"I do trust you," she whispered, "with my life."

"Then let me handle it."

"What if he won't listen to reason?"

"He'll listen."

Sarah didn't like the look in his eye. "You're not going to punch him out or something, are you?"

Evan laughed out loud. "No, though the thought has crossed my mind too many times to count." He shook his head slowly. "No, it's time for Ansell and me to come to terms with each other. Once and for all."

Evan picked up the envelope from the table and took it over to the wall phone. He punched out the number written on the front. "Ansell Walcott, please."

"Lara said he was out of town."

"I'll leave a message. Let him know I'm interested so he doesn't get any ideas of printing the photos before he talks to me." He listened for a moment, then asked, "When will he be back?"

Evan nodded. "Okay. Fine. Tell him Evan Forester called." He paused. "Yeah. He has the number."

Their gazes locked as Evan cradled the receiver. "Now we wait. And see."

The night before Lara's wedding, Sarah and Evan sat cuddled on the lounge chair on her front porch. They looked out upon a huge yellow-and-white striped tent, which was situated between the two yards just to the right of center. The tables and folding chairs were stacked inside, waiting for the army of caterers to appear at first light to begin setting up.

"I don't know how I let you talk me into going to this," Evan said.

"It'll be wonderful. Just wait and see."

He lifted her chin and looked down into her eyes. "Promise?"

"Do I detect a little nervousness, Mr. Forester?"

"No...well, maybe just a little. Walking her down the aisle and all. It may be Lara's wedding, but I think it's really my coming-out party."

"I think you're right. Lara said that when she sent out the invitations with your address listed, there wasn't a negative RSVP in the batch."

"The curious citizens of Wayside."

"You can't blame them," she said.

"I think we should christen that tent before the wedding? What do you say?" he asked, nuzzling her neck.

"You don't mean . . ."

Sarah's phone began ringing. She extricated herself from Evan's embrace and ran inside to answer it. Evan stared at the black starry sky, feeling content and happy . . . except for one item of business still to be handled—Ansell Walcott and his nasty little story.

Sarah appeared at the screen door, but didn't come back out onto the porch. Evan slipped out of the chair. "What is it?"

"Ansell was on the phone." She graced him with a wry grin. "Said he thought he'd find you here."

"Is he still on the line?"

She shook her heard. "No, he had to go. Said he'd meet with you tomorrow around noon. He left the name of the motel he's staying at."

"Tomorrow's the wedding."

"I told him that," Sarah said. "He didn't seem to care."

Evan took a deep breath and nodded. "Okay. I'll meet him between the church and the reception."

"Evan—"

"Don't," he said and pulled her into his arms. "I'm glad he's called. I want this over with once and for all. I feel as if the sword of Damocles has been hanging over our heads this past week. I want us to be free, Sarah." He looked down into her eyes. "And by this time tomorrow, my love, I promise we will be."

Sarah smiled up at him, wishing with all her heart that she could be as sure as he.

It was a perfect day for a wedding, but Sarah was too nervous to notice. She sat on the stool in front of the organ and looked down at her fingers poised over the keyboard. They were shaking. She took a deep breath to try to calm herself. Not only was it her debut as church organist, but she hadn't slept a wink last night, worrying about what would happen today with Evan and Ansell.

What if Evan couldn't talk him out of using the pictures? The thought made her as nauseous now as it had last night, and she couldn't bring herself to imagine what would happen to her in this town if they were printed.

The girls came running down the side aisle, bumping into her to stop themselves. "Mommy, Mommy, Lara's here!" Alys shouted. "She looks beautiful!"

"Alys, please lower your voice. You're in church."

"Lara is here. She looks beautiful," she whispered so loudly the people in the first pew chuckled indulgently.

Sarah smiled back at them, then turned her attention to the girls. "Now both of you go back where you belong. They'll be starting the ceremony soon."

"Okay, Mommy," Ariel said, pulling at her sister.

"Quietly," Sarah admonished, nodding at them as they tiptoed back to the front of the church to take their places in the bridal procession.

Sarah began to play a soft, tranquil piece that Lara and Willy had picked out to precede the wedding march. She knew it well and as her fingers glided along the keys her mind wandered.

She and Evan had gone their separate ways last night. They both needed time and space to prepare for today. She knew she was lucky to have the girls chattering and keeping her too busy at times to think. Not so Evan. He had all the hours of the night to get through.

They drove separately to the church, Evan in his dark gray tuxedo climbing into the pickup truck, she in her beige floral print dress slipping into the station wagon with the girls strapped in the back seat. When they'd arrived at the church, she thought she'd have a few moments alone with him to ask if he'd decided what to say to Ansell when they met after the ceremony, but such was not the case. The Reverend and Mrs. Winthrop were so pleased to see him finally at church, they monopolized the conversation until it was too late to talk. She and Evan were pulled in two different directions, and she hadn't seen him since.

An usher caught her eye, and the signal was given. Sarah began playing the wedding march, and the congregation stood, obscuring her vision of the center church aisle. She stretched and craned her neck, managing to at least partially see the girls drop white and pink rose petals on the white runner as they walked side by side to the altar.

She smiled her approval at them as they arrived, and they smiled back. Her heart burst with pride for how well-behaved and absolutely beautiful they were both inside and out, and she knew by the looks on their little faces that they were equally pleased with themselves.

By the time Lara arrived at the altar on Evan's arm, Sarah had completed the piece. She stood with everyone else and watched a serene Lara and nervous Willy exchange vows. Evan sat in the front row, turning his body not to face the altar, but so that he would be in her direct line of vision.

As the couple said their "I do's," Evan's eyes seem to bore into hers with an intensity she'd never seen before. She wondered if he was trying to tell her something. She was moved by the solemnity of the ceremony, but part of her was detached and frightened, as well, because she wasn't sure if that look came from his own personal apprehension for what he had yet to do this day.

There was no time to ruminate over what was to be. As the couple was pronounced husband and wife, Sarah began playing again, forcing herself to concentrate on the music. She continued playing until the church emptied, then made quick work of storing the sheet music before rushing to the church doors to collect her children, catch a glimpse of the bride and groom, and have a few minutes with Evan before he went off to his meeting.

"Do you know what you're going to say to him?" she asked as she cornered him at last.

"I know exactly what I'm going to say to him."

"How about telling me, then?" she asked.

"Later."

"Evan—"

"The girls are waiting. Lara and Willy want to take pictures down by the lake before the reception starts. Go along with them. I'll be as quick as possible." He bent over and gave her a quick, hard kiss on the lips. "I'll meet you there."

And then he was gone. Sarah headed back to the house, following along behind Lara and Willy, and waited as patiently as she could without biting every nail off her fingers while pictures were taken of the bridal party by the lake.

Once that was done, they had a few minutes' break before the guests were due to arrive. Sarah checked in her house to see if there was a message from Evan on her answering machine. There was not. She ambled outside, warning the girls not to get dirty as they ran around the tent.

Lara motioned her over. She sat on a chair outside the tent and shook off her shoes. "Oooh," she sighed as she wiggled her stocking feet in the cool grass. "This feels great." Seeing Sarah's concerned face, she asked, "Have you heard from Evan yet?"

"No, not yet. It's been over an hour. How long can this take?"

"With Ansell? Who knows?" She leaned over and squeezed Sarah's hand. "Evan knows what he's doing. He won't let you down. Have faith in him."

"I do," she said with a glance to the driveway where he usually parked his truck. "I just wish he would get here."

The guests began arriving before Evan, and each time a car pulled in, Sarah was on her feet. As the crowd grew, she became distracted, trying to make conversation, keep the girls in check and watch for Evan all at the same time.

Ariel ran up to her and hugged her legs. "Hi, sweetheart," Sarah said as she brushed the chestnut bangs back from her daughter's forehead. "Everything okay?"

"Where's Evan, Mommy?"

"He'll be here soon."

"Is he hiding from all these people?" Ariel asked with more wisdom in her eyes than a five-year-old deserved to have.

"Maybe," Sarah said with a smile. "You never know. I'll call you when he gets here. Now go find Alys." She patted her gently on the rear as she ran off. "And keep clean!"

Another half hour passed before she spotted Evan. He just appeared out of nowhere by her side. Startled, she asked, "When did you get here? I didn't see the pickup."

"Couldn't get anywhere near the driveway. I had to park on the road." He took her arm. "Got a minute?"

"Are you kidding?" she said, and grabbed his arm.

They made their way through the crowd, up his porch steps and into his house. He spun her around once they got inside, pulled her into his arms and kissed her. Wrapping her arms around his waist, she kissed him back with everything she had.

"Thanks," he said, "I needed that. Been waiting all day for it, in fact."

He leaned forward to repeat the action, but Sarah held him at arm's length. "No, you don't! I'm ready to jump out of my skin. What happened with Ansell?"

"Oh, that."

"Yes, that."

He grinned at her, slipped his hand into the breast pocket of the tuxedo jacket and took out an envelope. "For you," he said as he handed it to her.

"Are these—?"

"Negatives and all."

Sarah yelped and threw her arms around his neck. This time, she kissed him, a long, deep, hot, thrusting, melting, full-on-and-in-the-mouth kiss that was worthy of the most talented French courtesan. Evan actually blushed.

"If I had thought you would react like this—"

"So tell me everything! What did he say? What did you say?"

"It was strange in a way. I hadn't seen Ansell face-to-face in a long time. All those old memories were just that, old memories of the person I was then—angry, bitter and wanting to be left alone." He ran a finger down her cheek. "But all that's changed now. I've changed. Because of you. None of that old stuff matters anymore, so it was easy for me to forgive him."

"I'm so glad you came to terms with him. It's good to leave the past behind." She smiled a slow, sad smile. "I know that firsthand."

"We've both been doing a bit of soul-searching this summer, haven't we?" he asked.

"Yes, and I'd love to continue this deep conversation, but first you have to finish telling me how you got him to turn the photos over to you?"

"I made him an exchange offer I knew he couldn't refuse."

"What kind of offer?" Sarah asked.

"I promised him an exclusive on the wedding, pictures and all."

Sarah's brow wrinkled. "Lara's wedding? Why would he want pictures of Lara's wedding?"

"Not Lara's. Ours." Sarah's mouth opened, but no words emerged. "That is, if you'll have me. If you can take looking at this face for the next fifty years or so. And it would have to be at least that long. If you say yes, I'll never let you go." When she still didn't answer, his face fell. "Sarah, I'm asking you to marry me. For heaven's sake, *say* something..."

She swallowed, blinked, waved her hands in the air, then jumped up and wrapped her arms around his neck. "Yes! Yes! Yes! Ye—"

"I want to make love with you. Right here. Right now," he said softly.

"Oh, Evan, so do I...but..." She turned her head toward the noise from outside.

"I know. But later on, when everyone's gone home, and the girls are asleep, I'm going to pick you up and carry you into that big tent out there and show you exactly how much I love every delicious part of you. We're going to give new definition to splendor in the grass, my love."

Sarah laughed a nervous, excited, anxious laugh. "I can't wait." She ran a loving palm down the side of his face. The side with the scar. He didn't grab her hand, didn't flinch, and her heart swelled in her chest at how far he had come...how far *they* had come. "Oh, Evan, I love you so much."

"Deal?" he asked.

"Deal," she said.

He held out his hand. "Come on, let's stash these photos somewhere safe and show ourselves. Lara is probably already fuming at me for missing so much of the wedding.''

Sarah watched him hide the envelope in the cupboard. "Lara's been great."

Evan nodded as he grabbed hold of the doorknob. "I know that. If it weren't for her—"

"We wouldn't have met."

They stared at each other for a long moment. Evan was filled with an emotion that was so new, so different from anything he'd ever experienced before, it made him shake inside.

"Come here."

Sarah backed away. He followed. "Uh-uh." She held up her hand to stop his advance. "We can't, really, we can't . . ." she whispered and he reached up and threaded his fingers through her hair to hold her head still for his kiss. "Not now . . ."

"Oh, yes. Right now."

He kissed her with his lips, his mouth, his tongue, his body, pouring every bit of himself into it. And, as she responded to him, it was as if a plug had been pulled. He felt all the emotional baggage begin to seep away, drain from him—his mind, his heart, his soul. There was no past anymore, no scars that meant a damn, nothing but Sarah agreeing to be in his life. The idea that she would be his wife, that he would wake up beside her each morning, that his life would be filled with her every moment of every day, made him dizzy. That he would have a family . . .

There was a knock on the door, and they broke apart. Evan twisted the doorknob to find Alys and a young boy just about the same size standing before him.

"Hi, Evan," she said, then turned to her mother. "Mommy, where's Ariel?"

Sarah looked down at her daughter. "I don't know, honey. She's around here somewhere."

"No, I can't find her. Me and Tommy here want to play hide-and-seek with her."

"Maybe she went into our house."

Alys shook her head. "No, we looked there, too."

"Well, where can she be?" Sarah asked.

"I don't know," Alys answered.

Sarah caught Evan's eye. "She usually isn't a roamer," she said, trying to keep the worry out of her voice.

Evan squeezed her hand. "We'll find her. I'll go this way, you go that way."

They spent the better part of the next half hour searching the grounds, the tent, the two houses and down by the lake. Ariel was nowhere to be found. Neither was Ralph.

They met in the center of the lawn again as Lara was coming off the makeshift dance floor with Willy. "Whew!" she said as she wiped her brow. "Do I look as wilted as I feel? No, don't answer that." She fanned herself with her hand. "Hey, what's wrong, you two?"

"Ariel. Have you seen her?" Sarah asked.

Lara looked at Willy. "No, not recently. Have you?" Willy shook his head.

Sarah was worried now, and didn't even bother to hide it. "Where could she be?"

"When was the last time you saw her?" Willy asked.

"Here. Right here, in fact. She was asking where Evan was. I told her he would be here soon."

"And that was it?" Evan asked.

"No, she asked if you were hiding from all the people." Sarah smiled at her daughter's words. "And I said not to worry about him. She's very protective of Evan, you see, and—"

"I think I know where she is," he said, and with that, he turned and headed for the path on the side of the house that led to his special fishing spot.

Sarah, Alys, Lara and Willy were close behind. "Where are you going?" Sarah asked as she caught up with him.

"To the boat. If she thinks I'm hiding away, that's where she'd look. She probably took Ralph with her."

The rest of the guests noticed the bride and groom heading into the woods, and began to question what was going on. One by one, they followed, and soon the entire wedding party was traipsing single file in high heels and dress clothes down the narrow path toward the clearing where Evan kept his rowboat.

Evan ran ahead, knowing he was on the right track when he heard Ralph barking. The first to arrive at the clearing, he saw the dog running back and forth on the dock, seemingly in a turmoil. "It's okay, boy, it's okay. Where's Ariel?" he asked as he petted the dog, trying to calm him down.

It was then he noticed that the boat wasn't tied to its usual spot. He looked around and froze. His heart sank at the sight of the rowboat drifting out toward the middle of the lake. He strained to see if Ariel was in the boat, then noticed a bit of pink lace hanging over the side.

Sarah caught up with him as did Lara, Alys and Willy. "Where is she?" she asked.

"There," he said. Without thought, he kicked off his shoes and shrugged out of his tuxedo jacket as he took a running dive off the dock into the lake.

"Evan!" Sarah shouted, unaware at first what he meant, until she, too, caught sight of the rowboat. She brought her fist to her mouth. "Oh, God, no!"

She felt a tug on her sleeve. "Mommy...?"

Alys's lower lip was trembling, and her eyes were filled with tears. Sarah knelt down next to the frightened child and took her in her arms. "It's all right. Evan's going to get her. She's going to be just fine, you'll see." Sarah repeated the phrase, over and over again, as much for herself as for the child.

There were gasps and shouts as the wedding party arrived on the scene, but Sarah paid no attention. She held on tightly to Alys as Evan reached the rowboat. All eyes were glued on the scene unfolding. Evan tipped the boat, and Sarah could see Ariel lying on the bottom.

He turned and waved to the group on land. "She's okay," he shouted, and began trolling the rowboat back toward shore.

Willy and a few of the other men ran knee-deep into the water to grab at the boat as Evan approached them. As he reached inside to lift Ariel out, a cheer went up in the group.

Sarah felt her heart begin to beat again. "Thank God," she whispered in Alys's hair.

As she stood, Lara took hold of Alys's hand. "Go," she said to Sarah, who ran forward to meet them.

Ariel was crying, but held on to Evan's neck tightly as he carried her to shore. Dripping wet, he held her close to him. "When I got to the boat, she was fast asleep. I think she's more scared than hurt." Sarah tried to extricate her child from Evan's arms, but Ariel would not let him go. "It's okay," he said. "I'll carry her."

When they got to the waiting group, Lara caught his eye. "Can't give up being a hero, can you?" she asked with obvious pride and affection.

Evan smiled a half smile. "It seems to be what I do best," he joked, then added with a half smile, "on this day."

Sarah looked at him. "Do you mean today's—?"

"The anniversary date of the accident," he finished, then nodded toward this cousin. "Lara's perverse sense of humor."

Sarah opened her mouth to say something to both of them, but was preempted by her daughter. Ariel bent forward and kissed Evan's cheek. "Thank you for saving me, Evan," she said in her contrite little-girl voice.

"You're welcome," he answered, saving the lecture for later when she was less upset and more likely to remember his warnings.

Sarah felt the tears that had been so close rise to the surface. She leaned into him, and he wrapped his other arm around her. She, like her daughter, felt safe with him near.

When Sarah's lips brushed his cheek, Lara's eyes met Evan's, and the cousins exchanged a message. Sarah had kissed him on his scar. And he'd let her.

He knew then what a long way he'd come from that first day when the Widow Wyeth and her children arrived on his doorstep. He saw a life before him now—a family, maybe even a new Forester or two in Wayside, after all—where all there had been before was a huge gaping void. Sarah brought him back into the world by bringing a world to him.

Evan recognized the emotion behind the shine in his cousin's eyes. As their gazes met and locked, he mouthed the words *thank you,* to her. He acknowledged her nod and smile before he returned his attention to Sarah and Ariel.

Alys tugged on Lara's dress to get her attention. "Now Evan is Ariel's hero," Alys said with a wide, baby-toothed smile.

Lara scrunched down, unmindful of the mud on her wedding gown's hem, and wrapped her arm around the little girl. "Oh, Alys, you know something? I think he's Mommy's hero, too."

* * * * *

The spirit of the holidays...
The magic of romance...
They both come together in

HOLIDAY HONEYMOONS

You're invited as Merline Lovelace and Carole Buck—two of your favorite authors from two of your favorite lines—capture your hearts with five joyous love stories celebrating the excitement that happens when you combine holidays and weddings!

Beginning in October, watch for

HALLOWEEN HONEYMOON by Merline Lovelace
(Desire #1030, 10/96)

Thanksgiving—
WRONG BRIDE, RIGHT GROOM by Merline Lovelace
(Desire #1037, 11/96)

Christmas—
A BRIDE FOR SAINT NICK by Carole Buck
(Intimate Moments #752, 12/96)

New Year's Day—
RESOLVED TO (RE)MARRY by Carole Buck
(Desire #1049, 1/97)

Valentine's Day—
THE 14TH...AND FOREVER by Merline Lovelace
(Intimate Moments #764, 2/97)

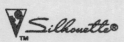

Silhouette®
™

There's nothing quite like a family

REUNION
HANNAH · MICHAEL · KATE

The new miniseries by
Pat Warren

Three siblings are about to be reunited.
And each finds love along the way....

HANNAH
Her life is about to change now that she's met
the irresistible Joel Merrick in HOME FOR HANNAH
(Special Edition #1048, August 1996).

MICHAEL
He's been on his own all his life. Now he's
going to take a risk on love...and
take part in the reunion he's been
waiting for in MICHAEL'S HOUSE
(Intimate Moments #737, September 1996).

KATE
A job as a nanny leads her to Aaron Carver,
his adorable baby daughter and the
fulfillment of her dreams in KEEPING KATE
(Special Edition #1060, October 1996).

Meet these three siblings from

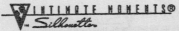

Silhouette SPECIAL EDITION®
and

▼ **INTIMATE MOMENTS**®
™ *Silhouette*

Look us up on-line at: http://www.romance.net

REUNION

This October, be the first to read these wonderful authors as they make their dazzling debuts!

Women to Watch

THE WEDDING KISS by Robin Wells
(Silhouette Romance #1185)
A reluctant bachelor rescues the woman he loves from the man she's about to marry—and turns into a willing groom himself!

THE SEX TEST by Patty Salier
(Silhouette Desire #1032)
A pretty professor learns there's more to making love than meets the eye when she takes lessons from a sexy stranger.

IN A FAMILY WAY by Julia Mozingo
(Special Edition #1062)
A woman without a past finds shelter in the arms of a handsome rancher. Can she trust him to protect her unborn child?

UNDER COVER OF THE NIGHT by Roberta Tobeck
(Intimate Moments #744)
A rugged government agent encounters the woman he has always loved. But past secrets could threaten their future.

DATELESS IN DALLAS by Samantha Carter
(Yours Truly)
A hapless reporter investigates how to find the perfect mate—and winds up falling for her handsome rival!

Don't miss the brightest stars of tomorrow!

Only from ▼ Silhouette®

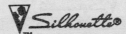

Emparejada con un príncipe

Kat Cantrell

Editado por Harlequin Ibérica.
Una división de HarperCollins Ibérica, S.A.
Núñez de Balboa, 56
28001 Madrid

© 2014 Katrina Williams
© 2016 Harlequin Ibérica, una división de HarperCollins Ibérica, S.A.
Emparejada con un príncipe, n.º 129 - 25.5.16
Título original: Matched to a Prince
Publicada originalmente por Harlequin Enterprises, Ltd.

I.S.B.N.: 978-84-687-7622-4
Depósito legal: M-5538-2016
Impresión en CPI (Barcelona)
Fecha impresion para Argentina: 21.11.16
Distribuidor exclusivo para España: LOGISTA
Distribuidores para México: CODIPLYRSA y Despacho Flores
Distribuidores para Argentina: Interior, DGP, S.A. Alvarado 2118.
Cap. Fed./Buenos Aires y Gran Buenos Aires, VACCARO HNOS.

Capítulo Uno

Cuando el sol estaba a punto de ocultarse sobre el cielo de Occidente, Finn dirigió el helicóptero a la costa. Su turno había terminado y, como siempre, no se pudo resistir a bajar lo suficiente hasta el mar y provocar que el poderoso chorro de aire rizara la azulada superficie del Mediterráneo.

Una garza se alejó de la turbulencia tan rápido como se lo permitieron sus alas, deslizándose por las corrientes de aire con poética belleza. Finn jamás se cansaría de la vista que se dominaba desde la cabina. Jamás se cansaría de proteger la costa del pequeño país que era su hogar.

Cuando aterrizó sobre la equis, apagó el rotor y salió de la cabina antes de que las aspas del Dauphin se detuvieran por completo. El rostro solemne del chófer de su padre lo observaba desde la distancia. Finn no necesitó saber más para comprender que su padre requería su presencia.

—¿Has venido a criticar mi modo de aterrizar, James? —le preguntó Finn con una sonrisa. Sabía que no. Nadie volaba un helicóptero con más precisión y control que él.

—Príncipe Alain —dijo James inclinando la cabeza con deferencia—. Su padre desea hablar con usted. He venido para llevarle.

Finn asintió.

–¿Tengo tiempo de cambiarme?

No sería la primera vez que Finn se presentaba ante el rey con su uniforme de guardacostas de Delamer, pero lo llevaba puesto desde hacía diez horas y tenía las piernas mojadas por un encontronazo con el Mediterráneo mientras rescataban a un nadador que había calculado mal la distancia a la costa.

Todos los días, Finn protegía a la gente mientras sobrevolaba un magnífico panorama de reluciente mar, montañas en la lejanía y pedregosos islotes a poca distancia de la costa.

James le indicó el coche.

–Creo que sería mejor que fuéramos inmediatamente.

El hecho de que su padre quisiera verlo seguramente tenía que ver con una cierta fotografía en la que Finn se tomaba chupitos de Jägermeister en el vientre de una bella rubia o con las acusaciones de corrupción a las que se enfrentaban dos de sus compañeros de correrías.

Un *blogger* había bromeado con que el título oficial de Finn debería ser príncipe Alain Phineas de Montagne y de Escándalo. Al rey no le resultaba tan divertido. El monarca había tratado de combatir la mala prensa con el anuncio oficial del inminente compromiso de Finn, una medida desesperada para conseguir que su hijo sentara la cabeza.

Hasta aquel momento, no había funcionado. Tal vez si su padre pudiera anunciar el nombre de la afortunada novia, la medida podría surtir efecto.

Finn se detuvo en seco ¿Y si su padre había elegido a alguien? Esperaba que no. Cuanto más pudiera posponer lo inevitable, mucho mejor.

Sin embargo, era consciente de que su vida no le pertenecía y de que debería plegarse a la voluntad de su padre, fuera esta cual fuera. No obstante, Finn, como siempre, encontraría el modo de salirse con la suya.

Se metió en el coche y se acomodó en el asiento trasero. Trató de contener el miedo mientras el edificio administrativo de los guardacostas de Delamer desaparecía a sus espaldas y el paisaje del hermoso país se desplegaba a través de las ventanas.

La estación más turística había comenzado oficialmente. Unos llamativos puestos se alineaban en el paseo marítimo, por el que paseaban parejas de la mano y jóvenes madres empujando sillas de bebes. Para Finn, no había un lugar más hermoso en toda la Tierra. Le daba a Dios las gracias todos los días por el privilegio de vivir allí y por tener la oportunidad de servir a su pueblo. Era su deber y lo hacía de buen grado.

El coche se aproximó a las majestuosas verjas del palacio en el que Finn había pasado toda su vida hasta que su madre le permitió mudarse. No había tardado mucho en darse cuenta de que estorbaba. El palacio era el hogar del rey y de la reina y, después, de Alexander y Portia, el príncipe heredero y de su esposa. Finn estaba tan abajo en la línea de sucesión que no existía posibilidad alguna de que pudiera ser rey. No le preocupaba.

Una cuadrilla de trabajadores se afanaba en los jardines que rodeaban el palacio para mantener el famoso diseño de cuatro pisos que rodeaba la fuente principal, que sostenía una estatua del rey Etienne I, que consiguió la independencia de Delamer de Francia hacía ya dos siglos.

Otro empleado, también de aspecto muy solemne, condujo a Finn al despacho que su padre utilizaba para asuntos informales. Un alivio. Eso significaba que Finn podría prescindir del protocolo en aquella ocasión.

Cuando Finn entró, el rey levantó la mirada de los papeles que tenía sobre el antiguo escritorio, que había sido un regalo del presidente de los Estados Unidos. Finn prefería los regalos que se podían beber, en especial si venían con un corcho.

Con una ligera sonrisa, su padre se levantó y señaló el sofá.

—Gracias por venir, hijo. Me disculpo por no haberte avisado con más tiempo.

—No hay problema. No tenía ningún plan. ¿Qué ha sucedido? —preguntó Finn mientras se sentaba en el sofá.

El rey Laurent se cruzó de brazos y se apoyó en el escritorio.

—Tenemos que progresar en lo de encontrarte una esposa —dijo.

Finn se rebulló en el incómodo sofá.

—Ya te dije que me contentaría con quien tú eligieras.

Mentira. Él simplemente toleraría a quien su padre eligiera. Si su esposa y él terminaban siendo amigos, tal y como había ocurrido con sus padres, genial. Sin embargo, aquello era pedirle mucho a un matrimonio concertado. No era que Finn no hubiera conocido el amor. Lo había vivido con la única mujer por la que se había permitido sentir algo.

El rostro de Juliet, enmarcado por un sedoso cabello castaño, inundó su pensamiento. Tragó saliva. Cien rubias con chupitos no eran capaces de borrar el recuerdo de la mujer que lo había traicionado de la manera más pública y humillante posible.

—Sea como fuere, se me ha sugerido una opción que no había considerado. Una casamentera.

—¿Una qué?

—Una casamentera de los Estados Unidos se ha puesto en contacto conmigo a través de mi secretaria. Ha pedido una oportunidad para trabajar para nosotros haciendo una unión de prueba. Si no te gustan los resultados, no nos cobrará.

A Finn le olía mal aquel asunto.

—¿Y por qué te has parado a considerar algo así?

¿Se trataba de otro plan para someterlo a su padre? ¿Había pagado el rey a aquella casamentera para preparar una unión con una mujer que fuera leal a la corona y que, por lo tanto, él pudiera controlar fácilmente?

—Esa mujer le presentó su esposa a Stafford Walker. He hecho suficientes negocios con él para saber que sus recomendaciones son sólidas. Si esa mujer no hubiera mencionado su nombre, jamás habría considerado la idea —suspiró el rey mientras se frotaba el entrecejo con gesto cansado—. Hijo, quiero que seas feliz. Me gustó lo que esa mujer me dijo sobre un proceso de selección. Tú necesitas a alguien muy concreto, que no tenga mala prensa. Esa mujer me prometió emparejarte con la esposa perfecta para ti. Me pareció un buen trato.

Un fuerte sentimiento de culpa se apoderó de Finn.

—Lo siento. Has sido muy paciente conmigo. Ojalá…

Había estado a punto de decir que ojalá supiera por qué había causado tantos problemas, pero conocía perfectamente la razón. Unos ojos del color de la hierba fresca, una piel resplandeciente y una obstinación más fuerte que las verjas de palacio.

Tal vez aquella casamentera pudiera encontrar a alguien que pudiera sustituir a Juliet en el corazón de Finn. Podría ocurrir.

—He hecho que investiguen minuciosamente a esta casamentera, Elise Arundel, pero te recomiendo que lo hagas tú por tu cuenta. Si no te gusta la idea, no lo hagas, pero yo he tenido tan poca suerte para encontrarte una candidata… En realidad, candidatas no faltan —añadió el rey sonriendo por primera vez desde que Finn entró en el despacho—. El problema es que no existe la que pueda contigo.

Finn sonrió también.

—Al menos en eso estamos de acuerdo.

Finn se parecía mucho a su padre. Los dos tenían grandes corazones y unas personalidades más grandes aún, todo ello con un gran sentido del deber que formaba parte innata de ellos como miembros de la realeza. Amaban profundamente a Delamer y al pueblo al que servían.

El padre conseguía hacerlo con gracia y propiedad. Finn, por otro lado, tendía a tener fallos que a los fotógrafos les encantaba inmortalizar. Por supuesto, una fotografía jamás podría reflejar el corazón roto que lo empujaba a buscar la manera, fuera la que fuera, de borrar el dolor.

Lo comprendía todo y no le importaba la idea de casarse, en especial para salvarse de la vorágine de los medios. Encontrar a una mujer a la que pudiera amar al mismo tiempo sería una bendición añadida. Sentar la cabeza y tener hijos le atraía si pudiera hacerlo con alguien que le diera lo que tan desesperadamente necesitaba: un refugio en el que pudiera ser un hombre en vez de un príncipe.

Las probabilidades de que una casamentera encontrara a la candidata ideal... Bueno, tenía más posibilidades de apostar mil al rojo y ganar.

—Hablaré con la señora Arundel.

Finn se lo debía a su padre. Debía tratar de encontrar el modo de detener lo que le causaba sufrimiento. También se lo debía a su país. Debía reflejar una imagen positiva de los Couronne en la prensa internacional. Si eso significaba aceptar a la candidata que eligiera la casamentera y procurar que todo saliera bien, así lo haría.

Los ojos del rey reflejaron alivio. Su padre lo quería mucho y deseaba lo mejor para él. ¿Por qué no podía él hacer lo que debía, como hacían siempre sus hermanos? Alexander sería el rey algún día, y tenía siempre presente lo que era su deber. El comportamiento del heredero estaba por encima de todo reproche. Alexander jamás les había causado a sus padres un momento de preocupación.

Finn, por el contrario, era el hermano juerguista. Por suerte, no se le necesitaba. Un matrimonio ventajoso sería su oportunidad para hacer algo bien, algo que fuera de valor para la corona.

—A ella le gustaría que volaras a Dallas, Texas, para conocerte en persona —dijo el rey—. Tan pronto como sea posible.

Dallas. Finn nunca había estado allí. Por lo menos se podría comprar un sombrero vaquero.

—Tengo turno mañana, pero puedo ir pasado.

El rey le colocó una mano en el hombro a Finn.

—Me parece bien.

Finn bajó la cabeza y se encogió de hombros.

—Ya veremos. ¿Qué es lo peor que me puede ocurrir?

Finn se arrepintió inmediatamente de haber pronunciado aquellas palabras. El escándalo lo perseguía sin que pudiera librarse de él. La traición de Juliet había sido el primero, pero ciertamente no el último. Simplemente había sido el que más le había dolido.

Ese había sido el desencadenante de todo. Ella le había hecho tanto daño… Finn la amaba desesperadamente y descubrió que ella no sentía lo mismo. Si ella le hubiera amado, jamás habría participado en una protesta contra todo lo que era importante para él: su padre, el ejército y las bases de la estructura de gobierno a las que había jurado lealtad eterna.

Menuda ironía… Las dos cosas que más le gustaban de Juliet eran la pasión y el compromiso que ella tenía por su familia. Sin esos sentimientos, ella sería un ser sin interés ni brillo. Sin esos sentimientos, la protesta no habría tenido lugar.

No importaba. Juliet se había encargado de aplastar todos los sentimientos que tenía hacia ella. A excepción de la ira. De la ira aún disponía a montones.

Con cierta tristeza, dejó que James lo llevara de vuelta a la base de guardacostas donde tenía aparcado su Aventador. Toda su vida se podía resumir en una única frase: una espada de doble filo. Fuera como fuera como la blandiera, terminaba cortándole. Sería hombre y príncipe hasta el día en el que muriera. Parecía que el destino le impedía satisfacer ambas facetas al mismo tiempo.

Sin embargo, un pequeño hilo de esperanza le empujaba a creer que aquella casamentera podría ayudarle a cambiar las cosas.

Juliet Villere no comprendía la fascinación de los estadounidenses por la conversación sobre temas triviales. Resultaba muy aburrido.

El salón de baile estaba a rebosar. No era el lugar en el que le apetecía estar, lo que, unido además al deseo de evitar seguir hablando sobre el ridículo juego que los confusos estadounidenses denominaban fútbol, la empujó a terminar en un rincón. La pared le protegía la espalda y le proporcionaba un estupendo escudo para evitar las miradas que le hacían arder la piel.

¿Por qué no le había dicho nadie que una transformación exterior no la transformaba también mágicamente en su interior? Ni el maquillaje ni el elegante vestido podían convertir a Juliet en alguien a quien le gustara el lápiz de labios. Ni las fiestas.

Sin embargo, estaba en deuda con Elise Arundel por haberla aceptado cuando salió huyendo de Delamer para buscar algo que pudiera curar por arte de magia el dolor continuo que le había producido la traición de Finn. Aquella era la única razón por la que había accedido a asistir a aquel evento de tanto postín, que contaba con muchos de los clientes de Elise. Tal vez ella no se diera cuenta si Juliet se marchaba de la fiesta y regresaba a la casa de Elise, donde Juliet residía hasta que la casamentera le encontrara un esposo en los Estados Unidos. Solo estaba a un par de kilómetros de allí y había practicado a andar con tacones lo suficiente como para que no le dolieran los pies.

Entonces, se percató de que Elise la estaba observando.

–¿Te estás divirtiendo? –le preguntó Elise al llegar a su lado.

–Sí, mucho.

Elise se percató inmediatamente de la ironía de aquellas palabras y sonrió.

–Te invité a esta fiesta para que puedas practicar a relacionarte socialmente. Esconderte en un rincón no te va a ayudar a conseguirlo.

–No tengo nada que decir sobre fútbol… –dijo ella mientras se colocaba la cinturilla del vestido verde que Dannie Reynolds, su nueva amiga, le había ayudado a elegir–. Por eso, me estoy relacionando con los beneficios de la soledad.

Elise se echó a reír.

–En ese caso, baila con alguien. Así no tendrás que hablar.

Juliet sacudió la cabeza. Ella tan solo había bailado con Finn y no quería que aquello cambiara.

Un dolor agudo y fuerte le atenazó el estómago. Cruzar el Atlántico no le había ayudado a olvidarse de él. Finn le hizo pedazos el alma hacía más de un año. ¿No debería haberse olvidado ya de él?

Sin embargo, el anuncio de su inminente compromiso le había hecho el daño suficiente para hacerla huir de Delamer a Dallas.

—No veo por qué tengo que bailar con uno de esos hombres.

Como no veía motivo para tener uñas postizas ni para pintarse los labios. Sin embargo, no le correspondía a ella cuestionar la fórmula que Elise utilizaba en su empresa.

—Ninguno de ellos será mi pareja —añadió—. Y, además, solo piensan en el deporte.

Juliet hizo ademán de poner mala cara, pero recordó que no podía hacerlo. En realidad, se suponía que tampoco debía ser tan franca a la hora de hablar. Su futuro esposo querría una esposa refinada que tuviera habilidad para mezclarse con la alta sociedad, no una mujer que resultara descarada.

¿Cómo iba a poder fingir de ese modo durante el resto de su vida? Seguramente, del mismo modo que fingía que el corazón no se le había roto cuando perdió al hombre que amaba, a su hermano pequeño y la vida que llevaba en Delamer.

Podía soportar cualquier cosa si eso conseguía emparejarla con un esposo que pudiera ayudarla a quedarse en los Estados Unidos y así no tener que ser testigo de cómo Finn se casaba con otra mujer.

Elise sacudió la cabeza y soltó una carcajada.

–No, no. No te contengas. Dime lo que sientes realmente. ¿Qué te parece si te ahorro más suspense y te digo que tengo pareja para ti?

Juliet sintió que el corazón se le paraba. Ya estaba. La razón por la que había ido a Estados Unidos.

¿Cómo sería su futuro esposo? ¿Le gustaría nadar y navegar? ¿Podría ella pedirle que la llevara de vacaciones a la playa? ¿Le importaría que su familia viniera a visitarla ocasionalmente? ¿Tendría una bonita sonrisa y se reiría mucho?

Lo más importante, ¿sería ella capaz de sentir algo por él para poder llenar el vacío que había dejado Finn en su interior?

Aunque Elise le garantizara una unión por amor, seguramente sería demasiado esperar que ese hombre pudiera reemplazar a Finn.

Tendría que conformarse. No le quedaba otra.

Tragó saliva para aplacar la quemazón que de repente sintió en la garganta.

–No te ha llevado mucho tiempo. Terminé el cuestionario ayer mismo.

Elise se encogió de hombros y se volvió a mirar hacia la pista de baile. Al hacerlo, le dio a Juliet un suave golpecito con el hombro.

–A veces, en cuanto cargo el perfil, no se me relaciona con alguien que ya esté en el sistema y tenemos que esperar hasta que entren nuevos clientes. En tu caso, saltó inmediatamente.

Juliet quería preguntar el nombre y, al mismo tiempo, quería esconderse debajo de la mesa.

Aquel hombre seguramente esperaría una cierta

clase de mujer, una que pudiera servir de anfitriona en sus fiestas, relacionarse con sus amigos y sonreír constantemente mientras charlaban sobre fusiones de negocios y pagos de impuestos. Y de fútbol. Esa mujer no era ella.

Quería marcharse a su casa. Entonces, pensó de nuevo en la vida que tendría en Delamer. Allí, vería todos los días el helicóptero de Finn volando por el cielo azul. O se encontraría con fotografías de él cortando la cinta en una nueva escuela... Jamás olvidaría aquella fotografía...

Una niña que asistía a la escuela primaria que él había acudido a inaugurar se le acercó y le rodeó el muslo con los brazos justo en el momento en el que Finn cortaba la cinta. Al terminar, Finn se inclinó sobre ella para darle un beso en la mejilla. El momento quedó inmortalizado por medio de las cientos de cámaras y de teléfonos móviles que estaban presentes.

Juliet no podía olvidar aquella muestra de la naturaleza cercana y encantadora del príncipe. Era un hombre tan agradable, con un sentido del humor que a ella le encantaba... hasta que se dio cuenta de la testarudez y la obstinación con la que Finn se negaba a ver el daño que él le había hecho al ponerse del lado de su padre. No había manera de razonar con Finn, y eso mancillaba el resto de sus buenas cualidades.

En Delamer, había también recordatorios constantes del vacío que la muerte de su hermano Bernard había dejado.

Cualquier esposo era mejor que todo eso.

15

–¿Qué ocurre si no me gusta el hombre que tu ordenador haya elegido? –le preguntó Juliet.

–No hay verdades absolutas. Si no te gusta, encontraremos a otra persona, aunque me podría llevar un tiempo. Sin embargo… Me gustaría que mantuvieras la mente abierta sobre las posibilidades. Este hombre es perfecto para ti. Jamás he visto dos personas que fueran más compatibles. Ni siquiera Leo y Dannie estaban tan bien alineados y mira lo bien que ha salido esa unión.

Juliet asintió. Dannie y Leo Reynolds eran ciertamente una de las parejas más enamoradas de todos los tiempos, y ni siquiera se habían visto antes del día en el que se casaron. Si Elise decía que ese hombre era la pareja perfecta para Juliet, ¿por qué dudarlo?

–Esta noche tenía un motivo adicional para invitarte a esta fiesta –confesó Elise–. Tu pareja estará aquí también. Vendrá muy pronto. Pensé que si os conocíais en un acto social te quitaría a ti presión.

Su pareja.

Juliet había esperado poder tener tiempo para conocer detalles sobre él antes de conocerlo. Se tocó el cabello. Al menos, conocería a su futuro esposo mientras estaba absolutamente impecable. Una pequeña victoria.

Respiró profundamente. Su hermano Bernard querría que fuera feliz, que siguiera con su vida. El recuerdo de la sonrisa de su hermano le dio ánimos.

De repente, un revuelo entre todos los presentes captó la atención de Juliet. Los invitados estiraban el cuello para tratar de ver y susurraban entre ellos mientras señalaban hacia la puerta principal.

–¿Qué es lo que pasa? –preguntó.

Elise susurró una palabra muy poco femenina.

–Esperaba poder tener algo más de tiempo para explicarme. Es tu pareja –dijo tras aclararse la garganta–. Ha llegado temprano. Creo que eso es una buena cualidad en un hombre. Es decir, además de todas las otras que tiene, claro está. ¿No te parece?

Su futuro esposo, asumiendo que todo fuera según el plan, acababa de entrar en el salón de baile. El pulso de Juliet se desató.

–Claro. ¿Pero por qué me parece que estás tratando de convencerme de algo? ¿Es que tiene dos cabezas o algo así?

–Para encontrar tu pareja, he hecho algo muy poco ortodoxo –confesó Elise mientras se mordía el labio. Entonces, agarró a Juliet del brazo–. Algo que espero que comprendas. Ha sido una prueba. Decidí que si el ordenador no os emparejaba, no te diría nada. No te contaría nada y os encontraría otra pareja a cada uno de los dos.

–¿De qué estás hablando? ¿Qué has hecho?

Elise sonrió débilmente.

–Has hablado tanto de él… Comprendí que aún lo tenías en tu corazón. No me podía considerar una casamentera si no os daba la oportunidad de redescubrir por qué os enamorasteis en un principio.

Juliet comenzó a sentir un sudor frío.

–¿De quién te he hablado yo?

–Del príncipe Alain. De Finn –respondió Elise. Entonces, señaló la entrada–. Él es tu pareja.

–¡Dios mío, Elise! –exclamó Juliet con incredulidad e ira a la vez–. Dios mío…

Efectivamente, allí estaba Finn. En el salón de baile. Él era su pareja. No el apacible estadounidense que se conformaba con ver el fútbol y que la salvaría del sufrimiento que Finn le había causado.

–Abre la mente –le recordó Elise. Entonces, le agarró la mano para obligarla a dar un paso al frente y tiró de ella hacia la puerta del salón–. Ven a saludarle. Dame diez minutos. Deja que os explique a los dos y luego me puedes regañar todo lo que quieras por lo que he hecho. O podéis pasar ese tiempo recuperando vuestra relación. Tal vez incluso dándoos una oportunidad. Vosotros elegís.

Juliet observó con avidez la multitud, buscando un rostro familiar. De repente, se encontró con un fuerte cuerpo vestido de traje oscuro y flanqueado por un discreto equipo de seguridad que se dirigía hacia ella.

Finn. Exactamente como lo recordaba su corazón.

Alto, guapo, seguro de sí mismo. Con toda seguridad el hombre que podría soportar el peso de una corona a pesar de que era improbable que así fuera. Músculos duros y definidos ocultos bajo un esmoquin que no conseguía disimular la belleza de su cuerpo. El cabello oscuro tenía, a pesar de que siempre lo llevaba muy corto, cierta tendencia a rizarse cuando lo dejaba crecer un poco. Y aquella maravillosa sonrisa…

Hasta que se detuvo delante de Elise y vio a Juliet. La sonrisa se heló un poco al mirar alternativamente a las dos mujeres.

–Señora Arundel, me alegro de volver a verla.

Finn extendió la mano y asió la de Elise antes de darle un suave beso en la mejilla como si fueran viejos amigos. Entonces, se dirigió a Juliet.

–Señorita Villere. Qué sorpresa tan agradable. No sabía que estaba usted en este lado del mundo.

A pesar del hielo de su voz, Juliet sintió que el estómago le daba un vuelco, como le ocurría siempre que estaba junto a Finn.

–La sorpresa es mutua –le aseguró ella, casi sin poder respirar. Las paredes del salón parecían cerrarse sobre ella y arrebatarle así el aire que flotaba en la sala–. Sin embargo, me reservo todavía la opinión sobre si es agradable o no.

Su lengua la había vuelto a traicionar. De repente, fue consciente del modo en el que la miraban muchos de los presentes y comprendió que muchas personas eran testigos de la reunión pública entre el príncipe Alain y una mujer que sin duda conocía. No se tardaría mucho en buscar fotos y vídeos, además de noticias sobre el escándalo.

La expresión de él se ensombreció.

–Asegúrese de informarme cuando lo decida. Si me perdona, tengo un asunto que tratar con la señora Arundel que no es de su interés.

Capítulo Dos

No dejaba de mirar a Juliet, atravesándola con unos ojos azules y duros como el acero.

Tras la muerte de su hermano, Finn la abandonó cuando ella más lo necesitaba. Juliet jamás se lo perdonaría.

—¡Yo no he tenido nada que ver con esto! —dijo ella con las manos en las caderas—. Pensaba que te ibas a casar. ¿Qué le ha pasado a tu princesa? ¿Por qué le has pedido ayuda a una casamentera?

Un músculo se tensó en la frente de Finn.

—Mi padre quiere que me case en cuanto encuentre una candidata. Eso es lo que estoy haciendo aquí. Me prometieron la candidata perfecta. Ya lo veo.

¿Finn no estaba prometido? ¿Ni siquiera tenía candidata alguna en perspectiva? Juliet se había marchado de Delamer basándose en algo que ni siquiera era cierto.

—Sí, lo mismo digo yo. Eso fue lo que me prometieron a mí.

Se volvieron a mirar a Elise los dos a la vez. Ella sonrió y los acompañó a los dos a un lugar más reservado. Los guardaespaldas de Finn se quedaron cerca, tratando de pasar desapercibidos.

—¿Recordáis la pregunta sobre el amor que había en el perfil? —les preguntó—. Os pregunté a los dos a qué estaríais dispuestos a renunciar para conseguirlo. ¿Cuál fue tu respuesta, Juliet?

Ella se cruzó de brazos y miró a Elise con desaprobación. Entonces, repitió su respuesta.

—No se debería renunciar a nada por amor. Debería ser algo que no requiriera esfuerzo alguno. Si no, no es amor verdadero.

Nada de compromiso. ¿Por qué tendría ella que reorganizar todas sus creencias para acomodarse a un hombre demasiado testarudo? El hombre adecuado para ella debería reconocer que había tratado de desbaratar el estado de cosas solo porque se había visto obligada a hacerlo.

El hombre adecuado para ella debería saber que él lo había sido todo para ella.

—¿Y tú, Finn? —le preguntó Elise.

La mirada de él se suavizó. Suspiró. Habló mirando directamente a Juliet.

—No se debería tener que renunciar a nada. El amor debería ser fácil y natural, como respirar. Nadie te pide que dejes de respirar para que el corazón pueda latir.

Él lo había hecho. Quería que olvidara que Bernard había muerto sirviendo al ego del rey, llevando puesto el mismo uniforme que Finn se podía todos los días. Juliet cerró los ojos y apretó con fuerza los párpados. Entonces, apartó aquel pensamiento. Era demasiado.

—Fácil y natural. Esa parte no ha sido difícil.

Con esas palabras, los aspectos buenos y más especiales de su relación con Finn iluminaron la oscuridad que se había apoderado de ella por dentro.

Todo había sido fácil entre ellos. No había requerido ningún esfuerzo. Si Bernard no hubiera tenido aquel accidente, probablemente Finn y ella estarían felizmente casados.

—No, no lo ha sido —dijo Finn sin apartar los ojos de Juliet. Parecía estar buscando algo que se parecía mucho a lo que Juliet deseaba constantemente: el modo de poder regresar atrás en el tiempo.

Desgraciadamente, eso era imposible. Pensó de nuevo en la razón por la que ella había salido huyendo a los Estados Unidos. Se marchó de Delamer porque pensaba que Finn se iba a casar con otra mujer. Si aquello no era cierto, ¿qué más cosas tendría que revaluar?

Elise extendió las manos y las colocó suavemente sobre el brazo de cada uno de ellos, uniéndolos.

—¿Recordáis lo que dijisteis sobre lo que estáis buscando en una relación?

—La tranquilidad en la tormenta —contestó Juliet. Su ira fue desapareciendo para verse reemplazado por un pequeño hilo de esperanza.

—Un lugar en el que yo pudiera simplemente estar, sin el resto de las presiones de la vida —dijo Finn con la voz algo ronca—. Así fue como respondí a esa pregunta.

—¿Y qué? Respondimos un par de preguntas de la misma manera. No es de extrañar.

Finn asintió.

—A mí me habría sorprendido si no hubiéramos respondido de un modo similar.

Siempre habían pensado igual. Eran dos corazones latiendo como si fueran uno. Cuando salían juntos a navegar, las palabras sobraban. Se coordinaban perfectamente. Se conocieron mientras salían a navegar con amigos mutuos. Luego se enamoraron cuando los dos salieron a la mar una y otra vez en el barco de Finn.

—En ese caso —dijo Elise alegremente—, tal vez sería mejor preguntar si los dos os podéis olvidar del pasado y ver cómo podríais haber cambiado. Estáis en Estados Unidos. Lo que os separaba en Delamer aquí no importa. Estáis a salvo. Tomaos tiempo en terreno neutral para averiguar si ese amor sin esfuerzo sigue existiendo.

Aquello era completamente innecesario. Juliet nunca había dejado de amar a Finn y estar allí, en su presencia, un largo y frío año después parecía remarcar el hecho de que jamás dejaría de hacerlo. Sin embargo, eso no significaba que pudieran estar juntos.

—¿Eres consejera de pareja o casamentera? —le preguntó a Elise sin poder contenerse.

—Las dos cosas. Hago lo que sea necesario para que una pareja encuentre la felicidad.

Felicidad. Aquello no había formado parte de su lista de requerimientos cuando fue a ver a Elise, desesperada por encontrar una solución que terminara con su dolor. Sin embargo, en vez de un esposo estadounidense, se le había dado la posibilidad de tener una segunda oportunidad con Finn.

En realidad, él era el único hombre al que se le pudiera considerar su media naranja. El único hombre al que ella había querido dar acceso a su corazón. Esa era la verdad y, de algún modo, Elise se había dado cuenta.

Menudo programa de ordenador el de Elise... Juliet había esperado un poco de magia. Y tal vez había conseguido su deseo.

—Elise tiene razón —susurró Finn—. Estamos en terreno neutral. Aquí la política no importa y es una fiesta. Baila conmigo.

Juliet asintió, esperando de corazón que aquella rendición no fuera la mayor tontería que hubiera hecho nunca.

Elise se apartó de ellos. Ni siquiera trataba de ocultar el alivio que llevaba reflejado en el rostro.

Los ojos de Juliet se llenaron de lágrimas al sentir que algo parecido al optimismo se apoderaba de su alma. Disfrutaría de aquellas horas con Finn y tal vez estas les conducirían a algo más. Tal vez el tiempo y la distancia habían diluido sus diferencias.

Tal vez él había comprendido por fin que lo que su apoyo y fuerza significaban para Juliet. Hacía un año, ella había perdido mucho más que un hermano. También había perdido el amor de su vida.

Finn condujo a Juliet hasta la pista de baile. Aquello fue un pequeño milagro en sí mismo, dado que las rodillas no le respondían.

Todo aquel asunto era ridículo. Desde el momento en el que una casamentera se había dirigido a su padre, Finn había sospechado algo. Sin embargo, jamás se habría imaginado el resultado de aquel viaje a Dallas.

¿Qué diría el rey cuando se diera cuenta de lo que había hecho sin querer? Finn había sido empa-

24

rejado con una mujer que le había causado a su familia mucho sufrimiento y que había provocado un escándalo cuyos efectos eran imposibles de limitar.

Sin embargo, Juliet y él habían vuelto a reunirse, emparejados por el que se suponía que era un programa de ordenador infalible. Todos a los que había consultado hablaban maravillas del proceso de EA International, de Elise y de lo mucho que se involucraba con las personas a las que ayudaba. Por eso, Finn se había sometido a las pruebas de Elise, había realizado el perfil y había respondido a todas las preguntas.

Ver que Juliet volvía a estar en su vida sin advertencia alguna... Lo más sensato habría sido darse la vuelta y marcharse sin mirar atrás. Quedarse allí era la manera más sencilla de asegurarse haber perdido por completo la cabeza al final de la velada.

Le había pedido a Juliet que bailara con él tan solo porque los buenos modales se le habían inculcado desde el nacimiento. Elise había organizado aquella fiesta y eran socios en los negocios. Tal solo era una cortesía hacia ella.

Sin embargo, en aquellos momentos ya no estaba tan seguro de que fuera la única razón. Al ver a Juliet de nuevo, se había despertado en él una oleada de sentimientos que había creído enterrados hasta entonces. Entre esos sentimientos, destacaba el deseo de recibir la cabeza de Juliet en una bandeja... después de haber disfrutado de su cuerpo en una cama.

Tomó a Juliet entre sus brazos y los dos empezaron a bailar. Tardaron instantes en encontrar el ritmo que siempre habían compartido. Miró su rostro, aquellos ojos verdes que jamás había olvidado y sintió que algo se aflojaba en su interior.

Era Juliet… Y se había transformado.

Los cambios eran externos. A él le gustaba exactamente el aspecto que ella tenía la última vez que la vio, pero, ¿y si había cambiado en ella algo más que su cabello?

La tenía entre sus brazos. Resultaba difícil seguir aferrándose a la ira que llevaba arrastrando un año entero.

—Pareces diferente —comentó—. Sorprendente. Y muy hermosa. Te has maquillado.

Ella parpadeó y sonrió. Incluso su altura era diferente. Finn le miró los pies y vio que llevaba unas sensuales sandalias en los delicados pies. Las hebillas le rodeaban los tobillos destacando aún más lo bien torneadas que tenía las piernas. De repente, se imaginó desabrochando aquellas hebillas con los dientes.

Dios. Bailar se había convertido oficialmente en una forma de tortura.

Ella seguía siendo la misma chica que le había dado una puñalada por la espalda y, al mismo tiempo… No lo era. La tensión se apoderó de él.

—Gracias. Elise me dio unos consejos para resultar más femenina —respondió ella. Entonces, extendió la mano y le mostró unas uñas pintadas de color coral—. No esperes que ice ninguna vela con estas manos.

Finn sonrió sin poder evitarlo. Si ella se iba a comportar como si no hubiera ocurrido nada, él también podría hacerlo.

—Yo haré todo el trabajo duro. Mirarte es suficiente recompensa para todos mis esfuerzos.

Ella alzó las cejas muy sorprendida. Apretó con fuerza la mano que tenía en la cintura de él.

—¿Te gusta mi nueva imagen?

Finn era capaz de sentir aquellas uñas a través de la chaqueta. ¿Cómo era eso posible?

—Me gustaba la Juliet de antes. Sin embargo, la nueva también está muy bien. Estás muy guapa. ¿Qué te ha animado a hacer esto?

Uñas largas, cabello recogido, un sugerente vestido con la espalda al descubierto. En aquellos momentos, merecía la pena volverse a mirar a Juliet varias veces.

—Es parte del acuerdo con Elise. Ella tiene muchos clientes masculinos muy influyentes y con un perfil muy alto, y esas personas esperan un cierto refinamiento en sus posibles parejas. Se pasa un par de meses mejorándonos, aunque tengo que admitir que se pasó mucho más tiempo conmigo que con las demás. Soy una mujer nueva. Cenicienta a tu servicio. ¿Acaso no te dijo cómo funcionaba esto?

—No en esos términos. Era más bien una garantía general que la mujer con la que me emparejara sería capaz de enfrentarse a todo lo que supone ser una princesa.

En el caso de Juliet, aquel jamás había sido un factor. A Finn no le podría haber importado menos si ella no respetaba el protocolo de la familia real o si jamás se había maquillado. No le había importado porque, érase una vez, entonces estaba enamorado de ella.

—¿Te desilusiona haberte encontrado conmigo?

—Sinceramente no sé lo que siento —respondió él con una carcajada—, pero desilusión no es.

Juliet podría haber sido una gran princesa. Siempre había comprendido la necesidad que Finn tenía de escapar de su posición social en ciertas ocasiones. Finn se entregaba al cien por cien a su trabajo protegiendo a los ciudadanos de Delamer, participaba de buen grado en eventos benéficos y no se sentía culpable en absoluto por tener sus momentos alejado del ojo público. Muchas mujeres no lo comprenderían. Insistirían en disfrutar de lo mejor.

A Juliet le había bastado con una cita en la playa o con salir a navegar. E incluso quedarse en casa, que era una de las cosas que más le gustaban a Finn. No. En realidad no era una sorpresa que el ordenador los hubiera emparejado.

Ver lo mucho que seguía aún deseándola a pesar de la llama presente de la traición le sorprendió mucho.

—¿Y tú? —le preguntó él—. ¿Ha decidido ya el jurado si volver a verme es una sorpresa agradable?

—El jurado está ocupado tratando de no tropezarse con tus pies con estos tacones.

Aquella respuesta hizo que él sonriera y se relajara. Mientras los dos mantuvieran el sentido del humor, se encontraban en terreno neutral. La noche era joven.

—Vayamos a tomar una copa de champán. Me muero por saber cómo terminaste en la base de datos de una casamentera de Dallas.

Cuando se dieron la vuelta para salir de la pista de baile, un flash comenzó una rápida sucesión de disparos.

Finn suspiró. Con la diferencia horaria, la llama-da de teléfono de su padre llegaría a medianoche, a menos que la secretaria del rey no se percatara de la historia, lo que era poco probable.

Finn le pediría a Elise que lo emparejara con otra persona. Más tarde.

Juliet esperó hasta que él la condujo al bar y le entregó una copa de champán Veuve Clicquot antes de responder.

—Es culpa tuya que yo buscara a Elise.

—¿Mía? —le preguntó él mientras brindaba chocando su copa contra la de Juliet antes de tomar un buen trago del espumoso—. Ni siquiera sabía que Elise existiera hasta hace unos días.

—Fue el anuncio del compromiso. Si tú ibas a seguir con tu vida, yo también tenía que hacerlo y no podía hacerlo en Delamer. Por eso estoy aquí —añadió.

Juliet extendió las manos. Al verle de nuevo las uñas, Finn no pudo evitar imaginar lo que sería sentirlas en la cintura cuando se hubiera despojado de la chaqueta y la camisa.

De repente, la temperatura del salón de baile pareció subir rápidamente.

—Como ya te he dicho, no hay compromiso. Todavía no. Mi padre y yo hemos acordado que ya era hora de que yo pensara en sentar la cabeza y comenzara a buscar esposa. Y aquí estoy.

Aquello ponía las cosas en perspectiva. Los dos habían tratado de superar el escándalo y la ruptura buscando alguien nuevo.

—Por mucho que he tratado de evitarlo, he visto las pruebas fotográficas de por qué tu padre pensaba que necesitabas sentar la cabeza. Te has convertido en el príncipe juerguista. No me parece propio de ti. Por supuesto, nos divertimos mucho bailando en las discotecas, pero normalmente nos marchábamos después de una hora o así. ¿Acaso no íbamos a las fiestas en las que te gustaba quedarte?

—Yo no quería quedarme en ninguna. Tan solo pensaba en conseguir que nos quedáramos a solas.

—Algunas de las fotografías resultan difíciles de asimilar —admitió ella. Finn no necesitó que se explicara más.

Siempre había sabido que, seguramente, ella vería todas las fotografías que le hacían con otras mujeres y oiría hablar de sus hazañas. Sin embargo, jamás había considerado que llegarían a hablar al respecto. En realidad, no había mucho del año anterior que le enorgulleciera.

—Dado que estamos repartiendo la culpa, eso fue tuya.

Ella lo miró con sorpresa.

—¿Cómo?

—Bueno, culpa tuya del todo no, pero yo estaba tratando de ahogar los recuerdos. Centrarme en el futuro. Seguir con mi vida, como tú dijiste.

—¿Y funcionó?

—En absoluto.

Sus miradas se cruzaron. Finn sintió un hormigueo en los labios. Quería estrecharla entre los brazos y besarla hasta que ninguno de los dos pudiera recordar nada más que lo bien que estaban juntos.

Juliet se tomó el resto del champán como si no se hubiera dado cuenta de lo que había pasado en cada instante. Finn deseó poder decir lo mismo al sentir cómo la sangre le abandonaba la cabeza para dirigirse al sur y formar una espectacular erección.

–¿Y ahora qué hacemos? –le preguntó ella.

–Ven a cenar conmigo. Mañana por la noche –replicó él con voz ronca–. Por los viejos tiempos.

Ninguno de los dos pensaba que aquel emparejamiento fuera buena idea. Finn lo sabía, pero no se podía resistir a disfrutar de una horas prohibidas con Juliet. Fuera lo que fuera lo que ella había hecho en el pasado, no podía marcharse de aquel salón sin volver a verla nunca más.

–Debería dejar que me examinaran la cabeza, pero está bien.

Por suerte, la aceptación de Juliet llegó en el momento adecuado. Una esbelta mujer y su amiga estuvieron a punto de empujar a Juliet por el entusiasmo que mostraron al intentar hacerse una foto con él.

Juliet siempre sería la mujer que había quemado una bandera de Delamer frente a las verjas de palacio. Sus compatriotas no olvidaban fácilmente los actos de deslealtad a la corona.

Ni él tampoco.

El hecho de cruzar un océano no creaba una dinámica diferente entre dos personas. Juliet no vería nunca que él no podía ir contra su padre ni comprendería nunca que, como segundo hijo suyo, Finn no tenía mucho que ofrecer a la corona aparte de un apoyo incondicional.

Si Juliet lo comprendía algún día, se le perdonarían todos sus pecados. Le perdonaría todo el mundo y él también.

Eso ocurriría el día que nevara en Delamer durante el mes de julio. Hasta entonces, disfrutaría de Juliet, ignoraría el resto y, después, le pediría a Elise que le buscara otra pareja.

Capítulo Tres

Juliet miró fijamente al espejo y trató de concentrarse para aplicarse la sombra de ojos del modo en el que Dannie y Elise le habían enseñado. Desgraciadamente, era incapaz de centrarse.

El mejor modo de describir el estado en el que Finn la dejó la noche anterior era asombrada y sin aliento. Ese estado no había logrado despejarse en las veinticuatro horas subsiguientes. El aroma limpio de Finn flotaba alrededor de ella, evocando recuerdos compartidos con él para llegar dolorosamente a la conclusión de que no sentía nada por ella. No le había importado su dolor al perder a su hermano. Lo único que le importaba a Finn era ponerse el uniforme de guardacostas de Delamer y lucirlo con orgullo nacionalista.

Era una locura. ¿Por qué había accedido a aquella cita?

Elise asomó la cabeza por la puerta del dormitorio de Juliet.

—¿Ya estás casi lista? Oh. ¡Pero si aún no te has vestido! ¿Qué te vas a poner?

—Quiero ponerme algo que le demuestre a Finn lo que he tenido que soportar en esta transformación por él. Cuanto más sexy, mejor.

—En ese caso, ponte el vestido amarillo. Y te he

traído algo –añadió Elise mostrándole un estuche de terciopelo.

Perpleja, Juliet lo abrió. Se trataba de un colgante de corazón realizado en plata que pendía de una cadena a juego. Otro corazón colgaba del primero, como si estuvieran aferrándose el uno al otro para no caer.

–Es muy bonito. Gracias.

Elise se lo puso alrededor del cuello.

–Les regalo siempre a todas mis clientas un collar. Me alegro de que te guste.

Cuando el coche aparcó frente a la casa de Elise, Juliet se avergonzó ligeramente al darse cuenta de que llevaba asomada a la ventana quince minutos esperando a que llegase.

Abrió la puerta principal de la casa. La mirada de apreciación que Finn le dedicó borró todo lo demás.

–Hola.

–Vaya… –dijo él simplemente.

Un ligero hormigueo por todo el cuerpo acompañó el rubor que cubrió las mejillas de Juliet.

–¿Sí? ¿Estoy bien? Elise ha elegido el vestido.

Y todo lo que llevaba debajo, aunque las posibilidades de que aquella cita fuera lo suficientemente bien como para dejar al descubierto la lencería de seda eran escasas.

Como respuesta, él le agarró la mano y la ayudó a salir de la casa.

–Hasta ahora, me gusta lo que veo. Ven conmigo para que pueda evaluar adecuadamente el resto.

Juliet se echó a temblar al sentir el tacto de la mano de Finn en el brazo. Aquel contacto le llegaba hasta lugares que él siempre había sido capaz de estimular con bastante pericia.

Dejó que él le diera la mano durante el breve trayecto, en parte porque quería fingir que todo era normal. Que aquello era tan solo una cita con un hombre muy interesante que podría transportarla a una noche llena de posibilidades.

La había ayudado a acomodarse en el asiento trasero del lujoso vehículo para luego sentarse junto a ella. Su potente presencia masculina resultaba abrumadora en un espacio tan reducido. Juliet estuvo a punto de sobresaltarse cuando él se inclinó hacia delante y le rozó el brazo. Tan solo iba a apretar el botón que levantaba la pantalla que los separaba del chófer, pero, para haber sido una gesto de tan poca importancia, el contacto permaneció en ella más tiempo del que le hubiera gustado.

El coche se apartó con suavidad de la acera y avanzó lentamente.

—¿Adónde me llevas? —le preguntó ella tras aclararse la garganta—. ¿A algún lugar de moda?

—De ninguna manera. No voy a compartirte con hordas de curiosos y de paparazzi.

—¿Están tus guardaespaldas en otro coche? Nunca se separan mucho de ti a menos que estés trabajando.

Finn le apretó la mano que no le había soltado.

—¿Acaso estás preocupada? Yo te mantendré a salvo.

Sin duda. Aquel era su trabajo. Disfrutaba protegiendo a la gente. Siempre había sido así.

Charlaron sobre asuntos sin importancia, como

el tiempo en Dallas, pero por suerte Finn no mencionó el fútbol. El único deporte que seguía era la Fórmula 1, pero respetaba que a ella le aburriera, por lo que casi nunca hablaba al respecto.

–Ya hemos llegado –dijo él cuando el coche se detuvo bajo un árbol.

Juliet miró por la ventana. Al otro lado de la carretera había un recoleto parque privado, en el que se habían colocado una mesa y dos sillas desde las que se dominaba una perfecta vista de la puesta de sol. Un hombre con gorro de chef parecía estar preparando algo de comida en una improvisada superficie de trabajo.

–Muy bonito –admitió ella. Entonces, miró a Finn–. Solo por curiosidad, ¿qué habrías hecho si hubiera estado lloviendo?

–Nos habríamos mojado. O nos habríamos marchado en el coche hasta encontrar un local de comida para llevar decente y habríamos cenado en el coche.

Juliet sonrió ante su pragmatismo.

–En ese caso, me alegro de que sea una noche despejada.

Finn respondió con una sonrisa que caldeó partes de su cuerpo que llevaban descuidadas más de lo aceptable.

–Después de la obscena cantidad de dinero que he tenido que pagar para alquilar el parque para esta noche, además de un quince por ciento más para conseguir comprar la reserva ya existente, no se podía atrever a llover.

Finn salió del coche y la ayudó a bajarse. El chófer

se marchó rápidamente después de que él le dijera que regresara al cabo de dos horas.

Juliet comenzó a avanzar por el sendero que llevaba al centro del parque, pero Finn le tiró de la mano para que tuviera que darse la vuelta y mirarlo.

—Tal vez deberíamos quitarnos algo de en medio.

—¿De qué se trata?

Estaba pronunciando aquellas palabras cuando sintió un repentino calor entre ellos. El brillo de anticipación que vio en los ojos azules de Finn respondió su pregunta.

—De esto.

Juliet se quedó inmóvil al ver que la boca de Finn comenzaba a descender. Una parte de su ser deseaba echar a correr antes de que fuera demasiado tarde, pero las piernas no le obedecían.

Entonces, los labios de Finn reclamaron los de ella, apoderándose de su boca poderosamente, exigiendo una respuesta. Así era Finn. Familiar y apasionado. Todo lo que ella llevaba echando de menos mucho tiempo. Juliet lanzó un gemido y se dejó llevar, desesperada por saborear lo divino, por fundirse con él.

La euforia le recorrió el cuerpo, inundándole los sentidos de agudo y húmedo deseo. Los dedos se abrieron paso ansiosos entre su cabello para que Juliet pudiera sujetarle la cabeza y conseguir que el beso explotase entre ellos con incandescente energía.

Sus cuerpos se fundieron, alineándose perfectamente, como siempre. Sí. Le había echado tanto de menos…

Había echado de menos cómo él nunca se contenía, su embriagadora presencia y cómo su fuerza capacitaba la de ella.

Finn deslizó los dedos bajo el finísimo tirante del vestido y le acarició suavemente la espalda. Si seguía así, la lencería terminaría después de todo haciendo acto de presencia. Sin embargo, Finn se apartó antes de que ella hubiera empezado a saciarse de la excitación que le producían sus caricias. Con la respiración acelerada, apoyó la frente sobre la de ella.

—Eso no ha hecho lo que esperaba…

—¿Y qué era lo que esperabas? —preguntó Juliet. A ella sí que le había hecho mucho.

—Que me permitiera cenar en paz en vez de distraerme pensando si seguirías sabiendo igual. Ahora, estoy bastante seguro de que lo único en lo que voy a pensar es en repetirlo.

Juliet ocultó una sonrisa.

—Si la cena va bien, podríamos repetirlo después del postre.

Finn entrecerró los ojos con un gesto seductor y muy sensual.

—Lo tendré en cuenta. ¿Cenamos entonces?

—Si insistes… —dijo ella, a pesar de que estaba segura de que no iba a poder comer. Los nervios que tenía en el estómago no le indicaban que fuera a ser posible.

Seguía existiendo la chispa entre ellos. El beso además había conseguido responder a una pregunta que seguía latente. ¿Podrían retomar la relación donde la habían dejado?

La respuesta era absolutamente afirmativa. Mientras pudieran solucionar el pasado. El escándalo. El profundo sentimiento de traición con el que Finn la había dejado.

De repente, Juliet no quiso seguir pensando en ello. No quería recordar lo abandonada que se había sentido.

Finn la condujo hacia la mesa y la ayudó a tomar asiento antes de sentarse él. Mientras el chef les servía unos deliciosos tomates aliñados con vinagre balsámico como primer plato, empezaron a charlar sobre temas sin importancia. La conversación estaba resultando muy agradable. Por suerte, Juliet parecía haber aprendido al menos algunas de las habilidades sociales que Elise se había esforzado tanto por inculcarle.

Desgraciadamente, no lograba sacarse de la cabeza el beso que habían compartido. Había pasado tanto tiempo desde la última vez que se besaron... Desde el escándalo.

Finn no se había contenido a la hora de buscar compañía femenina, pero Juliet había hecho todo lo contrario. Había adoptado la estrategia del avestruz. Si metía la cabeza en la arena el tiempo suficiente, sus impulsos femeninos terminaban desapareciendo.

Hasta aquel momento, su estrategia había tenido bastante éxito. Sin embargo, en dos segundos, Finn le había recordado que ni su fuerza de voluntad podría evitar que siguiera deseando los afectos de un príncipe muy habilidoso.

–¿Has dejado tu trabajo en Delamer? –le preguntó Finn cuando el chef terminó de servirles el segundo plato, una lubina con espárragos y quinoa.

–Sí.

Aquel monosílabo no comunicó la pena que ella había experimentado al dimitir de su puesto de profesora de inglés. Adoraba a los niños a los que daba clase y había esperado poder seguir ejerciendo su profesión en los Estados Unidos.

Entonces, cayó en la cuenta.

Elise no la había emparejado con un estadounidense. Si las cosas salían bien con Finn, ella podría regresar a casa, a su trabajo, al mar... A los brazos de Finn. ¿Sería posible un cuento de hadas así?

Con renovado interés, miró al hombre que estaba sentado frente a ella.

—¿Y tú, sigues volando helicópteros?

—Por supuesto. Lo haré hasta el día en el que muera. O hasta que me retiren. Lo que venga primero.

Aquel comentario no sorprendió a Juliet. A Finn siempre le había encantado volar, al igual que la parte de salvamento y ayuda de su trabajo. En realidad, su satisfacción era más que lo que hacía, para quién lo hacía.

—Hmm... —dijo ella mientras masticaba un trozo de pescado—. No iba a abordar este tema, pero no sé qué terreno piso en estos momentos. ¿Qué esperabas de la pareja que te proporcionara Elise? ¿Estás buscando esposa?

Finn dejó la copa en la mesa y la miró fijamente.

—No puedo seguir siendo el príncipe juerguista. Lo mejor que puedo hacer es un matrimonio concertado, como lo hicieron mis padres. Un medio para alcanzar un fin. Con eso me contento. ¿Y tú?

Aquella pregunta desató un escalofrío que no pudo controlar.

—Estaba dispuesta a casarme con quien escogiera Elise para mí. No me podía quedar en Delamer después de lo que ocurrió entre nosotros. El matrimonio era para mí también un medio para alcanzar un fin.

A Juliet le gustaría no seguir hablando más y simplemente disfrutar de la cita. Sin embargo, quedaban demasiadas preguntas sin respuesta.

—¿A qué viene esta cena? No se trata de una primera cita, tal y como habría ocurrido con las parejas que habíamos imaginado. Se trata de otra cosa. Tenemos una historia juntos que estamos evitando. Una historia importante y que debe resolverse.

Finn la miró con interés.

—¿Acaso quieres buscar pelea? Adelante.

—No, no quiero buscar pelea —replicó ella—. Ya nos hemos peleado bastante en nuestra relación. Quiero solucionar las cosas como adultos que somos. ¿Será posible?

Finn sonrió y le tomó una mano. Comenzó a frotarle suavemente los nudillos con el pulgar.

—Quedémonos tan solo con la Historia así con mayúsculas. Esta cena tiene que ver con el hecho de que tú y yo volvamos a conectar. Esa es la parte de nuestra historia que prefiero recordar.

—Está bien.

Juliet había esperado mucho tiempo. ¿Qué importaba unas horas más? Aprovecharía el tiempo pensando en lo que sabía que había hecho mal hacía un año. En vez de esforzarse para convencer a Finn de que hablara con su padre, tendría que haber afrontado aquel asunto de manera diferente.

Si Finn estaba de verdad buscando una esposa, ¿qué le impedía casarse con él para conseguir provocar los cambios desde el interior de las puertas del palacio? La princesa Juliet tendría mucho más poder para conseguir que el rey revocara el servicio militar obligatorio que la simple ciudadana Juliet Villere.

Tal vez entonces podría librarse de la abrumadora culpabilidad que sentía por la muerte de Bernard.

Cuando terminó la cena, Finn estuvo a punto de atragantarse al ver que Juliet se levantaba y se acercaba a su lado de la mesa con una sensual sonrisa y un brillo muy seductor en los ojos. Ella extendió la mano, que Finn aceptó en silencio, y le ayudó a ponerse de pie. Entonces, los dos se dirigieron a una sección del parque en el que la vegetación era mucho más espesa.

—¿Acaso te interesan ahora la fauna y la flora? —le preguntó él cuando el silencio se extendió demasiado tiempo.

—Estoy más interesada en cómo nos esconde la flora.

Juliet lo empujó contra un árbol y se pegó a él deliberadamente, haciendo que sus firmes senos se rozaran contra el torso de él.

Así que aquello era lo que Juliet tenía en mente… Evidentemente, recordaba lo bueno que había sido para ambos tan bien como él. Aparentemente, no tenía ningún problema en volver a hacer prender aquella parte de su relación.

—El beso de antes estuvo muy bien. A ver si consigues que este sea mejor —le ordenó.

Finn obedeció inmediatamente. La tomó entre sus brazos y comenzó a acariciarle suavemente la espalda. Las bocas se unieron y se alinearon perfectamente. El fuego no tardó en prender entre ellos.

Juliet.

El deseo se apoderó de él, empapándolo con un aluvión de necesidad. La tenía entre sus brazos, apoderándose de sus sentidos como si hubiera saltado de su helicóptero sin paracaídas.

Afortunadamente, Elise había hecho que se volvieran a encontrar, aunque solo fuera por una noche. Al día siguiente, los dos estarían emparejados con personas más adecuadas.

El beso se profundizó y Juliet se acurrucó contra él como si nunca se hubieran separado. El calor le envolvió la piel a Finn al sentir la perfección del hermoso cuerpo de Juliet contra el suyo. Lanzó un gruñido y le colocó una rodilla entre las piernas. Con el muslo, le tocó a ella inmediatamente el punto más sensible. El vestido ayudada. Los zapatos de tacón alto también.

Finn levantó los labios para murmurar:

—Te he echado de menos. ¿Podemos seguir con esto en algún lugar más privado?

Ella sonrió y asintió. Finn le agarró la mano y vieron que el coche acababa de regresar. Él la ayudó a acomodarse en su interior y prácticamente se lanzó dentro del coche.

Nunca se había podido resistir a Juliet. Por fin ya no tenía que hacerlo.

Además, parecía disfrutar de un respiro. El rey no le había llamado para exigir una explicación por las fotografías de la noche anterior. Aquella era su única oportunidad de saborear un trocito de cielo antes de rendirse a un matrimonio de conveniencia.

Contra toda lógica, había esperado que la mujer con la que Elise lo emparejara pudiera recomponerle el corazón roto. Las posibilidades que tenía de que eso ocurriera con la mujer que se lo había roto en primer lugar eran muy escasas, sobre todo porque él no volvería a entregárselo ni en un millón de años.

Por lo tanto, le daría a EA International otra oportunidad. Cuando tuviera una esposa a su lado, el público se olvidaría del príncipe juerguista y a él se le empezaría a conocer por algo de más valía.

El príncipe del pueblo. Le gustaba cómo sonaba.

Mientras tanto, podría disfrutar de Juliet y de todo lo bueno que había entre ellos sin tener que entrar en el doloroso pasado.

—Entonces, ¿deduzco que has pensado que la cena ha ido bien? —le preguntó él con una sonrisa—. Dado que has accedido a repetir el beso, quiero decir.

Juliet tenía el cabello algo revuelto por los dedos de Finn. Él se moría de ganas por retirarle las horquillas y dejar que aquellos sedosos mechones le cayeran por los hombros.

—Voy a permanecer abierta a lo que la noche me pueda traer, pero hasta ahora no ha estado mal —comentó ella mientras le observaba atentamente—. No nos estamos peleando. Como tú dijiste, estamos estableciendo vínculos.

No se estaban peleando porque, hasta aquel momento, habían evitado el problema. Finn estaba completamente dispuesto a seguir haciéndolo mientras fuera posible.

–Y si el chófer se diera un poco más de prisa, lo estaríamos haciendo aún más rápido.

Juliet se echó a reír.

–Tenemos toda la noche, pero mientras estamos en el tema, ¿lo de establecer vínculos significa que, esta vez, estás dispuesto a estar de mi lado?

Aparentemente, ella no tenía el mismo deseo de seguir evitando el pasado.

–Yo siempre he estado de tu lado.

–Si eso fuera cierto, jamás habrías adoptado la posición que tomaste –repuso ella–. Me habrías apoyado a mí y a mi familia cuando tratamos de hablar con tu padre.

Aquella era la Juliet que había visto la última vez en Delamer. Sintió que se le hacía un nudo en el estómago. Parecía que no les iba a ser posible seguir estableciendo vínculos.

–Lo dices como si no tuviera opción, como si tuviera que estar de acuerdo contigo para que no se considerara falta de apoyo –dijo él. Sin embargo, así era también como se sentía él. Como si Juliet no pudiera ver su lado de la historia. Inmediatamente, el pasado regresó con fuerza. El dolor y la ira con los que él había estado viviendo durante un largo año–. Tú tampoco me apoyaste a mí. Y yo nunca te pedí que fueras en contra de todo en lo que creías.

Juliet retiró con fuerza la mano.

–Eso es exactamente lo que querías que hiciera

yo –susurró Juliet. Una lágrima le cayó por la mejilla. Finn sintió que se le hacía un nudo en el estómago. Le dolía ver a alguien tan fuerte como Juliet llorando–. Que me olvidara de Bernard y que te apoyara todos los días mientras te ponías tu uniforme del ejército de Delamer. Todos los días, me recordaría que Bernard murió con el mismo uniforme y que yo no hice nada para vengarle. Todos los días, se me recordaría que tú elegiste ponerte al lado de la corona en vez de del mío.

El coche se detuvo frente a la entrada privada del hotel de Finn, que estaba situada muy discretamente en la parte trasera del edificio, dentro del aparcamiento subterráneo. Sin embargo, Finn no descendió del coche. Aún no habían terminado aquella conversación.

–La venganza lo describe todo muy bien. Tú me humillaste. Esa protesta llamó la atención por todo el mundo. Juliet… –se interrumpió–. Soy un Couronne. Tú quemaste la bandera del país en el que reina mi familia mientras estábamos saliendo. ¿No te das cuenta de lo que eso supuso para mí?

Por no mencionar que el hombre al que había afrentado era su padre. Finn quería mucho a su padre y a su país. Juliet había querido que él la eligiera a ella por encima de su honor.

–Mi familia ha cambiado para siempre por la política de tu padre. Bernard ya no está y… –susurró Juliet antes de que se le quebrara la voz–. Un hombre que me hubiera amado de verdad lo habría comprendido. Hubiera hecho lo que fuera para enmendar lo ocurrido.

Sin embargo, Finn no era un hombre cualquiera ni nunca lo sería. No se podía quitar la sangre real de las venas.

–Y la mujer que afirmaba amarme se habría dado cuenta de que yo tenía una obligación con la corona. No puedo ser nadie más que el príncipe Alain Phineas de Montagne, duque de Marechal, de la casa de los Couronne.

Pertenecía a una de las últimas casas reales de Europa y debía proteger el país que sus antepasados habían dejado en sus manos, por muy anticuada que esa noción pudiera sonar en el mundo moderno.

Aquello no había cambiado. Juliet era capaz de provocar que se sintiera loco por pasar de estar arriba a estar abajo en cuestión de segundos. Ella bajó también del coche. Parecía completamente decidida a seguir retorciendo aquella lanza en su corazón.

–Yo no quería que fueras otra persona. Te amaba.

Había hablado en pasado. Aquello no se le pasó por alto a Finn.

–Tú lo significabas todo para mí, Finn, pero estamos en tiempos de paz. La ley del Servicio Militar Obligatorio es algo ridículo. ¿Por qué no ves que tu obligación como miembro de la familia real es dejar de ser tan testarudo y pensar en la vida de las personas?

–Por la misma razón que tú no ves que el ejército forma parte de mí.

La ira se apoderó de él. A pesar del sensual vestido y del acertado maquillaje, Juliet seguía siendo la misma activista de siempre. Seguía decidida a alterar el corazón mismo de la institución a la que él le había jurado lealtad.

De repente, le resultó muy fácil resistirse a ella. No tenía el más mínimo interés en seguir a su lado durante el resto de la noche. Nunca se había plegado ante nadie.

Juliet lo observaba de brazos cruzados.

—Creo que podemos decir sin equivocarnos que la cita no ha sido un éxito.

—Haré que el chófer te lleve a casa de Elise.

En aquel momento, se escuchó un chirrido de neumáticos. Una furgoneta bajó a toda velocidad por la rampa y se detuvo a pocos centímetros del parachoques trasero del coche. En su interior, había cuatro hombres muy corpulentos, con la cabeza rapada y ropa oscura.

—Juliet, métete en el coche —le dijo mientras la protegía con su cuerpo. Los cuatro hombres se dirigían hacia ellos con talante amenazador. No debería haberles dado la noche libre a sus guardaespaldas. Aquel fue su último pensamiento antes de que el mundo quedara a oscuras ante sus ojos.

Capítulo Cuatro

Los ojos le escocían. Juliet trató de llevarse una mano a ellos para frotárselos, pero no pudo. Una pesada niebla le ensombrecía el cerebro. Algo iba mal. No podía ver ni mover las manos ni los brazos.

Parpadeó rápidamente para tratar de aclararse la vista. Estaba tan oscuro…

–Juliet, ¿me oyes?

Era la voz de Finn. Se apoderó de ella, despertando un montón de recuerdos, la mayoría de los cuales no eran aptos para todos los públicos. La voz de Finn en la oscuridad significaba tan solo una actividad. Placer. Roces de la piel de él contra la suya. Urgencia para llegar a lo más alto del cielo con él…

Un momento. ¿Qué estaba haciendo Finn allí?

–Sí –murmuró ella–. Te oigo.

El dolor se apoderó de ella en el momento en el que movió la mandíbula. Respiró profundamente y se giró para cambiar de postura… o lo intentó. Los músculos se negaban a cooperar.

–¿Qué–qué es lo que está pasando?

–Es un tranquilizante –le explicó Finn muy serio antes de lanzar una maldición en francés.

Los hombres de aspecto siniestro. La furgoneta. La prometedora cita que tan mal había terminado, para empeorar aún más después.

–¿Por qué nos han dado tranquilizantes?

–Para poder secuestrarnos sin resistencia –gruñó Finn–. Deberían estar dando gracias de que así lo hayan hecho. Si no, no les habría resultado tan fácil.

–¿Que nos han secuestrado dices? Eso solo ocurre en las películas.

–Bienvenida a la realidad.

El sarcasmo con el que él había hablado denotaba la frustración y la preocupación que sentía. Aquello no tenía buen pronóstico. Finn siempre sabía lo que había que hacer.

Juliet se movió hacia la derecha, que parecía ser donde estaba él.

–¿Te puedes mover? ¿Estamos atados?

A Juliet le resultaba difícil decirlo. No sentía nada. Por eso no se podía mover. La habían drogado. Y era incapaz de ver, tal vez para siempre.

Una fuerte mano masculina le apartó el cabello del rostro.

–No –dijo Finn–. Nos han inyectado suficiente narcótico como para que no hayan necesitado atarnos. Yo estoy bien. El cóctel no me afectó a mí del mismo modo que a ti.

Poco a poco, Juliet comenzó a vislumbrar sombras. Gracias a Dios.

–¿Dónde estamos?

–No estoy seguro. En una casa. Yo tenía miedo de dejarte sola por si necesitabas reanimación o volvían a presentarse esos tipos, así que lo único que he hecho ha sido mirar por la ventana.

Poco a poco, Juliet comenzó a distinguir la silueta

de Finn, junto con unos detalles adicionales. Paredes blancas. Una cama.

Finn le agarró la mano. Ella se la apretó con fuerza, agradecida de que los dedos le respondieran por fin.

—¿Hay guardias?

—Por lo que yo veo, no. No he visto a nadie desde que recuperé el conocimiento —dijo él. Entonces, indicó una puerta—. En cuanto puedas caminar, investigaremos un poco más.

—Ayúdame a sentarme —le imploró ella.

Finn le rodeó la cintura con un brazo y ella se apoyó contra él. Tras un par de intentos, consiguió por fin levantar las piernas y apoyarlas en el suelo.

Estaba descalza. ¿Le habían quitado los zapatos? No hacía más que acordarse lo mucho que costaban aquellas sandalias de cocodrilo. Además, le gustaban mucho.

—Ahora, ayúdame a ponerme de pie —le dijo ella. Los secuestradores podrían regresar en cualquier momento y los dos tenían que estar preparados. Finn era más fuerte y estaba mejor preparado, pero ella estaba lo suficientemente loca como para enfrentarse a ellos.

Finn negó con la cabeza.

—Tómate tu tiempo.

—Quiero salir de aquí. Cuanto antes averigüemos lo que hay que hacer para conseguirlo, mejor —afirmó. Le dolía mucho la cabeza, pero hizo lo que pudo por contenerse—. ¿A qué distancia crees que estamos del hotel?

Elise estaría preocupada. Tal vez ya había llamado

a la policía. Podría ser que las fuerzas especiales de la policía estuvieran poniendo Dallas patas arriba para buscar al príncipe Alain.

O… Podría ser también que Elise estuviera tan segura y encantada de haber realizado el emparejamiento de siglo que hubiera dado por sentado que Juliet y Finn estaban tan a gusto el uno con el otro que su pupila se hubiera olvidado de llamar. Probablemente Elise aún no se había dado cuenta de que habían desaparecido.

–Solo hay un modo de averiguar dónde estamos. Vamos.

Finn dio un paso al frente, pero las rodillas de Juliet cedieron. Sin perder el aplomo, él la tomó entre sus fuertes brazos. Juliet estuvo a punto de suspirar ante aquel gesto tan caballeroso.

Desgraciadamente, él seguía siendo el mismo de antes. Testarudo y obstinado. ¿Cómo había podido pensar que podría casarse con él, aun con la excusa de querer cambiar la política de Delamer desde el interior?

Finn la depositó con facilidad sobre el cobertor azul de la cama y le colocó con firmeza una mano en el hombro para que no se pudiera levantar.

–Son las primeras horas de la tarde, si nos podemos guiar por la luz que entra por la ventana. Probablemente llevamos cautivos unas dieciocho horas. Seguramente las fuerzas armadas de Delamer vienen de camino ya para ayudar a las autoridades locales. Quédate aquí. Yo iré a ver qué puedo averiguar.

–No eres el jefe por ser hombre.

–No estoy tratando de ser el jefe –replicó él frunciendo el ceño–. Estoy tratando de impedir que te rompas la cabeza. Si crees que puedes andar, vente conmigo.

Con un exagerado ademán, señaló la puerta.

Juliet decidió que no le quedaba más remedio que hacerlo, aunque solo fuera para demostrar que su alteza estaba equivocado. Lentamente, se puso de pie y fue dando pequeños pasos muy hacia la puerta.

Esta se abrió con facilidad, a pesar de que Juliet hubiera jurado que estaría cerrada con llave. Al otro lado, había un pasillo completamente vacío.

–Vamos.

Ella había dado un paso para atravesar el umbral cuando Finn se colocó delante de ella como si fuera su propio chaleco antibalas. Juliet hizo un gesto de desaprobación con los ojos. Por supuesto.

–¿Es que no tienes ni pizca de sentido común? –le espetó él–. Estamos en una situación muy peligrosa.

Si los secuestradores hubieran querido hacerles daño, ya lo habrían hecho. Finn era mucho más valioso para ellos vivo que muerto.

–Si hay algo peligroso acechando por estos pasillos, te va a dar a ti primero. Entonces, ¿quién me protegerá a mí?

–¿Qué te hace estar tan segura de que yo perdería? –susurró él mientras salía del dormitorio sin hacer ruido.

Siempre se movía con gestos muy elegantes, pero aquel modo de actuar, como si fuera un agente secreto, le resultaba más atractivo de lo que Juliet quería admitir. Echó a andar tras de él. Le costaba apartar la mirada del trasero.

–Una cosa. Si los secuestradores tenían tranquilizantes, seguramente tendrán pistolas. A menos que creas que están en esto tan solo por tener la oportunidad de tomar el té con un miembro de la realeza.

–Shh… –musitó él. Se detuvo donde el pasillo terminaba en una gran habitación. Asomó la cabeza para examinar el espacio–. Nadie a la vista.

Se trataba de un acogedor salón, con una chimenea y unos elegantes muebles.

–Esto no es lo que me hubiera imaginado que los secuestradores preparaban para mantener a sus cautivos.

Una espectacular vista del mar se divisaba más allá de unos amplios ventanales. La casa estaba sobre un acantilado desde el que se veía una particular tonalidad de azul que Juliet llevaba grabada en el corazón. Contuvo la respiración.

–Ya no estamos en Dallas –anunció Finn, a pesar de que era evidente–. Si nos han traído hasta el otro lado del Atlántico sin que yo me diera cuenta, esos narcóticos que utilizaron eran cosa seria.

–Estamos en una isla.

Juliet estaba en casa. En el Mediterráneo, cerca de todo lo que amaba. Había navegado lo suficiente por aquellas aguas para reconocer las colinas que se erguían tras la ciudad y el paisaje costero.

En casa. Nunca habría imaginado que volvería a verla. Las suaves olas del agua. Los ávidos pájaros. El cielo adornado de blancas nubes. Todos los matices poéticos del mar le inundaron el pecho y se lo apretaron con fuerza. Estuvieron a punto de arrancarle un sollozo.

–Sí –afirmó Finn mientras se acercaba a la ventana para mirar la línea costera que se veía en la distancia.

–A unas dos millas de la costa de Delamer hay, no sé, al menos cuatro o cinco islas en este cuadrante. Desde el suelo resulta difícil saber en la que estamos.

–No puede haber más de un puñado de personas que tengan casa en estas islas. Debería ser bastante fácil averiguar quién nos ha secuestrado –comentó ella sacudiendo la cabeza–. Desde luego, nos han secuestrado los más ineptos de todos. Nos han traído a nuestra propia casa.

–Ineptos… o muy listos. ¿Quién pensaría en buscarnos aquí? Se supone que los dos estamos en Dallas.

–Sí… en eso tienes razón.

–Además, como nos han dejado en una isla no tienen por qué quedarse aquí –dijo Juliet–. Es muy difícil que nos podamos escapar si nos han dejado sin teléfono móvil.

–Sí. Estoy seguro de que los secuestradores se han asegurado bien de llevarse todos los aparatos con acceso al mundo exterior.

Finn abrió la puerta corredera. Inmediatamente, la brisa del Mediterráneo inundó la estancia y embriagó a Juliet con su aroma marino. Lo había echado tanto de menos…

Salió con Finn al patio, que contaba con muebles de bambú y una chimenea exterior. Los gritos de las gaviotas eran para ella como escuchar su canción favorita por primera vez en mucho tiempo. Había lugares mucho peores para estar cautiva que una casa sobre un acantilado con vistas al Mediterráneo durante los primeros meses de verano.

Sin embargo, estaban cautivos de todos modos.

Finn agarró con fuerza la barandilla de hierro forjado que rodeaba el patio y se asomó.

—El embarcadero está vacío —anunció, tal y como era de esperar.

—Tal vez haya una canoa o algo en el almacén de la que se hayan podido olvidar los secuestradores.

—Deberíamos echar un vistazo. Sigo sin estar convencido de que estemos solos —comentó él—. ¿Por qué nos iban a dejar sin supervisión en lo que es esencialmente un lugar de vacaciones? Nada de esto tiene sentido.

—Lo del secuestro no tiene mucho sentido. ¿Acaso esperan con secuestrarte a ti, y a mí por añadidura, poder provocar cambios en las políticas del rey?

Ni siquiera cuando estaba más hundida por la muerte de Bernard se le habría ocurrido a ella poner en riesgo la vida de otro ser humano para conseguir cambios políticos.

—Lo normal es que nos hubieran secuestrado para pedir un rescate —dijo Finn—. No todo el mundo busca provocar cambios políticos, ¿sabes? No obstante, me resulta simpático que inmediatamente hayas sacado la conclusión de que el motivo que nos ha traído hasta aquí es político.

Ella se tensó. ¿Por qué no le había dicho también ingenua ya que se había puesto a hablar de ella?

—No tienes que burlarte de mí. Veo que no estás de acuerdo conmigo.

—No me estoy burlando de ti. Hablaba muy en serio. La pasión que tienes por tus principios es una de las cosas que más me gustan de ti.

Finn le colocó un dedo debajo de la barbilla para obligarla a mirarlo. Ella se lo permitió, aunque echó la culpa a su cerebro aún narcotizado. Sin embargo, ningún tipo de tranquilizantes le impediría sentir el aleteo que sintió en el corazón cuando él le dedicó una mirada líquida, insoldable, hermosa. Lo peor era que parecía que Finn le estaba diciendo la verdad.

Juliet apartó la mirada sin realizar comentario alguno. ¿Qué podía decir al respecto? Era el resumen perfecto de su relación. Finn apreciaba su pasión, pero no sobre lo que ella la experimentaba. Juliet amaba el sentido de la lealtad de él, pero no a lo que se lo había jurado.

Finn apartó la mano y se puso a mirar de nuevo el mar.

Parecía que el círculo vicioso en el que se encontraban no se podría romper nunca. La tristeza volvió a apoderarse de Juliet. Tal vez debería seguir el ejemplo de los secuestradores. Ellos habían mostrado una cruel determinación por alcanzar sus objetivos, fueran estos cuales fueran. Ella debería hacer lo mismo. Por Bernard.

Si eliminaba sus sentimientos de la ecuación, tal vez podría averiguar el modo de conseguir la reforma que quería. Sin embargo, primero debía descubrir la manera de marcharse de aquella isla.

***

Finn se entrelazó los dedos en la nuca para no tener que volver a tocar a Juliet. Evidentemente, a ella no le gustaba el contacto. Comprendía por qué: la tormenta de la discusión de la noche anterior aún flotaba entre ambos.

Se había visto obligado a verla dormida, rezando para que se despertara pronto, para que sus captores no regresaran con malas intenciones. No tenía ningún problema en hacerle daño a otros para proteger a Juliet, pero prefería mil veces no tener que hacerlo.

Por suerte, ya estaba despierta, pero sentía un incontrolable deseo de tomarla entre sus brazos para asegurarse de que ella estaba bien.

Juliet se aclaró la garganta.

—Deberíamos separarnos para registrar la casa.

—¿Estás loca? ¿Por qué diablos crees que te perdería yo de vista?

Juliet frunció el ceño y se recogió el cabello con su propio pelo.

—Porque tenemos que marcharnos de aquí lo más rápido posible y registraremos todo esto antes si lo hacemos separadamente.

—De eso ni hablar —le espetó él—. Si vamos rápido conseguiremos el mismo fin.

Con una mirada de desolación, ella comenzó a bajar las escaleras que llevaban hacia el mar. Lo hacía con velocidad, como si estuviera desafiándole a que la siguiera. Finn la siguió con facilidad hasta que los dos llegaron por fin a la playa. Sin decir nada, recorrieron la costa rocosa. Finn no dijo nada sobre el hecho de que Juliet fuera descalza. Si ella se hubiera mostrado más cooperadora, se habría ofrecido a buscarle los zapatos, que seguramente estaban en el armario de la habitación donde se habían despertado. No obstante, dudaba que las sensuales sandalias fueran la mejor opción para caminar por la playa.

—Aquí no hay nada —dijo ella mientras se ponía las manos en las caderas.

La brisa le sacaba mechones de cabello del improvisado recogido y hacía que estos le golpearan suavemente el rostro y el cuello.

Al verla, la sangre se le aceleró.

Seguía deseando tomarla entre sus brazos y entregarse al placer olvidándose de todo. Apartó la mirada.

—Nos queda mucho terreno por recorrer. No te rindas todavía.

—No me estaba rindiendo. Estaba evaluando la situación. Deberíamos encontrar algún modo de encender un fuego. Seguramente habrá personas navegando. Además, alguien te habrá sustituido, ¿no? Las señales de humo son una opción más segura que buscar un bote.

—Es una buena idea —mintió él.

Jamás funcionaría. Todo el mundo sabía que las islas que estaban frente a la costa de Delamer eran propiedad de gente muy rica e influyente. ¿Quién se entrometería en el dominio privado de otra persona para investigar lo que supondrían que era una fogata en la playa?

Sin embargo, aquello sin dudas era mejor que no hacer nada.

Regresaron al patio y entraron en la casa. Se dirigieron a la cocina para buscar cerillas o un encendedor.

Juliet asomó la cabeza desde la alacena.

—Bueno, si no nos rescatan pronto, al menos no nos moriremos de hambre. Ven a ver esto. Aquí hay suficientes provisiones para alimentar a todos tus compañeros guardacostas durante un mes.

Finn se reunió con ella y comprobó que ciertamente las estanterías de la alacena estaban muy bien surtidas. De repente, la curiosidad se apoderó de él. Salió de la alacena y se dirigió al frigorífico.

—Aquí lo mismo. Nuestros secuestradores se han asegurado de que comeremos muy bien.

En el frigorífico había carne, pollo, verduras, leche, mantequilla… Todo estaba muy fresco y los envases sin abrir.

Juliet se acercó a él y examinó el interior.

—Esto me intranquiliza. ¿Cuánto tiempo esperan tenernos aquí?

—Ojalá lo supiera…

La frustración se apoderó de él. Empezó a pensar en las cosas que le gustaría que fueran diferentes. «Ojalá no les hubiera dado la noche libre a Gómez y a LaSalle. Ojalá hubiera invitado a Juliet a cenar en la habitación de mi hotel. Ojalá tuviera tenido cinco segundos más para reaccionar cuando la furgoneta se detuvo…».

Sabía que aquello solo conseguiría ponerle más nervioso.

—¿Por qué no vas a ver si hay cerillas en la chimenea?

Cuanto más lejos estuviera ella, menos podría afectar sus sentidos.

Juliet se marchó y él se metió las dos manos en los

bolsillos. Un papel crujió bajo sus nudillos. Sacó un sobre con el sello del rey en el centro. Un sobre que no tenía en el bolsillo la noche anterior.

Una extraña sensación se apoderó de él.

Deslizó un dedo bajo el sello y sacó una página doblada. Tal y como sospechaba, el papel llevaba una nota escrita del puño y letra de su padre.

Siento las molestias que os estoy causando, pero un suceso inesperado me ha llevado a revaluar la situación. La familia Villere está consiguiendo volver la opinión pública en mi contra. Por eso, espero que utilices bien el tiempo que te estoy dando con Juliet. Arregla las cosas con ella y utiliza tu relación para influirle a ella y a su familia para que dejen de inflamar a la gente con su campaña política. Cásate con ella y asegúrate de que queda claro que la familia Villere está al lado de la corona. Es la unión más beneficiosa para todo el mundo.

Por fin, Finn sabía por qué no había tenido noticias de su padre sobre las fotografías que se tomaron en la fiesta de Elise. El rey había preparado el secuestro.

Finn sintió que se le hacía un nudo en la garganta. Así se explicaba que sus captores los hubieran dejado en un paraíso sin supervisión alguna. Era una reclusión forzada para que Finn tuviera la oportunidad de seducir a Juliet y conseguir que ella se alineara con él en vez de con su familia. El secuestro le permitía reclamar su inocencia en lo ocurrido y, además, les daba la posibilidad de unirse más para soportar las circunstancias.

Era una picardía muy ingeniosa. Y una locura.

Finn arrugó el papel en la mano. Su padre había ido demasiado lejos. Habían drogado a Juliet y le habían hecho sentir miedo. ¿Para qué? Para que Finn pudiera realizar un milagro y convertirla en una defensora de la corona. Si eso fuera posible, Finn lo habría hecho hacía un año.

—He encontrado las cerillas —dijo ella alegremente desde el salón.

Las cerillas eran ya innecesarias dado aquel nuevo desarrollo de la situación. Nadie los estaba buscando. Nadie se fijaría en un poco de humo que proviniera de aquella isla. Finn estaba seguro de que se trataba de la Île de Etienne, en la que Alexander y Portia eran dueños de la única vivienda que ocupaba el pequeño trozo de tierra. Aquella jaula de oro era el nido de amor del heredero y de su esposa. Por eso Finn no había ido nunca hasta allí.

¿Significaba eso que su hermano formaba también parte de aquel complot? ¿Estaban esperando todos los miembros de la familia real a ver cómo Finn se ocupaba de aquella situación?

El mejor modo de combatir la táctica del rey era decirle a Juliet qué era exactamente lo que estaba pasando.

—Un fuego no nos va a ayudar, Lisa. Tienes que…

—No. Escúchame tú a mí —replicó ella—. No lo sabes todo porque estés en el ejército. Puedes sentarte si quieres y esperar a que se presenten esos tipos, pero yo no voy a hacerlo. Quiero irme a mi casa.

Con eso, ella se dio la vuelta y salió de la cocina. Su hermoso trasero hacía menear muy sensualmente el vestido amarillo. La fuerza con la que cerró la puerta corredera para salir al exterior resonó por toda la casa.

Finn se sentó en un taburete y se agarró la cabeza entre las manos. ¡Qué mujer más obstinada y testaruda! Esas cualidades le habían causado un inconmensurable dolor hacía un año y sería un idiota si volvía a repetir.

Lo último que quería hacer era salir tras ella. Lo único bueno de aquella situación era que no tenía que hacerlo. Al menos, la nota del rey le aseguraba que no había peligrosos delincuentes que pudieran regresar en cualquier momento para hacerles daño.

Se levantó. Decidió que no formaría parte activa en aquel engaño y que no se casaría con Juliet para influir en ella y hacer que se volviera contra su familia. Sus diferencias solo se resolverían de verdad si ella lo escogía de buen grado.

Y eso no estaba ocurriendo. Era demasiado testaruda y seguía poseyendo la capacidad de enfurecer a Finn.

Salió al exterior decidido a decirle a Juliet lo que había hecho el rey. Después, podrían trabajar juntos para escapar de aquel ridículo plan.

El humo surgía de entre las rocas. Se asomó y vio que Juliet estaba quemando una de las sillas del patio. Al futuro rey le faltarían algunos muebles cuando estuviera en la isla, algo que se merecía por haber accedido a prestar la casa para el descabellado plan de su padre.

—¿Has conseguido algo? —le preguntó Finn.

—Sí. ¿Acaso no ves que las fuerzas armadas de Delamer ya están desembarcando en la playa? –replicó con sorna–. No debes de ser tan importante como crees, dado que nadie ha venido aún a rescatarnos.

En realidad, Finn era más importante de lo que había pensado, razón por la cual los dos estaban en aquella situación.

–Traté de decirte que encender un fuego no serviría de nada.

–Pues a ver si se te ocurre a ti un plan que funcione, listo.

Finn abrió la boca para contarle la verdad. Sin embargo, algo, no supo bien qué, le hizo cambiar de opinión.

Él era importante. Más de lo que había pensado. Tenía en sus manos el futuro de Delamer. Su hermano no podía hacerlo. Y tampoco su padre. Solo Finn tenía la capacidad de conseguir que Juliet y su familia dejaran de atacar al rey y al ejército de Delamer.

Finn, el segundón, no era después de todo tan inútil.

El rey era más inteligente de lo que Finn había pensado. Si le decía a Juliet que el rey estaba implicado en el secuestro, echaría más leña al fuego. ¿Quién sabía lo que sería ella capaz de hacer entonces? El objetivo era conseguir que ella dejara de hablar mal de su familia, no empeorar la situación.

Además, si Finn no hacía lo que su padre le había pedido, el rey podría encontrar otro modo de ocuparse del problema de Juliet y de su familia, un modo que podría terminar destruyendo sus vidas.

Finn tenía todos los ases en la manga. Si hacía lo que su padre le había pedido, salvaría a su país y volvería a tener a Juliet en su vida y en su cama. Sin embargo, nunca en su corazón. Esa parte de la relación había terminado.

Juliet miró hacia el mar con el rostro preocupado.

—Estoy elaborando un plan —le dijo él.

Era cierto, pero no se trataba de un plan de rescate. Se trataba más bien de un plan de seducción. ¿Podría de verdad sacarlo adelante?

Miró a Juliet y se sacó la nota del bolsillo del pantalón para arrojarla al fuego. El papel se arrugo, ennegreció y empezó a arder.

Ojalá sus recelos sobre la tarea que tenía entre manos pudieran destruirse tan fácilmente.

Capítulo Cinco

Finn tosió por culpa de un poco de humo.

—Bueno, propongo que regresemos a la casa y comamos algo. Hablaremos de lo que vamos a hacer a continuación cuando nos hayamos recargado las pilas.

Juliet se cruzó de brazos y le miró a los ojos.

—Deberíamos quedarnos aquí, junto al fuego. Si viene alguien, podrían apagarlo y marcharse sin darse cuenta de que hay cautivos en la casa.

Finn contuvo un gruñido. Por supuesto, ella seguía preocupada por el rescate y, a menos que él le diera alguna pista de lo que ocurría en realidad, continuaría haciéndolo. Sin embargo, aún no se lo podía decir, al menos hasta que averiguara lo que él quería hacer.

—Está bien. En ese caso, iré a preparar algo y lo traeré aquí. Tomaremos un picnic en la playa.

Ella lo miró con sospecha.

—No sabes cocinar.

—No estoy hablando de una comida completa. ¿Bastará un bocadillo para tu delicado paladar?

—Claro —respondió ella con una ligera sonrisa. Entonces, se dejó caer sobre una roca—. Aquí te espero.

Furioso, aunque no sabía muy bien con quién, Finn untó de mantequilla de cacahuete y mermelada unas rebanadas de pan y envolvió los bocadillos en servilletas. Aquella situación le molestaba. La comida no iba a conseguir suavizarla.

Tras colocar la comida en una bandeja, junto con un par de vasos de agua, regresó junto al fuego. Desgraciadamente, no había conseguido encontrar una solución que apaciguara su conciencia.

–Cómete el bocadillo. Después, comenzaremos a hacer fuegos alrededor de todo el perímetro de la isla –le dijo él–. Estoy bastante seguro de que esta es la Île de Etienne. Si conseguimos que alguien se fije, ver varios fuegos le hará venir a investigar.

Juliet levantó las cejas y, tras tomar un sorbo de agua, dijo:

–Es una idea genial. Gracias por el bocadillo.

Finn asintió y se metió el bocadillo en la boca. Cuando antes terminara, antes podrían marcharse de allí. Nadie le había dicho que tenía que esperar a que su padre fuera a recogerlos. Podría buscar su propio rescate. Así, no estaría a expensas del alocado plan del rey ni le tendría que contar a Juliet lo ocurrido y dañar más aún de ese modo las relaciones con la familia de ella.

Mientras tanto, si podían encontrar la manera de estar juntos sin pelearse continuamente, algo que dudaba, el matrimonio no sería una posibilidad tan lejana.

Los dos subieron la escalera hasta llegar al patio y arrojaron a la playa todos los objetos de madera que pudieron encontrar. Por lo que a Finn se refería, Alexander le podría pasar la factura a su padre.

El acantilado rodeaba la mitad del perímetro de

la isla y luego bajaba gradualmente hasta el nivel del mar en el lado sur, que miraba hacia África. Sin embargo, los dos estuvieron de acuerdo en que tendrían más posibilidades si colocaban los fuegos en la costa más cercana a Delamer. Los barcos de pesca y de mercancías pasarían por la mañana. Si los fuegos no generaban ningún interés por ese lado, centrarían los esfuerzos en el sur a la mañana siguiente.

El primer fuego estaba situado cerca de la escalera, por lo que empezaron a extender los montones de madera a lo largo de la costa norte. Se coordinaban perfectamente, sin necesidad de hablar. Juliet parecía leerle el pensamiento a Finn a la hora de amontonar la madera para que él pudiera encenderla después.

Finn tenía una extraña sensación de *déjà vu*, de que el año anterior había sido una horrible pesadilla de la que se había despertado suspirando de alivio porque Juliet y él estaban juntos y seguían enamorados. Seguían siendo felices.

Al mismo tiempo, el dolor de la traición de ella le oprimía el pecho, justo en el lugar donde se suponía que tenía que estar el corazón. La protesta había ocurrido y ellos ya no estaban juntos.

Finn no disfrutaba nada de aquella paradoja.

El improvisado recogido que Juliet había hecho con su cabello se había soltado hacía tiempo. Las mejillas se le habían ruborizado bajo el sol de la tarde. Ella no se quejaba, pero Finn se apostaba algo a que tenía cortes en los pies.

Así era el modo en el que ella lo desafiaba: con una fuerza silenciosa que Finn tan solo podía admirar y esforzarse por emular.

–Deja que termine de colocar estos fuegos. ¿Por qué no regresas a la casa? –le sugirió él después de un rato.

–¿Para qué? –le preguntó ella mirándole por encima del hombro mientras se dirigía hacia el siguiente fuego, que harían de una mesa auxiliar.

–Para que puedas descansar. Date un largo baño caliente. Estoy seguro de que podrás encontrar algo de música que poner en el cuarto de baño. Te estás quemando con el sol y no hacen falta dos personas para preparar estos fuegos. No te preocupes. Si viene alguien, me aseguraré de que no nos marchemos sin ti.

Ella se detuvo en seco y los dos estuvieron a punto de chocarse. Finn extendió las manos para sujetarla, pero ella se dio la vuelta. Le interrogó con una mirada brillante y curiosa.

–¿Te acuerdas de que me gusta escuchar música mientras me estoy dando un baño?

La esperanza que había en el tono de su voz despertó algo en el pecho de Finn.

–Lo recuerdo todo de ti.

A Finn no le había importado nada más que estar con ella: ni las obligaciones de su puesto, ni su trabajo, ni su familia… Todo había quedado en un segundo plano.

Quería recuperar aquellos momentos. Quería olvidarse del escándalo y disfrutar del paraíso que los rodeaba.

Tal vez el matrimonio no estaba sobre la mesa, pero el romance sí.

La respiración de ella había cambiado ligeramente.

El deseo nublaba su expresión. Como si Juliet hubiera leído sus pensamientos. El deseo se apoderó también de él.

De repente, Juliet ocupó el espacio de Finn. Sus labios se encontraron, dudando, rozándose. Entonces, cerraron con firmeza el espacio que los separaba.

Juliet se apoderó de él, inundándolo de necesidad. Finn le colocó las manos en la mandíbula para agarrarle la cabeza, poder profundizar el beso y saciarse del fuego que ardía en la boca de Juliet. Ella gemía contra sus labios, acrecentando la presión del deseo que él tenía en su cuerpo.

Le deslizó una mano por la espalda para cubrir el dulce trasero, moldeándolo a su cuerpo. Entonces, le levantó el vestido para poder sentir su piel. Era como la seda... Gruñó y ciegamente hizo ademán de agarrarle el bajo para quitárselo por completo. Cuando estuvo preparado, se detuvo unos segundos para darle a ella la oportunidad de detenerle, buscando la respuesta a la pregunta que flotaba en el aire.

Con el aroma del mar, del fuego y de Juliet engulléndole los sentidos, Finn rezó para que la respuesta fuera afirmativa.

El peso y la presión de los maravillosos labios de Finn sobre los suyos debilitó profundamente a Juliet. Finn pareció notarlo y la estrechó con fuerza, sujetándola contra su cuerpo.

Toda la ansiedad y el miedo que había sentido

desde que se despertó en una cama extraña desaparecieron. Finn estaba allí, con ella. No importaba nada, tan solo perderse en las sensaciones de la brisa del mar y de él. Todo era muy fácil. Sin esfuerzo, como siempre había sido entre ellos.

Ningún otro hombre la había hecho nunca sentirse como él. Era como si una poderosa marea le recorriera el cuerpo y lo electrificara al insuflarle energía en la sangre.

Tenía ya el vestido subido hasta la cintura. Los dedos de él le acariciaban la carne, rozándole los muslos y el vientre. Sí... Ansiaba sentir las manos de Finn por todas partes.

A medida que el beso fue alargándose, su corazón subió hasta lo más alto.

Para luego caer en picado.

No podía dejar que Finn la afectara de aquel modo. No se trataba de una segunda oportunidad. Ya lo había intentado en la cena de la noche anterior y no había funcionado.

Se apartó de él con un esfuerzo increíble, sacudió la cabeza y se volvió a colocar el vestido.

–Mmm, tenemos que...

Finn la soltó y señaló la casa con la cabeza. Su rostro carecía por completo de expresión.

–Ve dentro. Yo terminaré aquí.

–No. No me voy a dar un baño cuando puedo colaborar en el rescate.

–En ese caso, regresa a la casa y mira a ver si puedes acceder a Internet a través de la televisión. Estoy seguro de que he visto también una consola de juegos. Prueba con las dos cosas.

–A sus órdenes, teniente –le dijo ella saludándole al estilo militar para ocultar el alivio que le producía tener la excusa perfecta para alejarse de él. Y no volver a besarlo.

Tenía que mantener la cabeza fría y centrarse en la huida, no en el hormigueo que sentía en sus partes más femeninas y su alma femenina tan solitaria.

Lo dejó en la playa y subió las escaleras cojeando para llegar a la casa. No podía dejar de pensar en el beso. Después de la cena, los dos habían estado de acuerdo en que no podían ser pareja. De algún modo, ella le había enviado las señales equivocadas o los dos se habían visto presa de la pasión del momento, como dos supervivientes en una película de desastres, atraídos inexplicablemente el uno al otro a pesar de las duras circunstancias.

Sin embargo, cuando él la besaba, se olvidaba de todo.

Tenía que marcharse de aquella isla, lejos de él. Sería lo mejor para los dos.

La televisión no tenía conexión a Internet, pero sí tenía un servicio de cable que ofrecía más de trescientos canales. Buscó uno de noticias para ver cuánta importancia se le estaba dando a su desaparición.

Después de comprobar durante quince minutos que no se mencionaba la desaparición del príncipe de Delamer, Juliet se rindió. Todavía no se había dado cuenta nadie de que había sido secuestrado. ¿Qué clase de secuestradores esperaban tanto tiempo para dar publicidad a sus exigencias?

Tal y como había dicho Finn, había también una Wii en la estantería, pero quedaba algo oculta en la parte posterior. Solo la aguda visión de él como piloto de helicóptero podría haberla visto allí. La encendió, pero, a pesar de intentarlo muchas veces, no pudo conectarla a Internet. Los secuestradores habían sido bastante concienzudos. No obstante, la consola tenía tantos juegos que no sufrirían aburrimiento alguno en aquella jaula de oro.

Tras lanzar un suspiro, apagó la consola y se pasó varios minutos abriendo puertas y cajones para buscar un portátil o un móvil, algo que pudiera utilizar para contactar con el exterior y pedir ayuda.

La puerta de acceso al patio se abrió y se cerró, anunciando el regreso de Finn.

—¿No debería quedarse uno de nosotros en la playa por si viene alguien? —le preguntó ella—. Si no quieres volver tú, lo haré yo.

No quería estar en la misma habitación que él, sobre todo cuando tenía un aspecto tan delicioso y salvaje por haber estado a merced de los elementos.

—Se está haciendo tarde —dijo él mientras se remangaba—. Dudo que haya nadie navegando. Si nos ve uno de mis compañeros, aterrizará en el lado sur para investigar. Te aseguro que no podríamos pasar por alto el ruido de las aspas de un helicóptero. Creo que nos podemos quedar en la casa.

Torpemente, se dirigió hacia el sofá y se dejó caer sobre él.

—Creo que deberíamos pensar en la cena.

—Una ducha tampoco estaría mal.

—¿Me estás sugiriendo que necesito una? —bromeó ella.

Le resultaba tan natural bromear con Finn cuando, en realidad, ser víctima de un secuestro no tenía nada de gracioso.

La sonrisa que él le dedicó no consiguió aliviar la consternación de Juliet.

–Yo necesito la ducha, si me quieres acompañar, no tengo ningún problema.

Juliet no puedo evitar pensar en el cuerpo desnudo de Finn, con el agua cayéndole por los fuertes músculos mientras se enjabonaba.

–Ah… –susurró. Cerró los ojos para parpadear, pero no le ayudó. Las imágenes eran cada vez más eróticas–. Gracias. Me encuentro bien.

Finn soltó una carcajada como si hubiera adivinado la dirección de los pensamientos de ella.

–Yo me voy a quedar con el dormitorio que hay al final del pasillo. Tú puedes quedarte con el que viste cuando te despertaste. Hasta dentro de un rato.

Instantes después de que Finn se marchara, se escuchó el agua corriendo por las tuberías. «No voy a pensar en Finn desnudo. No voy a pensar en Finn desnudo», se repetía ella mentalmente mientras se levantaba del sofá para ir a ocuparse de la cena.

Sin mucha energía, examinó el frigorífico y luego la alacena. No encontraba inspiración. Se había pasado dos meses de horas de entrenamiento para ser la perfecta esposa con Elise y Dannie, tiempo que incluía muchas sesiones en la cocina. Elise le había explicado que las esposas perfectas sabían mucho más que cocinar. Conocían los ingredientes, cómo emparejar la comida y el vino…

Ciertamente, algo había aprendido, pero no parecía capaz de sacar información alguna de su cerebro. En vez de tratar de pensar, se decantó por una pechuga de pollo. Parecía fácil meterla en el horno y cocinarla a… cierta temperatura. Siempre le había confundido la conversión que tenía que hacer en los Estados Unidos entre grados Celsius y grados Fahrenheit. Y allí estaba en Europa, utilizando de nuevo los Celsius. Aquello era suficiente como para empujarla a tomar una copa.

Le pareció un buen plan. Fue a buscar en la bodega, que estaba junto a la cocina. Comprobó que estaba plenamente equipada con vinos que ni siquiera ella conocía, pero que imaginaba que eran especiales y muy caros. Eligió un burdeos y esperó que a los secuestradores les diera un ataque al corazón cuando se dieran cuenta de que faltaba la botella del reserva de treinta años.

Regresó a la cocina y se sirvió una copa del tinto. Comenzó a canturrear mientras colocaba el pollo en la bandeja con una mano y bebía con la otra.

—Eso sí que es bonito de ver. Estás canturreando una cancioncilla muy alegre.

Juliet miró por encima del hombro. Finn estaba en la puerta de la cocina, con un hombro apoyado contra la pared. Aún tenía el cabello húmedo de la ducha. Llevaba puestos unos vaqueros y una camiseta azul marino, que le sentaban a la perfección.

—¿Los secuestradores han traído tu equipaje? —preguntó ella extrañada—. ¿Han traído también mis cosas?

El vestido amarillo había adquirido la tonalidad de un linóleo de diez años. Una larga mancha marrón de algo que no era capaz de identificar le ensuciaba la falda.

–Me temo que no –respondió él con una resplandeciente sonrisa–. Encontré esta ropa en el armario que hay en mi dormitorio. También hay ropa de chica, así que te he dejado algo sobre la cama. ¿Qué estás preparando?

–Pollo.

–¿Y qué más? –preguntó él tras una pequeña pausa.

–¿Es que tiene que haber más?

–Es que me muero de hambre… ¿Qué tal un poco de pan o…? –sugirió él mientras rebuscaba en el frigorífico y sacaba una lechuga–. ¿Una ensalada?

–Puedes contribuir con lo que quieras a la cena. Toma un poco de vino –le ofreció ella magnánimamente–. Es un burdeos. Hay que aprovecharse de la hospitalidad de nuestros secuestradores.

–Perfecto. Alexander siempre está hablando de los méritos de esa bodega. Veamos si tiene razón.

Se sirvió una copa de vino y comenzó a trabajar en la cocina junto a Juliet. Sirvió ensalada en boles y cortó trozos de pan de la barra que había sacado de la despensa.

Ella fingía no observarle, pero… ¿Por qué un hombre resultaba tan sexy en la cocina? Tal vez solo era Finn, con su fluida elegancia y su hermoso y musculado trasero que aquellos pantalones prestados hacían resaltar como si se hubieran diseñado para hacer soñar a las mujeres.

El temporizador del horno sonó y la ayudó a salir de una fantasía solo apta para adultos que tenía como protagonistas la encima, el vestido amarillo subido hasta las caderas y los vaqueros de Finn en el suelo.

¿No se suponía que no debía pensar en él desnudo?

Emplató todo rápidamente para que Finn no se diera cuenta de la pícara sonrisa que tenía en el rostro y se sentaron a cenar. La espectacular puesta de sol encendía el cielo de Occidente y casi consiguió que la cena con su antiguo amante fuera soportable.

Finn charlaba sobre nada en particular y ganó puntos por no mencionar el pollo seco e insípido que tenía en el plato. Además, a Juliet le daba la sensación de que le habían explicado que el pollo y el vino tinto no van bien juntos, algo que alguien que asistía con regularidad a cenas formales con jefes de estado seguramente conocía. Finn no se le insinuó ni flirteó con ella.

Tal vez no era tan malo verse encerrada allí con él.

—Es la segunda noche seguida que cenamos juntos —comentó ella. Inmediatamente, deseó no haber pronunciado aquellas palabras. No quería que él pensara que le gustaba la idea.

—Sí —respondió él tras dedicarle una larga mirada que, sin duda, significaba que había interpretado la observación que ella acababa de hacer del modo equivocado—. Solíamos comer juntos siempre…

—Bueno, esperemos que sea la última vez —dijo ella—. No lo digo porque seas un compañero de mesa terrible, sino porque espero que nos rescaten pronto.

—Sabía a lo que te referías —comentó él mientras tomaba un bocado—. Cuando estés en tu casa, ¿piensas quedarte?

–En realidad no lo he pensado...

–Le podrías pedir a Elise que te buscara una pareja diferente –sugirió. Dejó el tenedor y comenzó a beber un poco de vino–. Es decir, si aún quieres encontrar un esposo en los Estados Unidos.

–No.

Resultaba sorprendente, pero cierto, a pesar de no haber tomado ninguna decisión consciente al respecto. El hecho de que huyera de Delamer había sido provocado por el falso anuncio de compromiso de Finn. Había optado por una huida cobarde, y eso ya no iba con ella.

Se apresuró a seguir hablado para que Finn no pensara que aquella decisión tenía que ver con él.

–Estar de nuevo aquí... No puedo volver a marcharme de Delamer, pero no tengo trabajo ni un lugar en el que vivir.

–Eso se resuelve fácilmente –dijo él encogiéndose de hombros–. A la nueva escuela le falta profesorado cualificado. Y estoy seguro de que podría recurrir a algunas personas para encontrarte un apartamento.

–¿Y por qué ibas a hacer algo así?

¿Porque tal vez pensaba que ella iba a darle una segunda oportunidad?

–No seas tan suspicaz. Vi tu cara en la playa. Sé lo que el agua significa para ti. Francamente, me sorprendió que te marcharas –observó él mientras miraba la puesta de sol durante un largo instante–. Convencí a mi padre para que construyera esa nueva escuela. Por ti.

Juliet estuvo muy cerca de derramar la copa de vino.

–¿Cómo has dicho? Eso no es verdad. La antigua escuela estaba saturada. Todo el mundo lo sabe.

–Sí, pero llevaba saturada mucho tiempo y nunca se había hecho nada al respecto. ¿Cómo crees que se convencieron los poderes públicos de que una nueva escuela era vital para el futuro de Delamer?

Juliet recordó la foto en la que él cortaba la cinta y el beso de la niña. El príncipe Alain había cortado la cinta porque fue él quien hizo posible la escuela.

–Nunca dijiste nada. Yo me había estado quejando del tamaño de las clases desde que nos conocimos.

La mirada azul de Finn capturó la de ella. Juliet no pudo apartar el corazón de aquellas profundidades.

–Era una sorpresa. Quería asegurarme de que el proyecto iba a salir adelante antes de mencionarlo. Ocurrió cuando nos separamos.

–Yo no… pero eso significa… –murmuró ella. El cerebro y la lengua parecían estar funcionándole independientemente–. ¿El rey se oponía y tú lo convenciste?

–No se oponía. Ya sabes lo caro que resulta construir en Delamer, dado que se tienen que importar todos los materiales de construcción. Una escuela no estaba a la cabeza de la lista de prioridades. Yo le ayudé a darse cuenta con toda la munición que tú me diste durante las veces que hablamos al respecto. Me resultó fácil.

–¿Y lo hiciste por mí? –susurró ella.

–Por ti y por mi pueblo. Si no hubiera pensado que era necesario, no habría apoyado la idea. Sin embargo, Delamer necesita niños preparados que crezcan y se conviertan en miembros productivos de la sociedad. Que nos ayuden a competir en un mercado global en el que habrá cada vez más oportunidades. Tenemos que empezar ahora si queremos que Delamer siga siendo relevante.

Juliet jamás había dicho nada de todo aquello. Su principal consideración había sido hacer bien su trabajo y asegurarse de que los niños tenían el mejor ambiente posible para aprender. Finn había sacado sus propias conclusiones, creando una imagen más amplia que ella no se había parado a considerar.

Juntos habían conseguido algo que merecía la pena. Por supuesto, ella no había participado activamente, pero… ¿Y si había hecho más de lo que esperaba? ¿Cuánto más podrían conseguir los dos juntos?

Resultaba evidente que Finn la había escuchado y que no le importaba defender una causa cuando creía en ella. Por algún motivo, no había creído en las súplicas que ella le había manifestado sobre la reforma del ejército. ¿Por qué no?

Sin embargo, preguntar podría proporcionarle respuestas que no le gustaban. Ninguna razón que él pudiera darle tendría más sentido que la anulación de la ley del servicio militar obligatorio. Creer en las razones que él pudiera darle sería una traición para la memoria de Bernard, algo que ella no aceptaría nunca.

En lo más profundo de su ser, ella se preguntó en secreto si la muerte de su hermano había sido culpa suya. En una familia de seis, era responsabilidad de Juliet como la mayor de todos ayudar a los demás. Se había pasado mucho tiempo con su hermano, pero, evidentemente, no le había enseñado lo suficientemente bien como para permanecer vivo.

Sus padres lloraban la pérdida de su único hijo seguramente más de lo que ella podría nunca imaginar. Se habían apoyado en ella para asegurarse de que ningún otro miembro de la familia sufriera el mismo final. La mirada de sus ojos cuando les dijo que Finn se negaba a cambiar de opinión la había destrozado para siempre. Después de perder a Bernard y a Finn, se había jurado que no le quedaba nada por lo que sufrir.

Nada podría arreglar lo ocurrido excepto la segunda oportunidad de la que disponía para cumplir el deseo de sus padres y llevar a cabo lo que esperaban de ella. De algún modo, tendría que persuadir a Finn para que eliminara el servicio militar obligatorio en honor de Bernard. Las razones que Finn hubiera podido tener para no hacerlo en un principio eran completamente irrelevantes.

Aunque esas razones la condujeran de nuevo a los brazos de Finn.

Capítulo Seis

El día siguiente amaneció sin progreso alguno ni en el rescate ni en el romance. No es que Finn hubiera esperado mucho en ninguno de los dos sentidos, pero resultaba difícil que su cuerpo asimilara que Juliet estaba durmiendo bajo el mismo techo sabiendo que las posibilidades de que ella visitara su dormitorio en medio de la noche eran nulas.

Lanzó un gruñido y se dio la vuelta sobre la enorme y solitaria cama.

Desgraciadamente, el beso no dejaba de turbar sus sueños. El tacto de la carne, los movimientos de la lengua…

La cena de la noche anterior había sido una tortura, especialmente después de que le confesara que había construido la escuela por ella. El gesto que se reflejó en el rostro de Juliet lo afectó más de lo que hubiera podido imaginar y mucho más de lo que estaba preparado para aceptar.

Había estado a punto de sugerirle que salieran a tomarse el resto del vino al patio con la esperanza de que la velada pudiera dar un giro más apasionado, pero ella se cerró en banda y se excusó para lo que quedaba de noche.

—Buenos días —le dijo Finn alegremente desde su puerta cuando Juliet salió de su dormitorio. Ella tenía profundas ojeras y parecía haber dormido tan mal como él.

¿Porque había estado despierta añorándolo como él a ella, pero había sido demasiado testaruda para admitir que lo deseaba? Finn sabía que le deseaba, a pesar de lo que fuera lo que le había hecho apartarse. Nadie podía besar a un hombre como ella lo había hecho sin que significara algo.

—Es de día. Es lo único que puedo decir al respecto —gruñó antes de alegrar el rostro un poco—. Al menos, me he dado una ducha caliente. Gracias por la ropa.

El jersey y los pantalones eran un poco grandes para ella, pero los llevaba con estilo. El gusto de Portia era bastante conservador, pero era la futura reina y se veía sometida a un escrutinio constante.

—Vamos a desayunar —dijo él—. Luego iré a comprobar la costa sur de la isla. Se me ha ocurrido otra idea para tratar de llamar la atención, pero tengo que ver si funciona.

—Parece prometedor. Y misterioso. Me muero de ganas.

Juliet sacó un par de barritas de la alacena y las untó de mermelada mientras Finn preparaba café. Sacaron todo al patio, junto con unas rodajas de melón. Allí, soplaba una suave brisa que le revolvía el cabello a Juliet. Finn sonrió. El sol de la mañana cubría Delamer con una capa plateada. La vista era maravillosa.

Finn quería tener su propia isla. Cuando regresaran a casa, haría todo lo posible por comprar una. Su futura esposa, fuera quien fuera, estaría encantada de tener un nido de amor. Desgraciadamente, no se podía sacar de la cabeza la imagen de Juliet en el embarcadero el día anterior, cuando se le soltó el cabello del improvisado recogido. Era como una hermosa criatura marina, demasiado etérea para poder ser capturada.

Se le formó un nudo en la garganta que le impidió tragarse el trozo de pan.

Cuando por fin logró tragárselo, se puso de pie.

—¿Has terminado?

—Sí, si me puedo llevar el café. No me había dado cuenta de lo flojo que es el café en los Estados Unidos —dijo mientras aspiraba con fruición el aroma del café que tenía entre las manos—. ¿Qué es lo que has pensado? ¿Más fuegos?

—No. Piedras. Si podemos encontrar las suficientes, podemos escribir SOCORRO para que se pueda ver desde el aire. Si alguien de la patrulla pasa por aquí, lo verá seguro. Cuanto antes lo hagamos, mejor.

—Genial.

Ella desapareció en la casa y volvió a salir con una taza tipo termo. También se había puesto un par de botas Timberland de Portia.

—Por cierto, todavía no hemos salido en las noticias. Eso de escribir sobre la arena me parece buena idea, dado que nadie sabe ni siquiera que estamos secuestrados.

Finn debería decirle la verdad, pero, ¿cómo podía hacerlo sin ponerlo todo en peligro? Si los rescataban pronto, se habría soltado del anzuelo.

Se marcharon y pronto tuvieron un buen montón

de piedras. Al igual que con los fuegos, trabajaron entendiéndose perfectamente, pero en esta ocasión, Finn prefirió no guardar silencio.

—¿Y si no volvieras a la enseñanza? —le preguntó retomando el hilo de la conversación de la noche anterior—. ¿Crees que podrías ser feliz con otro trabajo?

—Estoy segura de que podría encontrar algo que se me diera bien también.

—¿Por qué no piensas en algo que te gustaría hacer en vez de algo que se te diera bien?

Habían completado de hacer la S, por lo que Finn comenzó a trazar la O. Juliet colocó las dos piedras que tenía en las manos. Entonces, soltó un gemido de protesta,

—¡Ay! —exclamó mientras se examinaba una mano.

—¿Te encuentras bien?

—¡Qué tontería de uñas postizas! —exclamó frunciendo el ceño al ver el hilillo de sangre que le separaba la uña del dedo índice en dos partes—. Se me ha enganchado una entre las piernas y se me ha partido hasta la carne. Ni siquiera sabía que eso podía ocurrir.

—¿Y por qué te las has puesto?

Juliet se encogió de hombros. Pareció olvidarse, de la uña aunque le tenía que doler.

—Me ha dicho que eso es lo que hacen las mujeres. Se supone que tenemos que tenerlas pulidas y bien arregladas.

—No tienes que ponerte uñas postizas para resultar atractiva, ya lo sabes.

—Lo sé. Jamás te importó que yo no fuera muy femenina, algo que siempre agradecí mucho. Supongo que por eso nos emparejó el ordenador de Elise.

En realidad, los había emparejado porque compartían creencias y maneras de ser muy similares. Por eso comprendía que ella se hubiera mostrado tan disgustada e irracional cuando su hermano murió. Si hubiera sido a la inversa y Alexander hubiera sido el que entró en un campo electrificado, Finn habría reaccionado del mismo modo que ella.

Los modales importaban poco comparados con otras cosas, pero si pudiera convencerla de lo equivocada que había estado al adoptar la postura que tomó, la situación de ambos sería muy diferente.

El romance y el matrimonio podrían estar encima de la mesa.

El tiempo curaba las heridas y permitía tener perspectivas diferentes. Tal vez ella podría ver por fin las cosas más racionalmente. ¿Podría Finn dejar de pasar la oportunidad de tantearla? Podría decirle a su padre que lo había intentado.

—Tú nunca has salido en la cubierta del *Aurélien* —comentó él.

—No —respondió ella. Se arrodilló para colocar la siguiente piedra con sumo cuidado.

Esa fue la reacción que ella tuvo al repentino cambio de tema. La tensión de la espalda y los abruptos movimientos le dijeron a Finn que ella había reconocido el nombre del barco donde su hermano murió.

Estuvo a punto de echarse atrás, pero aquello era demasiado importante como para no afrontarlo.

Se sentó junto a ella y colocó las piedras un poco más, a pesar de que ya estaban perfectas.

—Es una fragata de defensa aérea. Estoy seguro de que la has visto desde la costa. Tiene muchos cañones y lanzamisiles sobre la cubierta. Un equipamiento extremadamente complicado y muchos niveles que pueden resultar muy confusos.

—Sí, la he visto.

Juliet no se lo iba a poner fácil. En parte por eso Finn no le había hablado nunca al respecto.

—Repasan el protocolo de seguridad constantemente —dijo. Eligió las palabras adecuadamente, pero sin censurarlas—. Cada soldado tiene la responsabilidad de comprender las reglas y cumplirlas.

—¿Estás a punto de decirme que Bernard no lo hizo? —le interrumpió ella.

—Yo no estaba presente, pero los informes son concluyentes. Entrevistaron a todos los marinos que estaban a bordo en aquellos momentos. No se puede entrar en las salas electrificadas sin la protección adecuada.

—Mi hermano no debería haber estado en ese barco —replicó ella mirándole a los ojos con una expresión desolada en el rostro—. Quería estar en la guardia costera, como tú. Te adoraba. No se cansaba de alabar tus habilidades como piloto ni lo heroicamente que rescataste a un nadador.

Aquello era un golpe bajo. Finn no era un héroe ni nadie que se mereciera adoración.

—El modo de entrar en la guardia costera es cumplir los tres años de servicio militar obligatorio —le recordó él—. Yo también lo hice. Odié cada segundo que pasé como marino, pero te recuerdo, Juliet, que la mitad de Delamer hacer frontera con el mar. Nuestra presencia naval es muy importante, y ahí es donde se necesitan hombres. Nuestra población es muy pequeña. ¿Cómo si no podríamos conseguir los marinos que necesitamos?

–¿Crees que la palabra SOCORRO es suficiente? ¿Deberíamos poner algo más? –preguntó ella mientras se ponía de pie para ir a recoger más piedras.

Finn no sabía si seguir con el tema. Sinceramente, el tema era algo delicado también para él. Había sentido mucha simpatía hacia Bernard. Se había imaginado convirtiéndose en su mentor si el muchacho hubiera llegado a los guardacostas después de cumplir sus tres años.

El sollozo de Juliet le hizo decidirse. La tomó entre sus brazos y la acurrucó contra su cuerpo. Ella se resistió durante unos instantes, pero luego se abrazó también a él. Las lágrimas le caían a Finn sobre el hombro, pero no le importaba.

–Bernard era un tío estupendo. Yo también lo echo de menos.

–Me gustaría dar marcha atrás en el tiempo, ¿sabes? –susurró ella–. Hacer que nunca hubiera ocurrido.

–Lo sé… Fue una tragedia, pero tenemos que seguir adelante con nuestras vidas, cielo.

Juliet se separó de él inmediatamente. Evidentemente, las palabras de Finn no habían sido las adecuadas.

–Seguir con nuestras vidas. Buena idea. Esto ya está –dijo mientras se secaba las pestañas con un dedo–. Tú espera aquí a que pase uno de tus compañeros en sus rondas. Yo iré al norte de la isla para ver si pasa algún barco. Tal vez pueda llamar la atención de alguno.

En aquella ocasión, Finn decidió dejar pasar el tema. Observó cómo ella se marchaba y lanzó una maldición. De algún modo, la dinámica entre ellos se había hecho más complicada. Le daba la sensación de que cuanto más tiempo se quedaran juntos en aquella isla, peor se haría.

Juliet se marchó deseando poder dejar de llorar, pero le estaba resultando imposible.

Al principio, mientras colocaban las piedras, se había sentido en paz con Finn, como si el hecho de trabajar juntos les ayudara a creer que no había pasado nada.

Entonces, él lo había estropeado todo.

¿Por qué había tenido que hurgar en su herida de aquel modo para luego mostrarse comprensivo y ofrecerle un hombro en el que llorar? No fue así después de la muerte de Bernard.

El dolor que sentía en el pecho no se aliviaba, a pesar de que trataba de respirar profundamente mientras contaba hasta cien. Normalmente, eso siempre le funcionaba. Aquel día no.

Tenía que alejarse de Finn permanentemente. Él estaba alterando su sentimiento de bienestar.

–Vamos, un barco… –musitó.

¿Cuánto tiempo tendría que esperar a que se acercara un barco lo suficiente a la isla como para ver a una mujer solitaria sobre la playa?

–Te he traído un paraguas de la casa.

Ella se dio la vuelta. Finn estaba allí, ofreciéndole un paraguas abierto. El verano era una estación seca en el Mediterráneo. Solo a Finn podría habérsele ocurrido buscar un paraguas. Solo a Finn podría habérsele ocurrido resguardarla del sol mientras Juliet esperaba allí a que se produjera un milagro.

—No te he oído bajar por la escalera —dijo ella.

—Parecías estar muy centrada en tu tarea. Siento haberte asustado.

Juliet sacudió la cabeza y aceptó el paraguas que él le ofrecía.

—Gracias.

—Hace una mañana preciosa, ¿verd…?

—Pensaba que ibas a esperar al otro lado.

—Se puede escuchar un helicóptero desde aquí lo mismo que desde allí. Pensé venir a asegurarme que estabas bien.

—Bueno, como si no pudiera cuidarme yo sola.

—No. Porque estabas llorando —le corrigió él—. No quería disgustarte.

—Estoy bien. Solo estoy cansada —mintió para excusarse—. Estar secuestrada me está pasando factura.

—Sí. Y también la conversación. ¿Acaso era mejor no hablar al respecto?

—No lo sé…

En ocasiones, Juliet quería hablar sobre ello y nadie mejor para comprender la angustia que había soportado que Finn. Él conocía a su familia, sabía que ella había ayudado a criar a Bernard, sabía que ella era la mayor de los seis hijos de los Villere. Su sentido de la responsabilidad por sus hermanos había marcado su vida.

Finn la conocía muy bien. Por eso dolía tanto estar separados.

–¿Qué resolvería hablar de ello?

Finn se encogió de hombros.

–Ayudaría a aliviar la pena. Es algo que no tuve la oportunidad de hacer la primera vez. Quiero estar a tu lado. Permítemelo.

La idea fue creciendo dentro de ella hasta que no pudo reprimir el sí. Aquella había sido la parte más dura del año anterior. No poder recurrir a Finn en la que había sido una de las peores rachas de su vida. Se había pasado mucho tiempo con sus padres, pero ellos se tenían el uno al otro. Sus hermanas estaban sumidas en su propio proceso de duelo y ninguna de ellas había ayudado a criar a Bernard. Habían perdido a un hermano que amaban, pero no era lo mismo que perder a un muchacho al que se había ayudado a moldear y a educar.

No era lo mismo que culparse por no haberle enseñado lo suficiente, que culparse por haber expuesto a un muchacho dulce e impresionable a un hombre como Finn, al que Bernard idolatraba y que le inspiró a seguir sus pasos.

Sin embargo, nadie podía entenderlo. Ni siquiera Finn.

El vacío que Finn había dejado ansiaba aceptar la promesa que él le había hecho de estar a su lado. Siempre habían estado juntos los dos. Juntos para siempre.

Dos corazones latiendo como uno.

Ella dio un paso atrás y agarró el paraguas con las dos manos. Finn no podía darle la absolución. Ni siquiera podía darle el apoyo incondicional que ella necesitaba desesperadamente. Y entonces, Finn se había tratado de comportar como si Bernard tuviera la culpa por no seguir las reglas.

Se aferró a eso para no volver a caer en brazos de Fin en aquella ocasión.

—Es demasiado tarde para estar a mi lado. De igual modo, es demasiado tarde para nosotros. Hemos terminado, igual que esta conversación.

Finn apretó los labios.

Por fin le había hecho comprender. Ojalá pudiera hacerle entender también que la testarudez de él era lo que se interponía entre ambos. Lo único que tenía que hacer era dejarla a un lado y ponerse a su lado contra su padre, contra el rey.

Si él lo hiciera, Juliet estaba convencida de que eso sería la clave para su mejoría. Le permitiría dejar de culparse.

Desgraciadamente, aquello no iba a ocurrir nunca.

Sorbió por la nariz y se aclaró la garganta.

—No viene por aquí ningún helicóptero y, evidentemente, estamos demasiado lejos para que nos vea ningún barco que salga del puerto de Delamer. La única manera de escapar de esta isla es nadando. Y eso es lo que voy a hacer.

—¿Vas a ir nadando?

—Sí. A la costa. No puede haber más de dos millas si me dirijo directamente al lado francés, a Saint Tropez.

—Nunca en tu vida has nadado una distancia como esa. ¿Qué te hace pensar que lo puedes hacer ahora?

—Claro que soy capaz de nadar dos millas. Lo he hecho muchas veces —replicó ella.

–Hay una gran diferencia entre hacerlo en aguas poco profundas que entre esta isla y Saint Tropez –afirmó él. Entonces, le agarró con fuerza los hombros–. Juliet, estamos en una zona rocosa. Crees que no hay obstáculos, pero estás muy equivocada. Estás hablando de nadar en línea recta en mar abierto.

–Tendré cuidado –insistió ella. Estaba convencida de que era la única opción que tenían.

–No se trata de tener cuidado –replicó él mientras se mesaba el cabello–. Rescato personas en esta agua todos los días. ¿Sabes la razón fundamental por la que no pueden llegar a la costa solos? Porque han sobrevalorado su fuerza contra la corriente.

–Entonces, no crees que pueda hacerlo.

Juliet quería escuchar cómo Finn lo admitía. Quería que él le dijera que no confiaba en sus habilidades y que no se trataba del agua.

–No tiene nada que ver contigo. Se trata de estar a salvo y no correr riesgos innecesarios. Incluso te podría golpear un barco.

–¿Pero qué estás diciendo? Si precisamente la falta de barcos es uno de nuestros problemas. Al menos si me choco con uno, el barco me vería.

–Te estás tomando este asunto con mucha ligereza, y no deberías. Así muere mucha gente.

Juliet de repente comprendió el verdadero motivo de la preocupación de Finn. Le preocupaba que ella muriera. Y entonces, verdaderamente sería demasiado tarde.

Sintió que se le hacía un nudo en el corazón y estuvo a punto de extender la mano para tranquilizarle.

No quería que fuera demasiado tarde.

Quería encontrar el modo de volver a estar con Finn, reconquistar de nuevo la felicidad de estar enamorada, de compartir sonrisas, de las tardes perezosas... Olvidarse de todo lo ocurrido y seguir hacia delante.

Sin embargo, ella no podía olvidar. Finn y ella eran como dos fuerzas enfrentadas, que se empujaban la una a la otra con toda su fuerza y, al mismo tiempo, sin ceder un ápice de terreno.

Incluso pensar en estar con Finn significaba que tenía que alejarse de él antes de que hiciera algo que no pudiera borrar. Algo de lo que ella se lamentaría.

El paraguas se le cayó de las manos.

—Quedarnos aquí no es una opción. Hemos probado con los fuegos, con las piedras sobre la arena... Todavía no ha venido nadie y los barcos se quedan demasiado lejos. Tenemos que probar otra cosa.

Se recogió el cabello y se quitó las botas, pero Finn le agarró la mano antes de que pudiera meterse en el agua.

—Espera. Estamos a salvo aquí. No hay peligro de los secuestradores. Si fueran a regresar, ya lo habrían hecho. Tenemos mucha comida. ¿Por qué no fingimos que estamos de vacaciones y nos relajamos unos días?

—Estás loco. Somos prisioneros —le espetó ella—. El lujo de la jaula no lo cambia. No me puedo quedar aquí y fingir que todo va bien aunque estemos secuestrados. Enviaré a alguien a por ti en cuanto pueda.

—Juliet, hay algo que necesitas saber —le dijo Finn

mientras le apretaba la mano con fuerza para que no se soltara–. No tienes que ir nadando a ninguna parte porque… mi padre está detrás de todo esto.

–¿Detrás de qué? –le preguntó ella con incredulidad. De repente, Juliet lo comprendió todo y se soltó de él–. ¿Del secuestro? ¿Tu padre nos ha secuestrado?

Finn suspiró y se entrelazó los dedos en la nuca, como si necesitara ayuda para mantener la cabeza erguida.

–Sí.

–Espera un momento… ¿Y tú sabías que tu padre era el que nos había secuestrado? ¿Desde cuándo?

–Desde el primer día –admitió él–. Tenía una nota en el bolsillo.

Finn lo había sabido desde el principio y no se había molestado en decírselo. Juliet lanzó una maldición.

–Hemos estado tratando de conseguir que nos rescaten, encendiendo fuegos… Y tu padre sabe que estamos aquí… Nos dejó tirados en esta isla a propósito… ¿Por qué le ha hecho algo tan horrible a su propio hijo? ¿A mí?

–Es complicado… Vio la fotografía que nos hicieron en la fiesta de Elise. Todo ha surgido de ahí.

–¿Está tratando de mantenernos alejados de la prensa? ¿Es que no puede soportar ver fotos de su precioso hijo junto a una extremista como Juliet Villere?

–No se trata de eso, Juliet. Guarda silencio durante cinco segundos y escúchame.

Aquellas palabras terminaron con la paciencia de Juliet.

–¡Deja de darme órdenes! Tú lo has sabido desde el principio. Has tenido oportunidad de hablar. Ahora me toca a mí –rugió ella. Por una vez, Finn cerró la boca y se cruzó de brazos para permitir que ella aireara su frustración–. No entiendo cómo puedes ser hijo de un hombre con la sangre tan fría como el rey. Jamás lo comprenderé. Nos ha puesto en peligro, igual que puso en peligro a Bernard. Estoy cansada de que ni tu padre ni tú veáis el problema. No voy a quedarme sentada esperando a que él realice su siguiente movimiento.

Con esas palabras, se lanzó al agua.

La fría temperatura del agua le cortó la respiración. No importaba. Podría hacerlo. Tenía que hacerlo, aunque no fuera nada más que para demostrarle al rey Laurent que no era capaz de controlarla.

Comenzó a nadar y se fue alejando lentamente de la isla. Brazada, respiración. Brazada, respiración.

Hacía tanto frío…

Se atrevió a mirar atrás y vio que apenas había recorrido unos trescientos metros. Decidió que era mejor no ir comprobando el progreso. Era mejor no saber lo que había recorrido y limitarse únicamente a nadar. Llegaría a la costa opuesta en algún momento.

Notó un pequeño hormigueo que se le extendía desde los dedos hacia las manos. No… Se le estaban durmiendo. Los estiró con cada brazada, esperando así incrementar el flujo de sangre.

Entonces, le dio un calambre en un costado y tragó agua. Comenzó a toser mientras se sujetaba la cintura y trataba a duras penas de avanzar en el agua, con la esperanza de que el dolor desapareciera tan rápidamente como había llegado. No fue así. El calambre volvió a azotarla con fuerza y estuvo a punto de hacer que se hundiera.

El mar que tanto amaba se había vuelto contra ella.

No. El mar era el mismo que siempre. Su estancia en Estados Unidos le había pasado factura y estaba en muy baja forma para nadar en aquellas condiciones.

Las piernas le ardían con el esfuerzo de mantener la cabeza por encima del agua. Apretó los dientes y nadó un par de metros más, pero una ola la hundió bajo el agua y le hizo tragar otra bocanada de agua marina. La tos volvió a impedirle que avanzara, pero insistió.

Cuando consiguió empezar a nadar de nuevo, otro fuerte calambre le sacudió el abdomen. Se dobló por la cintura involuntariamente.

Tenía que regresar.

Se dio la vuelta y comenzó a nadar de nuevo, en aquella ocasión en dirección a la Île de Etienne.

No iba a conseguir llegar. Moriría en el intento, tal y como Finn había predicho.

Comenzó a llorar de arrepentimiento. Tenía tantas cosas de qué arrepentirse. Hacía un semana que no llamaba a su madre. Jamás volvería a ver cómo otro niño formaba sus primeras palabras en inglés. Jamás tendría un hijo propio…

Lo peor de todo era que jamás tendría la oportunidad de decirle a Finn que aún seguía enamorada de él. ¿Por qué se había aferrado a la ira durante tanto tiempo?

Justo cuando pensaba que iba a perder el conocimiento, Finn apareció en el agua, tiró de ella y tras colocársela en la postura adecuada, comenzó a llevarla hacia la costa.

Juliet se quedó inmóvil y se dejó flotar, respirando desesperadamente y tratando al mismo tiempo de expulsar todo el agua posible. No iba a morir. No era demasiado tarde.

Capítulo Siete

Finn metió a Juliet en la cama en la que él había dormido la noche anterior porque era más grande. Le colocó dos mantas encima, maldiciendo la incapacidad de Alexander para tener un mísero termómetro en toda la casa.

La piel de Juliet ardía. No había duda de que tenía fiebre, pero a Finn le habría gustado saber cuánta y si le estaba subiendo o bajando.

Qué mujer tan testaruda. ¿Por qué había tenido que tratar de llegar nadando a Saint Tropez?

Sabía por qué. Juliet se negaba a creer que él pudiera tener razón, incluso en algo tan importante como si ella sería capaz de derrotar al mar que él conocía tan bien como la palma de su mano.

Había sido su repentina confesión la que la había empujado a hacerlo.

No había tiempo para dejarse llevar por las lamentaciones. Se quitó la ropa mojada en tiempo récord y se vistió con otra seca. Se metió entre las sábanas y observó cómo ella respiraba . Se dijo que tan solo quería estar cerca de ella por si le necesitaba.

Era una mentira.

Después de haber estado a punto de perder a Juliet en el mar, no podía separarse de ella. Le agarró con fuerza la mano bajo las sábanas. Estaba tan débil… El cabello húmedo se le extendía sobre la almohada y Finn deseó haber pensado en secárselo antes de meterla en la cama.

Tenía un aspecto tan frágil y hermoso… Finn no podía soportar pensar en que podía perderla.

El tiempo fue pasando. Una hora. Dos. Juliet se movía ocasionalmente, para luego quedarse completamente inmóvil, hasta el punto de que en un par de veces él se asustó tanto que tuvo que tomarle el pulso para asegurarse de que estaba bien.

Ciertamente, el rey no habría imaginado que su plan saldría de aquel modo en ningún momento, pero Finn estaba furioso con su padre.

Juliet estaba enferma y no tenían modo alguno de comunicar con el mundo exterior para conseguir medicinas o llevar a Juliet al hospital. La incapacidad de poder hacer algo le pesaba más que la fatiga y la preocupación. No había resultado fácil nadar contracorriente y luego además llevar a otra persona a la costa, todo ello mientras se sentía aterrado ante la idea de que Juliet hubiera sucumbido ya a los peligros ocultos del mar.

Cuando el sol empezó a ponerse, el hambre lo obligó a levantarse de la cama. Fue corriendo a la cocina y se comió dos galletas, se bebió dos vasos de agua y regresó a la cama para seguir con su vigilia.

Un tirón de la mano le sobresaltó. Abrió los ojos y, automáticamente, miró el reloj digital que tenía en la mesilla de noche. Las tres de la mañana. ¿Se había quedado dormido?

Miró a Juliet con la ayuda de la luz del cuarto de baño, que había dejado encendida. Ella parpadeó.

–Hola –susurró él mientras le acariciaba suavemente el rostro. Aún estaba muy caliente, pero tal vez no tanto como antes–. ¿Cómo te sientes?

Juliet se acurrucó sobre la mano de Fin deliberadamente, como si quisiera estrechar más el contacto. Entonces, se lamió los labios y tragó saliva un par de veces.

–Como si alguien me hubiera dejado caer en un volcán.

–Has tenido fiebre. Probablemente se trate de algo de lo que te contagiaste en Estados Unidos y que ha tardado tanto tiempo en dar la cara –dijo él.

Le acarició suavemente la mandíbula. La mitad inferior de su cuerpo de repente necesitó un buen sermón que le recordara la enfermedad de Juliet y lo inapropiado que resultaba sentirse excitado por una mujer que estaba demasiado débil como para poder responder adecuadamente.

Demasiado tarde. Su cuerpo había cobrado vida. El agotamiento y el estrés le habían bajado las defensas de tal manera que ninguna reprimenda surtía efecto. Sufriría de frustración sexual además de todo lo demás. Fantástico.

Esperaba que ella no se diera cuenta.

–Me has salvado –murmuró ella agradecida.

–Sí. ¿Qué otra cosa podría haber hecho?

–Dejar que me ahogara. Me lo merecía.

–Pues estuviste a punto…

–¿Cómo… cómo pudiste llegar tan rápido? Estaba bastante lejos de la costa.

–Te estaba siguiendo. En el agua. Cuando tú te lanzaste al mar, me lancé yo también.

–Oh… –susurró ella. Entonces, cerró los ojos un instante. Volvió a abrirlos con considerable esfuerzo–. No creíste que pudiera conseguirlo.

–No.

–Entonces, ¿por qué me dejaste ir?

–Porque no tengo por costumbre obligar a las mujeres a hacer nada. Y también porque tenías que intentarlo.

–Eso es… interesante –dijo ella. La voz se le quebró y ese hecho preocupó enormemente a Finn.

–Aún es de madrugada. Deberías descansar y no preocuparte por nada. Duerme. Yo estoy aquí.

–No tienes que cuidar de mí –musitó Juliet–. Yo debería cuidar de ti.

–Yo no estoy enfermo. La próxima vez que tenga fiebre, dejaré que seas tú la que me meta en la cama. ¿De acuerdo?

Juliet le apretó la mano a Finn. Entonces, se relajó y comenzó a quedarse dormida. Desgraciadamente, el sueño eludía a Finn. Al alba, Juliet parecía tranquila, por lo que se arriesgó a dejarla sola como para darse una merecida ducha.

El agua caliente le caía por los músculos, tranquilizándoselos. No se había dado cuenta de lo mucho que necesitaba un descanso de la incómoda postura en la que había estado tumbado en la cama, medio tumbado contra el cabecero. Era la postura mejor para vigilar a Juliet.

Allí, en la ducha, por fin solo, el terror que había mantenido dominado se soltó por fin. Comenzó a salirle del pecho y estuvo a punto de hacerle caer de rodillas.

Podría haber perdido a Juliet. En aquel momento, se dio cuenta de lo mucho que quería aquella segunda oportunidad que su padre le había dado. De algún modo, tenía que encontrar el modo de derribar el muro que los separaba, no porque el matrimonio fuera a ser ventajoso, sino porque, verdaderamente, no creía que pudiera funcionar el resto de su vida sin ella.

Aquel era el as que el rey tenía bajo la manga. Finn seguía enamorado de Juliet. El secuestro había llevado a la superficie todos aquellos sentimientos.

¿Y si pudiera encontrar el modo de hacer que Juliet cambiara de opinión? No había momento ni lugar mejor en la Tierra para intentarlo que estando atrapados en aquel paraíso.

Su corazón tembló ante la posibilidad de un futuro con la mujer que amaba a su lado con todas las diferencias que los separaban resueltas. Matrimonio. Familia. Un lugar en el que pudiera alcanzar una cierta normalidad, lejos de la opinión pública.

Desgraciadamente, aquel empeño parecía harto difícil. Juliet se había mostrado dispuesta a salir nadando de una cómoda isla que compartía con él. Ni siquiera le había dado la oportunidad de explicar el resto del plan de su padre. Eso indicaba claramente que Juliet no quería nada con él. La reconciliación parecía imposible por mucho que él la deseara.

Cuando regresó al dormitorio, Juliet se había incorporado sobre las almohadas y estaba viendo la televisión. El color le había vuelto al rostro, aunque no todo lo que a él le habría gustado.

–Buenos días –dijo ella con voz ronca–. Me duele la garganta.

–Te traeré algo de beber. ¿Te parece?

Ella asintió y Finn le llevó un vaso de agua del cuarto de baño.

–Mejor –afirmó Juliet tras tomárselo de dos tragos.

–¿Cómo te encuentras? –le preguntó Finn mientras le tocaba la frente con el reverso de la mano. Seguía caliente.

–Vamos a dejarnos de andar por las ramas, ¿de acuerdo? No me voy a levantar de la cama en un futuro cercano. ¿Va a conseguir eso que dejes de revolotear por aquí?

–No estoy revoloteando.

Ella le miró y le indicó su lado de la cama con un movimiento de cabeza.

–Siéntate.

Finn lo hizo.

–Simplemente estoy preocupado por ti.

–Y te lo agradezco, pero no me voy a escapar. En mi estado actual, no me puedo marchar nadando a Saint Tropez, pero no estoy tan débil como para que tengas que estar pendiente de todos mis deseos.

Juliet estaba tratando de demostrar que podía hacer todo lo que se decidiera a hacer. Admirable. Sin embargo, aquella era también la razón de que, en aquellos momentos, no estuvieran casados ya y con dos hijos.

Juliet era incapaz de admitir que se había equivocado. Finn podría tener la capacidad de amarla, pero no necesariamente la fortaleza.

Ella apretó el botón del mando en varias ocasiones y luego lo dejó y se acurrucó en la cama, inclinada hacia el lado de Finn.

—¿Te he dado las gracias?

—Puedes mostrar tu gratitud poniéndote bien y haciéndome una buena cena.

—Lo intento… Estoy tan cansada…

Juliet deslizó las piernas por entre las sábanas hasta que estuvieron pegadas a las de él. Pareció no darse cuenta. A pesar de que los separaban varias capas de tela, la piel de Finn ardía como si no se interpusiera entre ellos obstáculo alguno.

Desesperado por salir de la cama antes de que hiciera alguna locura, le dijo:

—¿Te sientes lo suficientemente bien como para darte un baño?

—Me gustaría —respondió ella abriendo los ojos—. ¿Me ayudarías?

—Pensaba que no me querías revoloteando —replicó él.

—Si te lo pido, no estás revoloteando, tonto —susurró ella con una delicada sonrisa que produjo un efecto devastador en Finn—. Tengo la piel muy reseca. No creo que pueda llegar a todas partes.

—Te ayudaré a llegar al cuarto de baño, nada más.

Juliet se llevó una mano a la frente con gesto frágil.

—Te necesito… por favor.

Aquella súplica le impidió a Finn decirle que no. Fue corriendo al cuarto de baño y abrió el grifo para llenar la bañera de agua templada. Echó medio frasco de un gel oriental que tenía Portia esperando que la espuma cubriera a Juliet lo suficiente para que él pudiera marcharse del cuarto de baño con la dignidad intacta.

El exótico aroma del sándalo y del jazmín transformaron el cuarto de baño en un lugar lleno de seducción. Y eso que había buscado mantener la dignidad. Si hubiera empapelado las paredes con fotografías eróticas no habría conseguido un efecto tan sensual.

Por si la tortura no fuera ya suficiente, puso la radio, que estaba montada en la pared, y encontró una emisora de jazz. El sonido pesado y seductor del saxofón llenó el espacio con sus notas.

—¿Finn? —preguntó ella desde el dormitorio.

Al escuchar aquella voz profunda y ronca, él sintió que la tensión se acrecentaba. Cerró los ojos un instante, pero no encontró la fortaleza que esperaba. Decidió refrenar su imaginación. Se dirigió a la cama, sacó de ella a Juliet sin apenas mirarla. No quería ver la camiseta que le había puesto la noche anterior, que en aquellos momentos parecía suplicar que las manos de un hombre la levantaran tan solo un poco para dejar al descubierto todos los secretos que ocultaba.

Lanzó un gruñido y se volvió de espaldas.

—Métete en la bañera. Entera. Dime cuando estés completamente cubierta por la espuma.

—Lista.

Finn miró de reojo y, efectivamente, vio que ella estaba sumergida en el agua hasta el cuello y que tenía la cabeza apoyada en el borde de la bañera y los ojos cerrados.

La peor pesadilla y la fantasía más erótica se unieron en una.

—Fiebre, fiebre, fiebre…

Tardó de recordar el modo más rápido de bajarla. Lanzó una maldición. Debería haberle preparado un baño templado... tal vez frío y con cubitos de hielo. ¿O esa era la cura para una erección desbocada? A él desde luego le vendría bien.

Juliet abrió los ojos.

–Sé que tengo fiebre. Me siento fatal.

–No estaba habla... No importa. Deja que te lave el cabello. Tú puedes hacer el resto.

Se puso en la mano suficiente champú para lavar la cabeza de cuatro mujeres y le enjabonó el cabello tan rápido como le fue posible.

–Ya está. Ahora, enjuágate.

Con lo que parecía ser un esfuerzo considerable, ella metió la cabeza debajo del agua y volvió a emerger con los ojos cerrados. Finn le dio una toalla y estaba a punto de ponerse de pie y marcharse cuando ella le tocó una rodilla con la mano.

–No te vayas. Frótame la espalda.

El cabello mojado le cubría la zona en cuestión.

–Pensaba que habíamos quedado que eso lo harías tú.

–No. Tú me diste la orden de que no podía salir fuera del agua. No puedo levantar los brazos tanto.

Juliet volvió a ofrecerle la espalda. Se suponía que aquello era un proceso de limpieza, no los juegos previos al encuentro sexual. Finn tragó saliva y enjabonó la esponja. Tal vez si no la tocaba, no pasaría nada.

La esponja se deslizó por la espalda de Juliet, haciendo que ella exhalara un gruñido. El deseo se apoderó un poco más de Finn, a pesar de que él no lo deseaba. Tenía el cuerpo en estado de máxima alerta. Le habría gustado dejar la esponja y acariciar aquella maravillosa espalda con los dedos. Una cadena de plata le rodeaba el cuello a Juliet. Él no podía dejar de mirar el punto en el que se reunía con la piel. Aquel colgante era nuevo. ¿Cómo sería la combinación del frío metal con la carne caliente?

Lo tocaría un poco. Había pasado tanto tiempo... Podría sentir de nuevo la piel de Juliet.

Sin embargo, no lo hizo. Y no por la fiebre.

Si se reconciliaban, Finn no quería que ocurriera de ese modo, llevando a cabo los deseos de su padre. No quería que Juliet pensara que estaba con ella por la política que rodeaba a las dos familias.

Aquellas circunstancias no se podían transformar en un vínculo que creara una relación duradera. En su opinión, la única posibilidad verdadera que tenían era escaparse primero y luego ver cómo iban las cosas cuando estuvieran de nuevo en Delamer.

Siguió frotándole la espalda. Ella gimió de nuevo. ¿Tenía que hacer ese ruido, como si le estuviera acariciando uno de los senos?

Ella gimió de nuevo y dejó caer la cabeza sobre las rodillas.

–Tengo la piel muy sensible, probablemente de la fiebre. ¿Te puedes dar prisa?

–¿Te estoy haciendo daño? –preguntó él horrorizado.

Mientras él estaba teniendo ensoñaciones eróticas, Juliet estaba sufriendo. No se lo podía creer.

–No. No demasiado. Es que... me molesta.

–¿Quieres que pare?

Finn esperaba de corazón que la respuesta fuera afirmativa. Sin embargo, por otro lado… Echaba de menos el placer de estar acariciando simplemente a una mujer. Juliet era capaz de dárselo. No había ni una sola rubia en el planeta con la que lo pudiera conseguir.

—No pasa nada —dijo ella mirándole por encima del hombro—. Puedes seguir.

Claro que podía. Sin problemas.

El sudor le caía a él por la espalda. ¿Por qué se estaba haciendo aquello? El dolor sufrido a lo largo del año anterior aún estaba latente. Debía de ser masoquista.

—Gracias —susurró ella—. Me alegro de que estés aquí.

Una calidez que no tenía nada que ver con el sexo se le extendió por el torso. Sí. Eso era. Quería hacer que ella se sintiera mejor, a pesar de lo que eso pudiera suponerle a él.

Su trasnochado sentido del honor le volvía loco algunas veces.

—Yo también. Si no, te habrías convertido en pasto para tiburones.

Finn se tragó todos los demás comentarios que hubiera podido hacer y rezó para que la fiebre le remitiera y pudieran marcharse de la isla antes de que él no pudiera contenerse más.

Después de un considerable esfuerzo, Juliet se vistió con otro conjunto que encontró en el armario y permitió que Finn la llevara al sofá del salón. Allí, se cubrió con una manta y apoyó la cabeza en el hombro de él. Le gustaba dejar que Finn la cuidara. Pero lo negaría hasta la muerte.

Le dolía todo. El pecho, la cabeza, los brazos y las piernas…No tenía ni ganas de ver la televisión.

—Siento que tengamos que ver esta película tan aburrida.

—No pasa nada. No me gusta que te sientas tan mal.

La tierna sonrisa de Finn se le entrelazó en el vientre y llegó un poco más abajo, caldeándola agradablemente por dentro.

Finn le había despertado algo muy poderoso y profundo, que la afectaba de un modo terrible y maravilloso a la vez.

Juliet odiaba necesitar a nadie, y mucho más a Finn. Él no había estado a su lado cuando más lo necesitaba. ¿Y si se permitía confiar en él y Finn volvía a defraudarla?

Sin embargo, seguía enamorada de él, de eso estaba segura. Y eso lo odiaba también.

—Yo…

Un ataque de tos le impidió seguir. Menos mal. ¿Qué podría haber dicho?

«Me siento en conflicto con lo que me haces sentir. Gracias por rescatarme, pero, ¿te podrías ir al otro lado de la isla hasta que yo decida cómo no estar enamorada de ti?».

Finn le agarró la mano y se la sujetó contra el regazo. Tenía la atención puesta en ella y no en la película. Como en los viejos tiempos. Avivaba una deliciosa llama en lugares realmente deliciosos, lugares que ella prefería que no se vieran afectados cuando unos sentimientos tan confusos y poco bienvenidos le rondaban el corazón.

–No tienes que hablar.

El pulgar le acariciaba los nudillos y aquel contacto la iluminó. Unido al revuelo emocional que sentía, ver una película juntos cada vez le iba pareciendo peor idea. Sin embargo, no podía soportar la idea de estar sola en la cama, deseando que algo o alguien la hiciera sentirse mejor. Alguien como Finn.

Él le había dado un baño, aunque habría preferido no hacerlo. No le culpaba. Ella no se había portado muy bien en la playa y, después, Finn la había tenido que rescatar. Ella también estaría enojada.

–Me siento fatal, pero puedo hablar –dijo a pesar de acompañar sus palabras con un ataque de tos.

Finn la miró con una sonrisa, como si estuviera recordándole que ya se lo había dicho. A Juliet le pesaban demasiado los brazos como para poder levantarlos, y mucho menos darle un golpe. Por lo tanto, se conformó con mirarle con desaprobación.

–¿Por qué no te centras en descansar en vez de tratar de hacerme ver que estoy equivocado? –le sugirió él mientras le apartaba un mechón de cabello del rostro–. Cuando antes te pongas buena, antes podremos centrarnos de nuevo en escapar de aquí.

Parecía tan molesto por tener que cuidar de ella como Juliet porque él tuviera que hacerlo.

–Mira el lado bueno. Estamos en esta hermosa casa. No hay peligro del que preocuparnos. Podemos relajarnos mientras yo me pongo mejor. Será divertido.

—Creo que eso fue lo que te sugerí antes de que te lanzaras de cabeza al agua —comentó él.

—Y estoy de acuerdo contigo.

—Ojalá ese fuera el inicio de una situación duradera —murmuró él—. Dado que esta película es tan aburrida, ¿te parece que juguemos a algo en la Wii?

Esa era la razón de que a Juliet siempre le hubiera encantado quedarse en casa cuando estaban saliendo. Finn siempre tenía buenas ideas. Todo se convertía en algo divertido o en el prólogo del acto sexual. Normalmente las dos cosas.

—Claro —replicó ella. Apartó inmediatamente de la cabeza aquellos pensamientos. Lo último que necesitaba era pensar en lo mucho que echaba de menos ciertas habilidades de Finn—. Mientras no sea demasiado complicado o uno de esos juegos de guerra con mucha sangre y disparos. Ah, y nada de zombis ni alienígenas.

—Pues eso más o menos elimina... —comentó mientras examinaba los títulos—. Todos. Espera. Tenemos Super Mario Brothers. Ese está bien.

Finn preparó el juego y comenzaron a pasar niveles, riendo mientras batallaban contra los malos. Los coloridos gráficos y la animada música les transmitió una sensación de paz. Todas sus penas desaparecieron cuando se dejaron llevar por el fantástico mundo de los videojuegos.

Se convirtieron en un equipo formidable. Cuando ella se adentraba en el territorio enemigo, él la seguía, apoyándola en su lucha.

Como había hecho en el agua el día anterior.

Si no hubiera sacado el tema de Bernard y luego

le hubiera confesado la traición de su padre, tal vez no se habría tirado al mar. Sin embargo, lo que importaba era que él había estado a su lado, a pesar de que ella le dijo que era demasiado tarde.

Juliet no podía dejar de pensar al respecto. En Finn y en todas las cosas maravillosas que comprendían su carácter.

Eso le hacía cuestionar todo.

—Pan comido —dijo ella cuando consiguieron terminar un nivel particularmente difícil.

—Me sorprende que te esté gustando esto —comentó Finn mientras apretaba el icono para ir al siguiente mundo—. Dado que el objeto del juego es rescatar a la princesa Peach.

—¿Ese es el objetivo? —preguntó ella frunciendo el ceño—. Pensaba que era pasar al siguiente nivel.

—Los niveles tienen que terminar. En el último, Mario rescata a la princesa de la jaula.

—Entonces has jugado a esto antes.

La desilusión se apoderó de ella. De algún modo, se había imaginado que jugaban tan bien porque eran un equipo. Pero su éxito era producto de la familiaridad de Finn con el juego.

—He jugado algunas veces con Portia —dijo él apartando la mirada, como si se sintiera culpable de no haberle contado aquella información antes—. Es su favorito y no me pide que juegue con ella con frecuencia. Solo cuando Alexander no está… Es solo un juego —añadió él mientras le golpeaba el hombro con el suyo.

—No. Es machista y está lleno de estereotipos. ¿Cómo es que no secuestran a Mario?

Finn la miró con incredulidad.

—Porque Mario y Luigi son los protagonistas del juego. Si quieres jugar a algo en el que la mujer sea la estrella, prueba Tomb Raider.

—¿Y por qué no puede hacer la opción de cambiar al que se secuestra en el juego? —preguntó—. Sería estupendo cambiar los personajes y meter a Mario en una jaula.

Cuantas más mujeres creyeran en sí mismas y en su fuerza, mucho mejor. A Portia le gustaban los bailes, tomar el té con la reina y verse rescatada por su príncipe azul. A Juliet no. Ese pensamiento le puso un nudo en el estómago.

Tal vez a Juliet no le gustara que la rescatara el príncipe, pero él había tenido que hacerlo de todos modos. ¿La menospreciaba él por no haber hecho lo que tenía la intención de hacer? Seguramente si no hubiera tenido un resfriado, habría conseguido llegar a Saint Tropez nadando. Esa era su excusa y pensaba aferrarse a ella.

Finn sonrió y dejó el mando. Entonces, se recostó contra el sofá.

—Estoy seguro de que a Nintendo le encantaría conocer tus ideas sobre cómo dejar de perpetuar el estereotipo de princesas que siempre necesitan que se las rescate.

—Tú ni siquiera me tomas a mí en serio, con lo que una empresa japonesa mucho menos. Seguramente no tienen ni una sola mujer en los puestos ejecutivos.

Finn le agarró un mechón de cabello y se lo metió detrás de la oreja. Juliet no pudo contener el temblor que evocó aquel contacto. No quería, pero el estómago se le tensó de anticipación y de miedo. La mezcla de sensualidad, solidez y ternura que había en Finn la asustaba y la excitaba al mismo tiempo. ¿Cómo era eso posible?

–Claro que te tomo en serio. Me encanta lo apasionada que eres… sobre todo, tus firmes opiniones definen tu carácter.

–No te gusta cuando tengo opinión sobre algo. En especial no te gusta cuando…

Juliet se mordió el labio con fuerza.

«En especial no te gusta tiene que ver sobre cómo deberías haberte comportado hace un año.

–Me encanta todo lo que tiene que ver contigo, Juliet –dijo él–. Me encanta que, aunque eres muy fuerte, me permitiste rescatarte. Me encanta que, a pesar una incansable determinación, estés dispuesta a pedirme que te ayude a darte un baño. Por eso somos un buen equipo. Jugamos con las fortalezas del otro y reconocemos nuestros propios límites.

Dios santo. Si Juliet se había preguntado alguna vez porqué se había enamorado de Finn, él había hecho pedazos su curiosidad. ¿De dónde había sacado tanta poesía?

–Tú no tienes límites –gruñó ella para ocultar la emoción que le habían producido las palabras.

–Eso no es cierto. Tú casi me hiciste que me olvidara que los tengo antes, en el cuarto de baño susurró.

Comenzó a acariciarle la mandíbula con el pulgar. A pesar de todo lo que había ocurrido entre ellos, o tal vez por ello, Juliet anhelaba perderse en los sentimientos, dejar sus inhibiciones y temores y perderse en los brazos de Finn, en su cuerpo, en sus embriagadores besos, tan llenos de placer que no importaba nada más.

¿Por qué no podían estar juntos, con todas las dificultades del mundo exterior olvidadas? Solo los dos, alimentando sus hambrientas almas.

¿No era eso lo que estaba ocurriendo en aquellos momentos? Estaban cautivos. Entonces, ¿por qué no aprovechar el tiempo que tenían juntos para disfrutar las partes buenas de su relación?

Nadie había dicho que tenían que besarse y hacer las paces. Tal vez podrían solo besarse… entre otras actividades. El rey Laurent no dictaba las reglas. Juliet podría estar con Finn tanto si al padre de él le gustaba como si no.

Sin un futuro del que preocuparse ni familia a la que desilusionar, ella no tenía que preocuparse de confiar en él. Si mantenía su corazón bien protegido, Finn no podría volver a rompérselo. Nada de sentimientos.

Lo único que tenían que hacer era mantenerse alejados del pasado y centrarse en el presente. Pan comido.

Capítulo Ocho

Más tarde aquel mismo día, Finn se tomó un respiro y dejó de estar pendiente de Juliet para darse una ducha fría. Le ayudó a aliviar un poco el ansia que se había apoderado de la mitad inferior de su cuerpo, pero no del todo. Sospechaba que tan solo una Juliet desnuda y dispuesta podría eliminarlo por completo. Eso o un estado de coma.

Cuando salió de su dormitorio, Juliet no estaba en el sofá, donde la había dejado viendo una película romántica. Unos ruidos provenientes de la cocina despertaron su curiosidad. Se dirigió hacia allí y sorprendió a Juliet tratando de someter una sartén y un poco de carne.

La observó durante un minuto, disfrutando de la visión trasera de una esbelta y descalza Juliet. Sin embargo, ella seguía enferma y él había regresado otra vez a su estado de tensión sexual.

—¿Por qué no estás descansando? —le preguntó él.

Juliet se sobresaltó y dejó caer un cazo sobre uno de los azulejos de mármol italiano y lo partió por la mitad. Portia iba a pedir la cabeza del rey.

—No me sobresaltes de esa manera.

—Lo siento —replicó. Pataleó el suelo unas cuantas veces, fingiendo que acababa de llegar—. Ahora estoy en la cocina, ¿de acuerdo?

–De acuerdo –replicó ella con una sonrisa antes de volverse de nuevo al fogón–. No estoy descansando, me pediste que te preparara la cena.

–¿Sí? –preguntó él. ¿De verdad? ¿Cómo se había atrevido a pedirle que repitiera lo del pollo?

–Antes, cuando me dijiste que podría mostrarte mi gratitud haciendo la cena.

Era cierto.

–No estás lo suficientemente bien como para levantarte del sofá. Vamos.

Finn le agarró de la mano y tiró de ella hacia el salón sin prestar atención a las eróticas sensaciones de piel contra piel.

–Pero tienes que comer –protestó ella mientras le hacía detenerse en seco.

–Llevo alimentándome solo desde hace doce años –replicó él. Aún seguían de la mano–. Me las arreglaré. ¿Y tú? ¿Tienes hambre? Te puedo calentar un poco de sopa.

–No, gracias. He comido unos biscotes. ¿Me he dejado el fogón encendido?

Juliet se asomó por encima del hombro de él mientras se mordía el labio inferior.

Finn la miró y sintió que su boca palpitaba. Aquellos labios eran deliciosos, tal y como bien sabía por experiencia personal.

–Si te lo has dejado encendido, yo me ocuparé.

–Estoy segura de ello. ¿Hay algo de lo que no puedas ocuparte? –replicó ella con ironía.

A Finn se le ocurría una al menos…

Ella suspiró, levantando los senos sugerentemente. Antes de que él perdiera la cabeza, dio un paso atrás, pero sin soltarle la mano. Juliet las miró y apretó la suya con fuerza. Entonces, dio un paso al frente y cerró el espacio que los separaba.

—Espera. No te vayas. Si no quieres que te prepare nada de cenar, siéntate conmigo en el patio para que podamos ver juntos la puesta de sol.

El deseo en estado puro se apoderó de él.

—Yo… probablemente no deberías salir…

¿Contemplar la puesta de sol? ¿Juntos? Seguramente no se había parado a pensar que sería un escenario muy romántico. Aquella era una complicación que él no necesitaba.

—Sigues estando enferma —añadió.

—En realidad, no me siento tan mal —musitó ella a pesar de que seguía estando un poco pálida y débil. Acababa de pronunciar aquellas palabras cuando inclinó la cabeza a un lado, sin fuerzas.

Finn lanzó una maldición y la tomó en brazos. Entonces, la llevó al sofá antes de que ella pudiera pronunciar una objeción más.

—Al menos, siéntate antes de que te caigas. Si estás decidida a mostrarme tu gratitud, ponte buena. Es una orden.

—Sí, señor —dijo ella realizando un saludo militar. Entonces, se acurrucó entre los cojines y se tapó con una manta—. ¿Estás contento?

En absoluto. Cada nervio de su cuerpo le vibraba de deseo insatisfecho.

—Encantado. Tenemos mucho tiempo para contemplar las puestas de sol cuando te pongas bien.

Ella parpadeó inocente y sugerente al mismo tiempo. Finn deseaba tanto acurrucarse con ella…

—En ese caso, siéntate conmigo —sugirió ella con una pequeña sonrisa que él no pudo rechazar.

Como necesitaba desesperadamente una distracción, Finn se sentó en el cojín y encendió la televisión. Carrera de Fórmula 1 en Singapur, uno de sus circuitos favoritos. Automáticamente fue a apretar el botón para cambiar de canal, pero se lo impidió la mano de Juliet.

—Está bien —dijo ella. Entonces le quitó el mando de la mano—. Me gustaría verlo contigo.

—Te preguntaría si te encuentras bien, pero ya sé la respuesta. Debes de tener más fiebre de lo que pensaba si estás dispuesta a ver una carrera de Fórmula 1.

—Ya te he dicho que no me encuentro tan mal. Dime una cosa. Siempre me he preguntado cómo sabes qué coche va primero si todos van dando vueltas por el mismo circuito una y otra vez —comentó mientras apoyaba la sien sobre el hombro de Finn para mirar la pantalla.

—Tienes la lista de posiciones en la pantalla.

—Ah, entonces es más fácil de lo que creía que sería. ¿Y por qué algunos de los coches son idénticos y otros son diferentes?

—Hay equipos —respondió él. Había perdido todo el interés por la carrera. Inclinó la nariz hacia el cabello de Juliet e inhaló el fresco aroma de Juliet y del champú que él había utilizado para lavarle el cabello. El recuerdo de su cuerpo desnudo y húmedo bajo todas aquellas burbujas despertó en él una lenta tortura.

Ella lo miró perpleja, aunque parecía interesada.

–Los equipos tienen más de un conductor –aclaró él–. Mismo coche, mismo equipo.

Durante los próximos quince minutos, Juliet le hizo más preguntas y escuchó pacientemente las respuestas. De vez en cuando realizaba algún comentario bastante acertado.

–¿Estás pensando solicitar trabajo como miembro del equipo? –le preguntó él al ver la cantidad de preguntas que ella realizaba–. En Mónaco hay un circuito. Podrías ir y venir en treinta minutos como máximo.

–Ni hablar –respondió ella riendo–. Me daría pavor tocar un coche que vale un millón de dólares.

–Entonces, ¿a qué se deben tantas preguntas?

–Es algo que te gusta. Quería saber más al respecto –dijo encogiéndose de hombros.

Entrelazó los dedos con los de él, como había hecho cientos de veces antes de que terminaran su relación. Unido a las palabras que acababa de pronunciar, el efecto fue potente.

Entonces, entornó la mirada.

–¿Qué te parece si, en vez de prepararte la cena, te quisiera mostrar mi gratitud de otro modo?

La pregunta vino acompañada de un suave movimiento de dedo índice sobre el pectoral. No quedó duda alguna de a qué se refería.

¿Qué estaba haciendo? Primero la Fórmula 1 y luego eso. La fiebre debía de estar cociéndole el cerebro.

–Tienes fiebre –le recordó él–. Ni siquiera debería estar tan cerca de ti.

–Me parece recordar que me has besado en las

121

últimas veinticuatro horas en más de una ocasión, y bastante concienzudamente.

Juliet observó ávidamente la reacción de Finn. Él se esforzó mucho por no dársela, pero estaba seguro de que la inmediata erección que se le formó no le pasó desapercibida. Ninguna tela en el mundo era capaz de ocultarla.

–Afróntalo –murmuró ella. Redujo al mínimo el espacio entre ellos y entonces, tiró la manta para acurrucarse contra el torso de Finn–. Ya te he contagiado todo lo que te tenía que contagiar. ¿Qué malo hay en otro beso? Para demostrarte mi gratitud…

Finn le miró los labios, que estaban muy cerca de los suyos.

–Dijiste que habíamos terminado. En la playa. ¿Acaso el hecho de que estuvieras a punto de morir te supone dificultad a la hora de tomar decisiones?

Aquel no era el plan. El rescate primero. La reconciliación más tarde. Había demasiadas cosas de las que no habían hablado para hacer algo así en aquellos momentos. ¿Cómo podría él decirle a Juliet que su padre quería que se casara con ella? Necesitaba tener la mente muy fría para tener aquella conversación.

Ella sonrió y se colocó la mano sobre la mejilla.

–En vez de suponerme dificultad, me ha hecho ver las cosas más claras.

–¿Cómo? Yo sigo siendo un príncipe y…

–Calla –susurró ella mientras le sellaba los labios con el pulgar para hacerle guardar silencio–. El príncipe Alain no está aquí. Yo solo veo a Finn.

Finn. Sí. Allí en la Île de Etienne, él se podía olvidar de las complejidades de aquella espada de doble filo y no ser nada más que un hombre. Ya podrían volver a la realidad cuando les rescataran. En aquellos momentos, podía dejarse llevar…

Involuntariamente, las manos de Finn buscaron el rostro de Juliet, decidido a tocarla, desesperado por establecer un vínculo con ella. Sus manos tocaron una piel fresca. Por fin.

—Creo que ya no tienes fiebre.

—¿Esta es la parte en la que yo te digo que ya te lo había dicho? —preguntó ella con una sonrisa. Entonces, comenzó a besarle la garganta.

—Claro. Puedo soportarlo.

—¿Y esto? ¿Puedes soportarlo también?

Juliet tiro de él hasta que sus alientos se cruzaron y le rozó los labios. Tan solo un ligero contacto e, inmediatamente, Finn solo pudo pensar en la hermosa mujer que tenía entre los brazos.

—Sí —murmuró él suavemente—. Puedo soportarlo todo…

Le enredó los dedos en el cabello y profundizó el beso con la intención de saciar el deseo desbocado que tenía por Juliet. Ya se ocuparían de las implicaciones más tarde.

Ella gimió y se inclinó sobre él como si no pudiera acercarse lo suficiente. Le acariciaba el cuello con los dedos y los deslizaba por debajo de la camiseta para extenderlos sobre la cintura.

Finn quería sentir aquellas manos por todo su cuerpo y quería tocarla del mismo modo para poder saciar la sed que tenía de la mujer que tanto había echado de menos.

Le colocó las manos en la garganta y le hizo inclinar la cabeza para poder profundizar el beso. Ella era deliciosa.

La esencia de Juliet se apoderó de sus sentidos. Ella se sentó encima de Finn y comenzó a rozarle el torso con los senos sin dejar de besarle. Las lenguas se enredaron una y otra vez para darse placer mutuamente.

Finn se moría de ganas por hundirse en ella y dejar que toda la pasión que sentía por Juliet explot...

Con esfuerzo considerable, apartó la boca de la de ella.

—Tenemos que tomárnoslo con calma, cielo.

—¿Tomárnoslo con calma? ¿Por qué?

La confusión de ella se mezcló con la frustración de él, añadiendo peso a la ya imposible situación que el padre de Finn había creado.

—Porque...

Le costaba incluso respirar por el fuerte deseo que le dominaba. Se mesó el cabello antes de volver a colocarle la mano sobre el tentador trasero.

—No hay ni un solo preservativo en toda la casa.

Juliet se quedó inmóvil al escuchar a Finn.

—¿No hay preservativos?

Fin de su plan para desnudar a Finn y dejarse llevar por una breve aventura sin ningún tipo de ataduras.

—Ni uno. He mirado. ¿Tú tomas la píldora o algo así?

—No. ¿Por qué iba a hacerlo?

—Bueno, porque has ido a una casamentera a buscar esposo. Merecía la pena preguntar.

En realidad, había ido a una casamentera porque estaba huyendo. La intimidad con un hombre no había ocupado su pensamiento en ningún momento.

–¿Entonces ya está? ¿No podemos hacer nada?

Juliet acompañó la pregunta deslizando el dedo hacía abajo por el torso de Finn. Él contuvo el aliento cuando las uñas de ella rozaron la impresionante erección.

–Si hubiera sabido que esas uñas postizas me iban a hacer eso, te las habría hecho poner hace mucho tiempo –dijo. Le apartó la mano del regazo y se la colocó sobre el corazón–. Tienes que contenerte.

–Podemos tener cuidado –susurró ella meneando las caderas y frotándose sin vergüenza alguna contra él. El deseo se apoderó de ella y se arqueó involuntariamente para rozar de nuevo el torso de él con los sensibles pezones.

Finn gruñó y levantó las caderas para unirse más a ella en sus movimientos.

–Cuando estás desnuda, no puedo tener cuidado, en especial si sigues haciendo eso. Me he pasado el último año a merced de los tabloides. Un embarazo sorpresa sería la guinda del pastel.

–Lo siento. Voy a parar –dijo ella. Comenzó a levantarse, pero Finn la inmovilizó con manos de hierro.

–Te he dicho que te lo tomes con calma, no que pares.

Su mirada azul buscó la de ella y la miró fijamente mientras movía en círculo las caderas apretando la erección contra ella.

–Entonces, si me haces el amor muy lentamente, no me quedo embarazada.

Lo de lentamente iba a dejar de ser una opción. La sonrisa que se reflejó en los labios de él hizo subir un poco más la excitación de ella.

–Me preocupa más la parte de no estar casados y menos la del embarazo.

–¿Qué estás diciendo? ¿Que si estuviéramos casados no sería un problema?

–Si te quedas embarazada, nos tendríamos que casar –susurró él acariciándole el torso, acercando peligrosamente los pulgares a los senos de ella–. No es negociable.

El cerebro de Juliet no era capaz de seguir lo que estaba pasando, y mucho menos con las partes más interesantes de Finn frotándose con las suyas. Ansiaba que él le tocara lo pezones.

–¿Me… me estás proponiendo matrimonio?

–No precisamente –dijo él frunciendo los labios–. Se trata más bien de una promesa en el futuro.

No era capaz de controlar sus sentimientos ni lo que experimentaba su corazón. Quería que él la amara en el sentido físico. En el emocional. Lo deseaba tanto que a su cuerpo no parecía importarle cómo lo consiguiera.

Aquel fue un momento verdaderamente malo para darse cuenta de no había sido capaz de ocultar bien sus sentimientos. ¿Por qué había pensado que podía?

–¿Por qué no podemos hablar de esto más tarde? –murmuró ella. Se inclinó hacia él hasta que los pulgares de Finn le rozaron los erectos pezones. El placer se apoderó de ella e inundo sus sentidos–. Yo solo quiero estar contigo, sin toda las complicaciones. ¿Es posible?

–Entre nosotros no.

–Porque tú eres el príncipe Alain. Siempre lo mismo –susurró ella.

La mirada de Finn buscó la de ella, llena de deseo y con un brillo significativo.

–Porque sigo enamorado de ti. Eso lo estropea todo. Ojalá hubiera una manera de olvidar lo ocurrido en el pasado y poder vivir tan solo el momento. Lo haría fuera como fuera.

Ella parpadeó para contener las lágrimas.

Finn seguía amándola.

El corazón se le abrió de par en par para recibir aquel sentimiento con alegría. Algo dulce y maravilloso le recorrió todo el cuerpo.

–No debería haber dicho eso –dijo él meneando la cabeza–. Yo…

–No pasa nada –musitó ella. Aún tenía un nudo en la garganta que le impedía pronunciar que ella también seguía enamorada de él.

Entonces, por fin, consiguió encerrar sus sentimientos. No podía decirle que estaba enamorada de él. Así le había dado antes el poder de hacerle daño.

Sin embargo, en aquella ocasión no tenía que hacerlo. Él le había ofrecido la solución perfecta. No tenían que revivir la historia ni mencionarla siquiera. Podían vivir el momento, dejarse llevar por el placer de cada uno y ocuparse más adelante del futuro. Mucho más adelante, en especial la parte sobre los sentimientos.

Lentamente, se levantó la camiseta y observó cómo la expresión de él se oscurecía.

–Olvidémonos de lo que ocurrió hace un año y disfrutemos simplemente juntos. Si hay consecuencias, ya veremos. En estos momentos, aquí y ahora, sé Finn para mí. Aunque solo pueda ser por una noche.

Capítulo Nueve

Una noche.

Finn observó cómo Juliet se dejaba al descubierto los senos. No llevaba sujetador. El pulso le latía en la sien con un ritmo errático que parecía más bien un código morse que un latido diseñado a mantenerlo con vida.

El deseo que se reflejaba en el rostro de ella le aceleró la sangre y acrecentó al máximo su propio deseo. Juliet tenía unos pechos muy hermosos, de puntas rosadas que él quería lamer hasta que ella gimiera de placer.

—¿Estás segura? —le preguntó.

Si Juliet elegía estar con él, no importaría que el rey los hubiera unido aposta. No importaría que ella se quedara embarazada mientras comprendiera que el matrimonio sería el siguiente paso.

—Estoy segura —dijo ella inmediatamente. Con decisión. Resultaba muy excitante saber que ella lo deseaba tanto.

Sin embargo, comprendió que había cometido un error de gran importancia.

—No estás permitiendo que el hecho de que yo te haya dicho que te amo te nuble la capacidad de decisión, ¿verdad?

—No —respondió ella, con una sonrisa dubitativa

en los labios, como si no fuera capaz de decidir si quería sonreír de verdad–. Esto tiene que ver contigo y conmigo y con lo que deseamos.

Finn sabía exactamente lo que quería. Aquella noche tan solo deseaba ser Finn.

–¿De verdad puedes olvidar? –le preguntó.

Ella levantó un dedo.

–No hay pasado. Ni mañana. Esta noche, tan solo estamos tú y yo. Esa es la única regla.

Le pareció una regla estupenda. Si no había mañana, el plan de su padre no era un factor a tener en cuenta. Además, la familia de Juliet jamás se pondría al lado de la corona, fuera lo que fuera lo que ocurriera entre ellos.

Juliet se echó hacia delante y colocó los labios sobre los de él para besarle. Los cielos se abrieron y vertieron luz en su debilitada alma. O tal vez era la fuerza de Juliet la que se la infundía a la suya.

La rodeó con los brazos y se aferró a la mujer que amaba para grabar aquel momento en su memoria y recordarlo más tarde y poder saborearlo. Ella era la única mujer de entre las que habían estado con Finn que él había considerado lo suficientemente capacitada para soportar las presiones y dificultades de estar con un príncipe. Ella jamás se derrumbaría.

Incapaz de contenerse un momento más, la besó con cada gramo de su pasión contenida. Ella gimió y se abrió bajo su asalto. Ansioso por saborearla, Finn entrelazó la lengua con la de ella y la estrechó contra su cuerpo para poder sentir sus magníficos senos contra su torso.

–Necesito esto fuera –musitó ella, y le quitó la camiseta a Finn.

En cuanto la dejó caer al suelo, Juliet le colocó las manos en la cintura y empezó a desabrocharle los pantalones. Con la prisa, estuvo a punto de arrancárselos.

Sí. Por fin desnudos.

Finn la hizo levantarse y se bajó los pantalones. Entonces, observó cómo ella hacía lo mismo antes de estrecharla contra su cuerpo. Por fin estuvieron piel contra piel. Finn gruñó de placer al sentir el cuerpo desnudo de Juliet contra el suyo y volvió a poseer su boca con un beso salvaje.

Ya no había necesidad de tomárselo con calma. Ni tenía intención de hacerlo.

La arrinconó contra la pared y le colocó un muslo entre las piernas para frotar su feminidad. Gozó al encontrarla húmeda y preparada para él. Conocía el cuerpo de Juliet tan bien como conocía el suyo. Sabía cómo tocarla, cómo le gustaba, cuándo detenerse y cuándo moverse con más rapidez.

Todo era familiar en ella, pero eso lo hacía más excitante. No había confusiones.

–Date prisa –gimió ella acrecentando la urgencia de Finn–. Hace ya tanto tiempo… Quiero sentirte.

Los deseos de Juliet eran órdenes. La levantó contra la pared y le separó los muslos para comenzar a torturarla con la punta de su erección. El cuerpo de Juliet ardía contra el de él de tal manera que Finn tuvo que cerrar los ojos para controlar la lujuria que se había adueñado de él. No pudo contenerse más. La hizo bajar un poco y la penetró lentamente, tratando de darle tanto placer como fuera posible antes de explotar dentro de ella.

Sin preservativos, la sensaciones eran abrumadoras. Se apoderaban de él como un potente *tsunami* de placer. Juliet se agarró a él con las piernas y le hundió los talones en el trasero para animarle seguir con idéntico fervor.

—Increíble —susurró ella—. Eres increíble…

—Tú también…

Juliet movió las caderas y lo acogió aún más profundamente. Finn sintió que las rodillas le temblaban de tanto contenerse.

—Juliet —murmuró él.

Ella le agarró la mano que le quedaba libre y se la llevó a la entrepierna. Entonces, entrelazó los dedos con los de él para guiarle. A Finn le encantaba cuando ella llevaba la iniciativa. Cuando se daba placer a sí misma. Era poderoso, hermoso. Apasionado. Y lo volvía loco.

Cuando más frotaba él, más se arqueaba ella echando la cabeza hacia atrás y gritando de placer. Juliet alcanzó el orgasmo con un poderoso temblor que le apretó a él exquisitamente y le obligó a dejarse llevar por fin.

Los dos cayeron al suelo. Finn la tomó entre sus brazos y la estrechó con fuerza. Los húmedos torsos de ambos trataban de respirar. Finn le apartó el cabello del rostro y respiró profundamente. Por fin, su cuerpo, su mente y su alma estaban en paz.

Aquello era lo que más había echado de menos.

—Tal vez la próxima vez conseguiremos llegar al sofá —musitó ella.

–Tal vez la próxima vez me des la oportunidad de llegar cerca del sofá.

Le besó la sien con delicadeza. Por primera vez en la historia de su relación, ninguno de los dos tenía ningún lugar en el que estar. Podrían estar haciendo el amor todo el día si querían.

Y Finn quería. El pasado no existía y el futuro aún no había llegado. No tenía que pensar en ninguna de las dos cosas.

Llegaron a la cama. A duras penas.

Juliet cayó sobre las almohadas y gimió de placer cuando Finn comenzó a deslizarle la lengua por el muslo muy lentamente, como si tuvieran todo el tiempo del mundo. No era así. Aquel paraíso tenía las horas contadas y, además, Juliet deseaba tenerlo en su interior inmediatamente.

–¿Cómo consigues que sea tan agradable? –murmuró ella. Entonces, gimió de placer cuando él comenzó a mordisquearla con la presión exacta para hacerla gozar.

El placer le recorrió el cuerpo rápidamente, pero Finn se detuvo justo a tiempo para evitar que ella alcanzara el orgasmo. Antes de que pudiera protestar, la tumbó boca abajo y la penetró por detrás. Sí… No solo era la postura favorita de Finn, sino que también era la de ella.

Juliet cerró los ojos de placer cuando él le levantó las caderas para poseerla más profundamente. Le había puesto la boca en el hombro y le arañaba la piel con la incipiente barba.

Finn salió de su cuerpo y volvió a hundirse en ella lenta, muy lentamente. Juliet juntó los tobillos para incrementar la fricción, tal y como a los dos les gustaba. Finn gruñó de placer e incrementó el ritmo tal y como ella necesitaba, a la velocidad que él sabía que llevaría a Juliet al orgasmo. Ella apretó una vez y no necesitó más. Las estrellas le estallaron delante de los ojos, cegándola durante un instante.

Finn gruñó y se desmoronó encima de ella. El clímax vibraba dentro de ella deliciosamente.

Juliet había perdido la cuenta del número de veces que él la había dejado completamente saciada. La primera vez, contra la pared del salón, había sido una experiencia increíble, y qué podía decir de las demás. Recordaba que él era buen amante, pero la realidad eclipsaba la memoria. Era increíble e incansable. Cuando se excitaba, no era delicado, pero a ella le gustaba un poco duro. Conseguir que un hombre perdiera ligeramente el control hacía que una mujer se sintiera muy sexy. Además, ella le daba tanto como recibía, y eso solo acrecentaba la pasión de él que, a su vez, alimentaba la de ella.

No era de extrañar que fueran una pareja perfecta. Encajaban como los corazones del colgante de Elise. Entrelazados por la pasión.

Se separaron por fin. Tenían la respiración entrecortada. Él se colocó el brazo por encima de la cabeza y cerró los ojos, tumbado sobre la cama como la fantasía erótica de una chica mala, desnudo y espléndido. Juliet bebió aquella imagen e, igual de descarada, disfrutó de cada segundo.

Los pectorales de Finn se flexionaban y se relajaban cuando respiraba. Tenía también los abdominales bien marcados, resultado de lo que debían de ser horas de ejercicio.

Al mismo tiempo, la tristeza se apoderó de ella. Finn había desarrollado aquellos músculos a lo largo del año pasado. Mientras estaban separados.

Habían acordado una única regla. Debían olvidar el pasado.

—Vayamos fuera —sugirió ella, decidida a olvidarse de nuevo de todo.

Finn abrió un ojo y la miró con cautela.

—Está oscuro. Debo de haberme oxidado un poco si quieres salir al exterior en vez de quedarte en la cama conmigo.

Juliet se echó a reír.

—Yo no he dicho nada de vestirnos. No tenemos vecinos ni paparazzi cerca. Estamos en el mes de junio y la temperatura es perfecta. ¿Cuándo volveremos a tener las mismas circunstancias?

Finn la miró sorprendido.

—Sexo bajo las estrellas. Me gusta…

Se levantó de la cama y tiró de la colcha. Entonces, los dos salieron del dormitorio. Juliet lo siguió y pensó en lo bonito que era el trasero desnudo de Finn. Suspiró. Sería genial si ella pudiera contar con poder verlo cuando quisiera.

¿De quién había sido la genial idea de estar juntos sin pensar en el futuro? De ella…

Cuadró los hombros y cerró la puerta corredera a sus espaldas.

Un impresionante panorama de estrellas iluminaba la tranquila noche, impresionante en todo su esplendor. El suave murmullo del agua proporcionaba un melódico acompañamiento. Una brillante luna colgaba del cielo hacia el oeste, iluminando el camino a España.

—Vaya… —dijo ella—. Deberías darme puntos extra por haber tenido esta idea.

Finn se tumbó en la colcha y la invitó a que se tumbara a su lado.

—Estaba pensando en todas las maneras en las que podía darte las gracias. Es maravilloso.

Juliet se acomodó a su lado y él la abrazó. Le cubrió suavemente el costado con el brazo y comenzó a acariciarle la curva de la cintura. Sin embargo, no había… fuego. Resultaba cómodo. La tranquilidad se apoderó de ella.

Podría ser así cuando regresaran a Delamer. Estaban ignorando muy bien el pasado. ¿Por qué no podían seguir así?

Las estrellas brillaban. Ojalá pudieran volver atrás. Si los dos se amaban, ¿por qué no podía ser suficiente?

—¿Y si te dijera que me puedes llamar? —le preguntó ella de repente—. Después de que nos marchemos de esta isla.

Podrían probar salir a cenar otra vez, tener una conversación civilizada y marcharse a casa de él para hacer el amor hasta el amanecer.

—Ya hemos pasado un poco esa etapa, ¿no te parece? A finales de mes, podríamos estar prometidos.

Se lo imaginó de rodillas, ofreciéndole un diamante más grande que una estrella. Los pulmones le ardían por contener el aliento, esperando conseguir así que aquella imagen desapareciera.

Finn no quería casarse con ella, pero lo haría por deber.

Qué romántico. ¿Cómo se había convertido aquella noche tan sencilla en algo tan complicado? No quería que Finn le pidiera matrimonio porque se sintiera obligado. Tampoco quería que aquel idilio se terminara nunca.

Se sentó y se volvió para mirarlo.

—¿Y si no me quedo embarazada? ¿Fin? *¿Au revoir* y eso de «ya te llamaré»?

—¡Qué cara más dura, Juliet! Tú fuiste la que se me insinuó, que fue como ofrecer vino a un alcohólico y pedirle que no se lo tomara.

—¿Acaso debería disculparme?

Finn lanzó una maldición.

—¿De verdad es esta la conversación que quieres tener?

—No lo sé. Todo es raro y alocado.

Finn suspiró.

—¿No piensas que podamos estar juntos a largo plazo?

—Sí —susurró ella. Estaría mintiendo si le dijera que no.

—Entonces, hagamos que ocurra, con o sin bebé que nos obligue. Si eso es lo que quieres.

Inmediatamente, la idea arraigó. Respiró profundamente y lo pensó. No podía tener las dos cosas. O rompían de nuevo o estaban juntos. Él tenía razón. No había posibilidad de darse tiempo a ver cómo iban las cosas. Su relación era demasiado profunda para eso. Siempre lo había sido y siempre lo sería.

—No te puedes casar conmigo. A tu familia y a la mía les daría un ataque al corazón.

Efectivamente, su madre tendría un ataque de nervios. Por eso la Île de Etienne era perfecta. Nadie tenía que saber que había disfrutado de una breve aventura con Finn.

Juliet no se podría casar con él nunca. Temía que pudiera ser capaz de utilizarlo para conseguir sus propios fines. Se mordió el labio. Sin embargo, si se quedaba embarazada, ¿estaba dispuesta a mentirle sobre quién era el padre? Eso no sería posible. Y Finn jamás ocultaría que era el padre de su hijo. Ella tampoco querría criar a un niño sola o privar a su hijo de todos los gozos de tener una familia normal.

Sintió ganas de llorar. Lo único que había buscado era una aventura sin complicaciones con un hombre muy guapo que le hacía hervir la sangre. ¿Era aquello mucho pedir?

—Eso no es cierto —replicó él—. Si tú estuvieras embarazada, ni siquiera pestañearían. Además, la opinión que mi padre tiene de ti se ha suavizado.

—¿Cuándo ha ocurrido eso?

—Cuando vio nuestra foto juntos. Estaba en la nota. Se ha dado cuenta de que sigue habiendo algo entre nosotros.

—Por supuesto. Por eso nos dejó aquí tirados, para que no pudiéramos dañar más su imagen si nos volvían a fotografiar juntos.

—Esa no es la razón. Nunca me diste la oportunidad de explicarme. Mi padre hizo que nos trajeran aquí para que pudiéramos pasar tiempo juntos, lejos de todo. Para ver si nuestra relación seguía siendo posible.

–¿Y por qué haría algo así?

–Debió de resultarle evidente que yo no quería un matrimonio concertado. Sin embargo, sigue queriendo que siente la cabeza. No obstante, yo jamás habría soñado que… Bueno, por eso traté de conseguir que huyéramos de aquí. No quería que nos reconciliáramos de esta manera, haciendo justo lo que él quería. Lo sien…

–No dejes que tu padre siga controlando nuestra relación –dijo ella–. Esta noche estamos solo nosotros. Mañana ya nos ocuparemos de todo lo demás, incluso de tu padre, del pasado y del futuro. Déjalo estar por el momento.

Ella trató de hacer lo mismo, pero, por mucho que se esforzó, no consiguió recuperar la paz. No podía dejar de preguntarse qué era lo que iba a hacer que el día siguiente fuera diferente del año anterior.

El destino no podría haber conspirado para ponerlos juntos a Finn y a ella y luego separarlos cruelmente.

Tal vez otras mujeres esperaban que el destino se adueñara de su destino. Juliet Villere no. Y tampoco iba a desperdiciar aquella segunda oportunidad

Al día siguiente, ella sería, de algún modo, la diferencia. Tenían que resolver sus puntos de fricción de una vez por todas y no volver a hablar del pasado. Ella quería recuperar su relación intacta, exactamente como había sido, una relación en la que pudiera estar segura de que Finn la iba a anteponer a todo lo que ocurriera en su vida.

En ese momento, estaría completamente segura de que la amaba de verdad. Y para siempre.

Capítulo Diez

Cuando Juliet se despertó por la mañana, apenas había abierto los ojos cuando notó a Finn pegado a su cuerpo, con la intención claramente reflejada en la mirada.

—Buenos días —murmuró ella mientras se acurrucaba contra su cálido cuerpo para disfrutar de un instante de pura armonía que no tenía nada que ver con el sexo.

Un instante fue lo único que disfrutó. Finn la tuvo veinte minutos ocupada.

—Buenos días —respondió él por fin.

Saciado y decidido a empezar perezosamente la mañana, encendió la televisión y abrazó a Juliet para ponerse a ver lo que echaran en aquel momento. Tenía el cabello revuelto y el torso desnudo, todo músculos y deliciosa piel. Juliet se podría acostumbrar a despertarse así por las mañanas.

Finn se incorporó con los ojos pegados a la televisión. Juliet miró hacia la pantalla y vio que se trataba de un programa de noticias. Estaban hablando de un barco de guerra de aspecto siniestro, cuya cubierta estaba repleta de mortíferas armas.

Finn subió el volumen para escuchar mejor.

—… frente a la costa de Grecia, a poca distancia del ejército recientemente reunido. Los líderes mundiales se van a reunir en Ginebra esta tarde para hablar de un ataque preventivo sobre las fuerzas del país.

Finn se tensó y la miró. Juliet sintió que el pulso se le aceleraba.

–¿De qué están hablando?

–No lo sé, pero sea lo que sea, no es bueno –respondió cuando el presentador pasó a hablar de una demostración pacífica en Atenas para protestar por la agresión–. Ese barco de guerra está estacionado en el mar Jónico. Desde aquí, podríamos darle con una piedra.

Juliet ansiaba agarrar el mando y lanzarlo al otro lado de la habitación. Agresión militar. Su tema menos favorito. Evidentemente, la presencia de aquel buque de guerra en el Mediterráneo era importante para Finn.

–Busca otro canal que hable al respecto –le sugirió ella–. Tienes que saberlo.

Finn asintió y fue buscando hasta que encontró otro canal de noticias. Se enteraron de que el gobierno de Alhendra, un pequeño y rico país situado entre Albania y Grecia, había lanzado unos misiles contra un barrio civil en Preveza, una hermosa región costera de Grecia. Había habido muchos muertos y la sed de venganza de los poderes mundiales era muy grande. Había sido un acto de guerra sin provocación alguna que las Naciones Unidas no podía ignorar.

Juliet escuchó atentamente de la mano de Finn, tratando que él no notara lo mucho que le temblaba la mano. Se había informado de la muerte de Bernard con imágenes muy similares de un barco de guerra navegando a toda velocidad, cortando las oscuras aguas del mar.

Finn lanzó un gruñido de desesperación.

–No me puedo creer que esto esté ocurriendo y que yo esté aquí atrapado. Delamer podría estar en peligro. Cualquier región costera podría verse envuelta en el fuego cruzado. Nuestros barcos deben estar preparados para colaborar con nuestros aliados en cualquier momento. Al menos, deberíamos enviar a alguien a Ginebra.

Atrapado. Con ella. Finn prefería estar en casa, gozando con la gloria de las fuerzas armadas.

–¿No crees que tu padre ya se habrá ocupado del tema? Este es su momento.

También el de Finn. Era una oportunidad de oro para ensalzar las virtudes de las políticas militares de su padre. Para reírse de todo lo que ella había dicho antes cuando defendía que eran momentos de paz.

–Por supuesto que sí, pero necesita ayuda. Seguramente ya viene alguien a buscarme. Yo debería estar allí.

Juliet se había equivocado. Tenía que aceptar que el sentido del honor de Finn jamás le permitiría no estar junto a su padre. Tenía que encontrar el modo de aceptar que la muerte de Bernard no se vengaría con una reforma.

O debía no estar junto a Finn.

Eso iba a ser bastante difícil si estaba embarazada de él.

Bernard había muerto, pero Juliet seguía con vida. Su hermano no querría que llevara una vida miserable por él. Adoraba a Finn y jamás se enfadaría porque Juliet encontrara su futuro al lado del príncipe. Sus padres se acostumbrarían, o no, pero su familia no era la razón por la que su relación con Finn había fracasado hacía un año.

Había fracasado porque no había compromiso.

—Deberíamos poner más señales por si tu padre piensa dejarnos aquí un poco más —comentó ella con desilusión al comprender cómo había cambiado el día en cuestión de minutos.

Suavemente, Finn la obligó a levantar la cabeza para mirarla a los ojos. Juliet parpadeó para que él no notara la humedad que estaba intentando ocultar. La miró con una intensidad que provocó un temblor en ella.

—Te amo —murmuró él—. Eso no va a cambiar ocurra lo que ocurra.

Tanto si había concebido como si no. Tanto si sus familias intervenían como si no. Tanto si el mundo estaba al borde de la guerra como si no.

—Lo sé.

Ella también lo amaba de ese modo y lo estropeaba todo porque Juliet odiaba el fervor que él sentía por todo lo militar. Odiaba que él pudiera morir como Bernard y abandonarla de nuevo, pero aquella vez para siempre.

Reconocer que no había compromiso no era lo mismo que le pareciera bien. No podía ser, ¿verdad?

Tal vez aquello no era amor verdadero. Si no, no sentiría que uno, o los dos, tenían que renunciar a todo. O tal vez era prueba de que el amor no era suficiente.

–No. No creo que lo sepas. No creo que puedas comprender lo desgarrado que me siento en estos momentos.

–Lo sé bastante bien –comentó ella con una amarga carcajada.

–Sé que esto es duro para ti. Sé lo que te cuesta guardarte la opinión que tienes de mi padre y de mi trabajo. No renuncies a tus convicciones. Yo no quiero que lo hagas, en especial que cedas a algo en lo que no crees.

El pulso le latía a Juliet con fuerza. Finn jamás había dicho algo así antes. Casi sonaba como si la admirara por haberse enfrentado a su padre.

Tal vez Juliet había confundido las razones que Finn tenía para no alinearse con ella. Tan solo habían discutido, sin hablar nunca racionalmente. Juliet había gritado, acusado… La diplomacia no era su fuerte.

Si terminaban casándose, ella debería practicar a ser diplomática. ¿Qué mejor lugar para empezar que con la historia del pasado?

Si lo conseguían, podrían soportarlo todo. Ella se sentiría por fin a salvo, lo suficientemente segura para confesar que jamás había dejado de estar enamorada de Finn.

Finn no hacía más que esperar oír por fin cómo se acercaban un barco o un helicóptero para sacarlos de allí. Cuanto más se prolongaba el silencio, más nervioso se ponía.

Era impensable que el rey fuera a dejar allí a Finn

mientras los barcos de guerra comenzaban a atravesar el Mediterráneo. Al mismo tiempo, deseaba de todo corazón poderse mantener aislados del mundo real para poder sumergirse por completo en aquella nueva Juliet.

La miró. Estaba muy guapa vestida con un sencillo vestido rojo que hacía destacar mucho su cabello castaño. Estaban sentados a la mesa, desayunando como si fueran una pareja normal.

Algo había ocurrido para que estuvieran así. ¿Podría esperar que fuera suficiente?

Así era. Una peligrosa esperanza había comenzado a vivir en su pensamiento. Quería dejar a Juliet sin aliento con una romántica proposición de matrimonio antes de que ella le entregara una prueba de embarazo. Antes de que él tuviera que vestirse de uniforme y unirse a la armada de Delamer en una posible maniobra de combate. Su trabajo diario era rescatar a quien estuviera en peligro, pero era teniente de las fuerzas armadas y debía defender a su país incluso con su vida.

Debía asegurarse de que ella le daba el sí para que mereciera la pena soportar todo lo demás. Estarían juntos, harían el amor y nada más podría afectarles.

Sin embargo, no podía pedirle matrimonio tal y como había imaginado porque no habían hablado del pasado. Preferiría no hacerlo, pero, si se casaban, ella tendría que comprender las obligaciones que le correspondían como princesa. No podría seguir con sus protestas.

Además, ella aún no le había dicho que le amaba.

El momento no era el adecuado. No podía pedirle matrimonio hasta que todo lo demás se hubiera resuelto.

—¿Vas a comerte eso o vas a seguir masacrándolo? —le preguntó Juliet sacándole así de sus pensamientos.

—Las dos cosas —respondió él tras mirarse las manos, que parecían estar pulverizando lo que una vez había sido una rebanada de pan.

Tenían que hablar. Finn ya lo había pospuesto demasiado tiempo. Además de hacerlo sobre el pasado, Juliet tenía que saber que su familia había renovado sus ataques contra el rey. Él preferiría que ella lo supiera por él. Aquella era la única manera de que funcionara la reconciliación.

—Estás tan tenso —comentó ella—. ¿Has terminado ya de desayunar?

—Sí —respondió él. Si los dos habían terminado, sería el momento adecuado para iniciar aquella necesaria conversación. Cuanto antes, mejor.

—Bien.

Juliet se puso de pie tan de repente que la silla cayó al suelo. Entonces, apartó los platos de la mesa y se sentó a horcajadas encima del regazo de Finn, encajándose con él. Él experimentó una erección inmediatamente al sentir la entrepierna de Juliet, que irradiaba calor a través de las braguitas.

Tal vez podrían hablar más tarde…

Aliviado de encontrarse en la situación, le palmeó suavemente el trasero y se lo arañó con los dedos. Entonces, metió la mano por debajo de la sedosa tela para acariciarle la entrepierna.

La respiración de ella se aceleró y el deseo se

le reflejó en el rostro. Eso excitó profundamente a Finn. Ella comenzó a mover sensualmente las caderas y echó la cabeza hacia atrás para cabalgar con fuerza encima de él. Desesperado por sentirla, Finn apartó la suave tela que la cubría y le introdujo dos dedos en su cálida y húmeda feminidad.

Estaba tan caliente...

Quería sentirla por dentro. Tuvo que contenerse para evitar su propio orgasmo. Ella no dejaba de moverse encima de él, cada vez más rápido, gimiendo de placer. Se arqueaba sobre la mesa y separaba las piernas todo lo que podía.

—Eso es... —murmuró él.

Juliet tenía los ojos cerrados de éxtasis y su interior palpitaba contra los dedos de Finn. Alcanzó el clímax con un grito que le atravesó a él por la entrepierna, resultando doloroso y erótico al mismo tiempo.

Se derrumbó sobre el torso de él. La cabeza le cayó sobre el hombro de Finn mientras se frotaba con fuerza contra la inflamada erección de él. Juliet lo volvía loco.

—Desnúdate —le ordenó ella sin moverse ni ofrecerle ayuda.

—A ti te resulta fácil decirlo —susurró. A pesar de todo, la levantó con una mano y se desnudó. Sin gracia alguna, por supuesto, pero, ¿a quién le importaba?

Después, dado que ella no se movía, le levantó el vestido, le apartó las braguitas y la hizo bajar sobre él con un rápido movimiento. Comenzó a mover las caderas y fue llevándole cada vez más profundamente dentro de su cuerpo hasta que alcanzaron un orgasmo de proporciones épicas que se podía expresar plenamente tan solo con el «te quiero» que se le escapó a él de los labios desde lo más profundo de su alma.

Ella no se lo dijo a él también.

Finn se dijo que no importaba. Eran solo palabras. Decirlas o no decirlas no hacía que el hecho fuera menos verdadero. Ella lo amaba. De eso estaba seguro.

Cuando encontró la energía suficiente, se puso de pie y la levantó en brazos para llevarla a la cama. Allí, volvieron a viajar hasta la estratosfera, pero, en aquella ocasión, fue algo más amargo. Finn se negó a examinar por qué.

Más tarde, mientras estaban aún tumbados en la cama, él comenzó a acariciarle el cabello.

—Ya no estoy tan tenso…

—Misión cumplida —replicó ella mientras levantaba el rostro para mirarlo con una radiante sonrisa.

—Sabes que todo esto está a punto de terminar, ¿verdad?

—¿Qué parte?

—Lo de estar recluidos en esta isla.

—Sí. Deberíamos estar haciendo algo para que nos localizaran, ¿no te parece? —comentó ella mientras le daba un beso en los labios—. Me has distraído.

—Ha sido más bien al revés. Estaba a punto de sacar un tema completamente diferente.

—Sé que tenemos que hablar —dijo ella mientras se sentaba en la cama—. Creo que estoy preparada.

—Pues parece más bien que vas a subir los escalones que te llevan al patíbulo.

–Hemos estado posponiendo este tema por una razón. Es doloroso. No hemos hablado de Bernard ni de la protesta. Si vamos a estar juntos, tenemos que hacerlo. Simplemente no quiero. No se me da muy bien expresarme sin gritar.

La tensión había regresado multiplicada por diez.

–¿Y sobre qué hay que gritar? Acordamos olvidarnos del pasado y mirar hacia delante.

–¿Olvidarnos durante cuánto tiempo? ¿Hasta que te traigan a casa en una bolsa? –le preguntó ella mientras se cubría el rostro con una almohada. No logró ahogar el sollozo que lanzó tal y como había esperado.

–Eh… Eso no es gritar. Me prometiste que me ibas a gritar. Deja esa almohada y deja que te vea.

En realidad, prefería que ella gritara. Eso lo comprendía.

Al escuchar sus palabras, Juliet se echó a reír. Esa carcajada le tranquilizó más de lo que había esperado. Iban a superarlo. Eran más fuertes que hacía un año.

Juliet suspiró y soltó la almohada.

–Yo crecí invisible. Demasiados niños en la casa, supongo. Tú fuiste la primera persona que me vio. Que me amó por lo que era, no por lo que podía hacer por ti. Cuando Bernard murió, te negaste a escucharme, te negaste a ver que yo podría tener ideas válidas sobre cambios. Me dolió. Me sentí abandonada y perdida. No sé cómo superarlo. Cuando veo buques de guerra en la televisión, recuerdo todo lo ocurrido. Quiero estar contigo, pero necesito que tú también me elijas. Si no, no puedo.

Todo era muy racional. Un buen objetivo. De repente, él no estuvo tan seguro de que pudiera conseguirlo. Ciertamente, prefería los gritos.

–¿Qué te parece a ti, Juliet? ¿Cómo puedo ayudarte a sentir que te estoy eligiendo a ti? –le preguntó él.

–Necesito saber que honras nuestra relación por encima de todas las demás. Que estás de mi lado, en especial cuando se trata de un tema que destruyó a mi familia.

Le tomó el rostro entre las manos.

–Quiero que comprendas algo muy importante. Si yo fuera un hombre corriente, me arrastraría por encima de cristales rotos durante cien kilómetros para hacerte mía para siempre. Sin embargo, no es así. No quiero ser así porque ser el príncipe Alain Phineas de Montagne, duque de Marechal, de la casa de Couronne, es un privilegio. Y a mí se me ha honrado con él.

–¿Qué estás diciendo? –susurró ella–. ¿*Au revoir* y ya te llamaré?

–No –dijo él bajando las manos. Esto significa que estoy al otro lado de una enorme extensión de tierra. Necesito que nos reunamos en el centro si lo nuestro va a funcionar fuera de la Île de Etienne.

Ya estaba. Lo había dicho todo lo claramente que podía.

–Compromiso –asintió ella–. Si eso es lo que hace falta, puedo hacerlo.

–Veo que por fin lo comprendes –comentó él aliviado–. Que ves lo importante que el ejército es para mí. Forma parte de mi vida. Es parte de mi identidad.

–Pensaba que tu título era tu identidad –replicó

ella confusa–. Que honrabas tu linaje. No veo cómo, de repente, el ejército alza su fea cabeza en esta conversación. Una cosa no tiene nada que ver con la otra.

Juliet no lo entendía.

–Tienen todo que ver. El papel de Alexander está claramente definido. Va a ser rey. ¿Qué voy a ser yo? No hay nada especial en mí. Siempre seré el príncipe Alain. No hay nada que yo pueda hacer para contribuir excepto proporcionar defensa para el país en el que reina mi padre.

Eso y casarse bien. El pensamiento añadió una pesada losa a los hombros de Finn.

–Cariño mío –musitó ella. Los labios le temblaban–. Eres el hombre más especial que he conocido nunca. Alexander nació para ese papel, pero es tan limitado… Tú tienes la oportunidad de hacer del tuyo lo que quieras ser. Puede conocérsete como el príncipe que marca la diferencia en la vida de su pueblo introduciendo una reforma en el servicio militar obligatorio.

–El ejército es mi vida, Juliet –le espetó él–. Y la reforma no está sobre la mesa.

¿Por qué estaban teniendo de nuevo aquella conversación? ¿Para demostrar que la historia siempre se repetía?

–Entiendo –dijo ella–. Estás a favor del compromiso siempre que la que se comprometa a algo sea yo.

–Estoy a favor de que los dos mostremos afecto y respeto honrando la postura del otro. Si me amas, no puedes amar tan solo una parte de mí. Tienes que amarme entera, incluso la parte con la que no estás de acuerdo.

—Lo mismo digo —repuso ella. Entonces, respiró profundamente—. ¿Te has parado a pensar alguna vez que yo también estoy honrando a mi sangre? Bernard era mi hermano y su recuerdo se merece mis más fuertes convicciones. Tú me dijiste que no debería renunciar a ellas. ¿Te vas a echar atrás en eso ahora?

Por supuesto que lo había pensado. Finn también tenía un hermano.

—No. Lo decía en serio. La integridad es muy importante para mí. No te amaría si no tuvieras esas convicciones.

—También lo es para mí. El hecho de que tú te apegues tanto a las tuyas es en parte la razón por la que estoy aquí hablando contigo en vez de haberme largado.

Ya eran dos. Sin embargo, cuanto más hablaban, mejor sonaba la opción de largarse. Si no podían resolver los problemas allí sin presiones externas, ¿cómo iban a poder hacerlo en Delamer?

Tenían que derribar aquel muro allí y en aquel momento.

—La familia es tan importante como la integridad —afirmó él—. Para los dos. Honrar la postura del otro incluye ayudar a nuestras familias a comprenderlo. Supongo que comprenderás que si estamos juntos tu familia no podrá seguir oponiéndose a mi padre.

Desde el exterior de la casa, se escuchó el sonido inconfundible del rotor de un helicóptero.

Juliet se volvió hacia el sonido como si le hubieran lanzado un cable para salvarle la vida.

No. Todavía no.

Desear que no los rescataran no funcionó mejor que lo había hecho desear quedarse allí. Finn se había quedado sin tiempo.

Capítulo Once

El zumbido de un helicóptero había impedido que Finn terminara la frase, pero Juliet había oído lo suficiente para alegrarse y entristecerse al mismo tiempo de que, por fin, el rey hubiera enviado a buscarlos.

Una parte de ella deseaba montarse en aquel helicóptero. Lentamente, se volvió a mirar a Finn.

—¿Mi familia no se puede oponer a tu padre o soy yo la que no puede?

—Ninguno de los dos. No puedo tener más escándalos. Ni protestas.

—¿O qué? ¿Tu padre no nos permitirá estar juntos? No estamos en la oscura Edad Media.

¿Cuánto tiempo les quedaba hasta que alguien llegara a buscarlos? Ni siquiera estaban vestidos.

—Mi padre no es… —comentó Finn mientras golpeaba la cama con frustración—. Esto tiene que ver contigo, conmigo y con nuestro futuro. Si nos casamos, tú serás princesa de un país que requiere que un muchacho de dieciocho años sirva tres años en las fuerzas armadas.

—Sí —replicó ella mientras terminaba de ponerse el vestido. Lo miró por encima del hombro—, pero eso no significa que tenga que estar de acuerdo.

—No, pero no puedes manifestar libremente tu desacuerdo. De eso se trata.

–Bien. En ese caso, no te cases conmigo –dijo ella con un gran dolor de corazón–. Podemos estar juntos sin que te cases conmigo. Así resolvemos todos los problemas de una vez. Incluso hará que tu padre se alegre.

–A mí no me alegrará. Además, el hecho de estar en esta isla era una oportunidad para reavivar nuestra relación, ¿recuerdas? Mi padre quiere que nos casemos.

–¿Cómo has dicho?

Finn se acercó al borde de la cama y comenzó a vestirse sin mirarla.

–Ya te dije a qué venía todo esto.

–Lo del matrimonio no. Lo recordaría –dijo ella. Algo le parecía raro.

–Porque era irrelevante. Una noche, sin pasado y sin futuro. Esa era tu regla. Ahora estamos en el día siguiente y estamos hablando.

–Sí, porque ayer yo pensaba que lo único que teníamos que solucionar era el pasado. Tu padre quiere que nos casemos. ¿Qué es lo que no sé?

Finn cerró los ojos durante un instante.

–Digamos que eres mi matrimonio de conveniencia –Juliet sintió que el pulso se le aceleraba–. Tu familia ha renovado los ataques contra mi padre –le explicó Finn con expresión oscura–. Si somos pareja, su postura se neutraliza porque parece que tú estás al lado de la corona.

Juliet no se podía creer lo que acababa de escuchar. Todo aquello era una estratagema para conseguir que su familia diera un paso atrás. Las náuseas se apoderaron de ella.

–Y tú te has dejado llevar.

–No. Yo jamás utilizaría nuestra relación para influir en tu familia. Sin embargo, si estuviéramos casados, tú te darías cuenta del problema que supone seguir protestando contra las leyes de Delamer.

Aquel había sido el objetivo desde el principio. Conseguir que la familia Villere se callara.

–Me he acostado contigo. He tenido relaciones íntimas contigo. Creía que querías estar conmigo, pero todo era una mentira. ¿Cómo has podido hacer eso?

–Te di una elección. Yo traté de tomarme las cosas con calma a pesar de que te deseaba por esta razón precisamente. Para que supieras que la elección la tomaste tú y no yo.

«Si te quedas embarazada, nos tendríamos que casar»

Juliet sintió que la ira se apoderaba de ella y le hacía ver rojo. Lanzó la palabra menos femenina que se le ocurrió para verbalizar la frustración y decepción que sentía.

El hecho de que no hubiera preservativos en la casa estaba planeado. Y ella había caído en la trampa. Aquel plan no era solo del padre de Finn. Él lo había hecho propio y lo había convertido en algo diabólico.

–¡Yo tomé esa decisión sin saber todos los hechos! –gritó ella para no escuchar el ruido que hacía su corazón al romperse.

–Sabías todo lo importante –dijo él–. Como que te amo.

Eso era la más pura ficción.

—¿Y esta es tu definición del amor? ¿Mentirme y utilizarme?

El piloto del helicóptero estaba aporreando la puerta principal.

—Yo no te mentí. Jamás te consideré un matrimonio de conveniencia. En realidad, ni siquiera estaba seguro de que pudiéramos solucionar las cosas, y mucho menos así. Sin embargo, todo se precipitó. Quise que supieras el renovado fervor de tu familia por mí. No quise que te enteraras por…

—¿Finn?

Una voz resonó en el salón.

—Alexander —terminó Finn.

Alexander de Montagne, príncipe heredero de Delamer, apareció en la puerta del dormitorio con una expresión seria en el rostro.

—¿Qué le ha ocurrido a mis muebles de jardín?

—¿Esta es tu casa? —le preguntó Juliet.

Creía haber perdido la capacidad de escandalizarse, pero, aparentemente, el engaño iba mucho más allá de lo que había imaginado. Finn lo había sabido desde el principio. No era de extrañar que la casa estuviera completamente equipada.

Finn se dirigió a su hermano.

—¿Puedes darnos un minuto, por favor?

—Solo un minuto —replicó Alexander con voz severa. Entonces, dio un paso atrás y desapareció.

—Juliet, por lo que más quieras —le dijo Finn—. Podría haber hecho esto de un modo muy diferente.

Se acercó a ella.

—¿Y por qué no lo hiciste, entonces? —le espetó ella—. ¿Por qué no me lo dijiste?

–Yo… Sinceramente, no creí que te lo tomaras así.

–¿A qué te refieres? ¿Al hecho de que si me quedaba embarazada te casarías conmigo y me utilizarías para obligar a los Villere a mantener la boca cerrada?

Finn bajó la cabeza.

–Ese no era el plan. El plan era huir de esta isla. Entonces, cuando llegáramos a casa, yo iba a llamarte para ver si podíamos volver a empezar.

–Voy a montarme en ese helicóptero con Alexander porque tengo que hacerlo –repuso ella–. Cuando lleguemos a Delamer, voy a bajarme y no quiero volver a verte.

–No digas eso –susurró él–. Esta reconciliación era real. No dejes que las circunstancias te lo arrebaten. Podemos hacerlo funcionar.

Juliet soltó una carcajada.

–No ha habido reconciliación. Tal vez íbamos de camino a conseguirla, pero no te engañes. Aún teníamos muchas cosas que solucionar y esta última ha borrado todos los progresos. Sigues sin poder ver que no solo no te pusiste de mi lado, sino que te pusiste del de tu padre. No hay nada que puedas decir o hacer en un millón de años que pueda solucionar lo ocurrido, que pueda hacerlo funcionar. Nada.

–Existe aún la posibilidad del embarazo.

–Tal vez, pero ese embarazo no implicará ni una boda ni un final feliz. Aléjate de mí. Lo digo en serio.

Finn nunca lo sabría. Si Juliet se había quedado embarazada, jamás le pediría nada para mantener a su hijo. Durante el resto de su vida tendría que ver los ojos de Finn en el rostro de su pequeño. Aquel sería su castigo por haber vuelto a confiar en él.

—No puedes hablar en serio. Tienes las llaves de mi corazón y no es un cliché. Tienes la capacidad de abrirlo desde el exterior y entrar sin mi permiso. Solo te pido que utilices ese poder sabiamente.

Finn quería decir que Juliet podía hacerle daño y, efectivamente, ella tenía la intención de hacer que le doliera tanto como le dolía a ella.

Finn observó a Juliet de reojo mientras ella se acomodaba en el asiento del helicóptero sin hablarle a él ni a Alexander.

En cuanto Alexander aterrizó junto al palacio, Juliet saltó del helicóptero y se marchó sin mirar atrás.

—Doy por sentado que no hay ido bien —le dijo Alexander.

—Cállate. La idea del secuestro fue una estupidez desde el principio.

Finn no sabía si ir detrás de Juliet y arrojarse a sus pies o mantener el poco orgullo que le quedaba y permitirla que se marchara.

Decidió que no había nada que pudiera hacer más que dejarla marchar. Juliet no estaba enamorada de él. Probablemente no lo había estado nunca. Después de todo, si lo hubiera amado no habría participado en la protesta. Si lo amara, se lo habría dicho al menos en una ocasión, en especial después de que él se lo hubiera confesado a ella.

—Ya se lo dije a padre —comentó Alexander.

—¿Por qué no viniste a buscarme antes si sabías que no iba a funcionar?

Alexander le dio una palmada en el hombro mientras subían los escalones de palacio.

—Le dije que era una estupidez, no que no fuera a funcionar. En realidad, pensé que lo conseguirías.

—Estaba destinado al fracaso desde el principio porque Juliet es demasiado testaruda.

—Debiste de mirarte en un espejo.

—¿Qué se supone que significa eso? ¿Acaso crees que soy testarudo?

—Como un pez que se niega a salir del agua —replicó Alexander.

—Gracias por el sermón, hermano. Me has ayudado mucho —se mofó.

Incluso su hermano estaba en su contra. Deseaba poder huir, esconderse en algún sitio para lamerse las heridas, pero el príncipe Alain no tenía el lujo de poder hacerlo.

—¿Está padre en palacio? —le pregunto a su hermano—. Necesito que me informe sobre la situación en Alhendra.

—Sí —respondió Alexander—. Está en su despacho.

Finn se dirigió rápidamente a ver a su padre acompañado de su hermano. Al entrar en el despacho, el rey levantó la cabeza.

—Has escogido un momento excelente, Alexander. Finn, me alegro de verte, hijo mío.

El rey se puso de pie y se apoyó contra el escritorio, tal y como era su costumbre cuando tenía que enfrentarse a noticias difíciles.

—Hay una gran tensión con nuestros amigos de Grecia, Italia y Turquía. Vamos a tener que enviar nuestros cuatro buques de guerra, lo que no va a ser

160

bien recibido por la población de Delamer. Confío en que tengas buenas noticias para nosotros en ese sentido.

Finn negó con la cabeza.

—A Juliet no le pareció bien la idea de casarse conmigo.

El rey adoptó una expresión severa. Finn no había sido capaz de cumplir sus expectativas.

—Una pena.

—Sí, señor.

El rey lo miró como si de nuevo volviera a tener diecisiete años y lo hubiera llamado al despacho para preguntarle por qué no había bailado con la hija del rey de España o por qué no había sacado tan buenas notas en el examen de bachillerato como Alexander.

—Entonces, ¿se puede decir que la relación es irrecuperable?

—Sí, señor. En este momento, estoy seguro de que ha terminado para siempre.

El dolor que sintió en el pecho lo cegó. Tuvo que parpadear varias veces para impedir que le cayeran las lágrimas.

¿Cómo se suponía que iba a poder superar aquello? Juliet tenía la mala costumbre de romperle el corazón y él la de permitírselo. Sin embargo, en aquella ocasión, la culpa no era solo de ella.

—En ese caso —dijo el rey—, tenemos que encontrar otro modo de que nos seas útil.

—Estaré encantado de hacer lo que se requiera de mí —repuso Finn. Lo único que Finn quería era serle útil a su padre.

—Estaré encantado de hacer lo que se requiera de mí.

–Perfecto. Te ordeno que vayas a presentarte al puente de mando del *Aurélien*. Si no puedes inspirar a una chica para que se case contigo, tal vez puedas conseguir que un país se eche atrás.

–Claro que puedo –repuso Finn con gratitud.

–Ojalá yo pudiera estar allí también –dijo Alexander con cierta nostalgia.

–La primera línea no es tu lugar –respondió Finn tan delicadamente como pudo.

«Alexander nació para ese papel, pero es tan limitado…». Recordaba claramente las palabras de Juliet. «Tú tienes la oportunidad de hacer del tuyo lo que quieras ser».

Con cierto aire de intranquilidad, comenzó a apoyar el peso en cada uno de los pies alternativamente. Se había pasado gran parte de su vida sintiéndose inferior al príncipe heredero. Tal vez contemplaba el orden de nacimiento con una lente demasiado limitada.

¿Había conseguido Juliet ampliar tanto su visión a pesar de pasar juntos tan pocos días?

Inmediatamente, regresó a la Île de Etienne, cuando estuvieron tumbados sobre una manta con el cielo por techo y hablaban sobre conseguir que lo suyo fuera más duradero. La echaba tanto de menos que sintió que, durante un instante, se le doblaban las rodillas.

–Sí, a tu hermano se le necesita en casa –replicó el rey con una sonrisa. Finn lo miró sin comprender.

–Portia está embarazada –explicó Alexander.

Aquella afirmación dejó sin palabras a Finn. Los celos rivalizaban con la alegría que evocaba el anuncio de su hermano. Iba a ser tío, pero en ese momento le habría gustado ser el que anunciara una futura paternidad, el que tuviera el brillo de alegría en la mirada. Juliet podría estar embarazada y Finn había estropeado toda posibilidad de tener una relación con la madre de su hijo. Si había concebido, ¿se lo diría?

–Enhorabuena –dijo sin mucho entusiasmo.

–Gracias. Ella está teniendo... complicaciones. El médico le ha ordenado reposo absoluto porque existe la posibilidad de que pueda perder al bebé –comentó Alexander con gran preocupación por su esposa.

Mientras estaba retozando en su casa y bebiéndose su vino, a Finn jamás se le ocurrió que su hermano pudiera estar pasando por dificultades.

–Bueno, por supuesto que no puedes partir en ese barco con nosotros. Cuida de Portia y de tu hijo. Eso es lo más importante que tienes que hacer –afirmó Finn–. Yo me ocuparé de la defensa.

Si esa defensa requería que dejara su vida por su pueblo, lo haría si rechistar. Después de todo, Juliet era una de las personas a las que estaría defendiendo y, además, Portia estaba embarazada del futuro heredero al trono de Delamer.

De lo único de lo que se arrepentía era de tener que hacerlo cuando su relación con Juliet estaba tan fracturada.

Capítulo Doce

Estaba en casa. Juliet abrazó a su madre. El olor que esta tenía a pan recién hecho y a canela fue suficiente para hacerla entrar en calor.

—Estábamos preocupados —dijo su madre mientras le atusaba el cabello como cuando era pequeña—. Te hemos llamado tantas veces al móvil… Por fin, conseguimos localizar a Elise Arundel y ella nos dijo que te habías marchado de vacaciones con el príncipe. No esperábamos que fuera él tu pareja.

—Yo tampoco lo esperaba —musitó Juliet—. Siento que hayas estado preocupada, pero estoy bien.

Mentira. Se sentía completamente estragada por dentro.

Su madre la miró de arriba abajo por encima de las gafas de cerca.

—¿Dónde has estado? Elise nos dijo que no deberíamos preocuparnos, pero parecía que habías desaparecido de la faz de la Tierra. ¿Ha ocurrido algo con el príncipe Alain?

Juliet se sentía tan agotada que, a pesar de que tenía la oportunidad de despellejarlo vivo delante de sus padres, no podía abrir la boca. Solo quería estar con su familia, donde nadie tenía motivos ocultos y todo el mundo la amaba. Quería olvidar.

—Es una larga historia. No ha ocurrido nada con

Finn ni nada va a ocurrir. Te contaré el resto en otra ocasión.

Collette, la hermana pequeña de Juliet y la única de los hermanos que aún vivía en la casa, la miraba apretándose las manos.

—Entonces, ¿vas a volver a los Estados Unidos o te vas a quedar aquí? –le preguntó.

—Me quedo aquí por el momento. No sé qué es lo que voy a hacer.

—Oh –dijo Collette con el rostro contrariado–. Tenía permiso para ir a visitarte a los Estados Unidos. Esperaba que fueras a regresar.

—Estamos encantados de que estés en casa y puedes quedarte todo el tiempo que quieras –le dijo su padre mientras le dedicaba una mirada de reproche a Collette. Entonces, le dio un abrazo a su hija mayor–. Ahora que el rey ha anunciado que va a enviar fuerzas para participar en la coalición internacional contra Alhendra, tenemos que movernos con rapidez. Estamos organizando una protesta y tú eres nuestra mejor estratega. Es una pena que no te haya salido bien con el príncipe. Podríamos haberlo utilizado para apoyar nuestra causa.

Juliet sintió que se le doblaban las rodillas y se sentó en el sofá. Llevaba cinco minutos en su casa y sus padres ya querían iniciar una protesta... Comprendió que sus padres no eran mejor que Finn.

—Estoy bastante cansada.

¿Es que todo el mundo solo la quería por lo que podía hacer por ellos?

—Por supuesto que lo estás, cariño. Ya basta por el momento, Eduard –le dijo su madre. Entonces, llevó

165

a Juliet a la cocina para prepararle una humeante taza de café.

Durante el resto del día, nadie mencionó Alhendra ni las protestas contra el rey. Juliet fue tranquilizándose poco a poco, pero no podía dejar de pensar en Finn. Aún tenía el aroma de él en la piel. Tan solo hacía unas horas, habían estado tan íntimamente abrazados que era increíble que el aroma de la excitación de él no hubiera impregnado todo su cuerpo.

Decidió subir al cuarto de baño y darse una ducha. Se frotó a conciencia, pero el aroma a hombre no desaparecía. Se secó y se metió en la cama, con el edredón hasta el cuello. Fue entonces cuando empezó a llorar. A llorar por un cretino en quien jamás debería haber confiado.

Sin embargo, tan solo podía recordar el alivio sentido cuando él la sacó del agua. La preocupación que se reflejaba en su rostro mientras ella estuvo con fiebre. El brillo que tenía en los ojos cuando le confesó que seguía enamorado de ella.

Todo mentiras y manipulación.

A la mañana siguiente, tan solo había conseguido dormir unas pocas horas, pero había desarrollado una tremenda necesidad de hacer algo, lo que fuera, para sacarse al príncipe Alain de su corazón de una vez por todas. Si le hacía daño, mucho mejor.

Arrinconó a su padre en la cocina.

—Hablemos de esa protesta…

A lo largo de los siguientes días, Juliet arengaba a todos con tal fervor que le pusieron el nombre de la generala Juliet. Daba órdenes a todo el mundo para, en primer lugar, organizar una sonada protesta y, en segundo, conseguir la cabeza del rey en una bandeja. Figuradamente, por supuesto.

Si el rey Laurent ordenaba a los buques de guerra que regresaran a casa y mostraba compromiso para mantenerse al margen de los conflictos internacionales, eso también le valdría a Juliet. Entones, tendrían la oportunidad de suavizar el resto de las leyes militares. Por fin.

El hogar de los Villere bullía de actividad desde el alba hasta medianoche para conseguir ese fin. Juliet se entregaba de todo corazón a la causa porque así no tenía tiempo de pensar. No quería contar los días hasta que una prueba de embarazo le diera resultados fiables y determinara así el desarrollo de su futuro.

Por las noches, compartía la cama con una prima, su hermana o una sobrina, en ocasiones más de una, pero lo agradecía. Si no estaba a solas, no podía llorar.

Una tarde, Juliet estaba discutiendo por teléfono con un magistrado sobre un permiso para manifestarse cuando Gertrude le tiró de la falda y le entregó un paquete envuelto en papel marrón.

Juliet rezó para que fueran los panfletos que llevaba días esperando. Aún tenía el teléfono contra la oreja, por lo que se lo sujetó con el hombro para poder cortar el embalaje con las tijeras de cocina.

—Conozco que el plazo habitual es de cinco días, señor Le Clerq —le decía al magistrado—. Le pido una excepción.

Abrió la caja y el teléfono se le cayó al suelo. El paquete contenía unos zapatos. Sus zapatos. Las sandalias de cocodrilo que se había puesto para salir a cenar con Finn cuando aún albergaba una cierta esperanza. Las mismas que creía que había perdido cuando se despertó descalza en la Île de Etienne.

—¿Te encuentras bien? —le preguntó su tía Vivian desde el otro lado de la cocina.

Juliet le hizo un gesto con la mano. No era capaz de hablar. ¿Cómo era posible que se los hubieran devuelto? Miró el remitente.

Era Finn. Sintió que se le hacía un nudo en el corazón.

Ojalá pudiera devolverle todo lo demás que le había arrebatado.

Con las manos temblorosas, cerró la caja y la metió en la parte trasera de la alacena, donde nadie pudiera encontrarla. Después, puso encima una bolsa de patatas.

Incapaz de contestar a su tía, se marchó hacia el salón, donde el tío Jean Louis estaba dormitando delante de la televisión.

Tan solo necesitaba un par de minutos para recuperarse y lograr controlar las lágrimas. A nadie le serviría de nada saber que estaba disgustada o que un hombre la había afectado tan negativamente. Un poco de televisión la tranquilizaría inmediatamente.

El canal de televisión que había puesto su tío estaba hablando sobre la cantidad de barcos de guerra que se habían reunido en el Mediterráneo, frente a las costas de Grecia. Sabía que Finn estaba en uno de ellos. Eso significaba que se había tomado al pie de la letra la petición que ella le había hecho de mantenerse alejado.

Aquello fue la gota que colmó el vaso. Primero una lágrima. Luego otra. De repente, ya no pudo contenerse más.

Estaba a punto de marcharse de allí cuando la tía Vivian asomó la cabeza con el teléfono en la mano.

–¿No estabas hablando con alguien? ¡Oh, *cherie*! ¿Qué te pasa?

Juliet respondió negando con la cabeza y le indicó a su tía que regresara a la cocina. No era capaz de hablar.

Sin embargo, Vivian la ignoró. Se sentó a su lado y le dio un gran abrazo.

–No es tan grave como parece, ¿verdad?

Juliet apoyó la cabeza sobre el regazo de su tía y asintió. Seguía enamorada de Finn y, aparentemente, nada de lo que él hiciera, por malo que fuera, era capaz de cambiarlo.

–Ese joven es un imbécil –comentó Vivian.

Juliet giró la cabeza y miró a su tía. ¿Le había contado su madre todo lo ocurrido?

–¿Cómo has sabido que estaba llorando por Finn?

Ella sonrió e indicó la televisión.

–Es muy guapo, pero no debe de ser muy listo si ha renunciado a ti.

El rostro de Finn apareció efectivamente en la pantalla para responder las preguntas de un reportero. Vestido de uniforme con todas sus medallas de honor estaba arrebatador. Juliet no podía apartar la mirada de la pantalla.

Examinó ávidamente su rostro para encontrar

pistas, por pequeñas que fueran, de su estado de ánimo. ¿La echaba de menos? ¿Se arrepentía? Esperaba que estuviera despierto por las noches y que sufriera, tal y como le ocurría a ella.

Le pareció que, cuando sonreía, tenía arrugas alrededor de la boca y los ojos que le hacían parecer más mayor. Parecía agotado.

¿Cuándo desaparecería la necesidad de tranquilizarlo y de asegurarse de que se encontraba bien?

—La primera ronda de negociaciones ha ido bien —le decía al micrófono.

¿Negociaciones?

Finn siguió hablando.

—Me congratulo de ser uno de los miembros del contingente invitado a Alhendra. Esperamos conseguir un alto al fuego pacífico y alcanzar la resolución de esta situación.

¿Finn era un miembro del comité que estaba negociando con Alhendra? Juliet no se lo podía creer, pero así lo afirmaba el titular que acompañaba la imagen de Finn. No solo era miembro del comité, sino que había jugado un papel fundamental a la hora de buscar la solución del conflicto sin disparar ni una sola bala.

—¿Qué fue la clave para las negociaciones? —le preguntó el reportero.

—Llegar a un término medio —respondió Finn. Juliet sintió que se le hacía un nudo en el estómago. Lo mismo que le había pedido a ella, para luego negarse a mover ni un milímetro su posición.

Sin embargo, lo había realizado con éxito con un país entero. ¿Cómo?

No pudo dejar de pensar en aquella pregunta a lo largo de toda la noche. La protesta era por la mañana, y la iban a hacer ilegalmente, dado que ella no había conseguido lograr el permiso para conseguirla a tiempo.

Seguramente, volverían a arrestarla. Al menos en aquella ocasión no tenía nada que ver con Finn, con lo que le ahorraba a él ese bochorno.

¿Y por qué iba a importarle? Finn se merecía todo lo que ella pudiera echarle encima y mucho más…

Por primera vez, pensó en cómo se debía haber sentido él. Debió de haberlo considerado una traición y separación de bandos. Ella había elegido a su familia en vez de a él. Más o menos de lo que le había acusado a él de hacer en la Île de Etienne.

Los ojos le escocían por contener las lágrimas. Finn le había hecho mucho daño, pero eso no significaba que no la amara.

Buscó a tientas el cajón de la mesilla de noche y lo abrió para sacar un libro. Entonces, encendió la luz. Cada página contenía una flor prensada de todos los ramos que Finn le había regalado. Aquellas flores habían estado vivas en una ocasión, y ya deberían haber desaparecido. Era el ciclo de la vida. Sin embargo, ella las había guardado cuidadosamente para conseguir que se convirtieran en algo que durara mucho tiempo.

¿Había algo parecido que pudiera hacer para romper el ciclo en el que parecían destinados a viajar Finn y ella? Lo único que sabía era que sin él estaba muy triste, y quería que dejara de ser así.

Se aferró al libro y estuvo así hasta el amanecer.

Cuando el sol salió y entró a través de las cortinas, sintió una suave calidez en el cuerpo por primera vez desde que llegó allí. Estaba en paz con lo que tenía que hacer.

Debían cancelar la protesta.

Ella había empezado el ciclo y dependía de ella terminarlo. Su relación con Finn podría no recuperarse nunca de las estupideces que los dos habían hecho, pero ya se ocuparían de eso más tarde.

Tenía que detener la protesta.

Todos estaban en la cocina, preparados para la protesta y deseando ver rodar cabezas.

—¡Que descaro! —decía su padre mientras señalaba los titulares de los periódicos—. El palacio va a albergar un baile esta noche para celebrar el peso que Delamer ha tenido en la negociación con Alhendra.

—Vamos a retrasar la protesta hasta la tarde —anunció su madre—. Bloquearemos la carretera para que no puedan pasar los invitados. Será muy eficaz. Todos los invitados tendrán que esperar y, mientras tanto, se verán obligados a leer nuestras pancartas y a escuchar nuestras voces unidas contra el rey.

—Pero el conflicto ha terminado. Lo dijeron ayer en las noticias. ¿Por qué seguir con la protesta?

—Va en contra de todo lo que creemos —replicó su padre—. Darle gloria a la guerra y a la agresión con una fiesta para honrar a todos los que marcharon a ella para perpetuarla es casi peor que obligar a los jóvenes a hacer el servicio militar.

—El rey requiere el servicio militar porque Delamer es un país muy pequeño —afirmó ella. Su padre la miró como si hubiera perdido la cabeza cuando, en realidad, Juliet acababa de encontrarla–. Sin él, las fuerzas armadas serían ridículas.

Había escuchado cómo Finn lo decía una docena de veces, pero sin escucharle de verdad. Se tocó el colgante de corazones que Elise le había dado. Había emparejado a Finn y a ella porque eran exactamente iguales. Apasionados. Testarudos. Había acusado a Finn de permanecer inmóvil en su posición, pero, ¿cuántos pasos había dado ella para desbloquear la suya?

Los corazones del colgante se aferraban el uno al otro, sosteniéndose mutuamente. El amor verdadero no era a lo que uno renunciaba, sino a lo que se ganaba cuando se aferraba al otro. Ese era el mensaje de Elise.

–La mitad del país tiene el mar como frontera –prosiguió ella–. El servicio militar obligatorio ayuda a tener una fuerte presencia naval. Tal vez no sea el mejor modo de abastecer de personal al ejército, pero en vez de protestar, deberíamos ofrecer alternativas.

–¡Juliet! –exclamó su madre–. Tu hermano murió por esa filosofía.

–La muerte de Bernard fue un accidente. Tenemos que seguir con nuestras vidas, perdonarnos y dejar de culpar al rey. No fue culpa de nadie. Eso es precisamente un accidente.

El peso que llevaba un año sosteniendo le desapareció de los hombros. La muerte de Bernard no había sido culpa suya, pero ella la había aceptado inconscientemente por haber presentado a su hermano a Finn.

Se cuadró de hombros.

–La protesta es ilegal. No deberíamos hacerla solo por esa razón. Tal vez una protesta no sea el mejor modo de ocuparse de esto. Por una vez, probemos con la diplomacia.

–Lo que debería ser ilegal es el modo en el que el rey gobierna, y no una protesta civilizada. Tuviste la oportunidad de utilizar la diplomacia con el príncipe. Por eso lo vamos a hacer así –le espetó su padre.

–Si seguís adelante, lo haréis sin mí.

Con eso, Juliet se dio la vuelta y se marchó. Llamó a Elise por Skype, a pesar de ser aún de madrugada en Dallas.

–Juliet, ¿va todo bien? –le preguntó Elise al ver el aspecto descuidado de Juliet.

–Siento haberte despertado.

–No lo has hecho.

Elise no estaba sola. Eso era peor aún.

–Pues en ese caso, lo siento mucho más.

La casamentera se echó a reír.

–No. Estaba trabajando en un presupuesto. Ojalá tuviera una razón mejor para estar despierta a estas horas.

En el mes que Juliet vivió con Elise, ella no había salido con ningún hombre. Sin embargo, resultaba evidente que quería conocer a alguien. ¿Por qué no metía Elise su propia información en el ordenador y se encontraba una pareja?

–Bien, dado que estás despierta, necesito tu ayuda –dijo Juliet mientras se mordía el labio.

Le contó a Elise toda la historia, incluso la parte de sus propios errores. No resultaba tan fácil perdonarse, pero había dado el primer paso. Debía dar más y solo había un lugar adecuado y lo suficientemente público para poder hacerlo.

—¿Qué puedo hacer? —le preguntó Elise.

—Utiliza tu varita mágica y dame el aspecto de una mujer merecedora de un príncipe. Voy a ir al baile.

Capítulo Trece

A Finn le dolía la cabeza. La limusina no se había movido en diez minutos, pero no importaba. Cuanto más rápido fuera, menos tardaría en llegar a palacio y, sinceramente, no estaba seguro de cuántos halagos y palmadas en la espalda podría soportar.

El conflicto con Alhendra había terminado, pero la tensión que él sentía desde hacía días no había desaparecido.

La devastación que contempló lo acompañó a lo largo de las negociaciones y le dio energía y determinación. Los líderes de Alhendra no salían de la sala sin acceder a entregar sus armas. Sin embargo, tampoco permitiría que sus barcos ni los de ningún otro país dispararan sobre Alhendra como venganza.

Compromiso.

Y funcionó.

No obstante, la victoria era agridulce, porque Juliet no estaba a su lado.

Se asomó por la ventana de la limusina y observó la larga línea de tráfico.

–¿Qué es lo que pasa, James? –le preguntó al conductor.

–Hay varias personas en la carretera –respondió el chófer–. Parece que están bloqueando el tráfico.

–Iré andando desde aquí. Gracias.

Se bajó del coche. Gómez y LaSalle lo siguieron. Sus guardaespaldas no lo dejaban nunca solo. Cuando se fueron acercando a las puertas de palacio, fueron distinguiendo mejor los gritos de los que estaban bloqueando el tráfico.

«Paz y no guerra. No más barcos de guerra».

Los que se manifestaban llevaban pancartas. Se trataba de una protesta. Una gélida sensación se apoderó de Finn. Otra vez no.

Casi en contra de su voluntad, fue examinando los rostros de los manifestantes. No tardó en ver a Collette Villere, la hermana de Juliet. Sintió una profunda desilusión, pero, ¿qué había esperado? Por supuesto que se trataba de Juliet y su familia.

No tardó en comprobar que Juliet no estaba entre los manifestantes. Una ridícula esperanza se apoderó de él.

No. No la veía por ningún lado.

Sin comprender, avanzó hasta el palacio y subió los escalones. Dos lacayos le abrieron las pesadas puertas y le franquearon la entrada al imponente vestíbulo. Finn bajó los escalones que conducían a la planta baja y esperó a que otro lacayo anunciara su presencia.

Todos los presentes comenzaron a aplaudir al verlo. Finn sonrió. ¿Qué otra cosa podía hacer? Era su pueblo quien le aplaudía. Resultaba agradable ver que apreciaban sus esfuerzos.

Fue saludando a todos los presentes. Lo más increíble era que nadie parecía querer hablar de Alhendra, sino de la identidad de los que se manifestaban en el exterior.

Por suerte, nadie mencionó el nombre de Juliet.

Alexander se marchó para ir a casa a cuidar de Portia y el rey se puso a hablar de caballos con su hermano. Finn agradeció quedarse solo unos instantes. Desgraciadamente, la reina se acercó a él. Finn le besó ambas mejillas.

—Estás impresionante, madre. Es una fiesta estupenda.

—Me alegra que estés en casa sano y salvo. He mandado a algunos empleados a que se ocupen de ese... ese asunto. Espero que no nos molesten mucho más —dijo la reina con expresión sombría.

¿Cuándo terminaría aquello?

El conde de Ghent se acercó a hablar con la reina y Finn aprovechó la situación para ir en busca de una copa de champán. Le costó encontrar a un camarero, había más de ciento cincuenta personas riendo y celebrando.

Acababa de llevarse la copa a los labios cuando un murmullo se extendió por todos los presentes.

Allí estaba, de pie en lo alto de las escaleras. Al verla, Finn estuvo a punto de dejar caer la copa que tenía entre los dedos. Estaba resplandeciente con un reluciente vestido ligero y vaporoso, que parecía haber sido tejido con la seda de cientos de arañas plateadas. Era un vestido digno de una princesa. Llevaba el cabello recogido y estaba tan hermosa que Finn se quedó sin respiración.

¿Qué estaba haciendo allí?

«Está embarazada».

Aquello fue lo primero que pensó y la alegría se apoderó de él. No. Era demasiado pronto para saberlo. Solo podía haber una razón por la que había acudido a la fiesta.

Se le hizo un nudo en el estómago y se dirigió hacia ella con la intención de echarla personalmente del baile. ¿Cómo se había atrevido? Si pensaba que iba a llevar sus arengas contra el ejército a la fiesta de su madre, tenía más descaro y menos inteligencia de lo que Finn había pensado siempre. Juliet no iba a avergonzar ni a disgustar a su madre.

Los invitados se fueron separando para franquearle el paso. Estaba a unos cien metros de Juliet cuando sus miradas se cruzaron y vio algo delicado y brillante en los ojos de ella.

—¡Para! —le ordenó ella en voz alta. Su voz resonó por el salón de baile—. Espera ahí.

Juliet se recogió la falda con una mano y bajó la escalera con una gracia que él nunca había visto en ella. Se movía como una aparición. ¿Qué estaba pasando? ¿Se había quedado dormido y estaba soñando aquella escena?

Juliet fue acercándose poco a poco a él sin dejar de mirarlo.

—¿Qué es lo que quieres? —le espetó.

—Que te quedes ahí quieto mientras yo recorro este espacio para encontrar el término medio.

Finn cerró los ojos y tragó saliva, pero no consiguió aliviar el nudo en la garganta. Cuando abrió los ojos, vio que ella seguía avanzando hacia él.

Había acudido al baile para volverlo a intentar, no para avergonzarlo delante de todos los presentes. Ella no estaba participando en la protesta. Se había puesto de su lado. Era una disculpa en toda regla.

Entonces, ella se detuvo justo a mitad de camino. Lo miró fijamente. El mensaje estaba claro. Quería que Finn se reuniera con ella a la mitad.

Él se puso de rodillas y fue arrastrándose hacia la mujer que amaba.

Los murmullos de los presentes se disiparon cuando él llegó junto a Juliet y se incorporó sobre una rodilla para tomarle una mano. La miró a los ojos y vació el contenido de su alma.

–¿Qué estás haciendo? –le preguntó ella con un nudo de emoción en la garganta.

–Tú has hecho tu parte y yo he hecho la mía.

El corazón a Juliet le dio un vuelco en el pecho.

–Tú eres quien eres por tu sangre y yo, egoístamente, he tratado de interponerme, de ponerte a prueba para ver si yo era más importante que tu linaje, exigiendo prueba de tu devoción pidiéndote que te convirtieras en alguien normal. No quiero eso. Levántate. Quiero al príncipe Alain en toda su gloria.

Todos los presentes contuvieron la respiración. Un par de mujeres comenzaron a aplaudir. Una de ellas era la reina.

Finn se puso de pie sin soltarle la mano. Entonces, con expresión solemne, se dirigió a todos los presentes.

–El espectáculo ha terminado, amigos. Disfruten de la fiesta y de la increíble hospitalidad de mi madre.

Los invitados volvieron a centrarse en sus conversaciones, animados por la reina. Juliet tenía mucho que aprender de la madre de Finn.

—Baila conmigo —le dijo él.

—¿Es ahora cuando tengo que admitir que se me ha roto la hebilla del zapato? —preguntó ella a punto de soltar una carcajada—. No puedo andar…

Sacó el pie por debajo de la delicada tela del vestido para mostrarle las sandalias de cocodrilo.

—¿Es esa la razón de que te hayas detenido? Ibas a recorrer toda la distancia que nos separaba, ¿verdad?

—Sí. Era lo que te merecías. Siento lo ocurrido el año pasado y siento la protesta. Me equivoqué y no debería haberlo hecho. Te amo e hice muy poco para demostrártelo.

—Yo también cometí errores —susurró mientras se llevaba la mano de Juliet a los labios para besársela—. Tal vez mi sangre sea azul, pero el órgano que la bombea te pertenece a ti. Ni a mi padre ni a Delamer. Yo también te amo, más de lo que amo a nada o a nadie en el mundo. Siento no haber honrado mi relación contigo por encima de esas dos cosas.

—No quiero que tengas que elegirme por delante de ellas nunca más. Ese ha sido nuestro problema desde el principio. Demasiada presión para elegir entre absolutos. Escojamos el término medio.

—Probemos con el perdón, ¿te parece? Te ruego que me perdones por todo el dolor que te he causado.

Qué fácil. La respuesta había estado allí desde el principio. Perdón. Esa era la clave.

Finn sonrió.

—Ya te he perdonado. Ahora, ¿me perdonas tú a mí?

—Hecho. ¿Crees que esta vez vamos a conseguirlo?

—Por supuesto que sí. No podría volver a perderte de nuevo. Vas a casarte conmigo. No hace falta que te quedes embarazada, aunque me gustaría que ocurriera en el futuro.

Princesa Juliet. Ella sintió un escalofrío por la espalda.

—¿Se trata de una proposición de matrimonio?

—Más bien la promesa de una que se producirá cuando no me encuentre tan deslumbrado por tu maravillosa belleza —dijo—. Serás princesa de por vida, una componente de pleno derecho de la casa de Couronne. La princesa Juliet de Montagne, duquesa de Marechal, además de un montón más de títulos. ¿Podrás hacerlo?

Ella le apretó con fuerza la mano.

—La pregunta es si puedes hacerlo tú. Yo no soy tan diplomática como tú. Tengo opiniones sobre muchos temas y no me voy a contener a la hora de hacértelas saber. Tu pueblo podría no perdonarte nunca por casarte conmigo.

—Me perdonarán porque verán lo que yo veo. Serás la princesa del pueblo, la que cree apasionadamente en lo mejor para ellos. Estoy a tu lado. Cuando el sol salga mañana, todo el mundo lo sabrá.

—Igual que yo estoy al tuyo…

Finn la estrechó entre sus brazos y susurró:

—Vayámonos de aquí.

Juliet sonrió.

—Es el mejor decreto real que he escuchado nunca.

Echó a andar detrás de él cuando se le rompió la

sandalia del todo. Antes que su príncipe azul pudiera escapar, se quitó el otro y los dejó los dos sobre el suelo del salón de baile. Estaba segura de que donde Finn iba a llevarla, directamente al paraíso, los zapatos eran opcionales.

Epílogo

Finn abrió la puerta del patio con una cadera y salió con una botella de champán en una mano y las copas en la otra. La Île de Etienne se extendía a su alrededor en todo su esplendor. Juliet estaba sentada sobre una de las hamacas que habían elegido para reemplazar a las que sacrificaron en el fuego.

—Pensaba que tenías que hablar por teléfono —dijo ella después de abrir los ojos—. Esto parece una celebración.

—Y lo es —afirmó mientras llenaba las dos copas—. Alexander me acaba de enviar un mensaje. Todo está en orden. Île de Etienne nos pertenece.

—Bueno, técnicamente te pertenece a ti —comentó ella mientras Finn tomaba asiento en otra hamaca—. Las desfasadas leyes de tu padre no nos permiten tener una propiedad juntos a menos que estemos casados.

—Pues hablando de eso… —observó él—. Tal vez quieras mirar en esa dirección.

Juliet lo hizo y lo que vio la dejó sin aliento. Escrito sobre el impresionante cielo azul estaban las palabras CÁSATE CONMIGO JULIET en humo blanco. La versión de Finn de una proposición escandalosamente romántica.

Ella lo miró con los ojos llenos de afecto.

—¿Crees que le importaría escribir también mi respuesta para que lo supiera todo Delamer?

Finn sonrió.

—Si tú quieres… Vamos a estar en el ojo público toda nuestra vida. Será mejor que les demos lo que esperan.

—¿Se paga por letra? —preguntó ella mientras fingían pensar—. Ciertamente un «no» sería mucho más barato.

—Pues no he considerado cuánto me ha costado este.

Extendió la mano y le ofreció su corazón engarzado en oro. El anillo era una sencilla alianza engastada de zafiros, pero era una de las joyas de la corona de Delamer, que databa del siglo XVII.

—Ay, Finn —susurró ella con los ojos llenos de lágrimas—. Eso no es que sea caro. Es que no tiene precio.

—Ni que lo digas. Tuve que prometerle a mi madre que le darías un nieto antes de que pase un año para que me dejara llevármelo —bromeó. Entonces, le ofreció la otra mano, que ella agarró sin dudarlo—. Tú eres mi paz en la tormenta y te necesito. ¿Quieres casarte conmigo?

Ella parpadeó para contener las lágrimas.

—¿Estás seguro? No voy a dejar de tratar de convencer a tu padre para que apruebe leyes en las que los chicos puedan elegir entre el servicio militar obligatorio y el servicio social que les sirva para la carrera que vayan a terminar estudiando.

Finn soltó una carcajada sin poder contenerse. Su vida iba a estar llena de discusiones y de mucho sexo de reconciliación.

–No quiero que deje de ser así. ¿Qué te parece esto? Dieciocho meses de servicio y dieciocho meses de servicio social si lo prefieren en vez del servicio continuado de tres años.

–Me parece estupendo –admitió ella con una sonrisa–. Me gusta.

–Llevo mucho tiempo tratando de decirle el bien equipo que formamos. Ahora, ¿te vas a casar conmigo o me voy a morir aquí esperando a que te decidas?

–Me casaré contigo –afirmó ella apretándole la mano–, pero solo si me prometes que tendré las llaves de tu corazón para siempre.

–Me temo que en eso no tengo mucho que decir –admitió Finn–. Las tienes desde el momento en el que te vi ahí enfrente –añadió señalando hacia Delamer, que se extendía al otro lado del Mediterráneo.

Allí, él era príncipe. En la Île de Etienne, con Juliet, era tan solo un hombre enamorado de una mujer. Lo mejor de ambos mundos.

–Bien. Eso significa que puedo entrar cuando quiera y amarte exactamente como te mereces.

Finn le colocó el anillo en el dedo y la besó para sellar el inicio de su final feliz.

No te pierdas *Emparejada con su rival*,
de Kat Cantrel,
el próximo libro de la serie
Felices para siempre, S.A.
Aquí tienes un adelanto...

En el mundo de los medios de comunicación, así como en la vida, la presentación primaba sobre todo lo demás. Por ello, Dax Wakefield jamás subestimaba el valor de causar una buena impresión.

La cuidadosa atención a los detalles era la razón del éxito de su imperio, un éxito que superaba a lo que él había podido nunca imaginar. Entonces, ¿por qué KDLS, la que había sido la joya de su corona, estaba teniendo unos índices de audiencia tan malos?

Dax se detuvo frente al mostrador de recepción del vestíbulo de la cadena de noticias que había ido a sacar a flote.

—Hola, Rebecca. ¿Cómo va Brian con las matemáticas este semestre?

La sonrisa de la recepcionista se hizo aún más amplia. Tras ahuecarse automáticamente el cabello, echó los hombros hacia atrás para asegurarse de que de Dax se percataba de su imponente figura.

Y claro que Dax se percató. Un hombre al que le gustaba tanto el cuerpo de una mujer como a él siempre se fijaba.

—Buenos días, señor Wakefield —gorjeó Rebecca—. En el último boletín de calificaciones ha sacado un aprobado. Ha mejorado mucho. ¿Cómo es posible que se acuerde de eso? Hace ya más de seis meses que le comenté lo de las notas de mi hijo.

A Dax le gustaba recordar al menos un detalle personal de cada uno de sus empleados para tener algo de lo que hablar con ellos. Un hombre de éxito no era solo el que tenía más dinero, sino el que dirigía mejor sus negocios, y nadie podía hacerlo solo. Si los empleados estaban contentos con su jefe, le eran fieles y se esforzaban al máximo por llevar a cabo sus cometidos.

Normalmente, Dax tenía pocas preguntas para Robert Smith, el director de la cadena, sobre los últimos índices de audiencia. Alguien estaba realizando mal su trabajo.

Dax se golpeó suavemente la sien y sonrió.

—Mi madre me anima a usar esto para el bien en vez de para el mal. ¿Está Robert?

La recepcionista asintió y apretó el botón que abría la puerta de seguridad.

—Están grabando. Estoy segura de que estará cerca del plató.

—Saluda a Brian de mi parte —le dijo Dax mientras atravesaba la puerta para adentrarse en el mayor espectáculo de la Tierra: las noticias de la mañana.

Los cámaras y los técnicos de iluminación iban de un lado a otro, los productores caminaban con mucha.

En medio de todo aquel bullicio estaba sentada la estrella de KDLS, Monica McCreary.

Estaba charlando frente a las cámaras con una mujer menuda de cabello oscuro que, a pesar de su corta estatura, tenía unas piernas espectaculares. Sacaba mucho partido a lo que tenía y Dax apreciaba el esfuerzo.

Deseo

VAN

La esposa de su enemigo

BRONWYN JAMESON

La amnesia le había robado los recuerdos, pero con solo ver la traicionera belleza de Susannah Horton, Donovan Keane evocó las apasionadas imágenes del fin de semana que habían compartido sin salir de la cama. Susannah había planeado aquel romance para arruinar un importante negocio, pero ahora Van tendría la ocasión de vengarse. En una sola noche conseguiría romper el compromiso de matrimonio de Susannah, recuperaría el negocio y se marcharía con todos los recuerdos que necesitara para seguir adelante.

Lo que no imaginaba era lo difícil que le resultaría olvidarla a ella.

Él estaba decidido a vengarse… pero aquella mujer era completamente inocente

¡YA EN TU PUNTO DE VENTA!

Acepte 2 de nuestras mejores novelas de amor GRATIS

¡Y reciba un regalo sorpresa!

Oferta especial de tiempo limitado

Rellene el cupón y envíelo a
Harlequin Reader Service®
3010 Walden Ave.
P.O. Box 1867
Buffalo, N.Y. 14240-1867

¡Sí! Por favor, envíenme 2 novelas de amor de Harlequin (1 Bianca® y 1 Deseo®) gratis, más el regalo sorpresa. Luego remítanme 4 novelas nuevas todos los meses, las cuales recibiré mucho antes de que aparezcan en librerías, y factúrenme al bajo precio de $3,24 cada una, más $0,25 por envío e impuesto de ventas, si corresponde*. Este es el precio total, y es un ahorro de casi el 20% sobre el precio de portada. !Una oferta excelente! Entiendo que el hecho de aceptar estos libros y el regalo no me obliga en forma alguna a la compra de libros adicionales. Y también que puedo devolver cualquier envío y cancelar en cualquier momento. Aún si decido no comprar ningún otro libro de Harlequin, los 2 libros gratis y el regalo sorpresa son míos para siempre.

416 LBN DU7N

Nombre y apellido	(Por favor, letra de molde)

Dirección	Apartamento No.

Ciudad	Estado	Zona postal

Esta oferta se limita a un pedido por hogar y no está disponible para los subscriptores actuales de Deseo® y Bianca®.
*Los términos y precios quedan sujetos a cambios sin aviso previo.
Impuestos de ventas aplican en N.Y.

SPN-03   ©2003 Harlequin Enterprises Limited

Él se llevó su virginidad y ella prometió vengarse

Sophie Durante esperaba frente a la lujosa oficina de Luka Cavaliere con el corazón acelerado. Cinco años antes, cuando la encontraron en la cama del magnate siciliano, su reputación y su orgullo quedaron destruidos. Luka estaba en deuda con ella y había ido a pedir una retribución. Para consolar a su padre moribundo, Luka debía hacerse pasar por su prometido.

Intrigado, Luka aceptó tan asombrosa proposición. Sabiendo que bajo la fría fachada de Sophie había una personalidad ardiente, intuía que la farsa podría ser muy placentera.

Pero hacer el amor estaba fuera de la cuestión… hasta que le hiciese admitir cuánto lo deseaba.

UN NOVIO SICILIANO
CAROL MARINELLI

Pasión y diamantes

Kelly Hunter

Tristan Bennett era alto, atractivo y enigmático. Y Erin, joyera de profesión, no sabía si era un brillante o un diamante en bruto.

Tristan disponía de una semana libre y accedió a acompañar a Erin a las minas australianas a comprar piedras preciosas.

Una vez que Erin y Tristan emprendieron el viaje, la atracción que sentían el uno por el otro les traía locos.

Erin sabía que eso solo le acarrearía problemas, a menos que ambos pudieran controlar su mutua pasión.

Una joya… en su cama

¡YA EN TU PUNTO DE VENTA!